HARP OF DESTINY

By

Elizabeth MacDonald Burrows

From the labyrinths of world libraries and the Roman Vatican,
the untold story of Jesus of Nazareth.

Cassandra Press
San Rafael, Ca. 94915

Cassandra Press
P.O. Box 868
San Rafael, Ca. 94915

Printed in the United States of America.

First printing 1991

ISBN 0-945946-13-9

Library of Congress Catalogue Card Number 91-75083

Front cover art by Gary Hespenheide. Copyright © 1991 Cassandra Press.

TABLE OF CONTENTS

Jesus' grandparents pray for a child. Birth of two Marys. Elder Mary is dedicated to the Temple. Mary is espoused to Joseph bar'Jacob. Angel appears to Mary. Mary conceives. Five Planetary conjunction. Jesus is born in a cave.

Baylonia Astronomers arrive in Jerusalem. Jesus is taken to the Temple. Journey to Egypt. Jesus' boyhood Tutored by Zacchaeus. Studies with Gamaliel. Enters the Essene Sect. Departs for India.

Jesus joins a caravan going east. Arrives in Nepal Studies Jain Religion. Enters Buddhist monastery. Departs for Egypt. Joseph dies. Letter to his mother. Returns to Israel. Decision in the wilderness.

Jesus teaches communion with the angels. Prayer to the Earthly Mother. The Holy Stream of Life. Angels of the sun, water and air. Letter to Abgarus Uchama. Teaches the disciples in secret.

Secret communions of the Heavenly Father. Angel of Peace. Parable of the rich man. Merger with the Holy Stream of Light. Jesus travels to his last Passover.

Jesus continues the secret teachings. Communion with the angels of the Heavenly Father. Return to Capernaum. Pathway to wisdom. Angel of Power. Merger with Holy Stream of Light. The final journey to Jerusalem. Angel of Love.

Final appearance at the Temple. Apocalyptic prophecies concerning the end. Parable of the ten virgins. Rite of the Last Supper. Garden of Gethsemane. Via Dolorosa, path of mastership.

Jesus is arrested. Snahedrin condemns Jesus. Taken to Pilate. Transcript of court trial. Pilate issues a death warrant. Copy of death warrant. Crucified. A great earthquake.

Jesus dies. Joseph Arimathea asks for the body. Placed in a tomb. Caiaphus afraid body will be stolen. Joseph Arimathea arrested. Jesus' body disappears. Jesus appears to his disciples. The last farewell.

DEDICATED TO:

Jesus of Nazareth, the man who
once walked the shores of Galilee.

DEEP APPRECIATION TO:

Professor Edmond Bordeaux Szekely, whose tireless effort in making this a better world for mankind, made this book possible, and to his wife, Mrs. Norma Bordeaux Szekely, who allowed us to use certain texts from her husband's translation of the Vatican manuscript pertaining to the unknown teaching of Jesus according to John. I wish to express my gratitude also, to the many dedicated workers whose efforts resulted in its completion.

Mr. Morris Bennet
Miss Janet Berglund
Mr. and Mrs. Chris Bundschu
Mrs. Lisa H. Crone
Dr. and Mrs. Dennis Dossett
Dr. John George
Miss Virginia Hoyt
Mrs. Robin Hughes
Mr. and Mrs. Leroy Lewis
Miss Sandra Lundstrom
Mrs. Carolyn Meyer
Mrs. Karel Mottley
Dr. Nancy Potts
Dr. and Mrs. Ralph Sand
Mr. Stafford Smith
Miss Vicki Ann Tinnes

PREFACE

Many years of study and research have gone into the preparation of this book, and the task of putting such a colossal amount of information into sequential order has proven almost insurmountable. It has now been 20 years since that fall of 1969 when the destiny of my soul became linked with that of the man in the scarlet robe. His first appearance to me, which occurred in September of that year, seemed to awaken me from eons of sleep with a subtle whisper from another place, another time. It was as though I had always known him, and somewhere within the hidden recesses of my mind there also seemed to exist a forgotten promise which had not yet been fulfilled. Shortly thereafter, I became one of those involved in the long search for the real Jesus of Nazareth, and like others, wanted to know more about this man from Galilee who had captured the hearts of a billion people. Although I had been raised in a traditional church and knew Jesus through the scriptures, this was no longer enough. By his appearance to me, he had become an undeniably tangible presence, and a powerful empathic connection was established between us. Because of this, I felt his pain, his longing, and his feelings through the outer shell of superficial research. I came to know him in a way I never dreamed was possible.

During those years of the long search, I left no stone unturned. Through many repetitive writings on Jesus' life contained in the vast labyrinths of world-renowned libraries, the skeleton of the man from Galilee began to gather flesh. Within a few years, it became relatively easy to discern which manuscripts were fraudulent, which were written by pseudo adepts, and which were authentic. The first two either deviated too much from the thread of historical conformability, or they followed a path of omission. It also became painfully apparent that a lack of knowledge pertaining to the hidden teachings of Christianity was the primary obstacle facing most people who sought to write about Jesus' life. Among these teachings, of course, were the mysteries which encompassed the path known as Christian Mastership, or the Resurrection of the Dead. This is understandable, of course, because the deeper teachings of Christianity have been among the most protected secrets of the Roman Vatican and have never been openly disclosed in the mass media. They would have remained so for me also had not a series of mystical events pierced the sanctuary which contained them.

Often it seemed as though I was working on a giant jigsaw puzzle which had no beginning and no end. Neither do I remember the exact moment when I became aware of the fact that the Bible was comprised of a dual teaching: the first revealing the metamorphosis of the soul in its graduation from human to divine, and the second, pertaining to the story of a man who had achieved it. When I finally realized this, the largest piece of the great mystery fell into place and opened up avenues of exploration heretofore unknown to me. It now became obvious that Jesus taught a secret, or mystical, teaching which was given to his disciples in private and a basic, or literal, teaching administered to the outer religious assemblies.

It is difficult to say which of the sacred manuscripts uncovered during the long years were the most exciting, although the *Gospel of Peace* is certainly among those at the top of the list. Originally discovered in the Archives of the Roman Vatican and translated from Hebrew and Aramaic by the renowned philologist and former Professor at the University of Cluj, Dr. Edmond F. Bordeaux Szekely, the *Gospel of Peace* certainly reveals the greatest of Jesus' private teachings. Recorded by John the Beloved, who is also responsible for *The Acts of John, The Gospel of John,* and *Revelation,* the Vatican manuscript cannot help but open doorways which can never again be closed. Although some theologians have a tendency to shun the manuscript because they are unfamiliar with it, this is a theological error, for in 1985 announcements of the reading of the *Gospel of Peace* were made over the Vatican radio by Mr. Mario Spinelli, a Vatican journalist.

There are over a hundred other books in my private library which have also been used as reference material for this book. Many of these are reprints of rare manuscripts, chosen for this work because they confirm the mystical overtones surrounding the life of Jesus. Some of these will not be recognized by traditional theology, because most writers have selected to follow the more common practice of reiterating the basic gospels. However, the gospels are not the only place where the teachings of the Master can be found, particularly in light of the discovery of the *Gospel of Peace.* Therefore, a true adventurer must approach the complex road of open exploration if he, or she, is to fulfill the quest of the soul to know the real Jesus better. Had I followed the path carved by preestablished ideas, I would have written nothing different, and my years of research would have been in vain. I might have chosen the path which the man in the scarlet robe had laid before me, but I knew that I might also have to combat centuries of fundamental concepts. For a time this created a considerable conflict in my soul, which was further complicated by the growing problem of presenting the secret teachings of Jesus to the world. However, the powerful link between myself and the Master was too strong to be broken. I decided to offer what I consider to be the great path of Christian Mastership, which reveals the rich heritage of human evolution.

Elizabeth MacDonald Burrows
January 1, 1990

INTRODUCTION

Although Christianity believes itself to be a modern religion, its origin actually goes back to the beginning of creation and is woven in the birth of life's first born. As God, who rules over all kingdoms, moved through endless time to bring the universe into being, with its one hundred billion galaxies, he not only created, but also came to dwell in all life. He alone is the divine nature and immortal aspect of matter and man's eternal promise in the ever-changing panorama of nature. Therefore, there should be no disharmony among men, for God's laws are just, beneficent, and give to each that which has been rightly earned. When this great truth is really understood, religious differences will cease and men will walk as brothers on earth. As all of this comes to pass, the ancient prophecy concerning the end times will be fulfilled, and mankind will graduate into higher states of existence well prepared for a greater role in the universal plan.

Since the beginning of man's ability to discern, there have always been those rare visionaries who sought to discover the mysteries of life. Some of them succeeded in piercing the veil of the Holy Temple which divides the mortal world from its immortal counterpart, and gave birth to that special essence which separates greatness from mediocrity. These spiritual giants emerged from the shadows of history to keep the endless light of truth unbroken. Sometimes they were regarded as gods, other times as mythological beings who were of little importance. Surrounded by legends, the ancient masters blazed a trail by which anyone who is willing to surrender his hold on a temporal world can join the ranks of an illumined brotherhood who share in the co-creation of the world. Forming an invincible army, these wise men have occupied a special place in the shifting sand of evolution.

Following Moses' illumination on Mount Sinai, the illustrious Hebrew leader sought to establish a code of living (i.e., The Law) based on the forces of nature and the invisible forces of the cosmos. This proved no easy task, for the people were illiterate, childlike, and easily moved to dissension during difficult periods. He finally chose to follow the example of other great leaders before him and give two teachings. One set of principles was taught to the masses, and deeper mysteries were revealed only to the heads of the Twelve Tribes of Israel.

The Mosaic stamp of an esoteric, or secret, teaching even applied to the Tabernacle in the Wilderness. That is, the tabernacle was not only a place of worship for the people, but also a place of symbolic ritual for the initiated priests and elders. Symbolically, the tabernacle signified the three aspects of man: (a) his body, the outer court, (b) his soul, the room of the Holies, and (c) his in-dwelling spirit, or the Ark of the Covenant which was housed in the area known as the Holy of Holies. It was taught that the soul rested between the physical world of man and the immortal kingdom of spirit, and served as a bridge between heaven and earth. Therefore, the soul's development, or level of consciousness, depended on whether it centered on the human way of life (the outer court) or the spiritual way of life (the Holy of Holies).

It ultimately became evident to Moses that his elect would have to be trained in the mysteries of creation and that guidelines would have to be established to enable the heads of the Twelve Tribes of Israel to complete this transformation of human to divine. The process by which this great work could be achieved was symbolized by the seven-pronged candlestick, representing the seven days (cycles) of creation as they were revealed through the burning bush; i.e., darkness into light, light into matter, matter into vegetation, vegetation into fish and fowl, fish and fowl into animal, animal into man, and man into God (Genesis I and II).

At the same time the candlestick was also designed to reveal the nature of natural and cosmic law. When creation began, power brought forth the suns, love formed the cohesive force which united the universe and created the waters, after which wisdom guided the universe by its forward motion, thereby creating air. After this, eternal life was revealed through the evolutionary process of earth, while creative work assured the continuity of human life through farming and scientific advancement. Finally, when earth was brought to peace, her people would achieve joy beyond compare, and heaven would descend to earth as God was born in man, heralding the final day of creation.

So it came to pass, from the Egyptian pyramid to Moses' Tabernacle in the Wilderness, the greater truths of creation flowed from master to disciple and from teacher to student. However, they again came to rest with a secret order of people who called themselves Essenes, a name taken from the breast plate of the Hebrew priest which was called Essen, meaning righteous. While there have been many rumors concerning the possibility that Jesus was affiliated with this order during his youth, there was little to substantiate this until Professor Bordeaux Szekely presented his translation of the *Gospel of Peace*. This manuscript had originally found its way into the Archives of the Vatican and into the home of the Benedictine Monastery, Monte Casino, via the Nestorian priests who, under pressure from the advancing hordes of Genghis Khan, fled from east to west, bearing their holy icons.

The Essenes represented one of the three major philosophical groups which existed among the Jews during, and before, the time of Christ. Due to the extreme integrity of the sect, they gained the respect of both Romans and Jews. Unwilling to participate in the constant dissension among the various systems, they withdrew from involvement in contemporary customs to establish a community based on the original Mosaic principles. Any person requesting admittance into their order was first placed on probation for one year and issued a small hatchet, a white garment, and a girdle. Upon proving that he was able to keep the rules of the brotherhood, the probationer was allowed to partake in the rites of purification, after which followed two more years of trials before being fully admitted into common assembly. Later, the initiate was sworn to secrecy regarding the doctrines of the order, particularly those pertaining to the mysteries of angelology. After the preparatory trials were completed, the initiate was finally allowed to take his place among one of the four novice classes.

The order's principle doctrine was based upon two groups of seven laws: the first set pertained to such cosmic forces as love, power, and wisdom; the second set was founded upon the utilization of natural forces, such as sun, water, air, and food. These angels, or forces, corresponded exactly to the principles contained in the original laws of Moses and correlated to the mysteries of the seven-branched candlestick.

Although the Essenes sometimes have been criticized for their worship of angels because Paul did not sanction it, Dr. Bordeaux Szekely, who was responsible for breaking the Essene code of angelology, has clearly demonstrated that the teachings of Jesus on this subject and those of the Essenes are essentially the same. Since this doctrine comprises such an integral part of the secret teachings of the man from Galilee, its omission from Christian theology has left a very fascinating door unopened.

It is also quite apparent that the man from Galilee chose to follow the traditions of ancient wisdom which sought to reveal the foundation of natural and cosmic law. As the people of his time were illiterate and could not comprehend the deeper truths, he turned to those few men and women who could later carry on the great work. Those things which he taught in secret became the foundation of the Christian mysteries, and for the first few centuries after the crucifixion there did exist a superior class, or order, who were initiated into these mysteries. This select group, after the manner of the earlier brotherhoods, was bound by a solemn promise not to disclose or even converse about the mysteries, except in the presence of those who had been similarly initiated. They were called brethren, the faithful and devotees of the great work.

Christianity, as a whole, is unaware that their master taught both an outer teaching which was given to the masses and an inner teaching which was privately taught to his disciples on the shores of Galilee. The latter mysteries have been carefully protected by descendents of the apostles who were initiated into them. These secret teachings, also referred to as the Holy of the Holies, have been the pulse of the saints and prophets throughout the ages. They have been passed on from generation to generation to those select few who sought for the deeper meanings of life.

And the disciples came, and said unto him, Why speakest thou unto them in parables? He answered and said unto them, Because it is given unto you to know the mysteries of the kingdom of heaven, but to them it is not given.

St. Matthew 13:10-11

Because of persecution, the early Christian master initiates found it necessary to take great precaution and hold the meetings of the faithful in private places under concealment of darkness. They assembled at night to guard against the intrusion of false brethren and profane persons, or spies, who might cause their arrest. Moreover, they conversed together figuratively, using symbols lest the curious or eavesdroppers overhear. The formula which the early church pronounced at the moment of celebrating its mysteries was this: "Depart, ye profane! Let the Catechumens and those who have not been admitted go forth."

Early Christian literature is replete with references to the necessity of maintaining the secrecy of the mysteries. In the *Hierarchiae*, attributed to St. Dionysius, the first Bishop of Athens, the tradition of the sacrament was said to have been divided into three Degrees: purification, initiation, and accomplishment or perfection.

The *Apostolic Constitution* attributed to St. Clement, Bishop of Rome, describes the rule of the early church: "These regulations must on no account be communicated to all sorts of persons because of the Mysteries contained in them." It also relates to the Deacon's duty to keep the doors locked so that no uninitiated should enter, that the mysteries were open to the Fideles, or Faithful, only, and no spectators were allowed at Communion.

Tertullian, who died about A.D. 216, said in his *Apology*: "None are admitted to the religious mysteries without an oath of secrecy. We are especially bound to this caution, because if we prove faithless, we shall not only provoke Heaven, but draw upon our heads the utmost rigor of human displeasure. Far hence, ye Profane is the prohibition from all holy Mysteries."

Clement, Bishop of Alexandria, born c. A.D. 150, says in his *Stromateis* that he cannot explain the mysteries because he should thereby, according to an old proverb, put a sword into the hands of a child.

St. Augustine, Bishop of Hippo, who was born A.D. 347, mentioned in one of his discourses, "Having dismissed the Catechumens, we have retained only you to be our hearers; because, besides those things which belong to all Christians in common, we are not to discourse to you of sublime Mysteries which none are qualified to hear, but those who, by the Master's favor, are made partakers of them... To have taught them openly, would have been to betray them."

St. Chrysostom and St. Augustine speak of initiation more than 50 times. St. Ambrose writes to those who are initiated; and initiation was not merely baptism or admission into the church, but it referred to the Mysteries. The greater truths of religion were unveiled only to the baptized and initiated and kept secret from the Catechumens who were permitted to hear the scriptures read and ordinary discourse delivered. The secret teachings, reserved for the Faithful, were never discussed. When services and prayers ended, the Catechumens and spectators withdrew.

Theodoret, Bishop of Cyropolis in Syria, was born in A.D. 393. In one of his three Dialogues called Immutable, he introduces Orthodoxus speaking this: "Answer me, if you please, in mystical or obscure terms: for perhaps there are some persons present who are not initiated into the Mysteries." And in his preface to Ezekiel, tracing the secret disciplines to the commencement of the Christian era, he states, "These Mysteries are so august that we ought to keep them in great caution."

It is true that modern Christianity is yet in its infancy, and that the dawn of its greatness still lies ahead through the restoration of its secret teachings. Jesus, the Master, walked on earth and gave his life that the brotherhood of man be hastened. It was not his intent that his followers fight among themselves for possession of his robe, but that they learn to live according to his teachings and rise above petty competitiveness into universal oneness. Before the last days of human evolution are finished, this great world, which has been brought into being for the lessons of man, must come to one

accord, without inharmony between religious beliefs, philosophical differences, and scientific separation.

*And then shall the Sons of Men like true brothers give love
one to another, the love which they received from their
Heavenly Father and from their Earthly Mother; and they
shall become comforters one of another. And then shall
disappear from the earth all evil and all sorrow, and there
shall be love and joy upon earth. And then the earth shall be
like the heavens, and the kingdom of God shall come. And
then with the kingdom of God shall come the end of the times.*

Gospel of Peace
Vatican MS./Szekely
Section I, ch. III: 3-5

DESCRIPTION OF JESUS THE CHRIST

*A letter by Lentulus, an official for the Romans
in the time of Tiberius Caesar, to the Roman Senate.*

There hath appeared in these times, and still is, a man of great power named Jesus Christ, who is called by the Gentiles (peoples) the prophet of truth, whom his disciples call the Son of God: raising the dead and healing diseases, a man in stature middling tall, and comely, having a reverend countenance, which they that look upon may love and fear; having hair of the hue of an unripe hazel-nut and smooth almost down to his ears, but from the ears in curling locks somewhat darker and more shining, waving over his shoulders; having a parting at the middle of the head according to the fashion of the Nazarenes; a brow smooth and very calm, with a face without wrinkle or any blemish, which a moderate color makes beautiful; with the nose and mouth no fault at all can be found; having a full beard of the color of his hair, not long, but a little forked at the chin; having an expression simple and mature, the eyes gray, glancing and clear in rebuke terrible, in admonition kind and loveable, cheerful yet keeping gravity; sometimes he hath wept, but never laughed; in stature of body tall and straight, with hands and arms fair to look upon; in talk grave, reserved and modest (so that he was rightly called by the prophet) fairer than the children of men.

Christus-bilder 318
E. von Dobschutz
The Apocryphal 477
Translated by M.R. James
Provost of Eton University

The Alabaster Face   Burrows (cc)

There has appeared in these times, and still is, a man of great
power named Jesus Christ, who is called by the Gentiles the prophet
of truth, whom his disciples call the Son of God.

PART I

YOUTH AND LOST YEARS OF JESUS OF NAZARETH

PROLOGUE

On the eastern seaboard of the Mediterranean, in the heart of Palestine, lies the land which once belonged to Jacob and his 12 sons. This 7,993 square mile portion of the earth's surface has become perhaps the most famous area in the world, for it is known as the Holy Land and is the home of the spiritual giants who gave birth to the dominant religious culture of the modern world. Its name, Israel, was given to Jacob by an angel at Jabbok on the eve of his reunion with his brother, and its meaning is believed to be, May God Rule. Jacob, who also became known as Israel, passed the lands on to his 12 sons: Reuben, Simeon, Levi, Judah, Dan, Naphtali, Gad, Asher, Zebulum, Joseph, and Benjamin. Each, with the exception of Levi, received his inheritance in the *Promised Land* during and immediately following that epoch known as the Conquest. Reuben and Gad, together with the holy tribe of Manasseh, received the territory east of Jordan from Moses, while the priestly house of Levi acquired certain cities and lands within the territories of the other tribes. The tribes of Joseph and Benjamin held the region of the central highlands, which later became known as the Kingdom of Israel when the Hebrew monarchy was divided in 922 B.C.

The capital of the Holy Land is Jerusalem, which is the chief city of Palestine and sacred to the Christians, Jews, and Muslims. It originally developed as a central point among a complex of sacred places which encompassed the altars of Yahweh, Beersheba, Hebron, Bethlehem, Bethel, Shiloh, and Sheihem. Its principal temple has served as the platform for the great prophets and religious leaders of every era, including Isaiah, Jeremiah, and Jesus. To the Jews, it is the place which the Lord has chosen: to the Christians the place where Jesus was crucified, buried, and arose from the dead; while to the Muslims it is the setting for Mohammed's visionary ascent to heaven.

The city is situated in the central highlands of Judah C. 33 N.E. of the Mediterranean, C. 14 N.W. of the Dead Sea and C. 138 S.W. of Damascus. Today it is divided into two sectors: the old city rising on a quadrangle of rock enclosed on all sides by a great wall, and the new city which lies open in the surrounding hills and valleys.

Its lengthy history is exceeded only by the stories and legends of its mother country, and visitors from all parts of the world flock to it daily to absorb its mystique. The western spur holds the palace of Herod the Great, which was later the residence of Caiaphas, the high priest responsible for ordering the death of Jesus of Nazareth.

For many people, the Holy Land is perceived as a desolate collection of hills and valleys usually devoid of vegetation, but to the eye trained in the beauties of nature, the symmetric hills of Palestine reflect a peace which belies its history of war and dissension. During the Master's time, his home province, Galilee, was in the northern portion of Roman Judea, while Samaria rested in the rugged central highlands, and Jordan comprised the southern region, ending at the Idumaea border. As seen from the air, Palestine consists geographically of four parallel bands lying between the Mediterranean Sea and Arabian Desert, their lines demarcated by two mountain ranges. These are, first, the Central Range extending down from Mount Lebanon along the western side of the Jordan Valley; second, the Maritime Plains bounded on the south by the desert beyond Gaza; third, the area between the Central Range and the Mountains of Israel, which constitutes Israel's main land mass and forms the backbone of the land where Jesus lived; and finally, the Jordan Valley extending southward to form a plain separating Lebanon and Anti-Lebanon.

Temperatures in Palestine are varied due to the great difference in elevation between the 11,000-foot summit of Mt. Hermon and the surface of the Dead Sea, which is 1,200 feet below the level of the Mediterranean. The area's two seasons are determined by the incidence of rain. Summer runs from May to October and is hot and rainless, while winter is relatively mild in temperature with heavy rainfall.

From Jerusalem to Nazareth, one travels among the barren hills near the Dead Sea and past Jericho on the west side of the south Jordan River ten miles northwest of the Dead Sea. Next, the route takes the traveler past Jacob's Well into Samaria through the Plains of Esdraelon, finally reaching Nazareth which is situated in Lower Galilee. Beyond this lies Upper Galilee, Magdalal, and Capernaum, a small lake port on the northwest shore of the Sea of Galilee two and one half miles west of the mouth of the Jordan River. It was in Capernaum that the most famous of all men, Jesus who became known as the Christ, spent much of his time during the last years of his life.

CHAPTER I

HARP OF DESTINY

In the histories of the twelve tribes of Israel it is written that there was one Joachim, exceedingly rich: and he offered his gifts twofold saying: That which is of my superfluity shall be for the whole people, and that which is for my forgiveness shall be for the Lord, for a propitiation unto me.

Book of James 1:1

n 23 B.C. during the early reign of Herod the Great, an Idumaean ruler over Palestine who had been placed on his throne by Marcus Antonius (B.C. 83-30), there lived a devout couple named Anna and Joachim in the city of Bethlehem, Judea. It also happened that they were both direct descendents of King David ben Jesse, the most powerful king in the history of Israel. The woman, Anna, had been born in Bethlehem, the native city of the ancestral king. Her husband, Joachim, had been raised in Nazareth, a city situated on the southern range of Lower Galilee, about ten miles from the plains of Esdraelon. Although their marriage was exceedingly good, their hearts were overshadowed by darkness, for 25 years had passed since their espousal, and they had produced no children. In the eyes of the people their plight was looked upon as a curse from God, who was believed to close the womb of all women who were not found worthy to bear seed. Behind their backs, many of their kinsmen scorned them; a few offered supplication on their behalf. As time passed Anna, who had been a young teen when she married Joachim, approached her fortieth birthday in barrenness. In spite of this, however, she still continued her supplication to the Lord, hoping that He would bestow His grace upon her and her womb would be opened. And it came to pass, that the seasons vanished one by one without avail, containing in them the melting snows of Lebanon and the Feasts of Dedication.

It was written in the *Histories of the Twelve Tribes of Israel* that Joachim was an exceedingly rich man and quite able to provide his wife with a substantial home in the city of her birth. Although he felt great affection for her, he was seldom at home. As a shepherd, he spend a great deal of time in the surrounding countryside tending his flocks. Occasionally, it became necessary to take the sheep to distant pastures where the grazing was more abundant, particularly in the month of Tebeth (December/January) when the rain, hail, and snow touched the higher hills. During these periods, Joachim would put up his tent in the wilderness and watch the comings and goings of the sun as it made its daily pilgrimage from east to west. In the morning he led his flock forth from their sheepcote (an enclosure to protect the animals from thieves), calling to them, and by day he watched over their wanderings to assure that none went astray. As the sun set in the evening, casting its shadows across the broad expanse of Palestine's symmetrical hills, he led them back into their fold, counting each one as it passed under his shepherd's rod. Except on rare occasions, when other herdsmen passed near, the sheep master had no one to talk to. Thus he was a quiet man and spent a great deal of his time in contemplation and prayer to God.

In the year of B.C. 23, during the month of Chisleu (November/December), as the trees bared themselves because of the winter storms and the pastures turned green due to the heavy rains, Anna and Joachim prepared for their annual journey to Jerusalem to celebrate the Feast of Dedication. This particular feast was popular and joyous, for it commemorated the purification of Solomon's temple, removal of its polluted altar, and restoration of the worship of Jehovah by Judas Maccabeus (B.C. 164). The couple planned to give an offering of sheep to the high priest on their arrival at the temple in order to continue in the grace of the Lord. A man of noble character, Joachim always shared his worldly substance by dividing it into three parts. The first third went to the support of the holy center of Jerusalem and its officers, another third was distributed among strangers and the poor, while the final portion was reserved for family use.

The couple's family home was made of sand and limestone which burned and dried in the hot sun, while the beams of the building were made of sycamore. The house had a semblance of an upper story, providing sleeping rooms for kinsmen, and its walls were whitewashed outside and inside with gypsum. Although there were few openings into the building, the nature of its construction allowed relief from the hot sun, so the couple lived in considerable comfort and contentment. Now, as Anna and Joachim made ready for the short journey to the city of Jerusalem, Joachim picked up his tribal ensign denoting his alliance to the house of Judah, the fourth son of Jacob and Leah. Then he motioned to his wife that he was ready to leave. Gathering a small flock of sheep together which had been singled out for their offering to the temple, the couple hastened to the main thoroughfare connecting the village of Bethlehem to the primary caravan route below.

As Anna and Joachim began their descent, they were joined by others who were heading toward the Holy City for the festivities. Gradually forming into groups, they lifted their voices in song to honor Moses, their lawgiver, who had brought their people out of Egyptian bondage. Although the Feast of Dedication did not require everyone to journey to Jerusalem, many did so. The popular celebration brought traders from all over the land and offered everyone a fine opportunity to barter. By this time, Jerusalem was not only a religious center but also a great trade center for those who came from Egypt, Damascus, and Babylon. Therefore, the streets were constantly filled with traders who came from far and wide to sell their silks, incense, and rich tapestries.

The city itself sat on a plateau 2,550 feet high and 3,800 feet above the level of the Dead Sea. Its exclusive location off the main highways between Asia Minor and Egypt offered no river frontage like Babylon, Thebes, Rome, or Memphis, but it possessed a good water supply which was fed from the ancient Gihon Spring in the Kidron Valley. In the afternoons, the plateau was fanned by a breeze from the Mediterranean Sea, creating an annual temperature of 63 degrees, dropping to 25 degrees in the winter. Centrally located, Jerusalem was ideally situated for the capital of the United Kingdom of Israel.

It was customary for the men and women to dress in a similar manner, but on this day of the festive celebration many of the garments were adorned with special embroidery and occasional pieces of silk. The straight, apron-like clothing allowed freedom of movement and protection from the summer's oppressive heat. Both men and women tied bold pieces of cloth around their mid-sections, forming belts which added touches of individuality and color. Many of the women also added chains, jewels, and headdresses for ornament and protection. Since the month of Chisleu was the beginning of winter, the rains had started and the weather had turned much colder. Therefore, the men wore mantles over their dress, while the women wore shawls or broad garments similar to the outer cloaks worn by the men.

Many came from the surrounding countryside to join the travelers as they wound their way along the five-mile road from Bethlehem to Jerusalem. These too raised their voices in thanksgiving, and the power of their singing filled the distant hills and reverberated through the valleys. As the aggregation began their entry into the Holy City, the people felt a great deal of reverence for this land which had been established by their ancestors. Although Jerusalem was situated on only eight acres of land and was considerably smaller than Megiddo, the royal city of the Canaanites, it had been the center of the financial splendor of David and

Solomon. The history of the Twelve Tribes of Israel was written in every stone of the great wall surrounding the Holy City of the great kings, and even the mighty wars which resounded with the glory of victory and the agony of defeat had not daunted the hearts or pride of the people. They remembered the sons of Jacob who had bowed their backs under Egyptian tyranny, and how God who had heard their cries sent a deliverer. Now they too turned their eyes toward heaven, searching for a new Messiah to restore Israel to its people and redeem its greatness.

From some distance away, Issachar, the seventh son of Obede-dom and gatekeeper of the temple, watched the tribes approach with their offerings. His position had descended to him from his father, a Korhite Levite, also a gatekeeper, as had his father been before him. He nodded his head in greeting as the travelers approached, and then quickly turned his attention to their offerings. One by one, the tribal standards passed before him without interruption, until it was time for Anna and Joachim to pass through the gate with their herd. Arrogant over his lineage, Issachar harshly lashed out at the couple and inquired of them, "Why do you, who have brought forth no seed in Israel, appear among those who have? It is not lawful that you do so, for you have been judged by God to be unworthy to receive children. Our scriptures say, 'Cursed is he who has not begotten seed in Israel.' Therefore, you must first free yourself of this curse before you can come to God with your offerings."

The words of the gatekeeper pierced Joachim's heart with great pain, for he had long suffered humiliation because of his barrenness. To be singled out in front of his kinsmen in such a manner brought great humiliation. Turning from Issachar, he departed with his offering that he might search through the history of the Twelve Tribes of Israel to see if the priest had spoken the truth. What he discovered later did not alleviate his sorrow, for he found that the leaders of all tribes had brought forth children in the Holy Land. In view of this evidence, he knew that he could not return to his home and wife or face his kinsmen again. So he turned toward the dangers of the wilderness for solace. There the sheep master remembered how God had given Abraham and Sarah a son in the last days. So he set up his tent and prepared to fast until he received an answer from God, saying to himself, "I will not eat or drink until I am visited by the Lord, my God."

In the meantime, Anna, who had watched her husband depart in great sorrow, returned to the family home in Bethlehem and withdrew to her private quarters. Tears flowed from her eyes because her husband had not spoken to her when he left. Although she understood the pain Joachim was suffering, she too would have to endure a greater disgrace than before. Not only was her womb barren, but it was now necessary that she don widow's robes because her husband had left her. In agony she cried, "I do not know how I shall live through this terrible disgrace, for I am now a widow, and my womb is childless."

Now it came to pass that as the Lord's day (Sabbath) drew near, Euthine, Anna's maidservant, became deeply concerned over her employer's grief. Going to her, Euthine asked, "How long are you to humble your soul? The great day of the Lord is near and you should not mourn. Please take this headband which one of my former mistresses gave me for my work and put it on. Really, it is not fitting for me to wear it because I am your slave and it bears a royal mark."

Rudely pushing her away, Anna cried out, "Get away from me! I did not do this, but it is God who punishes me, so take back your headband. I do not know if one of your employers gave it to you, or one of your men, and I do not wish to share in your corruption by accepting this as a gift."

Shaking her head in disbelief, Euthine's dark eyes began to flash in anger, for her gesture was intended to be one of kindness toward Anna, whom she loved. Lashing out quickly, she said, "Why should I curse you because you have not believed me? After all, God has shut up your womb and has given you no fruit in Israel."

When Anna heard these words, she became even more distressed because not only did the women of Israel scorn her, but now her own maidservant as well. Hastily returning to the sanctity of her room, she removed her mourning garments, cleaned her hair, and reached for her wedding clothes. After putting them on, she went into the garden and took a position under a laurel tree. Wringing her hands, she closed her eyes and implored the Lord, crying, "O God of our fathers, bless me and hear my prayer, as you did bless the womb of our mother Sarah and gave her a son, Isaac."

As Anna's eyes turned toward heaven she spied a sparrow's nest in the uppermost branches of the tree. This filled her with even greater despair, for now it seemed that God considered even the birds of the air more worthy. Weeping loudly she cried, "Woe to the womb that brought me forth, for I have been born as a curse before the children of Israel. At the temple I was reproached, ridiculed, and thrust out of the temple. Oh Lord, I am not even given the privileges of the birds of the heaven, for they are allowed to bear young. Neither am I allowed to reproduce like the animals, or the fish, or earth, for even this earth brings forth its fruit in season to praise thee. Oh God, why have you placed such a burden on me?"

With these words her head dropped forward and tears fell from her eyes. As Anna sat weeping, her heart burdened with the hopeless chains of darkness and loneliness, a shadow fell over her. It came from the mist of timelessness and a light of some distant horizon which mortal man has seldom seen. Within its subtle radiance, there stood one whose countenance was as the sun, and peace and mercy flowed from him as water from a never-ending spring. His body was not solid, as the body of man, but comprised of subtle ethers as delicate as a gossamer web floating in the summer mist. When he touched her, her eyes were opened and she beheld this being who had been sent from far beyond the ravenous world of human life. Then the angel spoke to her gently, his voice like the whisper of the wind, and he said, "Anna, you must not grieve so, for God has heard your prayers. I have been sent to tell you that you shall conceive and bear forth a child who shall become known throughout the whole world."

As the childless woman beheld the angel of the Lord, she felt his peace reaching into the desolate wasteland of her soul, and her sorrow passed as a shadow in the light. Then disbelief and joy began to penetrate the deep caverns of disappointment and she reached out her hands to touch the countenance which stood before her, crying out, "As my God lives, and if you are not an illusion born of my desires, then I promise that I shall dedicate this child to God, and it will serve him all the days of its life."

After these words had been spoken, he who had come from the angelic kingdom began to dissipate, leaving but a fleeting promise where once his presence had stood. Shortly, doubts began to assail Anna, for she could hardly believe that God had heard her prayers and sent a messenger with such glad tidings. However, even as these questions burned through her mind, the melodious voice of the angel spoke again through her subtle senses, saying, "Be of good cheer Anna, for you have indeed found favor in the eyes of God. Now dry your tears, for your husband has also received the news that you will conceive and has come to make his sacrifices."

Throwing aside her veil with great joy, Anna rushed out of the garden and went toward the gate, which served as entry into the sheepfold. Standing there she saw the distant outline of her husband moving slowly toward her with his herd. Yet, because of their sad parting, she felt somewhat estranged and shy and wondered if his greeting would be as it was before their disgrace. But it came to pass that her fears were soon alleviated, for as Joachim neared she saw the mirror of the miracle within his eyes, and she ran towards him and fell upon his neck, sobbing, "Now I know that God has indeed blessed me. I am a widow no more and I, who have been childless, shall bring forth a child upon the soil of Israel."

On the following day after he had rested, Joachim made ready to take an offering to the Temple of Jerusalem, saying, "If God is reconciled to me, the plate which is worn on the mantle of the priest will manifest it to me." Turning to Anna, he bid her good-bye, and picking up his tribal standard he turned toward the City of Peace where he had recently been dishonored.

Once Joachim reached the plateau which held the seat of the Palestine government, he could look southward over the Judean hills. On the east the valley of the Kidron separated the plateau from the ridge of the Mount of Olives, while the Wadi Er Rababi bound the city on the west and south, meeting the Valley of Kidron near the lower Pool of Siloam. Jerusalem was the product of human effort and not one of geographical configuration, for it was the meeting place of east and west; poised on the watershed between the desert and the sea, she had united them. As G.H. Smith stated in his book, "Jerusalem is central, but aloof, defensible but not commanding...left alone by the main currents of world's history, she had been but a small highland township, her character compounded of rock, the olive, and the desert. Sion the Rockfort, Olivet and Gethsemane, the Oilpress, the Tower of the Flock, and the wilderness of the Shepherds would have been no more than names, had she not become the bride of kings and the mother of prophets."

Making his way through the narrow streets, the sheep master passed through the crowded streets to the temple. Then he came before the altar of the high priest, and falling on his knees, he prepared to give his offering in thanksgiving and gratitude for his redemption. Peering up at the dark blue miter, Joachim looked deeply into the gold diadem which bore the words HOLY TO JEHOVAH, saying to himself, "If the Lord God be reconciled to me, the plate which is worn on the forehead of the priest will manifest it to me."

Looking down upon the kneeling figure, the high priest stood quietly, a magnificent figure against the subtle light of the burning candles. Over his under girdle he wore a fine linen chethone which reached to his feet, and upon this was placed a blue Meeir, or long robe, also covering the full length of his body. This was tied around with a girdle embroidered with flowers of scarlet, and purple, and blue, and intertwined with gold. It appeared at the waist like a coiling serpent, although it hung loosely from the waist to the ankle so as to not hinder his movements. At the bottom of the garment hung fringes, in color like pomegranates, and between each pomegranate hung a golden bell. Besides this he wore an ephod which resembled the epomis of the Greeks. Woven to the depth of a cubit, it was comprised of several colors and intermixed with gold, yet left the middle of the breast uncovered. In the void place of the garment there was inserted a piece of material embroidered with gold and the colors of the ephod, called an Essen, or Oracle. As the priest now stood at the altar in his official dress, he served as a mediator between God and the people, and a part of his responsibility was to witness the offerings and sacrifices which were made for atonement and redemption. Therefore, he quietly watched over the prayerful figure of Joachim, awaiting a sign.

Still looking earnestly into the golden diadem, it came to pass that Joachim saw no sin in himself. Therefore, he knew that God had forgiven him for his iniquities and he rejoiced greatly, saying, "I know now that God has truly looked upon me with favor and has forgiven me."

After he had completed his prayers and rendered his sacrifice, the sheep master returned to Bethlehem, his heart light and content. As the weeks passed, he and Anna waited expectantly for the fulfillment of God's promise, and they were not disappointed. Soon Anna conceived, and in the ninth month on the fifteenth day of Adar (March) she gave birth to a girl child.

As the last pains of the long labor ended and Anna lay exhausted from the ordeal, she heard the crying of her child as it was prepared for presentation. The midwife had already cut the navel cord and was bathing the infant in water, after which she rubbed the child in salt and wrapped it in swaddling clothes. Although Anna was weak, her soul felt magnified and joy coursed through her heart as she asked the midwife, "What have I given birth to?" Looking down upon the tired woman, the midwife spoke with great tenderness, "You have brought forth a girl, Anna."

Reaching for her newborn, Anna exclaimed, "My soul is glorified this day, for I have been redeemed in the eyes of my people." And she named the child Mary, meaning obstinacy.

Not long thereafter, the family members and neighbors began to gather around the home of the new parents, for the news of the birth had traveled quickly throughout Bethlehem. In traditional fashion, the men surrounded the new father and danced and sang. Occasionally they joked about the fact that Joachim had brought forth a girl child instead of a son. However, this type of monologue did not daunt the new father, for he knew these things were spoken in happy jest. After this, a great feast was prepared and the people offered prayers of thanksgiving to God who had bestowed His blessings upon the childless couple.

And it came to pass, in the section of Canaan bequeathed to Judah, the fourth son of Jacob and Leah, the infant child was nursed by her mother. In the distance lay the Salt Sea, separated from Bethlehem only by the wilderness which was the former home of the aggressive Hittites. To the east lay the Great Sea and to the north, Nazareth and the Sea of Galilee. The child did not know that her destiny lay in the historic northern land near the Plain of Esdraelon, or that her name would be forever carried in the winds of history. For now, she was content to smile happily at her mother and father when they came near her and to sleep peacefully in the homemade cradle which had been lovingly carved for her. Her fair skin and dark hair gave promise to the beauty which would one day herald her as one of the most beautiful women in all of Israel.

After 80 days had passed, Anna went to the temple to offer a sacrifice of purification. Then she prepared a sanctuary in her bedchamber to make certain that nothing common or unclean touched Mary because she had been promised to God before her birth. When Mary was several months old, Anna placed her on the ground to see if she could stand alone, and as she took several tottering steps her mother caught her up in her arms, saying, "As the Lord my God lives, you shall walk no more upon the ground until you are taken to the temple."

Since Joachim was a prosperous man, Anna was able to engage young, undefiled, Hebrew maidens to carry Mary to and fro and insure that her feet did not touch the ground. A year passed, and along the northern boundary of Palestine the mountains of Lebanon gathered their annual snowfall and stood white against the winter skies. But their beauty diminished as spring came and the snows melted, filling the Jordan channel and causing the river to overflow in the lower plains. On the day of Mary's first birthday, Joachim ordered a great feast. He invited some of the priests and scribes from the Assembly of the Elders (also known as the Sanhedrin Council) to attend the celebration. When they had gathered, Joachim took his daughter in his arms and presented her to them, asking that she be blessed, saying, "O God of our fathers, bless this child."

After the ceremony was completed, the name Mary was added to the ancestral records of the tribes of Israel, and then Anna took the child to her sanctuary for feeding. While she tarried in her private quarters, with Mary nestled gently in her arms, she composed a song. Raising her eyes toward heaven, her voice filled with great thanksgiving, she sang, "I will sing a hymn to God, because he has visited me and taken away the taunts of the other women. He has given me fruit to bear as do the trees and plants, and I walk in shame no more on earth. Hear me, O you tribes of Israel, my offspring now lives and feeds among you."

After this Anna laid the child to rest and returned to attend those who came to the feast. Later, when everyone had departed, she and her husband fell upon their knees in joyous prayer to glorify God. Another year passed, and as the month of Ijar (April/May) approached, the rains ended. The white tamarisk tree yielded its pink and white blossoms, while the children of Israel went forth to harvest the wheat which had been sown in the early rains of November.

In the vineyards, the grapes also prepared to renew themselves for their winter vintage, and the temperatures escalated as summer began its customary pilgrimage across the land. Up above, the new moon shown in great splendor, as preparations were made to celebrate the Little Passover by those who had been unable to participate in Nisan. In remembrance of his promise to God concerning Mary, Joachim now went to Anna, saying, "Let us take Mary to the Temple of Jerusalem, that we might keep our promise to the Lord. I am afraid that if we wait any longer He will become impatient with us and our gift will not be acceptable."

When Anna heard these words a great heaviness penetrated her heart, and a pain filled her soul, leaving tears of longing amid the field of gratitude and promise. She had always known that this day would come to pass, for the clouds of separation had loomed in the subtle horizons of her commitment to God since her child's birth. Yet it seemed that time had passed so swiftly. Even though she had no intention of withdrawing her commitment to God, her motherly instincts now fought against the hour of release, and turning to Joachim with great sorrow, she asked, "Can we not wait until the third year, for then the child may not long for us so much?"

As Joachim looked at his wife, his eyes were filled with great understanding. Although he was firm in his decisions, he was also a wise man, and the deep lines of aging which etched his face played hide-and-seek with an overpowering sense of gentleness. As he listened to Anna's request, a sharp pain also filled his own heart, for his daughter had brought much joy to his household and was a sign from God that they lived in His grace. He knew that Anna's reason for delaying the temple presentation was one born of motherhood and not just concern over Mary's youth. Thus, even his own sorrow cast its rays across the compassion emanating from his soul and he spoke to Anna as a loving father to a child, "Very well Anna, we shall wait another year as you have asked."

The following year moved swiftly across the ancient land. The festival of the Little Passover, which celebrated the Hebrews' entry into the wilderness, had come and gone. So had the Feast of Dedication, and even the Feast of Tabernacles had given way to the winter rains and the plowing and sowing. The trees were bare, while the desert hungrily devoured the moisture and was transformed into abundant green pastures. In the meantime, the flocks had left the highland for the Jordan valley, while the cold spring rains sustained the growing crops. The countryside came alive from the bright splash of color exuding from the orange trees, bearing their ripened fruit as though in preparation for the forthcoming Feast of the Passover. Each passing month seemed to bring a sign, as well as a reminder, of the unfulfilled covenant between Anna and the God of Israel.

And it came to pass that Joachim, who had once yielded to the pangs of his wife's desire, felt that further delay in fulfilling the commitment to God would be unwise. He went to Anna, saying, "Anna, it is time for us to take Mary to the Temple of Jerusalem to be presented to God. Go now and call forth the daughters of the Hebrews who have not been defiled, for they must go with us to the presentation. Let each of them carry a burning lamp and proceed before us, lest the child turn backward and her heart be led away from the Lord."

In her own heart Anna knew that her husband spoke wisely and so she nodded her head, passively agreeing with his command. Then she went to her quarters to dress Mary for the presentation, seeking to subdue her sorrow. She found some comfort in the fact that Mary would be attended by her kinfolk, for her sister Bianca's daughter, Elisabeth, had become espoused to Zacharias of the Order of Abijah, and it was he who officiated as high priest in the temple where Mary would be raised as one of the temple virgins.

After Anna completed dressing Mary, she summoned some of the young Hebrew females who cared for her, and then she and Joachim also donned their finest apparel, lest God find them unworthy to present their gift. After these arrangements had been completed, they began their journey to the Holy City. It was a solemn parade, for the undefiled Hebrew maidens went before Anna and Joachim bearing unlit lamps. Neither did the couple speak to one another, or look down at the infant which Anna held in her arms. To do so might have brought regrets, and they wished to give their offering unblemished by sorrow or tears. God had shown his mercy and taken away their shame, and now they wanted their most priceless possession to be just as acceptable in His eyes.

On arriving at the temple, Anna and Joachim requested that the young Hebrew women light the lamps and go before them to attract the attention of the child, lest she look back. At the entrance stood a folding door of cypress wood with door posts of olive, each door being divided into an upper and lower section, after the manner of the Tabernacle in the Wilderness. Inside, the walls were covered with cedar and carved with buds and open flowers, while other sections of the design work were overlaid with pure gold.

As the aggregation entered the sanctuary of the *Holy* its silence permeated them, forbidding speech. The flickering lamps which passed before them added solemnity to the sacred occasion, and to Anna and Joachim's satisfaction the child did not look back. Ahead of them, just in front of the altar, stood Zacharias waiting to receive their gift, and when they approached the third step from the altar they lowered Mary to the floor. Reaching down for the child, the priest picked her up and cradled her in his arms, kissed her, and said: "The Lord has chosen you from among all of Jerusalem. Within your womb in the latter days you shall bear His redemption to all the children of Israel." Thereafter, Mary was referred to as the Virgin Mary, after the manner of the other young undefiled girls who served in the temple.

Upon hearing the prophecy of the priest, Anna and Joachim knelt before the altar praising God because the child had not turned back, after which they departed from the temple in great peace because they had fulfilled their commitment. At the same time, they knew that they would no longer share joyous interludes with their daughter. When they looked into her bed she would not be there, nor would the sound of her happy gurgling fill their home. However, even as they made their way quietly along the dusty road which took them to Bethlehem, other plans were being set in motion by a powerful and wise God. As they walked, they did not know that destiny would again occupy their daughter's bed, or that the delightful sounds of another infant would fill the emptiness of their hearts.

In the days which followed Mary's dedication, another vision came upon Anna, and an angel of the Lord appeared again, saying kindly, "Anna, you have found grace in the eyes of God and you will conceive again. You shall name this child Mary also, for she is being given to you to ease the wound in your heart."

When Anna beheld the angel and heard his words her spirit was uplifted, for the promise of the Lord that she would conceive again was beyond any wish she secretly harbored in her heart. Once more the miracle of child birth would fall upon the house of Joachim, but this time it would not leave shadows of emptiness behind. Therefore, Anna rejoiced greatly and went to tell her husband the glad tidings.

As the seasons passed her womb grew, and in the hour of her delivery she brought forth another girl child, naming it Mary, as it had been given her. Later when the time of espousal fell upon the younger Mary, she was betrothed to an influential fisherman named Zebedee, and gave birth to two sons, James, who would become known as *the Great,* and John, who would become know as *the Beloved.* At approximately the same time, on the outskirts of Jerusalem, their older kinsmen, Elisabeth and Zacharias, also gave birth to a son, whom they named John, but the world would call him *the Baptist.* In this manner the looms of destiny would weave their mysterious cloak, and the relatives of the Virgin Mary would be written in the blood lines of the Twelve Tribes of Israel.

During the 12 years which followed her dedication to God, the elder Mary lived under the guidance of the priesthood and partook only food which was especially prepared to maintain her purity. Her home was with the other virgins in the women's quarters of the temple, where she was supervised by one of the young women sanctified by the priesthood. During this time she was exposed to no outside influences and remained untouched by hatred, anger, and jealousy, as well as the conflicts which developed among the people of her land. The Virgin Mary was instructed not only in the gracious arts of womanhood, such as sewing, but also in the rituals of the temple. Due to the latter training, she was expected to participate in the daily absolutions and worship of God. The bud of future beauty made her fair to behold in the eyes of all who saw her.

As the twelfth year of Mary's life approached, deep concern surfaced among the members of the priesthood, for it was customary that the temple virgins be declared impure when the cycles of womanhood began. At this time, the virgins were no longer allowed to remain within the temple walls, and husbands were selected for them from among the eligible bachelors of the land. Although one of the high priests at the temple greatly admired Mary and offered her many gifts to marry his son, she remained steadfast in her consecration to God. This created a very unexpected problem for the priesthood, who were accustomed to being obeyed. Eventually, they gathered for council, saying one to another, "Behold, Mary is now 12 years old and she is still living in the temple. We must make some arrangements for her espousals, or she will pollute the sanctuary."

Although they convened for some time concerning the matter, they were unable to reach a common decision. Finally, it became evident that the problem should be turned over to the high priest, so they went to him, saying, "It is you who stands over the altar of the Lord. We have been unable to resolve the issue concerning Mary, the daughter of Anna and Joachim, who came to us 12 years ago. If suitable arrangements are not made soon we fear that she will bring grievous harm to us. Please go and pray concerning her, and whatever God asks we will do."

When he heard the complaints of his priests, Zacharias went to his chambers and put on the vestment of the 12 bells. Then he entered into the room of the of *Holy of Holies*,[1] which contained the Law, or the Ark of the Covenant. As he knelt in front of the mercy seat he began to pray, and an angel came down and stood upon the seat. The garments of the angel were as the morning sun, and his face was etched in gleaming light of endless worlds. When he spoke to Zacharias, it was in gentle tones, "You must seek out the prophecy of Isaiah to discover to whom Mary is to become bethrothed. Isaiah has said there shall come forth a rod out of the stem of Jesse, Son of Obed, Father of King David, and descendant of the tribe of Judah. From him there shall be born one like unto a flower, and the Spirit of God shall rest upon him and make him wise in all matters."

After Zacharias came out of the inner sanctuary, he went to seek through the books of the Twelve Tribes of Israel to find the names of any eligible bachelors in Israel. He knew that he must select one among them to become Mary's espoused husband. As she was a temple virgin and consecrated to the Lord, her marriage would have to be arranged with someone who would not only honor her position, but who was of royal lineage.

Now it happened that there was a man named Joseph ben Jacob, a descendent from the tribe of Judah and the house of David, who lived in Bethlehem. He was a carpenter of considerable renown and a respected member of the Sanhedrin Council, the supreme court of Israel. His wife had died a year before, leaving him a widower and father of six children. His four boys were named Judas, Josetos, James, and Simeon and his two daughters were named Assia and Lydia. (*History of Joseph*, 4th Century Egyptian and Arabic-Forbes Robinson's and Peeter's version). He was a tall, reserved man, pleasing in countenance, possessing sandy hair and a full beard of the same color, after the manner of some of the early Hebrews. Joseph was a man of few words and was greatly devoted to truth. By religion he was said to follow the practices of the Essenes, a Jewish sect which had withdrawn from the fundamental ritual and tradition to reestablish the original laws of Moses. His work, as well as his reputation, was so excellent that he was much in demand throughout all of Palestine.

When Joseph received Zacharias' summons to appear before him, he laid down his adze (a cutting tool with a thin, arched blade which is used for shaping wood) and picked up his tribal standard. He hastened immediately to Jerusalem, believing that a special meeting of the Council had been called. By the time he arrived, Zacharias had assembled the tribal rods of the eligible men before him and had begun his prayer to the Lord. Then Zacharias received a sign from heaven designating Joseph as Mary's future husband. He turned to Joseph and said, "Joseph, it has fallen to you to receive the temple virgin Mary as your wife. Now let us honor the wish of God, so take her in to the house of Joseph that she might serve you."

At first Joseph refused, saying, "I have grown children and am an old man. I cannot do as you request, for it will surely bring ridicule upon my head and the heads of my sons."

With serious countenance, Zacharias replied, "I have known you for many years, Joseph, and you are an old and trusted friend. Fear the Lord your God, and remember all that God did to Dathan, Abiram, and Korah when they mutinied against Moses in the

Wilderness of Peran. Remember how the earth was rent open and they were swallowed up because of their rebellion. And now fear, my friend, lest the house of Joseph become unsanctioned and trouble befall you because you have gone against the will of the Lord."

And being a just man, Joseph did as Zacharias requested and agreed to take Mary as his wife. When the betrothal had been arranged, he returned to Bethlehem to put his house in order that he might receive his young wife. Later, when the proper time had passed, he returned to Jerusalem for the marriage ceremony. And it happened that Anna and Joachim, Mary's sister, and other kinsmen also came from Bethlehem to attend the wedding, for they had been notified by the priest of Mary's impending union. However, the customary celebration of feasting, music, and dancing did not follow, for Mary's wedding was one of holy sanctification and not by human arrangement.

Later, following the ceremony which had been officiated by the high priest, Mary and Joseph returned to Bethlehem where Joseph accepted Mary into his house, saying, "Mary, I have received you from the temple of the Lord. Now I must leave you in my house and go away to work at my trade. Afterwards I will come again to you, but for now may God watch over you."

During the next two years Mary lived in the house of Joseph, first in Bethlehem and later in her father's native land, Nazareth. After leaving the temple, she gave much of her attention to rearing James, her husband's youngest child. Although considerable time had passed since the couple had become espoused, the marriage had not been consummated, primarily because Mary was still considered a temple virgin and bound by oath to remain undefiled throughout life. Therefore, as her fourteenth year approached, she had known no man.

One day, while sitting at the spinning loom, a thirst came over the young woman. Picking up a pitcher, she made her way to the communal well that she might fill the vessel and drink. As Mary lowered the pitcher into the water, she was suddenly startled by a voice, which spoke to her and said, "Mary, your ways have been pure and have found favor in the eyes of God. You will be blessed among women."

Turning to see who said these things, Mary was surprised to find no one there. Confused at hearing such an inner voice from the unseen world, she became very much afraid and hastened back to her house. Setting the pitcher down, she took up the thread again and began to draw it through the fabric she was working on, but as she did so there appeared a being clothed in light. Similar to him who had appeared to her mother, the angel was not solid after the manner of humankind. He appeared to be comprised of fine mist, glowing and pulsating like a distant star and his voice had a melodious quality unlike the harshness of earthly sounds. Even his presence emanated a gentleness and love which could not abide in human hearts. Immediately, the angel sensed Mary's fear and spoke to her kindly, saying, "Fear not, Mary. I am here to tell you that you will conceive a male child, and he will come forth from the highest regions of the angelic kingdom and the Spirit of God will dwell in him."

When she heard these words, Mary asked, "Am I indeed to conceive such a child and bring it forth in the manner of all women?"

"Not so, Mary," the messenger replied, "Your child shall be great among men, and shall be called the Son of the Highest. The Lord shall give unto him the throne of his father David and he shall reign over the house of Jacob forever, and of his kingdom there shall be no end. You will name him Jesus, meaning redeemer and savior." After these words had been spoken the angelic emissary disappeared like a ray of sun in a cloud swept sky.

As Mary sat working over the material for the temple, she pondered over the things she had heard, and wondered if these sayings would indeed come to pass. During this time, Joseph was away pursuing his trade in Capernaum, a city on the western shore of the Sea of Galilee, and had not seen his wife for some time. In the past, he had found her inclined to fanciful daydreaming, and at other times, she appeared to dwell in other worlds, which caused him grave concern. He was hoping that this frivolity would pass away as the girl matured, for he had little way of knowing that Mary would soon conceive and was destined to bring forth a son who was marked by Aaron and molded by the crown of David.

During his return trip to Nazareth, Joseph was not aware of the deep and mysterious things in his future, but the great power which moves the destiny of all life carefully observed him walking along quietly. Even as Joseph moved, the golden orb of day rose high in the sky toward its zenith, and a great soul waited in the timeless ethers to be born into matter. His brief sojourn in an earthly body would make it possible for those of human bondage to find the way of ancient wisdom and bring the brotherhood of man to earth. The sand in the unseen hourglass fell swiftly now, with barely enough grains to last one more year.

On arriving home Joseph went to his house where Mary dwelled with James. She was now 14 years old and, according to the customs of the land, considered to be of full womanhood. His hope that she had outgrown her mystical fancies was soon dispelled, for she related the story of the heavenly messenger who said she would bring forth a son from the most high. Joseph, shaking his head, left the house to ponder what should be done about his wife. Although he feared that she was becoming mentally unbalanced, he had studied the history of Israel and knew that communication from the higher angelic kingdom was possible. He now had to ask himself if it was wise for him to bring forth another child, or if Mary should be put away privately. Since she had nearly completed the period of purification prescribed by his own faith, he could take Mary as a wife, if it was the will of God. However, he hesitated to do so, first because she had been a temple virgin and he was bound by certain oaths, and secondly, because he was an old man.

As evening fell, the city became silent and the children ceased their fretting, while the movement of the animals surrendered to the night shadows. High in the heavens, the stars also cast their light and awaited the first rays of dawn. But it was another light which descended on Joseph's troubled sleep. Coming silently from a kingdom beyond time and space, a being appeared and stood by Joseph's bed. Then he reached over and awakened him. Looking up, still in dream-like state, Joseph could hardly believe what he saw, for the figure was clothed in shimmering transparent light. And it came to pass that the angel spoke, saying, "Joseph, son of David, do not fear me, for I have come to instruct you to take Mary as your wife, for that which is to be conceived in her is the Spirit of God. She shall bring forth a son and you are to call him Jesus, for he shall redeem his people from darkness and ignorance."

Then Joseph, having been raised from his sleep, did as the angel bid and took unto him his wife (St. Matthew 1:24-25), and knew her not again as she prepared to bring forth her first-born.

It also came to pass that some distance away, in the graceful hills outside of Jerusalem, Mary's cousin Elisabeth had also conceived and the time for her delivery was near. The forthcoming child was perceived as a miracle, for she and her husband, Zacharias, had tried to abide within the law, as well as to administer to those less fortunate than themselves. Yet they remained childless, and had finally passed the usual age for childbearing. Like their kinfolks, Anna and Joachim, they had felt great disappointment and wondered on occasion why they had been denied this fulfillment. Then, one day when Zacharias had gone into the temple to burn incense, a messenger from God came to him. At first the priest was afraid that he had done something wrong in the eyes of the Lord and was to be chastised.

"Do not be afraid, Zacharias," the angel said quietly, "for your prayers have been heard. Your wife, Elisabeth, will bear you a son and he is to be named John (meaning Jehovah is gracious). This birth will bring much rejoicing, for the boy shall be great in the eyes of God and will drink neither wine nor strong drink. He comes from the most high and will walk in the spirit and power of Isaiah. As he grows in grace, many of the children of Israel will come to him for redemption, and his name shall live forever in the chronological records of Israel."

Upon hearing these words, Zacharias was overcome with great doubts and so he questioned the figure which stood before him, asking, "How do I know that this is true, and that I am not seeing a manifestation born of my desires. We have prayed many years for such news, and now I am an old man and my wife is also burdened with years. It is hard to believe that such a benefaction is to be allowed now. Please answer me, how am I to know that these things will indeed come to pass?"

The holy emissary looked down upon the priest with understanding and compassion, for he was a good man. Then he spoke to Zacharias gently, saying, "I am Gabriel, who stands in the presence of God, and I have been sent to you with these glad tidings. Since you doubt, I will give you a sign that you might believe. Henceforth, your tongue shall not be loosed until the days of this prophecy have been fulfilled and your son is born. Now I must leave you, for I am called back to another world."

For a time Zacharias stood in the room of the Oracle, which was called the *Holy of Holies*. Outside, the other priests were greatly puzzled when he did not appear at his usual time, but before they could make a decision to enter the sanctuary they saw the priest approaching them. As he came near, he motioned that he was unable to speak, and they knew he had received a vision. Although he remained at the temple until his priestly obligations were completed, he then departed for his home, leaving Samuel to serve in his place.

As Zacharias walked along, his mind was so filled with the vision which had come to pass, that he paid little heed to the well-proportioned land surrounding Jerusalem. His home was located but a short distance from the outskirts of the city, in the territory known as the land of Judea. Judea was a mere 55-mile stretch of land extending from the beach of the Dead Sea to the hill country. Southeast of Jerusalem, situated on the edge of the wilderness and the west shore of the Dead Sea, was Engedi. From there a road stretched across the Kidron into Bethlehem and Jerusalem. Although physically considered the most barren province of Syria, Judea was nonetheless the most powerful and had drawn the greatest of kings and prophets into its bosom.

On his arrival home, Elisabeth showed much concern over her husband because he could not speak, although he appeared to be in good health. Motioning her to silence, Zacharias sat down and began to write. In his message he related the miracle which had occurred and that they must be patient, for his voice would be restored when the events of the day had come to pass. And in the days which followed, Elisabeth conceived and hid herself away for five months, saying, "The Lord has graced me and taken away my shame from the eyes of Jerusalem."

As the sixth month of Elisabeth's pregnancy approached, Joseph was called to the Council in Jerusalem. Since Mary was deeply concerned over the health of her cousin, she asked to be allowed to go with her husband and assist in the birth of the child. Traveling by burro, the couple made their way from Nazareth to the Queen City along the main caravan route. It was a pleasant time of the year, and as they traveled through Samaria they saw Mt. Ebal raising its lofty 2,950-foot crest in the distance. It was here that Joshua had recorded and read the Law of Moses, placing a curse upon the barren ridges of the rise, after which it was referred to as the Mount of Cursing. On the other side of them was the mountain of the Gerizzites rising 2,849 feet above the Mediterranean Sea.

From there the couple made their way past Jacob's Well and continued their journey through the symmetric hills of Palestine to Bethel and Ramah. After resting and getting fresh water, they proceeded along the final 12-mile stretch of the road which led into Jerusalem. As they entered the city, Joseph made the decision to take Mary to Elisabeth and Zacharias' home first, before attending the Assembly.

On their arrival, Elisabeth reached forth to embrace her younger cousin, and as she did so the child which she carried moved greatly in her womb. Then, inner sight and prophecy fell upon her, and she beheld that Mary's child would be great among men. "Bless you, Mary, and bless the fruit of your womb, for you will give birth to one great in stature like unto Moses, who brought forth the Law to the children of Israel. My own child leapt with joy when you approached."

Placing her arms around the young woman, Elisabeth led Mary and Joseph inside the ample dwelling of sandstone. Its whitewashed walls gleamed from their frequent treatment of lime, sending out a delicate scent of cleanliness. The tiled roof was flat, possessing a lattice-like railing to prevent falling, while the interior had a common hearth used for the preparation of meals. Just outside the single-slabbed door lay an attractive court which offered reprieve from the burning sun. Considered among the more prosperous homes of Jerusalem, the building offered comfort and spaciousness.

As the older woman led Mary into the guest chamber just opposite the entrance of the court, she asked, "What has brought you here at this time, Mary? It will not be many months before your own child will be delivered, and I am not certain you should be traveling, although I am pleased that you are here."

"I know," Mary replied, "but I received word that you had conceived and were in your sixth month. Therefore, I felt I should be with you until you gave birth, for I am young and strong. You have been of deep concern to me because of your age, so it is well that I am here to care for you."

On the next day, after he had rested, Joseph left Mary's kinsmen and went to Jerusalem to attend the Assembly.

Three months passed and finally Elisabeth went into labor. As she prepared to deliver, Zacharias went forth and brought a midwife from among the women who served the temple. As the hours passed, the pain grew more intense, but at last there came a final wrench more painful than all those which had gone before. And with this, Elisabeth expended the last of her ebbing strength, falling back on the bed in exhaustion as she was delivered. Then Zacharias was called to greet his new son and give thanks to God for his and his wife's redemption in the land of Israel.

Soon after this there was a great celebration, for the son of a priest was honored above other children. As a general rule, the descendant of the consecrated was also expected to enter into the priesthood when he was young in years. In this manner the lineage of the elect remained pure. So on the eighth day thereafter, the child was prepared for circumcision as was customary under the law.[2] On arriving at the temple, the couple took their son and climbed up the steps to the altar for the presentation. Reaching for the child, who was wrapped in a swaddling band, the officiating priest laid him on the altar and began to bare the infant for the holy ritual. Then he reached for a sharp silver instrument and cut off the foreskin, bringing forth a cry of pain from the tiny human which lay before him.

When the circumcision had been completed the boy was given the name of Zacharias, after his father. However, Elisabeth intervened, saying, "No, his name shall not be Zacharias, for I have received a vision that he shall be called John."

Since it was customary to issue a name which had been carried by a member of the parent's tribe, the priests objected, acclaiming to Elisabeth, "None of his kindred is called by this name." So he turned to Zacharias and inquired what name he would have the child called.

Asking for a writing tablet, Zacharias wrote, "His name is John," and in that moment his mouth opened and he spoke praising God and prophesying. "Blessed be the Lord God of Israel," he said, "for He has sent a son to us who shall be a redeemer of His people. He has lifted up a horn of salvation which will sound loudly throughout the kingdom, calling forth the people to conquer evil.

"This child shall save us from our enemies and from the hand of all who hate us. He will redeem us, as it was promised to our forefathers, and he will remember the Holy Covenant which God made to our father Abraham. For in those days, when Abraham offered his own son as a sacrifice, God said to him, 'I will bless you and I will multiply your seed as the stars in the heavens and as the sand which is upon the sea shore, and your seed shall possess the gate of the enemies. And in your seed shall all nations of earth be blessed because you have obeyed my voice.' He also promised our father Abraham that we shall be delivered out of the hands of enemies, to serve Him without fear in holiness and righteousness all the days of our lives."

Then Zacharias looked down upon his son and spoke again, saying, "You, child, shall be called the prophet of God and will go forth before his people. You will give light to those who sit in darkness and bring peace to those who walk in the shadow of death."

After hearing these things, fear descended upon those who dwelled nearby, for the news was broadcast through the hill country. And those who heard about the boy asked themselves, what manner of child would this be? However, the mark of God was with the child, for he had come from the most high and descended with the light of God in the power of Isaiah. Being so endowed, a decision was made that he should be raised in the Order of Abijah in accordance with the practices of his priestly father.

When Elisabeth became stronger, Mary, who was now in her sixth month of pregnancy, left the dwelling of her cousin and returned to the house of Joseph in Nazareth. There she abided until the winter rains were almost past, at which time an edict was issued from Caesar that all subjects of Roman rule should be taxed. This consisted of both a levy on income and a per capita impost. The head tax, being equal for persons both free and slave, was levied on subjects between the ages of puberty and 65. This, in turn, required that all persons be enrolled in the public records, together with their property and income. It therefore became necessary for Joseph to travel with his family from Nazareth to the city of Bethlehem, so that they might be enrolled and taxed properly in his ancestral home.

As it had been in the days when Anna and Joachim brought forth their seed upon the land, the Israelites, who were beginning to suffer under foreign jurisdiction, believed that the time of the Messiah was now at hand and the lands of their ancestors would be redeemed. They also felt that He who had been predicted by the prophets of old would come forth as a powerful king after the manner of King David and deliver them as Moses had delivered the Hebrews. Therefore, wise and learned men of the Law carefully studied the sky, seeking a sign in the heavens which would indicate the arrival of such a ruler. They did not know that, when the spring rains decreased, the cry of their Messiah would drift down from Heaven and flow across the sandy hills.

Now it also came to pass that in the year of 6 B.C., astronomers at the Sippar School of Astronomy in Babylonia discovered there would be several unique planetary conjunctions in which certain planets within the solar system would appear to merge. According to their calculations, this phenomenon would occur on three separate occasions during the next six-month period, and each would be conducive for the birth of a person of unusual capabilities. The first would take place on December 9th, 6 B.C. Julian; the second on March 1st, 7 B.C. Julian; and the final on March 24th, 7 B.C. Julian. Of the three dates, however, it was noted that on March 1st the sun would pass between the giant outer planets causing a cluster. This would culminate in its full potential when the moon swept through the configuration one hour after midnight. During these hours the heavens would be exceptionally well aspected for bringing the birth of a successor to King David. Continuing to study the movement of the heavenly bodies, the Magi became more and more convinced that March 1, 7 B.C. Julian, was the best possible date for the descent of a great king. Realizing that the moment they had been waiting for was now at hand, they made ready to journey to Jerusalem to witness this moment in history. In the meantime, it was not long before news of the impending event also spread throughout the land, eventually reaching the ears of Herod the Great.

Herod, who was the son of Antipater and descendant of the tribe of Esau, had originally been appointed procurator of Galilee. Later, he was made king through the influence of Marcus Antonius, although he did not succeed in asserting his royal rights in Palestine until he captured Jerusalem in 37 B.C. As a ruler, Herod was considered cruel, jealous, and vengeful. Moreover, it was rumored that he intended to destroy the anticipated Messiah, lest the new arrival usurp his kingdom. As Mary made ready to deliver her child, disease had captured the body of the king in the form of ulceration and worms, making him even more tyrannical in disposition. By now his greatest enemy, jealousy, ruled his life with an iron hand and caused him to viciously destroy anything or anyone who might hinder his continued domination over Palestine. Since such conditions prevailed over Israel, the land was fearful and unsettled at the time Mary and Joseph departed from Nazareth to be taxed according to the edict of Augustus Caesar.

Once again Joseph and Mary selected to travel along the main caravan route which ran between Damascus and Egypt. This was not the best time of the year for such a journey, for the month of Adar (February/March) was subject to rains, hail, and occasional snow. In the Jordan Valley, the cultivation had ended, and the barley crops waved their delicate heads as they ripened in the spring winds. It was a month of lesser celebrations, beginning with the fast because of Moses' death and ending with the feast commemorating the repeal of the decree of Grecian kings forbidding Jews to circumcise their children.

Although the city of Nazareth lay in a basin, once the travelers had reached the upper edge, the country's spectacular view lay before them. The plains of Esdraelon, green with the recent rains, spread out over the countryside, showing little evidence of its famous battles and sacrifices. The weather was relatively cold and would remain so until the month of Ijar (April/May) had brought forth its cloudless sky.

In the beginning of their journey, Joseph had placed Mary on the back of a burro, while he walked along beside her holding the lead rope. The animal, easy in gait and surefooted, jogged along amicably with little concern over its burden. They had gone but a short distance before the city disappeared, leaving little before them except the etched indentation of the road. Generally, there were only a few merchants traveling along the caravan route at this time of the year, but because of the tax edict the couple frequently met others making their way to Bethlehem. When this occurred, they exchanged greetings and sometimes traveled side by side for a time, discussing the weather, the crops, and the taxes.

The census, which was its official name in Rome, originally was held every five years. It fulfilled two important purposes: to provide important information for calling up men for military service and to collect much needed revenue. Without exacting tribute from its foreign possessions, Rome would never have been able to afford the luxury of its much admired and magnificent culture.

By the time Mary and Joseph neared their destination, many who did not have lodgings had gathered along the sides of the streets to prepare their evening meals. While the burning fires made a picturesque scene against the descending dusk, they also brought an ominous chill to Joseph's heart. It was obvious that sleeping accommodations would be difficult to obtain, and the older man was deeply concerned over the welfare of his young wife, who showed much strain from the long trip. Although the couple made numerous inquiries concerning quarters it soon became evident that there were none available. The journey from Nazareth had been a difficult one for the mother-to-be and soon labor pains began to press upon her body, doubling her up over the burro's neck. Originally, Joseph had planned to take Mary to the home of her cousins, Zacharias and Elisabeth, until after her delivery. There, she and the child would receive proper care. However, evening had now fallen and it was obvious that Mary would be unable to travel further.

Even though Joseph continued to make inquiries it was to no avail. He now became quite alarmed, for Mary showed evidence that the child would be born very soon. At last a kind inn keeper suggested that she be taken to a sheltered grotto on the outskirts of the city near Rachel's tomb. There at least they would find protection from the evening chill. Accepting this advice, Joseph hastily led the burro, carrying its precious cargo, toward the secluded oasis of the large cave. He helped his wife to dismount and led her inside to a place where the rocky walls sloped gently to the smooth contour of the floor. After making Mary comfortable, Joseph left his son James to watch over her and went back into the city to seek a midwife.

Earlier that day, the sun had moved into position between the giant planets of Jupiter and Uranus, linking their orbs together. Now, just past midnight, the moon joined the configuration and the sands of time emptied their last residuum through the hourglass. High in the heavens, a sign was given to the people, for the planets formed into a giant harp. As the spirit of night prepared to relinquish rulership to the sun, a subtle light seemed to suffuse the cave and the last grain of sand slipped slowly into the past. A cry of a child moved across the land, and the prophecy of the angel was fulfilled.

And, behold, thou shalt conceive in thy womb, and bring forth a son, and shalt call his name Jesus. He shall be great, and shall be called the Son of the Highest: and the Lord God shall give unto him the throne of his father David: And he shall reign over the house of Jacob for ever; and of his kingdom there shall be no end. St. Luke 1:31-33

Author's Addendum

Many believe that the birthday of Jesus of Nazareth falls on December 25, although the time of birth is not specifically mentioned in the Gospels. This has aroused a great deal of curiosity, primarily because there is no record of a census at that time or of unusual planetary configurations. In fact, for a time, it appeared that St. Luke was veering so far off the historical records some were prone to disregard his account. This possibility was given even more credit because Matthew, Mark, and John do not mention Jesus' birth. This seems rather strange, for John was a close relative. However, part of the puzzle was solved when it was learned that P. Sulpicius Quirinius, a Roman senator, was assigned to the official office of the first Procurator of Judea. As a result of this appointment, which was purely military, he led a campaign against the Homonadenses, a tribe in the Taurus Mountains in Asia Minor. It was recorded that his seat of government was established in Syria between 7 and 10 B.C. and this would have lead to an imperial edict for taxation, as opposed to a more provincial one.

On December 17, 1603, shortly before Christmas, the Imperial Mathematician and Astronomer Royal Johannes Kepler sat through the night high above the Hradcanian Mountains above Prague, observing the approach of two planets. Sometimes when such a conjunction occurs, the two planets come so close together that they appear as one. This reminded Kepler of something he had read by the rabanic writer Abarbanel referring to an unusual influence which Jewish astrologers ascribed to this constellation. It was believed that a Messiah would appear when there was a conjunction of Saturn and Jupiter in the constellation of Pisces. Searching back in time again and again, Kepler finally determined that such a configuration had indeed taken place in December of 6 B.C. Unfortunately for Kepler, when his calculations were progressed they did not correlate with later events in Jesus' life.

Finally in 1925, the German scholar P. Schnabel deciphered some Neo-Babylonian cuneiform of a famous professional institute in the ancient world, the *Sippar School of Astronomy* in Babylonia. Among an endless series of recorded observations, he came across a note concerning the position of certain planets in the constellation of Pisces. Jupiter and Saturn were carefully marked for a five-month interim during the year 7 B.C. In the year of 7 B.C., Jupiter and Saturn did in fact meet in Pisces and, as Kepler had already discovered, they met three times. One of these three dates fell at the end of February. At that time a clustering began and Jupiter moved out of the constellation Aquarius towards Saturn in Pisces. However, on April 12th, both planets rose in Pisces heliacally (astronomy term for rising star at daybreak). Therefore, the arguments over Jesus' correct birthday continued between both astronomers and theologians.

About 15 years ago, Don Jacobs, a Methodist minister, became fascinated with the discrepancies existing between Kepler's calculations, those of Schnabel, and calendar events which covered the last three years of Jesus' life. For over eight years, he sought to determine another date. By this time, modern technology had provided new ways to determine the exact placements of heavenly bodies during certain important historical events. Using such equipment, Reverend Jacobs worked diligently forwards and backwards over the configurations to find a period when planetary influences were sufficiently exacting to bring forth a person of extraordinary genius. He certainly gave particular attention to Kepler's calculations, but they were weak on two points: first, Kepler's calculations did not progress accurately, and second, a person born at that time would not have possessed some of the major attributes which were so prevalent in the personality of the man from Galilee. However, the Methodist minister, a Bible studies major at Southern Methodist University, was to be rewarded. One day, when he least expected it, a five-planetary conjunction showed up on his equipment. Interestingly enough, it correlated closely with the first dates which had been marked on the cuneiform deciphered by Schnabel. Taking the date of March 1, 7 B.C., 1:30 a.m., longitude 35E13 and latitude 31N42, Bethlehem, Judea, he was amazed to find that it not only coincided perfectly with the scriptures, but also indicated the birth of someone who would rise in genius above all others.

Why then, was Jesus given the birth date of December 25th by the early church? Actually, the reason is quite obvious, for that is the solstice when the old year dies and preparation begins for the rebirth of spring. It also heralds the Feast of Dedication and the grand illumination which signifies the advent of the seventh cycle of creation, or the birth of God in man.

1. The Jewish religion, as it is taught today, has little comprehension of the great wealth which Moses bestowed upon the world, for he taught in symbolism and mystery. Like the Christian faith, the Jews also rely on an outer teaching as opposed to a hidden teaching. The third compartment of the Tabernacle of the Wilderness (see introduction) contained the Ark of the Covenant. As the outer court represented the body, the sanctuary of the Holies represented the soul, and the Holy of the Holies signified the in-dwelling consciousness of God which contains the Law. The ark measured two and a half cubits long, a cubit and a half broad, and a cubit and a half high. The measurements, of course, symbolized the nature of the two selves (mortal and immortal) returning to the one God through the resurrection of the divine nature, or Law. The half measurements were derived from the time period existing between dawn and high noon, for sunrise was considered to portray the reenactment of creation, while the sun at high noon signified the return of God to his full glory, or when man brought forth the

fulfillment of the seventh day of Moses' prophecy by opening the inner spiritual nature.

2. The ritual of circumcision originated with Abraham, who taught that the spiritual nature of man must be separated from his carnal, allowing the lesser to be ruled by the higher. Since the foreskin of the male organ was considered susceptible to certain diseases when it was not cleansed properly, its removal represented a cutting away of the impurities of human life as a sacrifice to God (Genesis 17:11).

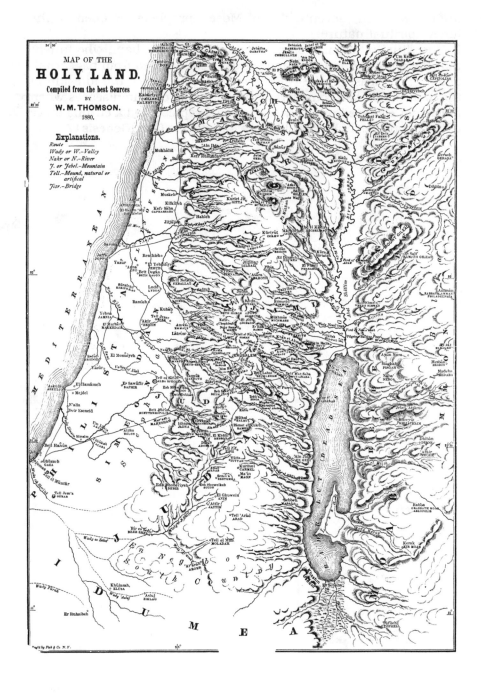

CHAPTER II

WILLOW IN THE WIND

Jesus saw the children who were being suckled. And he said to his disciples: "These children who are being suckled are like those who enter the Kingdom." They said to Him: "Shall we then, being children, enter the Kingdom?" Jesus said to them, "When you make the two one, and when you make the inner as the outer and the outer as the inner and the above as the below, and when you make the male and the female into a single one, so that the male will not be male and the female will not be female, then shall you enter the Kingdom."

Gospel According to Thomas
Log 22:20-31,35

n the dark and turbulent days of unknowing, when Joseph and Mary bar Jacob brought forth their seed to walk the hills of Palestine, the people were involved in long and jealous battles over issues of the Law. Although the scribes and Pharisees claimed supremacy, they were overshadowed by the encroaching authority of the Sanhedrin. By this time, the original teachings of Moses had been buried in ritualistic practices, which shone falsely amid the fine splendor of priestly robes like fool's gold. While the mysteries of the Ark of the Covenant lay in its dusty tomb like some forgotten burial shroud, the people's voices rose in constant and quarrelsome dispute. Even their king was crafty and revengeful and he, like the others, wanted domination not only over their lands, but over their souls. So much did he wish to feel the power flowing through the diseased and scab-encrusted tissue of his body, that he ordered his own son, Antipater, slain, as well as his favorite wife, Mariamne. It would be said of him later that it was better to be Herod's hog than to be his son.

In spite of the conflict of religious doctrine, however, there were those who had kept the flame of realism alive. Out of the stormy winds of war, the rains of death, and the nights of forgetfulness, giants of light walked upon the land and brought hope to those who struggled along the rocky crags of timelessness. These exceptional people withdrew from the mainstream of human agony to contemplate the reasons of existence, and by doing so they discovered the mysterious secrets surrounding the forward movement of divine order. In turn they recorded it in the battle of Asha, the pages of the Torah, and taught it among their own elect. During these periods, it was said that God descended to walk among men and grace them with his presence. In this manner, the ancient prophecy concerning the struggle of light over darkness and its ultimate victory lived as a flickering flame in the hearts of the people and their nation. And now it was destined to live again, for as dawn crept over the distant hills of Israel, the covenant of God was carried forth in the pain of a child's whimper.

At last Joseph sat in the grotto watching over Mary and their newborn son, he felt the deep sense of responsibility which had been placed upon him. He knew that his youthful wife had little comprehension of the role the child was to play. Even he could not perceive it entirely, but he did know that the soul which rested in the arms of his mother was as old as the lands which surrounded them, and that it had descended from worlds he little understood. He was but a mortal man, yet because of the mysterious circumstances preceding the child's birth, he was aware that the infant was more than this. He also realized that his primary purpose during his few remaining years of life was to protect and prepare his son to fulfill the purpose which had been created in him by the powerful Mover of the universe. Even though Joseph had studied the Laws of Moses with great diligence, as well as the histories of Israel's elect, he could not help but wonder about the years which lay ahead. Yet he was not afraid of the task which had been given him, for he was a kind man, as well as a man of strong principles, and he had lived the rigid principles of the law most of his life.

At last Joseph placed this matter in the deep recess of his mind to be scrutinized at a later time, for more immediate problems faced him. This grotto where his wife lay was not a suitable place for one who had just given birth, but now it was quite impossible for him to take her and the child to more comfortable quarters. Although Elisabeth and Zacharias' home was only a few miles away and they had been notified of Mary's delivery as soon as possible, Mary's difficult labor had left her greatly weakened and he was concerned over her safety. Naturally, as soon as the news of the child's birth was received, both Elisabeth, and Mary's mother, Anna, made haste to the cave, bearing necessary supplies to tend to the needs of the child and his mother. When they arrived, thereby alleviating some of Joseph's concern, the two women began to attend the young girl. As she worked, Elisabeth paused for a moment to look down upon the face of the child which had made her own fetus move with joy, and she wondered what sort of a soul had been placed in their midst. Even she, the wife of a priest, could not fathom the spirit which lay behind the closed eyes of the infant. She had been bred on mortal ritual and had not developed the capabilities to perceive light, and only light could perceive light. Yet, as she gently touched the tiny hand in wonderment her love enveloped it.

On the third day following the delivery, Joseph went forth to secure an oxcart to carry the new mother and her son out of the cave. Gently he picked Mary up and laid her on quilts which had been arranged in the bottom of the wagon, after which he reached for his son and placed him in her waiting arms. Meanwhile, the beast which was to pull the sacred load to its destination waited patiently. It was not long, however, before it saw the tall figure of Joseph approaching and felt the gentle tug of the lead rope. Slowly the cart started to move, the ample figure of Elisabeth walking beside it with a small bundle of things which had been used in the cave. However, Anna had been encouraged to climb inside and sit beside Mary. She was now approaching her sixtieth birthday, and an attempt to walk the few miles to Elisabeth's home would have proved somewhat difficult for her. Therefore she was quite content to buffet along beside her daughter, keeping her delighted eyes on the new grandchild. She felt blessed among women and her joy was twofold, for she who had been barren had given life to this young woman. In turn this child of her womb, who had redeemed her family in the eyes of the people, had now produced a male. Glorifying God, she thought, "Now the fruit of our seed will live in the history of Israel and walk on its sloping hills." Little did she know at this time, that her grandson would champion the souls of millions, or that one day his name would be revered second only to God.

On the eighth day following the birth, in compliance with the Hebrew custom, the newborn child was prepared for circumcision. As a general rule this was done by the father, but since Joseph and his family were guests in the home of Zacharias, and since he was a priest, it was agreed that the ritual should be performed by him. Selecting the robes of the priesthood, Zacharias placed them on his body in proper order, the breeches first, followed by the coat, and lastly the girdle. Then raising his hands he gave thanks to the Lord. After this he motioned for the knife which had been placed in a cup near his right hand. Picking it up he reached for the infant's foreskin. In one swift cut the task was accomplished, leaving the child crying lustily. Since he had already counseled with Mary and Joseph regarding a proper name, the priest blessed the child and named him Jesus, as it had been told him.

When the days of Mary's purification were completed according to the Laws of Moses, his parents took the infant to the temple of Jerusalem to be presented to the Lord God of Israel and to offer a sacrifice of a pair of turtledoves. There was in the temple at this time a pious and righteous servant of God answering to the name of Simon, who had long waited for the consolation of Israel. Although he was now an elderly man he still remembered a silent moment in his soul, when the Spirit of the Lord descended and said that he would not see death until he saw the Messiah. Now as Mary and Joseph brought Jesus into the temple to do for him according to what was commanded in the law, Simon received the infant in his arms, and praising God, he said, "Now dismiss your servant, O My Lord, in peace, according to your word. Behold, my eyes have already seen your mercies which you have prepared before the face of all people, a light for a revelation to the Gentiles and a glory to your people of Israel."

Blessing the child's parents, Simon said to Mary, "Behold this one is appointed for the fall and the rise of many in Israel and for a sign of dispute. And a sword will pierce through your own soul, so that the thoughts of the hearts of many may be revealed."

Then Hannah the prophetess, an 84-year-old widow and daughter of Phanuel of the tribe of Asher, stood up at that hour and also gave thanks to the Lord. After this she hastened from the temple and went forth to tell those who looked forward to the salvation of Israel, that she had seen the child who would lead Israel out of bondage. Many scoffed at her and relegated her prophecy to the fancies of an old woman, while others would not listen and walked away shaking their heads. Even those who did stop to hear the prophetess eventually turned away also, for they did not believe that the son of a carpenter could become a king. To them, the Messiah must be a great man who could restore the nation to the wealth and courts of David and Solomon. Therefore, a person who merely assisted in bringing the kingdom of heaven to earth was of little interest to them. Everyone knew that the realms of Jehovah lay someplace amid the twinkling stars, and that the ground which they walked upon was comprised of the iniquities of war and bloodshed. Yet, this did not daunt the aged woman, and when she saw Joseph and Mary coming out of the temple she bowed before them.

Following the presentation at the temple, Joseph and his family returned to the home of Elisabeth and Zacharias. They remained there but a short time, for during this interim a great tumult rose up in Jerusalem, and a rumor began to spread throughout the land that the long-awaited king had been born. To further complicate matters, astrologers from Babylonia soon arrived in Jerusalem to make inquiries.

Traveling along the main highway leading from Sippar to Damascus, Melchus, Casper, and Phadizarda, the Chaldean Magi, first entered the once famous city of Syria. Damascus lay about 70 miles from the seaboard on the east, of what would later be known as Anti-Lebanon. Close to the foot of the hills, in the valley of Abana, its panoramic land was caressed by the plain of Ghutah and cooled by the waters of the Abana River. Pausing there for a time to refresh themselves and their camels, they made preparations to complete the final phase of their journey. Having departed from their native home during the mid part of Shebat (January/February), they had encountered the beginning of the cool season, and heavy rains had sometimes impeded their progress. From Damascus they planned to follow the pleasant route along the Jordan River through Tiberias and Sythopolis.

After renewing their supplies, the Magi finally placed their camel packs atop the single hump of their long-legged transportation and mounted. When they struck the hindquarters of the beasts, the camels gave a great lurch, rose, and at the command of their riders, moved toward the natural highway running east to west, which served Galilee, Levant, and the Nile. According to the astrological charts, the conjunction of the stars had occurred over Jerusalem. Therefore, they hastened toward the Queen City, intending to make inquiries among the people.

Upon their arrival, they attracted much attention, for the three men's attire indicated they were not only from a foreign country but also men of profundity and artists of destiny. As of yet, the study of the stars was an unexplored science, not only in Israel but also in most of the known countries. For this reason, the strangers were looked upon as great and learned men. They passed among the people, saying, "We have seen a sign in the heavens and know that a great king has been born. Can you tell us where we might find him, for we have come bearing him gifts?" Then the rumors of the birth of a Messiah began to spread far and wide.

Herod was greatly concerned when he heard of these events, for the birth of a new king would be a great threat to his rulership. Calling forth the chief priests and scribes, he asked that they examine the scriptures and determine if such an occurrence could be true. Not long thereafter the pain of prophecy pierced his heart and his tortured soul, for when the holy men searched the scriptures they came to the book of Micah. In the ancient writings of their forefathers, were the ominous words, "But thou, Bethlehem Ephratah, though you be little among the thousands of Judah, yet out of thee shall he come forth unto me that is to be ruler of Israel; whose goings forth have been from of old, from everlasting." (Micah 5:2).

When he heard this, Herod decided to summon the learned travelers and inquire by what sign they had seen such a birth. They said, "Our calculations indicated that there would be a five-planet conjunction occurring near Jerusalem at this time. And it came to pass, that as we traveled we witnessed such a miracle. We saw five constellations move into one great cluster in the east just a few nights ago, and then they became as one star. We are quite certain that our configurations are correct and that a great ruler has been born in the land."

Upon hearing these words, Herod became angry and indignant. However, since he had received rumors and prophesies concerning the birth of John, the son of the priest Zacharias, he now thought that it was John to whom the astrologers referred. Immediately he began to scheme as to how he would kill this new threat to his throne. Thus wanting the Magi out of the way while he carried out his wicked plan, he urged them to return to the people and continue searching for the infant. "My scribes report that the scriptures state that such a one will be born in Bethlehem. Perhaps you should go there and seek him first, and if you find him return and tell me so that I may also go and worship him."

Accepting Herod's suggestion, the astrologers went directly to Bethlehem and inquired of the townspeople concerning new births, for they wished to behold the new king with their own eyes. It was not long before they heard talk concerning a young mother who had given birth to a son in a cave. Immediately they investigated the matter further and learned that Mary and the infant were housed nearby with some of her relatives. Although their excitement was mounting, they felt it wise to recheck the planetary configurations, this time for the exact time of birth, to make certain that they had not been in error. Laying the papyrus chart across the sand, they began checking their calculations. First they followed the earlier notes, and then re-evaluated the conjunction. Nothing had changed, the great star of the east rose but a short distance out of Jerusalem, and did indeed seem to hover over Bethlehem. Now, according to the rumor of the townspeople, the child in the manger had been born about midnight, near the time of the new moon. If this were true, then they knew they had found the one they were seeking. Looking with exaltation at one another, they immediately sought directions to the place where the infant was housed.

Upon entering the residence[1] the Magi saw the child in the arms of his mother, and casting themselves down before him they paid homage. For a time there was silence, and then the three men rose and offered their gifts of gold, frankincense, and myrrh. They gave gold as a tribute for rulership and wisdom, frankincense, the purest and rarest of incense, for love, and myrrh for the bitterness of mortal life. Then, bowing before Mary they took their leave. As she watched them depart, she looked down at her son, her heart bewildered and questioning.

After this, the three men went abroad among the people, speaking great things concerning the child. However, they sensed Herod's treachery, and having received warning in a dream that they should not return to the king, they left for their own country without stopping in Jerusalem.

Shortly thereafter, as Joseph lay sleeping in the night, a voice awakened him. Standing before him was a figure of a man clothed in subtle ethers. His countenance was barely perceptible, for so much light radiated around the figure that it was impossible to see him clearly against the penetrating darkness. For a moment, the angel looked down quietly at Joseph and then he spoke, saying, "Joseph, if you remain in Israel, your son is in grave danger. Therefore, you must take him to Egypt until the tumult has passed away. Wait there until you receive word that all is well. You will be notified by messenger when it is safe to return, and now I bid you make haste, for there is little time remaining."

Early on the following morning Joseph went to his wife and awakened her from sleep, saying, "Mary, I have been told that we must take Jesus to Egypt as soon as possible. If we remain here he may be taken from us, for word has spread that he is the Messiah. So come, we must not tarry, but prepare immediately for the trip. Since it will not be possible to return to Nazareth first, I will assign one of my sons to take care of our property there."

Seeing Mary's frightened look, Joseph spoke again gently, "Do not be so frightened Mary, there is sufficient time. Otherwise, we would not have been warned by an angel of God. Nonetheless, we must not delay longer than necessary, and now I take leave of you that I might go and arrange for the supplies that we need." After this he awakened Elisabeth and Zacharias and informed them of the situation.

While Mary packed their things and prepared Jesus for the long journey, Joseph and Zacharias went to select the animals which would be needed. They went first into Jerusalem to the bartering pens where there were asses for sale. Once there, they cut out a couple of the beasts which looked promising and checked them out, first opening the mouths to see if the seller was deceiving them concerning the age. After this they inspected the limbs and hoofs. The better animals were quite beautiful and had been bred for the purpose of bearing riders; therefore, they were perfectly surefooted, as well as high priced. Although some were small and cheap, they could not be considered for the journey, primarily because the return from Egypt to Israel had to be considered also. Finally, having selected two of the noble beasts from the pen, they began bartering. When this had been concluded to the satisfaction of both parties, the men went to purchase supplies, after which they returned to the house.

Although Zacharias did not question the necessity of the journey, he was still gravely concerned for the safety of the entire family. They would be entering a land as strangers and there was little assurance of their well-being. While Joseph had affiliations with the Essenes, who had a brotherhood in northern Egypt, there was always the possibility that he and Mary would not be granted asylum. Also, the child was very young and the summer months had begun. This meant the undertaking would be even more uncomfortable, for the heat would be intense across the desert. However, there was no other alternative, and early the following morning as the morning sun rose above the rolling hills they made ready to depart. The small retinue consisted of Joseph, Mary, the child, two riding animals and another, smaller, beast of burden which was relegated to the task of carrying clothing and supplies.

By this time Joseph had already helped Mary, who was carrying the child, to mount, but before mounting himself he reached to shake Zacharias' hand. Their eyes lingered on each other in deep friendship, perhaps because of their concern over the future, or perhaps because someplace deep within them there was a knowing that they would never meet again. Then Joseph mounted and with a click of his tongue, and a prodding of his slender stick against the animal's backside, they began to move away. Elisabeth and Zacharias watched them until they faded from view, a deep sense of sorrow and pain laying its heavy burden on their hearts. Then the priestly couple turned and went into their home, which now seemed to close around them with a strange aura of desolation.

Selecting one of the two common trade routes which ran from Jerusalem to Egypt, Joseph, carefully holding the lead rope to Mary's animal, turned onto the main highway going in the direction of Gaza. Although this was the longer of the two possible passageways, it allowed more frequent rest stops and lay nearer to the Mediterranean Sea. The shorter inland route through Beer-sheba would have been almost impossible for the animals because many of the watering places had dried up due to the summer heat. Although camels could have crossed the desert easily, they did not have as much practical use as the ass, and Joseph did not know how long they would have to remain in exile.

From Gaza, an ancient city on the old Canaanite border, the family moved southward along the inland Mediterranean route toward Raphia and the upper Sinai. Whenever possible, they stopped at one of the oasis which served caravans passing between

Babylon and the country of the kings. They filled their water containers and rested under the shade of the desert palms. As a general rule, there were others to talk to, so the men often gathered to discuss the law while the women tended to the children. The young seemed to disregard the summer warmth and continued to play their active games of childhood. However, as soon as the intense heat of high noon passed, the people gathered up their supplies and made ready to resume their respective journeys. Most of them were going either to Jerusalem or Egypt and, like Mary and Joseph, had selected this route because of the extreme temperature across the Arabia Desert, once known as the Wilderness of Zin.

Finally Joseph and Mary, who had been able to travel much of the way with others, reached Tahpanhes, an Egyptian frontier town at the easternmost mouth of the Nile River in the delta. This was a pleasant sight to them, for they would no longer have to be quite so concerned over the tiny infant which traveled with them. However, Jesus had weathered the journey extremely well, crying lustily when he was hungry or unclean. During these times, Mary had poured water onto a cloth and wiped his warm body in an effort to cool him, but now she felt great joy over the nearness of their destination.

From Tahpanhes, the family rode along the east fork of the river until they connected with the upper Nile at On (Heliopolis). By this time, the 4,000-mile river was in its higher stages because of the rains and melting snow which poured from the interior of Africa and the Mountains of the Moon. After so many days of solemn and almost desolate travel, Joseph and Mary welcomed the sight of the great Nile. Instead of the smooth contours of the desert, there were fishing boats and barges busily sailing up and down the river, and in the city, the voices of those who bartered rose above the movement of carts and animals. Joseph immediately went to secure lodging, that his family might enjoy the cool comfort of shelter and the welcome relief of a bed. After this had been accomplished, he took the animals to be tended, for he was kindly toward all beasts.

On the following morning, Joseph and Mary resumed their travels. They were now 19 miles north of Memphis, a journey which took two days. During this period Joseph again sought lodgings, and on the third day thereafter, they left Memphis and moved in the direction of a small settlement of Essenes who lived in the beautiful countryside near the banks of Lake Moeris as it had been told them. On their arrival they were warmly welcomed, and the people set about arranging a suitable dwelling for them. At first Joseph and Mary were housed by others, but later they were moved into a private place, and Joseph returned to the carpentry trade. Mary was not idle during the long months which followed, for she had been taught sewing in the temple and was a beautiful seamstress.

As the months passed, the child Jesus waxed strong and began to receive instructions from the Essene brothers who were assigned to teach him. He began to learn his letters, as well as develop some basic concepts pertaining to natural and cosmic law. He was fortunate in that his teachers were authorities on the Law and exacting in their attention for detail. Other times the boy followed after Joseph as he went about his carpentry work, for he was quick to learn and curious by nature. During these early days of childhood, his form was characterized by childish chubbiness, and the hidden destiny of his soul remained buried behind the dancing and somewhat mischievous eyes of youth.

After Joseph and Mary had left Israel, a heavy shadow of darkness fell upon Israel, for Herod perceived that the astronomers had duped him. Rising up in wrath, he sent his soldiers to kill all children who had been born during the time of the unusual planetary configuration. He particularly sought out John, the son of Zacharias, of whom he had been told many great things. Fortunately, Zacharias had been afraid that this might happen, and when the alarm sounded he instructed Elisabeth to take their son to a safe place and not to reveal the location to anyone. Thus when Herod failed to find the boy he sent his officers to the temple to ask the priest where John had been hidden. And it came to pass, that when the soldiers came to make inquiries, Zacharias did not actually know the whereabouts of John, and answered them accordingly, saying, "I am a priest of God and spend most of my time here tending the temple. I am afraid I do not know where my son is."

Departing, the officers returned to Herod. Their news did not please the king and he immediately gave the soldiers orders to return to the high priest, fearing greatly lest John should become king. Also, he had hated Zacharias for a long time, not only because of the priest's aversion to wickedness and his love of liberty, but also because he was rich man. By disposing of him, the king hoped not only to seize his effects but also to get rich off of someone who had the power to destroy him. Therefore, the soldiers were instructed to kill Zacharias if he continued to refuse to provide the information Herod sought. In that the priest still did not know where Elisabeth had taken John, he again responded to the soldiers inquiry by saying, "I am a servant of God, and if you shed my blood my spirit shall be received by God. But you and he who sends you shall be exiled from heaven and shall suffer reprisals for the slaying of an innocent man. There shall not be peace for you or those of like mind, for the Kingdom of God is for the good and noble. Now, do as you wish." The soldiers fell up on him, beat him, and stabbed him through the heart with a spear.

As the sun began its ascent in the heavens, bringing with it a new day, other priests arrived for the morning hour of salutation. They waited long for the high priest to appear that they might salute him, but when he was not forthcoming they hesitated to enter the sanctuary, lest their disregard of the rules find disfavor in the eyes of God. Finally, however, because of the serious delay, one of the priests decided to enter the sanctuary where Zacharias lay in his morning clothes surrounded by a pool of blood. On seeing the ghastly sight, he rushed to inform the others of the diabolical treachery. The priests were stunned when they heard the news and immediately went in to remove the body from the sanctuary and lay it out for burial according to the law. First they wrapped the remains in unguents and perfumes, then in fine linen cloth, after which they went to secure a vault. When the burial arrangements had been completed they went forth among the people to tell them that the high priest had been slain.

When the tribes heard of the brutal murder of their beloved priest, many rent their clothes and beat upon their heads in mourning. And it came to pass that the people grieved over the death of Zacharias for three days and three nights as the Law prescribed. On the third day, the priests took counsel among themselves to decide who should replace Zacharias. In the meantime, Elisabeth had also been notified of her husband's death and was stricken with grief. She dared not openly attend Zacharias' funeral, for there was too great a danger that she might be arrested and killed also. Therefore, her main concern now was to see that John was protected and cared for.

Finally, the tumult died down, for Herod had become ill with distemper, and a fever and intolerable itching had fallen upon him. Along with this he had colon pains, dropsical tumors on his feet, inflammation of the abdomen, and putrefaction of his privy member that produced worms. Still he struggled to live and hoped for recovery. Accordingly, he went over to Jordan, and made use of the hot baths at Callirrhoe, which run into the Lake Asphaltitis. While he was there, the physicians bathed his whole body in warm oil, letting it down into a large vessel full of oil. Immediately his eyes failed him, and he began to pass in and out of consciousness as though he were dying.

Not long thereafter, Herod returned to Jericho in such a state that death seemed imminent, but there still remained sufficient life to perform one more abominable act. He brought the most illustrious men in all of Israel together in the Hippodrome and shut them in. He then called for his sister Salome, and her husband Alexas, and made his speech to them, saying, "I know well enough that the Jews will keep a festival upon my death. However, it is in my power to be mourned for on other accounts and to have a splendid funeral, if you will be subservient to my commands. Send forth soldiers to encompass these men that are now in my custody and slay them immediately upon my death. Then all of Judea, and every one of their families, will weep whether they wish to or not."

For a while after this, Herod desired to live, but presently he was overcome with pain and was disordered by want of food and by a convulsive cough. In spite of this, he still sought to prevent a natural death by attempting to take his own life. However, Achiabus, his first cousin, came running to him and held his hand, hindering him from doing so. As soon as Antipater, Herod's son whom he had imprisoned, heard of this he took courage and attempted to entice the principal keeper of the prison to let him go. The guard, however, believing he might receive a reward from the dying king, went to Herod and told him, after which Herod changed his will and arranged for Archelaus, his oldest son, to become his successor. Then, he ordered that Antipater be slain. King Herod succumbed to death just five days after the slaughter of his son.

During the third year of Joseph and Mary's exile from Israel, they received word King Herod had died. Now they were instructed by emissaries of the angelic kingdom who watched over their son that they were to take Jesus and return to their native land. Leaving Egypt, they retraced their steps along the same caravan route which they had traveled before. However, as they neared Judea they heard that Archelaus, Herod's son by a Samaritan woman, now ruled over Idumea, Judea, and Samaria and was bringing much trouble to the land. Thus Joseph decided not to return to his holdings in Bethlehem, but went directly to Nazareth, then under the governorship of the late king's less tyrannical son, Herod Antipas.

By this time Joseph's older children, Josetos and Simeon, as well as both of his daughters, had married. Judas, the third son, resided near Jerusalem, while James the youngest, who later became known as the Just, left the house of Joseph in Bethlehem and came to dwell with Joseph and Mary in Nazareth. Shortly after the family had finally settled down, Joseph returned to his carpentry profession and eventually sought to teach the trade to both James and Jesus. During this same period, he also tried to instruct the two young boys in the ways of righteousness, particularly Jesus. In view of the astute ability of the latter to quickly comprehend the more complex aspects of nature, Joseph felt the constant need to protect his youngest son from the outside world. He knew that any inordinate attention toward the lad might place him in grave danger and that it was best for the family to sustain a low profile. Thus he sought to protect Jesus by subjecting him to a simple lifestyle, allowing no special privileges which might bring unexpected reprisals.

As a lad, Jesus was relatively handsome and became more so as maturity changed his features into those of a man. Because of his attractive countenance, he was destined to draw many female followers, and due to his authoritative demeanor, as well as his miracles, he would also command the respect of men. His hair was darker than his father's and reflected auburn highlights when the sun shown upon it. His eyes, which were a clear gray, showed the impishness of boyhood as well as keen alertness. However, his personality was unlike any other of his age, for he had the noble bearing of a ruler. Jesus commanded easily and accepted obedience from his peers gracefully, comporting himself in the manner of one possessing great authority. However, this seriousness did not displace his mischievousness, for this remained an integral part of his makeup throughout most of his life. His sense of humor, interwoven with an astute discernment, made him a favorite among old and young, rich and poor.

It was not uncommon during the early period of his life for Jesus to find himself in occasional conflict with his parents, primarily because of his avid curiosity and humanitarianism. One day when he was playing with other children by the edge of a small brook, he opened all the dove cages and allowed the birds to fly free, saying to them as they flew away, "Remember who set you loose."

Since the doves had been collected for the forthcoming Sabbath and were to be dedicated to the temple as sacrifice, the young boy immediately brought the wrath of the elders upon his head. Naturally the incident was immediately reported to his father, who promptly chastised his son, saying, "You should not have done this, for you have trespassed on the property of others. In spite of the circumstances, it was not lawful for you to do so."

Another time when Jesus was walking with Mary, his mother, through the midst of the marketplace of the city, he looked about and saw a master teaching his pupils. It also happened that a group of quarreling sparrows had gathered on the wall behind the teacher, and on occasion one would fly down into his lap. This made Jesus laugh, which in turn made the teacher very angry. Speaking loudly, the teacher called out, "Bring that boy to me."

One of the men standing near Jesus reached out and caught him by the clothing, and dragged the boy in front of the teacher. Glaring at him with dark piercing eyes, the Pharisee asked, "What right have you to laugh while I am instructing the people. Have you been brought up without any respect for the law, or your elders?"

It was fortunate that the young boy hid further laughter, for to have continued with such action would have brought even more disgrace on both him and his mother. By this time Mary, embarrassed over her son's actions, had stepped to the back of the crowd in an effort to remain less noticeable. To interfere with a Doctor of the Law in Jesus' admonition would have been considered in very poor taste. However, she soon realized that her simple retreat was not sufficient, for she heard her son say, "Master, see, my hand is full of corn, and when I saw the sparrows sitting on the wall behind you I showed the corn to them and scattered some of the kernels. This made the birds fly down to partake of it. But when they began to fight among themselves, just like those who are listening to you, I could not help but laugh."

On hearing these words the Pharisee became livid with rage, and motioned for Mary to come forth and take her son away. Jesus' analysis of the matter, as seen through the eyes of youth, all too obviously revealed the fight between scribes over the Law, and the teacher was greatly offended. The Pharisees believed that every soul was imperishable, but that only those of the righteous pass into another body, while those of the wicked were punished with eternal torment. Thus, as he watched the two disappearing figures, he was convinced that the brown haired lad would surely go to a place beneath the earth and be eternally imprisoned.

Now it also came to pass that, while Jesus was still a young lad, a rebellion against foreign domination began spreading throughout Israel. This resulted in the plunder of the royal palaces. Eventually, the Roman governor of Syria was called upon to intervene, and he hastened to the scene with a powerful army to reinforce the local garrisons. As the governor and his army approached Jerusalem, the rebels retreated with their smaller band of followers, but they were pursued and finally captured. Two thousand of their men were crucified. Joseph, fearing that the tumult might endanger his family, removed them from Nazareth and settled in Capernaum, a peaceful town on the western shore of the Sea of Galilee. Later, after the disruption caused by the revolt had subsided, he returned with Mary, Jesus, and James to his holdings in Nazareth, where they remained until Jesus was seven years old.

Since the city of Nazareth was situated on the primary caravan route which brought travelers from Samaria, Jerusalem, Damascus, Greece, Rome, Arabia, Syria, Persia, Egypt, and Phoenicia, Jesus was occasionally tempted to pass time among them. During the years of his youth, it was not uncommon to find him keeping company among strangers, both delighting and astounding them with his insight into matters of religious doctrine. Some of the wisest of these visitors, upon beholding the nature of Jesus, overstayed their allotted time in Nazareth in order to impart some additional fragment of knowledge to him.

From time to time, Chaldeans arrived among the travelers, and these were Jesus' favorites. The Chaldeans had descended from aggressive Aramaean nomads and originally came from an area near the birthplace of Abraham. Having gradually migrated into southern Babylonia, the Chaldeans had a foundation in both astronomy and astrology. The challenge of pursing the purpose of man's existence, as well as the destiny of his planet, were questions which had perplexed humankind from the beginning of intellectual awakening. Those who turned toward the stars found some of the answers through the precise law of cause and effect of planetary movement. It was, therefore, no wonder that the boy was fascinated by these unusual people, for as he sat and listened to them, he heard about the moon's effect upon both land and sea, how star clusters related to the seasons of the year, and how calendars were calculated according to earth's relationship to the sun, as well as the various star formations. The astronomers even assigned names to the months which were based upon the events of civil life, such as 'Simanu,' from the making of brick, and 'Addaru,' from the sowing of seed.

As the days passed, Joseph watched the growing differences between the ways of his son and those of other children and decided that it was time to take him to other teachers for more advanced instruction. Problems had already started to manifest in the boy's training, for Jesus had not only mastered the basic Hebrew letters, but also outdistanced all of his fellow students. As a consequence, he began to display impatience with the dreary formalism which characterized the traditional Jewish teachers. This, in turn, frequently brought the censure of his instructors upon him, for they all too often overlooked the essential spirit of the teachings in their zeal for literal interpretation.

And it came to pass that one of the teachers by the name of Zacchaeus, who marveled greatly that the young boy could speak so well on learned matters, went to Joseph and said, "You have a very remarkable child. I have come to you to ask that he be allowed to study with me. I will teach him the letters and school him in matters of the law. Also I will teach him reverence, to salute all the older people, honor them as grandfathers and fathers, and to love those of his own age, so that he does not become foolish."

Believing this to be a suitable arrangement, Joseph took Jesus to Zacchaeus' place of teaching. This did not seem to make Jesus resentful, and when they arrived at their destination the youth took his seat obediently among the other students. Zacchaeus, immediately wanting to impress his new pupil, taught the words of the first line which went with A to T. However, it soon became evident that the boy had already mastered the primary studies. The teacher was further astonished to find that Jesus had also easily assimilated everything that had been taught him, but not without some trial and error. For it happened, that after Zacchaeus carefully instructed the lad in all the letters from Alpha to Omega, Jesus looked at him questioningly and said, "I see that the first letter has lines and a middle mark which goes through the pair of lines. These converge, rise, turn in the dance, and are three signs of the same kind, subject to and supporting one another."[2]

Now when Zacchaeus heard so many such allegorical descriptions of the first letter being expounded, he was very perplexed, as well as astounded at such great teaching. He said to those who were present, "Woe is me, I am forced into a quandary, wretch that I am; I have brought shame to myself in drawing to myself this child. Take him away, therefore, I beseech you brother Joseph. I cannot endure the severity of his look, nor make out his speech at all. This child is obviously not earth-born; for he can tame even fire. Perhaps he was begotten even before the creation of the world. What belly bore him, what womb nurtured him, I do not know. Woe is me, my friend, he stupefies me. I cannot follow his understanding and I have deceived myself, wretched man that I am, for I strove to get a disciple and have found myself with a teacher. My friends, I think of my shame, that I, an old man, have been overcome by a child. I can only despair and die because of this child, for I cannot in this hour look him in the face. And when all say that I have been overcome by a small child, what have I to say? And what can I tell concerning the lines of the first letter of which he spoke to me? I do not know, my friends, for I know neither beginning nor end of it. Again I ask you, brother Joseph, take him away to your house. He is something great, a god or an angel or what I should say I do not know."

In spite of these events, Joseph did not speak to Zacchaeus concerning the lineage of Jesus, for he feared that such knowledge might still prove dangerous, even though Archelaus had been dethroned and banished into exile. Further, it was necessary that secrecy be maintained for the sake of the boy himself, who was still not totally knowledgeable concerning the destiny of his soul. However, Joseph also knew that it was now only a matter of time before God would reveal the past, present, and future to this youth who now stood before him. Realizing that the matter would require careful thought he took his son and returned home. Once there, he returned to his carpentry work to ponder this new twist of destiny.

Carefully noting the understanding with which the boy approached all things and that he was growing to maturity, Joseph resolved to find another teacher. As a member of the Sanhedrin, he knew well those who were reported to be the greatest Doctors of the

Law, and he went forth to seek one of them. Not wishing to alarm the scholar, he made no mention of the preceding events which took place in the home of Zacchaeus. And when Jesus was brought before the teacher, the teacher said to Joseph, "First I will teach him Greek, and then Hebrew." For the man had heard rumors concerning the boy and was afraid of him. Nevertheless, he wrote the alphabet and practised it with him for a long time. At first Jesus refused to answer, saying, "If you are indeed a teacher, and if you know the letters well, tell me the meaning of Alpha, and I will tell you that of the Beta."

On hearing this, the teacher became very annoyed and sought to strike the boy on the head. However, Joseph intervened and taking Jesus in hand, they again returned home. Joseph was now even more perplexed, for he knew that it would be wise to harness Jesus' youthful energies. If the power that was beginning to manifest in his son was not subdued in a proper manner, he feared that it would cause him trouble later in life. And while he was devoted to the original laws as they had been taught by Moses, he still bore more of the human frailties than this boy who had been placed under his guardianship. Therefore, he did not fully understand the mystery of the powerful soul inhabiting the slender body before him.

Openly concerned now over the reports from the two teachers, Joseph sought out his friend Gamaliel, a Doctor of Law and fellow member of the Sanhedrin, and explained some of the difficulties to him. By this time, Gamaliel had risen among the ranks of the Sanhedrin and was rapidly earning the reputation of being one of the greatest administrators of the law of all times.

Not only was Gamaliel the grandson of the famous Sanhedrin statesman, Hillel, but also the son of Pedahzur, captain of the tribe of Manasseh. As a direct descendent of aristocracy, he was beginning to take a leading position in the High Council, which was recognized as the supreme court of Israel for determination of questions pertaining to the teachings of Moses. Although not called upon to intervene in every case decided by the lower courts, once the Sanhedrin had rendered a decision in any case, the judges of the local courts were, at risk of death, bound to follow it. The court was comprised of representatives from the privileged families of Israel and included Pharisees, Sadducees, Essenes, Galileans, and other major cast systems. Although a Pharisee, the noted statesman rose beyond secular orientation and dedicated much of his life to the Council and to the teachings of the *Torah*, the body of literature containing the laws, teachings and divine knowledge of Judaism. It was later said of him that, after he died, the honor of the Torah ceased to exist and purity and piety became extinct. He eventually received the title *Rabban*, which was borne only by the leaders of the highest religion.

A remarkable classification of pupils corresponding to the fish of Palestine was ascribed to Gamaliel. In this arrangement, he enumerated the following kinds of pupils: (1) An unclean fish, considered by ritual as unfit to eat, a son of poor parents who has learned everything by hard study, but has no understanding; (2) A clean fish, a son of rich parents who has learned everything and possesses understanding; (3) A fish from Jordan, a pupil who has learned everything but does not know how to reply to questions; and (4) A fish from the great Mediterranean Sea, a pupil who has learned everything and also knows how to reply.

Now, when Joseph approached Gamaliel concerning the education of his son, the Pharisee listened most attentively and asked many questions. It was not uncommon that he be approached in such a manner, for his reputation as a teacher was beginning to grow throughout Israel. However, he was also aware of Joseph's fine reputation, and he had heard rumors concerning his son. Therefore, he wanted to meet Jesus himself, and so he said to Joseph, "Bring the boy to me that I might talk to him. I have heard things concerning him and would like to see if they are true. I cannot promise to teach him until we have met, but be of good cheer Joseph, I will do what I can for you."

Shortly thereafter, Joseph took Jesus to meet with the noted man, who questioned him on many things. He was not only astounded by the boy's answers, but also confounded,[3] and he accepted Jesus into studies concerning the Law with anticipation. After this, he not only taught Jesus Aramaic, Hebrew, Greek, and the orderly progression of the universe according to Mosaic Law, he also arranged for the boy to study with other learned men. It was quite natural that a close bond developed between the learned Doctor and his pupil, which endured throughout both their lives. Later, Gamaliel's deep understanding of the Law, and his sense of fairness, would cause him to defend his prodigy's followers when they were incarcerated. He even named one of his sons Jesus, who later became successor to Jesus, the son of Damneus, in the priesthood.

During the ensuing years of studies, Jesus grew in stature. He was slender, commanding, and usually assumed a role of leadership when playing with other children. Yet, there was something else which set him apart from others his age, and that was his wonderful light-hearted banter. Although he was somewhat a tease, he seemed to have the ability to be humorous, compassionate, and still a leader, all at the same time. It was not uncommon to see him organizing the play, or running ahead of others in races, or encouraging the children to enter the water for frolic. In spite of his youthful boyhood body, however, he still preferred the company of his elders. Among these was his mother Mary, who was acclaimed one of the most beautiful women in Israel. She supplied some of the sensitivity and understanding of womanhood which would later create a strong and unusual sense of equality in her son. Jesus would become one of the few men in early history to allow women into his inner circle of followers.[4]

By the time Jesus reached his twelfth year, the spirit of mastership which had lain dormant in the recesses of his soul occasionally burst forth like a fleeting ray of sun in the morning dawn. This caused a cloud of sorrow to spread in Mary's heart, and she experienced a sense of loss. Both she and Joseph knew as they watched their son mature, that he would be called on a journey someday and that they could not follow. This was painful to Mary, for Jesus was her only child. Joseph, on the other hand, still served as protector and directed Jesus with a firm hand, continuing with the preparation which would enable the boy to fulfill the special mission which had been assigned him. This task, although happily administered, was still a grave responsibility, and Joseph took great care to see that all things were done in the proper manner.

As Jesus approached his thirteenth birthday, the house of Joseph began making preparations for the annual Passover pilgrimage to Jerusalem. The Passover,[5] followed by the Feast of Unleavened Bread, was one of three great historical events sanctioned by Mosaic Law. As the lunar pastoral festival coincided with the lambing season, it fell upon the fourteenth day of the civil year in conjunction with the spring equinox (March-April). The Paschal lamb was killed on the evening of the fourteenth, heralding the beginning of the festival.

Thus it came to pass that, as spring descended once more on the graceful hills and the winter rains began to abate, Joseph, Mary, and Jesus, made ready to join the procession to Jerusalem. They planned to visit the home of Elisabeth while they were in the Queen City, which would enable Jesus to renew his friendship with John. If Joseph realized that neither he nor Elisabeth would live to see their sons reach full manhood, he not discuss it. He was like the sea, impenetrable and deep, so it was impossible for others to know what went on in his mind. Nor did he allow passions of the flesh to rule him, such as anger, excessive food, or heavy conversation.

Yet he was respected by everyone who knew him, for he was good, kind, and often went out of his way to help those less fortunate. Above all, Joseph was known best for his deep sense of integrity and honesty. A promise from him was like an oath, and when he spoke, his words were carefully weighed so that they had value. In making decisions concerning any wrong doing he was like granite, solid and firm, and seldom changed his mind once it was made up.

Since his religious affiliation prescribed the immortality and pro-gression of the soul, as well as obedience to natural and cosmic law, he carried out the task which had been assigned him with fortitude and calm understanding. Although he saw many things quite dif-ferently than his young wife, he was gentle with her, and it was for her sake they now prepared to travel to Jerusalem for the Passover.

As Joseph and Mary, with Jesus, joined others who were making their way to the Holy City, there rose much singing and chanting among them. The progress of the caravan was slow, for occasion-ally a child would wander off to explore some crack or crevice along the way, or an elder stopped to prod the sacrificial animals with his staff. In keeping with the requirement of the celebration it was deemed that on the tenth day of Nisan, the head of each family should select from his herd an unblemished male goat or sheep of the first year. On the fourteenth day, the animal was sacrificed at the hour between sunset and complete darkness. A bunch of hyssop was then dipped into blood and applied to the two posts and lintel of the house where the meal was to be eaten. Then, the whole animal, without breaking a bone, was roasted and eaten by the family, in-cluding slaves and strangers, if they were circumcised. The meal was served with unleavened bread, bitter herbs, and wild lettuce.

When the Holy City came into view, the caravan formed into an orderly column and began chanting and praying, while flute play-ers led the way. Although Joseph did not customarily participate in the sacrificial acts, Mary's family still followed the more custom-ary Hebrew traditions. For this reason, Joseph, who diligently respected the beliefs of others, observed the pageantry of the Passover celebration without showing disrespect for its formalized ritual. But the young Jesus, who stood near his parents when the festival began, removed himself quickly, his soul greatly troubled.

Immediately, the youth made his way toward the temple in order to seek out the great teachers of the law. Once he arrived at his destination, he went among the people in order that he might listen to the numerous discourses being presented by prominent and learned men. Most of these sat in the corridors of the temple sur-rounded by their respective students. If he preferred one to another, it passed unnoticed. Neither did the administrators of the Law pay any great heed to him, as he wandered from one gathering to the next like a nomad. However, as the days passed, Jesus, although courteous and respectful to the noted statesmen, began to ask inci-sive questions pertaining to the various doctrines being discussed. Therefore, it was not long before they did begin to notice the youth's unusual astuteness, and they took pleasure in answering his queries and expounding the law to his listening ears.

Joseph and Mary, believing their son to be with kin, had not been unduly concerned over his long absences. However, as the festival drew to a conclusion and many travelers prepared to depart from Jerusalem, it was discovered that Jesus had not returned. When Joseph and Mary inquired among their relatives and friends, they learned that the youth had not been seen for some time. Concerned, they made their way to the temple hoping to find him along the way. As they entered the sanctuary they noticed a crowd gathered nearby, and thinking their son might be found among the listeners, they approached its outer fringes. They spied him listening and asking questions in the midst of the Doctors of Law, and all that heard him were astonished at his understanding. Mary was upset that the boy should have caused them so much concern, but Joseph gazed at the youth sternly. He felt that the lad had acted in a manner which could cause him harm, if not now, later.

Jesus looked up and saw his parents standing nearby. After he finished what he was saying, he bid the Doctors farewell and then made his way toward them. As he did so, one of the teachers turned to Mary, and asked, "Are you the mother of this child?"

"Yes, I am," she responded nervously, for she did not know if the learned men had been offended by her son. In the past, there had been those who had been provoked into anger over Jesus' vexatious questions and this was awkward for her. She was a gentle childlike creature who had been protected from the hostilities of the outside world, first by the temple, and then later by her husband. However, it was not the boy's questions which proved difficult to her, but the violent way in which some people reacted.

Sensing her timidity, the man spoke kindly, saying, "You are most blessed that God has given you such a child. A wisdom such as he possesses is seldom found in one so young."

Taking the things which the Doctor of the Law said about Jesus and quietly storing them in her heart, she turned toward Joseph and made ready to leave the temple. Joseph did not speak to her or to Jesus, who had now joined them, for he was greatly troubled by what he had witnessed. He knew that serious complications could be forthcoming if the boy's lack of discretion were further permitted. As they left Jerusalem, Joseph remained in a contemplative mood. He felt the time was rapidly approaching when it might become necessary to commit Jesus to the care of one of the Essene communities, where he could mature under the disciplined guidance of Essene adepts. There he would be able to work and study until he had grown to manhood.

Although Joseph was not then aware of it, his fears were not totally unfounded. Even as he and his family traveled the familiar route toward Nazareth, some of the Pharisees and Rabbis were in private council. Of those who had gathered to discuss the remarkable lad, some desired that he be banished from Galilee because they were afraid that he was possessed by some evil influence.

Once Joseph and Mary returned to their home, Joseph brought up the possibility of taking Jesus to the Essene school on the Dead Sea for further study. Although Mary did not wish to have her only son taken from her, she also knew her husband spoke wisely. She was now almost 30 years old, and during the period since Jesus' birth there had been times of great difficulty. Therefore, she did not oppose Joseph in this matter, and soon thereafter he and Jesus left for the Essene monastery which was situated near Engedi.

The town, also called the City of Palm Trees, was located about 30 miles southeast of Jerusalem on the edge of the wilderness, which was full of rocks and caves and the source of the fountain from which the town derived its name. The fountain itself was on the mountainside about 600 feet above the sea and offered the followers of Moses the perfect opportunity to commune with their angels, or the forces of natural and cosmic law. Here in the quiet Jordan valley, where the saline streams flowed through the nitrous soil and heavy clouds formed from the sea's evaporation, the Essenes utilized the forces of nature in a manner still unparalleled in the modern world.

The Essene sect had formed approximately 200 years prior to Jesus' birth, and its members spent much of their time in study, both of the ancient writings and such special branches of learning as education, healing, and astronomy. They were direct heirs to Chaldean and Persian astronomy, as well as the Egyptian arts of healing, and proficient in the use of plants and herbs for curing man and beast. The Brotherhood also excelled in prophecy, for which they prepared by prolonged fasting. Living a simple life, they arose each day before sunrise to study and to commune with the forces of nature, first ritually bathing in cold water and donning their white robes. Following their daily labor in the fields, they ate their meals in silence, preceding and ending each with prayer. The evenings were devoted to study and communion with the heavenly forces. There were neither servants, nor rich, nor poor, as such conditions were considered a misuse of natural and cosmic law.

Living on the shores of lakes and rivers, the Essenes were mainly agriculturists, possessing a vast knowledge of crops, soil, and climatic conditions which enabled them to grow a great variety of fruits and vegetables in desert areas with a minimum of labor. Membership in the Brotherhood was bestowed only after a probationary period of a year followed by two years of initiatory work and seven more of study, at which time the initiate was allowed access to the full inner teachings. Before being permitted to partake of the communions, each initiate vowed to exercise piety toward

God, to observe justice to all men, to harm no one either of his own will or by the command of others, and never to reveal the angelology of the Brotherhood to the profane.

The initiates also committed themselves to work for good and against evil, to assist the righteous, and to show fidelity to all men, especially those in due authority. Swearing to be truthful, they kept their hands clear of theft and their souls free from unlawful gains, and they agreed that nothing would be concealed from those of their own sect. Anyone caught betraying his oaths to the society was separated from the group, suffering greatly thereby, even though the judgments exercised were accurate and just. Most honored among the Essenes, after God himself, was the name of their great lawgiver, Moses. As for death, if it was for the glory of their fellow man, they esteemed it better than living.

The later Essene initiations conveyed the abstract idea of the Law by means of a symbolic figure called the *Tree of Life*, which diagrammatically represented the great revelations which Moses received when he saw the burning bush in the desert. Moses, considered the spiritual progenitor of the Essene sect, had achieved an intuitive knowledge of the origin of the world and the beginning of all things when he entered illumination on Mt. Sinai. It was from this concept of earth's creation that he derived the laws governing daily life. He taught that all things are part of the whole, assembled by the cohesive law of attraction, and the seven elements or basic forces of life manifest through seven cycles of creation. (Genesis 1 & 2). The candles were lit every seventh day, on the Sabbath, to remind man of the seven phases of creation, the seven elemental forces of the sensible world as represented by the laws of nature, and the seven basic powers of the invisible world known collectively as cosmic law. Through proper utilization of these forces, a person was assured a long and healthy life, as well as the ability to transcend the world of matter and unite with the Creator.

The Brotherhood did not believe in the resurrection of the physical body, but rather that of the soul only. By meditation they endeavored to isolate the soul from the body and thereby return it to God by uniting the mortal consciousness with the inner divine consciousness. They also cultivated the science of medicine and kept the Sabbath more rigorously than other Jews. The teachings of these forerunners of Christianity were full of mystical parables, enigmas, and allegories. They believed in both the esoteric (inner) and the exoteric (outer) meaning of the scriptures.

Immediately, on Jesus' arrival at the Essene training center,[6] he was placed among the other young initiates and given a white apron to wear. It was a simple garment, reaching from the neck to the floor, its seams passing under the arm and down each side. The neck was cut in a circle with a slit in the front for easy entry of the head. When worn, this was tied with narrow ties made of the same linen material as the apron. The neck and the bottom were hemmed. The practice of wearing this style of dress would remain with Jesus throughout his life, and later appear in the multi-art forms which graced the world for over 2,000 years.

Upon entry into the school, the youth was directed to subject himself to the primary disciplines of the sect, which were obedience and exactness. After this he began his studies under the most learned masters of the sect. If he did not rebel over this training, it was because his soul was awakening and he found vast knowledge in a world directed by people who had risen above the level of the masses. Their teachings, although considered narrow by some, contained the necessary ingredients for awakening the dominant Spirit of God existing in all mankind. The mastership of such forces as sun, water, and air would become the central core of Jesus' miracles, and so he was content to practice the concentration and discipline necessary to harness them.

The years passed, and the youth grew in stature. He did not spend all of his time at the monastery, but occasionally went to visit his parents and his cousins, both in Capernaum and Jerusalem. However, it was Elisabeth and Zacharias' son, John, who became his favorite. By this time, John was preparing for a role in the priesthood after the manner of his father, and had received the doctrine of the Nazarenes.

By tradition, Nazarite meant crowned one, indicating one who had been ordained by God through the descent of spirit into the flesh. In many respects, the oath of the Nazarite was similar to that of the Essenes. Both required complete consecration and sobriety, as well as uncut hair. However, unlike the Nazarites, the Essenes based their practices primarily upon their understanding of those things which related directly to the physical body, as well as those things which related directly to the soul.

As the years passed, Jesus was able to visit his cousin a number of times, and during such periods he liked to expound on the law. It was he who was the leader and the talker, and his cousin the observer and the listener. John loved Jesus and never tired of watching him take the initiative. This later caused him to turn away from his early Nazarite instruction and join Jesus at the Essene monastery for study.[7] Even so, there were still a number of differences between the personalities of the two youths. Jesus was quick and lithe; John was slower and more robust in stature. This was not to say that he was fat, but his bone structure was larger and, later on, imposing. These were characteristics which belonged more to Elisabeth, than Zacharias, for the latter had been tall and quite thin as a result of regular, and sometimes austere, fasting. Elisabeth, on the other hand, was dark haired, olive skinned, and considered voluptuous. This combination gave John the lighter skin and hair coloring of his father, but the broad shoulders and heavier build of his mother. He also possessed the prophetic abilities of his family, although these were not yet fully developed. Later on, his sun-bleached hair would take on auburn highlights, and a long curly beard of the same color would almost blot out the features of his face. All that would remain visible would be intense blue eyes, which seemed to pierce the innermost core of the soul.

The two young men had one common trait, however, and that was their tendency to tease. Even when John grew into full manhood, his teasing attitude won him both friends and enemies, for he could speak of the most amusing observations with complete seriousness. He knew no limitations, possessed absolute moral sublimity, and no duty or danger shook his confidence. His courage was undaunted, whether in the presence of royalty or death. However, a recluse by nature, his sensitivity reached out in sympathy to those who suffered. At other times, John was stern and sometimes unyielding in his opposition to sin, and fierce as fire in his righteousness. As he grew in mastership through his studies, his command of the people was second only to Jesus', and he eventually drew followers from throughout Israel.

It was here in the stark wilderness of Judea, bound on the north by Samaria and on the south by the desert, that the spirit in Jesus rose into fullness. The mighty force which had lived quietly in him as a child could no longer be leashed to the web of human frailties and, rising like the morning sun from its bed of night, it began to rule over Jesus' soul. He felt it rising, and he started to remember the shadows of the distant past and to know the purpose for which he had been born. At first the feelings were perplexing, but as they gathered into concrete ideas, he became enraptured by them. By the age of 19 the narrow confines of the Essene community could no longer contain his irrepressible spirit. His instructors knew also, for they had watched his awakening and the quick manner in which he had managed to unite with the powerful forces of God. So they made arrangements for Jesus to leave their midst. Although they had been witness to the purpose being wrought in him, they showed no special favoritism. It was not that they did not think fondly of him, but they knew that too much attention to his capabilities could build the weeds of ego and reap havoc in the fertile field of his soul. Therefore, they bid him farewell with kindly words and impassive countenances.

First Jesus returned to Nazareth to visit his mother and father, the latter whom he would never see again. Having already said his farewells to John before leaving the Dead Sea, he now traveled to Capernaum with his mother. There, he said good-bye to his other cousins, John and James. By this time he had developed many of the traits of the impersonal life, for his years of discipline in the Essene community had broken any final threads of attachment to the human world. Every morning, before the sun was up, he had risen to work with the forces of nature. By day he studied with the learned Elders and worked at the carpentry profession which his father had taught him. By night he poured over ancient ikons and practiced the communions which would enable him to work with the more powerful forces of the cosmos. There had been little time during those years of asceticism for him to dwell upon mundane practices of the human world.

In spite of his studies, however, Jesus was not yet fully prepared to play out his destiny. During his life he had been sheltered, first by his family and later by the cloistered community. Now it was time to take those years of training and apply them in the open arena. It was necessary for him to become so adept in his work, that the lower forces emanating from the mundane world could neither distract from, nor be greater than, the power of a single man. This would not be a simple task, for groups of people, individuals, and races are bound by a common thread of attraction. In turn these create powerful forces, which are difficult for a single person to rise above. Therefore, Jesus decided to leave his homeland and travel among people in strange lands. To remain in Israel would make things more difficult, for the people would listen neither to youth nor to a carpenter's son.

And it came to pass, at the age of 19 the creative power of the universe took Jesus from his homeland to make him a subtle willow in the wind. As the young man turned his eyes toward the sun, the spirit of truth and mystery moved his feet toward Babylon, the home of the Chaldeans.

1. It has been commonly believed that the wise men, or magi-astrologers came directly to the cave at the time Jesus was born. However, this hypothesis is based only on the Gospel of St. Luke and does not correlate with other historical accounts of the birth. One must look closely at the contradiction which appears between St. Luke and St. Matthew concerning this event: "And when they were come into the house they saw the young child with Mary his mother, and fell down, and worshipped him" (St. Matthew 2:11).

It is well to remember that St. Matthew is the reported son of Alpheus, surnamed Levi, therefore he would have been a cousin to Jesus. There are other considerations also, such as the fact that Anna and Joachim's native home was in Bethlehem, as was that of

Joseph, and Elisabeth and Zacharias also lived nearby.

2. Alpha, the beginning, signifies the nature of God which created the soul and the body, and therefore the center line. In that God (spirit) created first soul and then the body, two outer lines are set on each side of the center line. This signifies the nature of God and the two aspects of man which are sustained by him. They naturally merged together into one in their descent into matter, thus forming the beginning of creation.

3. Hemmer and Lejay, *Evagiles Apocryphes.*

4. A. Guillaumont and Yassah Abd Al Masih, *The Gospel According to Thomas* (New York: Harper and Row, 1959).

5. The pageantry of this festival contained many hidden symbols which are still not understood by either Jewish or Christian theology today. While the seven-day Feast of Unleavened Bread signified the seven phases of creation according to Mosaic tradition, the lamb symbolized redemption through sacrifice. This same festival later evolved into the Christian Easter, and the paschal lamb was replaced with the symbol of a crucified man. In early Christianity, this symbol represented the immortal self, which descended from its heavenly abode to live in a corporeal body comprised of the four elements. The crucifixion, or passion, contained further mysteries, in that the crucified man was resurrected from the dead by surrendering his personal life (taken down from the cross). In uniting the body, soul, and spirit (three days in the tomb), he rises immortal and achieves mastership over the lesser ego (that aspect of himself which is bound to earth).

During this period, Judaism still closely followed traditional Hebrew practices, and therefore, on the twelfth day of the festival, the death of Joshua was celebrated. This twelfth day completed the cycles of purification (12,000 (Revelation 12:5)—the return of the two selves to the one God through the union of the body, soul, and spirit). This is to be distinguished from the doctrines of medieval Christianity, when many came to believe that all decomposed bodies would simultaneously rise from their tombs and the corresponding souls would again enter these physical vessels in order to present themselves for judgment.

6. According to the 1873 English translation of an ancient Alexandrian letter which was found by archeologists in a deserted library formerly inhabited by Grecian friars, Jesus entered his studies with the Essenes shortly after his appearance in the temple during the Passover. This would easily account for the lack of information concerning that period. To have simply gone into oblivion as a carpenter's apprentice is hardly a satisfactory answer, particularly in view of the stories concerning his childhood prior to that.

7. B.F. Austin, *The Crucifixion,* (Indo-American Book Co., 1919).

Light of the Spirit Burrows (cc)

And you will bathe in the light of the stars, and the Heavenly Father will hold you in his hand and cause a spring of knowledge to well up within you, a fountain of power pouring forth living waters, a flood of love and of all-embracing wisdom, like the splendor of eternal Light. And one day the eyes of your spirit shall open, and you shall know all things.

Gospel of Peace
Vatican M.S./Szekely
Section II: Ch. XI:52

CHAPTER III

MARK OF GOD

If those who lead you say to you, "See, the kingdom is in heaven," then the birds of the heaven will precede you. If they say to you, "It is in the sea, then the fish will precede you. But the kingdom is within you and it is without you.

Gospel According to Thomas
Log 3: 20-26

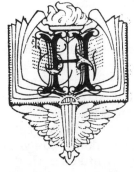aving packed the things he felt he needed, Jesus prepared to depart from his native land. He placed only a light load on the burro which would serve him, for he had learned great frugality during his studies on the Dead Sea. He also felt a deep sense of freedom, for the world of more formal study lay behind him. Ahead were new horizons and new experiences. Yet, even through the years of quiet discipline, he had remained a leader among not only those of his own age but those who sought for the purpose of life. While his youthful enthusiasm had been checked from time to time by his teachers, he possessed a deep understanding of all that had been taught him. Therefore, it was not uncommon for him to help others who could not perceive the mysteries resting behind the spoken word. Even Jesus' cousins did not escape the early experimental discourses, and when he came to visit they gathered around to listen to the stories of nature which he wove out of the tapestry of life.

As the young master stood beside the burro in the early morning sun, Joseph watched him with a sense of completion and loss, but Mary experienced confusion and sorrow. To her, Jesus was still very young and vulnerable to the forces of the unknown and the unexpected. If she could have changed things she would have, but her husband stood beside her, quiet and resolute, and she knew there was nothing she could do. As the rays of sunrise shone down on the slender, white-robed figure, it touched his hazelnut-colored hair and young beard, giving them a glint of deep bronze. The handsomeness of childhood marked his features even more distinctly, and as he saluted in final farewell, his face distinctively reflected delight over the new challenge.

Turning northeast toward Magdala, on the west shore of the Lake of Gennesaret (Galilee), Jesus began the first phase of a journey which would keep him away from Israel for 11 years. From there he traveled along the upper Jordan River toward Merom, Hazor, Kedesh, past Mt. Hermon on the northernmost boundary of the great river. His next destination was Damascus. This would be one of the few major stops on the long journey to the Far East. Damascus was situated not only on the border of desert, but also on a natural highway which ran east to west. Three great roads allowed travelers to depart from her ancient settlement, west, south and east. The western, or southwestern, which Jesus had taken, went by Galilee to the Levant and Nile. The southern, which left the city by the "Gates of the God," went toward Arabia, and the eastern toward Bagdad.

In Damascus, Jesus exchanged his burro for a camel, a more common mode of transportation for long journeys. Although he experienced some delay while he waited for a caravan going eastward, he spent the time bartering for supplies and experiencing the adventure which awaits those who have left their native lands for the first time. However, he carried no sense of loneliness, for he had lived away from home, in the midst of strangers for several years. Although his mastership was now only in the budding pangs of youth, he felt the tight bands on his head which linked with the world of those who guided him. This brought forth a sense of possession by a force and power which nurtured and sustained, and because of it his powers were increased. While his eyes and ears peered at the human world, the eyes and ears of his spirit were also open, and he saw into the angelic kingdom where those dwell who serve God without flaw. Yet, overshadowing all of this was the consciousness of the powerful mover of the universe.

It was natural that the Far East, particularly India, with its mystery and enchantment, would send out a call to the young protege of God. There, where dawn and sunset cast saffron colors into the sea, turning it into flaming orange, existed the legends of great spiritual giants. The ancient culture of this mystic land also contained the mysteries of the ages, guarded by esoteric teachings which forbade the uninitiated to enter. Throughout the country, from north to south and east to west, learned men met with their disciples and discoursed on the nature of life. Many met in the diversified temples which interspersed the landscape, but others met in caves, gathered in open spaces, and under trees. Those who entered discipleship learned that discipline was freedom, and that free will often produced vast prisons where escape was almost impossible because of attachments and sentiments.

From time to time, Jesus had come in contact with these dark-skinned people who came from the mystic land. Not only were their silks and spices among the rarest used in barter, but their stories of wise men and masters had infiltrated the common ground of learn-ing. Although few could speak the native languages of Israel, their tales filtered through the linguistic barriers like the juice of a grape wretched from its skin. Most of those who traded with these strange people who appeared to worship many gods, perceived only opposi-tion to the one God of their Lawgiver. Yet this did not deter the interest of people, and the vivid colors of the fabrics and rarity of their wares drew both the curious and the rich. However, it was not the memory of Indian wares which now drew the young white-robed figure, but the tantalizing aroma of mastership. Israel, which now followed the Book of the Law rather than Moses, their master, no longer offered clear truths concerning the reason and progression of life. Hampered by the nation's ritualistic practices, the actions of any young leader would be looked upon as seditious, for Israel would never allow anyone to be equal to, greater than, or even com-petitive with their Lawgiver. Such claims, particularly by one of their own, would ultimately result in death. In India, however, the status of mastership was both common and accepted, and there Jesus would have the opportunity to develop freely the role which he must later play.

It was not a long wait for Jesus in Damascus, for within a few days a small caravan made ready to depart for Babylonia. This nation which occupied the eastern end of the fertile crescent, lay between the two great rivers, the Tigris and Euphrates. While Baby-lon, Babylonia's principle city, rested on the Euphrates River, which served as the western boundary of Babylonia, the village of Baghdad was located 55 miles to the south, on the Tigris, or eastern boundary. As a cradle of civilization, the nation virtually sepa-rated the Mid East from the Far East. For this reason, the city of Babylon, its name meaning to confound, because of its confusion of tongues, became a meeting ground for most of the races in the known world.

As the caravan formed, Jesus prepared to mount the camel which now knelt on its horny pads in front of him. Although it was not the first time he had ridden such a beast, he was much more famil-iar with the four-legged burros which were the common means of transportation in his native land. Grabbing at the pack saddle, he hoisted himself upon the dromedary's protruding hump and hit the hindquarters lightly to make the animal rise. Raising the rump first, the camel almost threw Jesus over its head. But then it gave a wild lurch and managed to bring its two front legs into an upright position. As they moved off to join the others in the caravan, the Master felt himself swaying from side to side as the creature raised and lowered its broad feet, leaving shallow marks in the sand. Seated eight feet high and well above the heads of the few early risers who milled in the narrow streets, Jesus felt the current of anticipation which flowed from the others through him and mingled with his own.

It was early morning, but already the temperature had begun to rise. The voices of the camel drivers rose above the quietness of the city and, prodding their animals with sticks, they moved out, heading north eastward toward Palmyra (Tadmor), which would be the first major stop between Damascus and Babylon. A wilderness city built by Solomon, Palmyra lay in deep desert 176 miles from the caravan's destination. Serving as a center way station between Damascus and the Euphrates River, it was a site for vast commercial traffic. Surrounded by the broad expanse of the Arabia Desert, the city also served as doorway to the upper crescent, known as the land of Mesopotamia and Kingdom of Mari. From there the caravan would take a straight course across the northern part of the great desert to Mari, an ancient city on the Middle Euphrates. This was a natural trade route because it offered the shortest distance across the huge desolate wasteland and provided greater water accessibility.

For Jesus, it was a journey back into the history and lives of his ancestors. In 2161 B.C., Abraham, the progenitor of the children of Israel and descendant in the ninth generation from Shem, was born in the land of Chaldea. Later, Abraham traveled this same desert, departing from Haran for the land of Canaan. After this came Jacob, second son of Isaac, who left his homeland and crossed the wasteland to Mesopotamia to seek a wife among his kinfolk. He, in turn, brought forth the Twelve Tribes of Israel, of which even Jesus was a direct descendant. Thus, as the young Master lay near his camel, with his head propped upon the rigging, he rested in the cultural cradle of his nation. The stars shown above with clarity, their movement a part of the mystery he must come to understand. Questions poured through his mind pertaining to his purpose, the nature of God, and systematic process of nature. Although he had become a master, he was still in the fresh bloom of its awakening. As a seed becomes a tree, so did he have to mature from an infancy of light into a season of wisdom. However, these thoughts could not dwell in his mind, for the hours of travel were long and hard, and ultimately sleep became victorious over life's awakening.

The trip from Damascus to Palmyra took about three days, and from there to Babylon, twelve days. Although the camels could travel at a fast walking pace of over three miles an hour, they were not usually forced to do so during the hottest part of the day. Strange and obstinate creatures, they could negotiate the barren deserts for up to three weeks without water. The smooth-walled anterior section of the stomach had diverticula (small sacs), which served as storage areas for water. However, by the time the fluid was processed and stored in its holding sacs it had turned into a putrefied substance resembling pea green soup. Because of this, and because a camel was considered stupid, the wrath of their owners often fell upon them. Nonetheless, survival in the desert depended upon the camel, and some owners, like Jesus, became fond of their animals and treated them well.

Upon reaching Mari, the caravan delayed long enough to refresh both beast and man, and take on fresh water. From there they followed the Euphrates River to Babylon. For several, this *Gate of God* represented the end of the journey. On arrival the retinue dispersed and Jesus said farewell to some of his companions. Although he, along with others, would have to wait a few days to join a caravan leaving for the Far East, there was much to do in Babylon. It was not only a meeting place for the known world, but also served as a great cultural center. More importantly, for Jesus it was the home of the Chaldean astrologers, and both astronomy and astrology drew people from all parts of the known world. It also held all sorts of magicians, sorcerers, and diviners. Therefore, the young Master traversed the streets, mingled among the unusual, and sought out those who seemed to be men of learning. However, the Chaldean astrologers fascinated him the most, and he spent considerable time with them.

At last, word was received that a caravan had formed and would be leaving for the Far East. There was great activity in the camp where the camel drivers waited with their beasts, for supplies had to be checked and holding vessels filled with water. Although everyone was in high spirits, there was also an undertone of seriousness, for it would be a long and hazardous journey which would take over 300 days. During that time there would be sandstorms, possible bandits, and day after day of total isolation. At times, the stench of their bodies would be almost equal to that of the beasts they rode. Fresh water would become a scarce commodity, and what they carried with them would have to be preserved for drinking. Nevertheless, as dawn broke over the Temple of Bel, the riders mounted their animals and headed south along the Euphrates to the Persian Gulf.

By this time Jesus had become adept with camels. As he sat on his high perch swaying to and fro, he looked much like the others in the group. His skin was burned dark from the heat of the desert, while his hair disappeared under a carefully wrapped stripped turban.

Although he carried a mantle for warmth at night and in cold weather, he now wore only his white apron-like garment girded with a narrow rope, while his feet were clad in dark brown sandals and tied with leather thongs. The skin of his feet and hands was also darkened by the sun, but his gray eyes still set him apart from the piercing brown eyes of those from the Far East. Most of his time was spent in quiet thought, his eyes taking in the details of the terrain. During the day, there was very little conversation because of the distance between animals, but sometimes in the evenings the men asked the young Master questions. Although there were some language barriers at first, Jesus quickly learned to communicate. While the traders expected little from the 19-year-old, they were often surprised. His growing understanding of life, knowledge of nature, and keen mind won him considerable respect.

From the city of Ur, Abraham's native city in southern Babylonia, the caravan moved along the northern tip of the gulf. Here they branched off from the Euphrates and Tigris to follow one of the long narrow rivers running between the gulf and the Caspian Sea which would take them to the cities of Persepolis and Shiraz. This route, although more desolate than following the sea, was much shorter and took them around the southern part of the rugged chain of hills called the Zagros Mountains. The high valley stood above the sea 5,200 feet, like a silent sentinel above the vast wasteland of the Kuhha ye Zagros. There were a few caravansaries, or way stations, along the way, which provided housing for both men and beasts. These structures opened to a central court and were surrounded by porticoes, serving as dwellings, storage, and shops. While the animals were bedded down in the central section, the wealthier travelers occupied the surrounding rooms. Those who could not afford rooms made their beds with the animals or slept nearby in the open, using their camel packs for pillows.

And it came to pass that, after his arrival in India, Jesus went to dwell in the State of Nepal. Here were beauties he had never seen before. The territory was bounded on the north by Tibet, on the east by Sikkim, on the south by Bengal, and on the west by Kumaon, separated only by the Kali River. Along the northern frontier rose the highest peaks of the great Himalaya mountain range. In clear weather, he could see the magnificent snowcapped peaks running in an almost unbroken line all the way to Kathmandu. He also found the temperatures of his new home a vast contrast to the hot deserts where he had been raised, for even in the summer months from April to October it was seldom above 90 degrees. There was a price for this comfort, however, for the icy chill of winter caused the young Master to take refuge in the lower areas of Delhi, Mathura,

Kanpur, and Bangladesh. He had reached his twentieth birthday, and although he did not know it, this strange new land with its orchids, wild buffalo, and black bears would hold him in its bosom for almost four years.

There were three major religious beliefs in the northern sectors of India at that time: Hinduism, Buddhism, and Jainism. The vast soul structure of Hinduism embraced the caste system, an arrangement of mankind into a hierarchy of groups. These groupings were considered hereditary and nontransferable. At the top of the system was the aristocracy of India, the Brahmans, who were custodians of sacred learning and served as the priesthood. Between the Brahmans and untouchables were three other major caste groups: Kshatriyas, theoretically, temporal rulers; Vaisyas, merchants, or artisans; and Sudras, or servants. For reasons of both necessity and simplicity, Jesus chose to dwell among the lowly Sudras, placing his attention on Jainism which was an ancient monastic religion denying the validity of the Vedic and Pantheon, as well as the ritual and authority of the Brahmans. As the Brahmans reminded him a great deal of the *beau monde* of the Sanhedrin of his native country, he was content to study for a time with those who were in opposition.

According to Jain cosmography, the universe was eternal and moved through progressive ascents and descents. Its Canon was composed in the Ardhamayadhi language and transmitted orally from master to disciple. The leader, although not the founder, was Vardhamana Mahavira, who at the age of 30, in the thirteenth year of rigorous asceticism, won supreme knowledge. Although Vardhamana Mahavira was not a living man, he was acknowledged as a perfect master because he had transcended the necessity of descent into matter, or rebirth. The followers of the Jain philosophy and the other eastern religions believed in the soul's perpetual rebirth into matter, as well as the precise law of cause and effect. They further believed that salvation could only occur if the soul passed through the resurrection of the dead (uniting the two aspects of man, mortal and immortal), which released the soul from the perpetual rebirths because it had achieved perfect wisdom.

Of course, it was not long thereafter before Jesus began to see through the outer facade of the teachings. All too often those who taught repeated only the words of the masters before them and illumination remained as far from their reach as from the hearts of their disciples. He saw that the shadows of their unknowing often matched the vast shadows cast by the 29,028-foot Mt. Everest and the 27,790-foot Makalu, so he turned toward the other religions. However, these were no different. Repetition and ritual had woven a heavy cloak of bondage around the truth, which could only be restored by ripping asunder the prison chains which bound it. Therefore, the young Master now began to teach among the lowly cast of Sudras, and from their midst he drew his first devotees and disciples.

One day the Brahmans came to Jesus and asked, "Why do you live among the Sudras? Do you not know that there is nothing for them but death, and that we are forbidden to come near those who were created from Para-Brama's belly and feet?"

Responding to their inquiry, Jesus said, "Verily, I say to you, that God has created all men equal and all are dear to him. He alone has existed from the beginning of eternity, created and willed this universe into being. His existence is without end and there is no one like unto Him, either in heaven or on the earth. Further, you have separated Him in so many aspects that it has clouded your vision. Now you are no longer able to perceive the One. Although all things owe their existence to him, he alone is omnipotent and all-sufficient."[1]

Following this event, the young Master brought the wrath of the Brahmans upon him, for he was considered both a foreign intruder and a usurper. Fearful that there would be reprisals for the loving people who had fed and housed him during the two years he had been in India, he decided to travel westward. Leaving his home near Darjeeling, not far from the base of Kanchenjunga, he journeyed toward Guria Mandhato, a 25,355-foot summit near Lake Manasarowar. This was located north of Delhi at the edge of the eastern sector of Nepal. However, he did not tarry there, for his interest by this time was focused on a Buddhist monastery which was said to exist in the interior of the mountains near Kashmir. There, in a remote sanctuary governed by monks and lamas, Jesus settled down again to monastic servitude and severe austerity.

Hidden away in a valley between the high snowcapped peaks of the western ridge of the Himalayas, where the worlds of the unspoken word and meditation prevailed, Jesus spent his final months in India. Buddhism was not a major contender for religious domination at this time, as it was relatively new. Its philosophy was originated by Guatama Buddha, a royal prince who had reached perfect enlightenment after a number of years of the most brutal austere practices. Fortunately, Guatama finally realized that his torturous practices had accomplished little and, accepting a bowl of rice, he sat himself under a great banyan tree to eat. Shortly thereafter, he went through the expanded states of soul consciousness to enter the perfect state of Nirvana, or full atonement with the presence of God. Having now witnessed the fallacy of repetitious practices established by the various religions of India, he sought to overcome fundamentalism and restore the ancient teachings. Although of Indian origin, he was no longer accepted in his country because his teachings were considered heretical. Thus, it was no wonder that the teachings of Guatama appealed to Jesus, for he saw in them a reflection of the problems which existed in Israel.

During the years the Master lived in India, a subtle change took place in him. On his arrival, he had been full of the enthusiasm of youth, the unbridled energy of his awakening, and a naivete in the ways of mastership. These things had now passed away, and in their place existed a certain air of confidence, maturity, and a definite ability to more ably control the mighty forces of nature and cosmic law. The sixteenfold path of peace[2] of Guatama did not differ too greatly from those things which he had studied in the latter years of his residency in Israel, and for a time he was content. However, as the seasons passed, Jesus received the call to leave, and as spring burst forth and the snows began to melt in the lowlands, he picked up a long walking stick. Making his way down the steep mountain path, he journeyed toward Lahore, carrying a meager supply of rice, a goat hide of water, and a rough outer blanket for warmth. Soon after his arrival he managed to link with a caravan moving westward to Babylonia, and he bid farewell to a land which he would never see again.

At Babylonia a surprising thing occurred. Jesus, who had by this time developed a perfect link of communication between himself and the world of the angels, was told to go directly to Egypt. Although there was a considerable wait before he could join up with a caravan going in the direction of Cairo and the Nile River, he passed his time patiently among those encamped for similar purposes. As he walked around quietly in the city of many tongues he could not help but notice it had begun its decline. The majesty of the past showed perceptibly through its more dreary facade. Everywhere he traveled, he witnessed the decline of great empires due to the direct misuse of natural and cosmic law, and soon he would witness another. Egypt's great culture was also gradually sinking into the mire of its graceful sands and taking upon itself the cloak of established patterns which it would bear for centuries. Eventually, like the 492-foot colossal pyramid built by Khufu, founder of the Fourth Dynasty, the great wisdoms of the world who went to Egypt to study the secrets of the universe would turn toward other nations to be carried in the voices of the troubadours and the dreams of visionaries.

Almost two years later, the Master arrived in Kemet, known as the black land because of the contrast between the dark-colored Nile mud and the red sands of the desert. He was now 26 years old. The hardships of the long journey had further seasoned his mastership, and he no longer had need of possessions, home, or friends. Although he was popular, his years of seclusion had made him both a man of thought and a man of honor. He was strong where others were weak, for the years of his nomadic life had broken the last chains of youthful bondage, and a bed of sand, a ceiling of stars, along with the constant presence of the changing panorama of outside elements, was the only world he now knew. Through the stars, the Master perceived the creative principle of God at play, and in the beating of the rain, wind, and sands upon his body, he felt a certain unity with the powerful forces of nature. Later this enabled him to perform many miracles, for his unity made it possible to control and utilize such powers for healing and transforming others. These forces, although within the reach of all mankind, could not be mastered by most because buildings, restrictions, desires, and attachments blocked any direct contact or understanding.

The nation of Egypt consisted mainly of a narrow strip of land watered by the Nile. It extended from Memphis or Cairo as far as the first cataract and the pie-shaped area between the Mediterranean Sea, called the delta. This geographic configuration of the country gave rise to the term Upper Egypt, denoting the long, narrow fertile valley, and Lower Egypt, comprising the delta. The entire country was only about 550 miles long, from the Mediterranean to the first cataract and its average breadth about twelve miles, earning it the Greek reference "gift of the Nile." However, it was not its geographic location which set it apart from the rest of the world. It was also the home of the great kings, and Memphis, the ancient capital situated on the Nile River, held the mysteries of the great pyramids. The highest of these structures had long served as a place of learning and drew noted people from other lands, particularly from Greece.

Guarding the threshold of Cheops was the silent Sphinx, concealing within his structure the common belief that human had risen from animal. Not far away stood the mute structure of the pyramid as a symbol of man in the vast desert of unknowing until he raised the triangular capstone by uniting the body, soul, and spirit. Within its hallowed walls of sandstones, initiation rites concerning the mysterious transformation of man were taught by the ancient teachers. Over the grand gallery lay seven over-lapping layers of stone to signify the seventh day of creation when God would gather himself from all parts of the world and restore the world. Lastly, the King's chamber, the finale of the great mysteries, had four low compartments representing human release from the bondage of the four elements. A fifth compartment was peaked, signifying the grand crowning of humankind as it raised the capstone and became an illumined race like unto the sun at high noon.

The most famous of all of the ancient philosophies at this time, of course, were the Eleusinian mysteries. The rites and mystical interpretation of nature's most precious secrets spread out from their origins in east-central Greece to overshadow the major civilizations of the area and absorbed many of the smaller schools. These teachings became the avenue by which the traditions of creation were dispensed, and the Eleusinian initiates rose resplendent among the spiritual initiates of the world. Their rituals, like those of the later Christian mysteries, were divided as the lesser and the greater. The lesser related to the impure soul which was still encased in its earthly body by its material and physical nature. The crux of the Eleusinian argument was that man is neither better nor wiser after death than during life. If he does not rise above ignorance during his sojourn here, man goes on after death making the same mistakes he made here. If he does not outgrow the desire for material possessions here, he will carry it with him to the invisible world.

To the Eleusinians, birth into the physical world was the same as death. They regarded true birth as that of the spiritual soul of man arising out of the womb of its own fleshly nature. The following statement from Porphyry gives a fairly adequate conception of Eleusinian symbolism: "God being a luminous principle, residing in the midst of the most subtle fire, remains forever invisible to the eyes of those who do not elevate themselves above material life."

After spending several months in Lower Egypt, Jesus departed for Upper Egypt, making his way along the Nile River to Thebes, an ancient religious capital in Upper Egypt occupying both banks of the Nile. The great temples of Karnak and Luxor were situated along the right bank, and on the left, going north to south, lay the temples of Goornah and Colossae. These two metropolises had drawn some of the greatest men on earth into their hallowed halls of learning, among these, Pythagoras, Plato, and Pindar (the Greek lyric poet). Now Jesus also stepped into the shadows cast by the great temple pillars to walk in the hallowed halls of the noble. However, it was not long before he was recognized as a master and soon began to draw disciples of his own, once again bringing the wrath and jealousy of some of the teachers upon him. Others embraced this strange man of the East who had wandered in faraway lands and bore the distinctiveness of a king.

There was a great deal for Jesus to do in this faraway yet familiar land where he had dwelled in exile in his infancy. It was now essential that the past and present intermingle in his soul, for that which had been wrought by Moses during the time of Rameses II had to find a fertile field. Thus, under the dark shadows of ignorance, the laws which Moses had founded for the children of Israel were but stagnant pools of disease and if Israel was not to succumb to its cancerous spread, then the fresh sea of truth would have to purify the roots of the disease. Although Jesus knew that his destiny lay in his native land, he also knew that he must wait to be called back by the unseen world which guided him. There, in the vast regions beyond the boundaries of flesh, abided the great administrators of God, each bound by the common cause of man's necessity. Although the Creator was the indomitable energy behind the movement of the universe, the angelic emissaries were his hands and his feet. Through them, he directed the administration of worldly things, for they bore the light of His son [3] within them.

While Jesus was traveling in Egypt, he received the sad news that his father had died in Galilee and that his mother was grieving. By now he had little interest in remaining in Egypt, so he wrote his mother saying,[4]

Beloved Mother:

Be not grieved, for all is well for father, as with you. He has completed his present work here on earth, and has done so nobly. None in any walk of life can charge him with deceit, dishonesty, nor wrong intention. In his period of life here he has completed many great tasks and is gone from our midst truly prepared to solve the problems that await him in the future. Our God, the Father of all of us, is with him now as He was with him heretofore, but even now the Heavenly Hosts guard his footsteps and protect him on his way. Therefore, why should you weep and suffer? Tears will not conquer your grief, and your sorrow cannot be vanquished by any emotion of your heart and mind. Let your soul be busy in meditation and contact with him who is gone, and if you art not idle, there will be no time for grief. When grief throbs through the heart, and anguish causes you pain, permit yourself to rise to higher planes and indulge in the ministry of love. Your ministry has always been that of love. Therefore, let the past remain past. Rise above the cares of earthly things and give your life to those who still live with us on earth. When your life is done, you will find it again in the morning sun, or even in the evening dew, as in the song of the birds, the perfume of the flowers, and the majestic lights of the stars at night. For it will not be long before your problems and toils on earth will be solved also, and when all is counted and arranged you will be ready for greater fields of effort and prepared to solve the greater problems of the soul. Try then to be content until I come to you soon and bring to you richer gifts than any of you have ever seen, and greater than those made of gold or precious stones. I am sure that my brother will care for you and supply your needs and I am always with you in mind and spirit.

Your Son,
Jesus

Nothing remained for Jesus in this land of the pharaohs. He had reached the height of mastership, and while he lived in the mortal world, he was no longer of it. His use of the forces was par-excellent, and having united the body with nature, the soul with the unseen world beyond matter, he dwelled in the world of spirit amid the archangelic who administered the power for God. By this time, he also knew that he had descended from the higher unseen regions to fulfill a special mission, and he bore the confident countenance of one who knew his destiny. With these achievements, the dream of the Jewish people for a political heir to the throne of King David ben Jesse died forever.

Finally, bidding farewell to Egypt, Jesus prepared to return to Israel by caravan. His true Father was the eternal one which moved ceaselessly through the waves of universal order, and his true Mother, nature. The time had finally come when his assignment with destiny was to be fulfilled, and with Joseph's death the call to his homeland was urgent. Soon the dust gathered on sandaled feet and marked the edge of his white tunic, while the stars over Egypt whispered their witness to the mystery carried forth upon the wind. Above his lithe form they sighed over the memory of the Lawgiver who had stood upon the Mount in the final years of the pilgrimage of the children of Israel and said "A *prophet shall the Lord your God raise up unto you of your brethren like unto me; him shall ye hear.*" If Jesus was aware of this silent prophesy, stealing through the darkened nights of his journey out of Egypt, he betrayed no sign nor showed any anticipation as the caravan moved slowly along the Nile, veering off at Heliopolis toward Beer-sheba.

As the caravan approached Beer-sheba, a Simeonite town located in the southern part of Palestine, about midway between the Mediterranean Sea and the southern end of the Dead Sea, the Master set foot once more upon the soil of his homeland. This land which had once been a favorite residence of Abraham and Isaac, and the latter's home when Esau sold his birthright to Jacob, would now bear witness to the end of Jesus' life. A heaviness descended upon him and the joy experienced by a traveler returning home was absent, for when he entered Palestine he knew he had signed his death warrant.

After entering the city, the travelers halted for the night and set about feeding and watering the animals. The open arena where most of them would sleep was full of camels as well as traders and merchants, some of whom smelled as foul as the beasts which had carried them. By this time, however, Jesus was used to the gathering places of nomads and paid little heed to the pandemonium surrounding him. Therefore, when things had finally quieted down, he too took off his camel pack and made ready to pass the night as he had so many times before. When the light of the morning laid its warm touch upon the land on the following day, those who were not remaining in Beer-sheba to trade made ready for departure. Although some took the road to Egypt, others, including Jesus, departed for Israel, but he alone was traveling toward a final assignation with destiny.

Although Jesus fully intended to go to Nazareth to visit his mother, he decided to stop in Jerusalem to seek out his cousin John before continuing the journey. There he was informed by Elisabeth that John was baptizing in the Jordan Valley south of Jericho where the Jordan intersected with the Jabbok River. At first when he came and knocked upon her door she did not recognize him, for the weathered skin and lithe figure of a man had replaced the youth of the past. It was with a certain amount of amusement that Jesus informed her of who he was, and on hearing the good news the woman rejoiced greatly. Urging her nephew to stay for the night and rest she sought to prepare him a sumptuous feast. However, he stopped her from doing so because his system had too long been accustomed to a most frugal diet and the simplest of foods. Later he also found the bed strange and felt the heaviness of the partitions closing in around him. Even with the wooden shutters of the window open, the Master experienced a sense of separateness from the forces which had served as walls for him during much of his 11-year absence. His sense of discomfort during the night established a precedence, and, weather permitting, he would seldom sleep in any building in the future. During the next three years, as he wandered from place to place, he made his bed in the open pavilion of nature.

The following morning, having already exchanged his camel for the native vehicle of an ass, Jesus departed from Elisabeth's and made his way toward Jericho and the Jordan River. During the years of his cousin's absence, John had entered into the higher order of the Brotherhood and eventually went into the wilderness (the world of the unenlightened) to teach the redemption of man and to baptize. He too had changed throughout the years, for his youthful countenance had taken the form of a powerful man and his voice was equal to his bearing. For these reasons, he soon began to attract great multitudes from Jerusalem and all Judea, as well as the region around Jordan. In his ministry he urged the Jews to strive toward perfection and walk humbly before God. Baptizing by water to symbolize the purification of the body, he taught that this path of transmutation would lead to the baptism of fire, or the purification of the soul. As an adept of the deeper teachings of human existence, the Baptist well understood that obedience to the laws of nature would ultimately reveal the subtle cosmic laws which were the essence and cause of all life.

While John had some awareness of his forthcoming purpose as he baptized in the waters of the Jordan River, his mission had not been fully revealed to him. Had he known it, his assignment with destiny was second only to the one who was to follow. It was his task to bring the people together and prepare the way for Jesus, although he did not know that the prophesy of a Messiah would be fulfilled by one of his own kin. If he had failed to accomplish this, then a greater work could not be wrought, for the three years remaining in Jesus' life would have been insufficient to prepare and plant the field. Therefore, it fell upon John to lay the foundation, plant, and water, so that all would be in readiness when the time for reaping fell across the land. He peered into the faces of those who were called wise ones as he sought for the answer to this riddle. On each occasion he turned away, realizing that the search had not yet ended. Long hidden in the dark clouds of prophesy not yet fulfilled were the words of Elijah: And there shall come forth a rod out of the stem of Jesse, and a Branch shall grow out of his roots: And the spirit of the Lord shall rest upon him.

Often, as the indomitable man stood in the water to baptize, thousands of tiny fish gathered to nibble at his feet, making it difficult to remain solemn. The fish were common to the tepid waters and quite harmless, but they swarmed around his feet. From time to time, he had to shuffle his legs to frighten them off, because their mouths were small suction cups and they pressed these against their object of attack, becoming an extraordinary nuisance. Neither did he escape the ridicule of doubters, for some came to humiliate him and lay waste to the words he taught. Some, of course, succumbed to his words and entered the river to be baptized, believing that they would be saved from the terror he spoke about. When the priests and Levites came to John, they called out, "Who are you, that we may give an answer to those who sent us? What do you say of yourself?"

The scoffing was usually of little concern to John and he sought to answer these sword-like thrusts by calling back, "I am the voice of a man crying in the wilderness (unknowing and unenlightened world of matter), to make straight the path of the Lord as spoken by the prophet Isaiah. All which is less in you shall be raised and all which is high in you shall be brought low; and those of you who are crooked shall be made straight and the rough ways shall be made smooth. I promise you that all flesh shall see the salvation of God.

"You, who have been treacherous as vipers, has anyone warned you to flee from the day of judgment which will come upon all men before the end? Do not depend upon the protection of your Father Abraham to keep you from these days, for only good deeds, kind words, and kind thoughts shall be worthy offerings to God, who is ruler over all of Israel. In the days of atonement, every soul which has failed to bring forth good fruit shall be cast into the fires of purification (purification by the inner divine nature), as decreed by God."

Some of the people, hoping to free themselves from the terrible day of judgment asked him, "What shall we do?" John replied, saying, "He who has two coats, let him give one to him who has none; and he who has food, let him share it with those who are hungry."

Also the publicans, who were collectors of Roman tax money, came to be baptized and they asked of him, "Master, what shall we do?"

And John said to them, "You must take care that you extract no more from anyone than is decreed by law," and to the soldier who questioned him, he responded, "Do violence to no man, accuse no one falsely, and be satisfied with that which is paid you."

Many who came to the Baptizer, noting his wisdom, wondered if he were the Messiah whose coming had been prophesied since the days of old, and the one who would raise Israel. To such questions, John answered them, saying; "I indeed baptize you with water to purify your body, but he that comes after me is mightier than I, whose shoes I am not worthy to bear. He shall baptize your soul with the living spirit of God. The wind is in his hand and he will thoroughly purge the error of your ways and gather that which is good in you into the garner. So too will he burn the impurities within the soul with unquenchable fire, that fire which is eternal light and brighter than the brightest sun" (*Dark Night of the Soul*, St. John of the Cross).

It was now the summer of 24 A.D., and the twenty-ninth year of Jesus' life. As John called forth his followers for baptism on this particular summer day he had no intimation that Jesus was nearby. Entering the water up to his waist, he took his accustomed place near the mouth of the Jabbok River, which had once served as a boundary between the kingdoms of Sihon and Og. The weather was very hot and in the highlands the wheat harvest had begun. Around him the parched land revealed a dreary waste of withered stalks and dried grass. Although the warm waters of the Jordan River offered some relief from the intense heat, the air was very still. So intent was he on what he was doing that he failed to see the lone traveler making his way toward the river, his legs dangling in a relaxed manner over the sides of his burro and his feet almost touching the ground as the animal meandered along.

As Jesus approached the place where the Jabbok River empties into the Jordan, he saw his cousin standing in the water while a group of people waited to be immersed. Thinking both to surprise John, and also to see if he would recognize him, the traveler joined the ranks of those waiting for baptism. An early playfulness still resonated in the chords of Jesus' heart and his humor forbade dismissal of the tiny ray of amusement which danced across his eyes. The Baptizer, long accustomed to the routine passage of one face after another, paid little heed to the figure who had just joined them until he recognized the traditional white garment of an ascetic. Gazing upward to see who now stood before him in the river, he was surprised to find a pair of bold, but mirthful, gray eyes looking into his. Although he did not recognize Jesus at first, he sensed that the traveler was a master of the highest order. Therefore, he declined to baptize him, saying, "It is I who have need to be baptized by you; yet you come to me?"

With great solemnness Jesus replied, "Let it be so now, for it becomes us to fulfill all righteousness."

And it came to pass, that, as his cousin rose from the water, John saw a vision of a white dove[5] descend upon his head, signifying divine benediction. Then John heard the same inner voice which had spoken to Moses through the burning bush at Mt. Sinai, saying, "This is my son in whom I am well pleased."

At first John was puzzled and continued to look at Jesus, his eyes seeking to penetrate deeply beyond the world of matter into the deep recesses of soul. Then a subtle joy slowly began to spread throughout his countenance, for he not only recognized his cousin now, but also knew that the time of fulfillment had come to pass and his search had ended.

After this, Jesus tarried for a time to discourse among his cousin's followers. No one had met such a man, for his words were as a narcotic and his command as powerful as the sea. He spoke of things which none had ever known—death, the purpose of life—and in his presence there was the shadow of a force which seemed to dwell in worlds beyond them. When he spoke, no one else spoke. Even John sat quietly listening, for while he was a master also, he knew that his mastership was less. Yet he was content to dwell in the shadows, for in spiritual ascent he who is less serves he who is greater. Soon, however, the trip to Nazareth to be with his mother was pressing Jesus to continue on.

Two days after his baptism in the Jordan River, Jesus bid John and his disciples farewell and continued on his way to Nazareth. Although his forthcoming mission weighed somewhat heavily upon him, he assured John that he would return within a short time. As the two men stood facing each other, each acknowledged the falling sands of destiny within the silence of their souls. The

The Light of Life   Burrows (cc)

I am sent to you by the Father, that I may make the light of life to shine before you. The light lightens both itself and the darkness, but the darkness knows only itself, and knows not the light.

Gospel of Peace,
Vatican MS./Szekely
Section I, ch. III:14

Baptist was now aware that his mission was almost over and that it would be necessary for his work to decrease in order that greater work might be accomplished. By this time, he was also aware that his death was imminent and that his followers must be reconciled to the idea of supporting the work of one who was greater. As he watched Jesus disappear into the distant hills, he turned to two of his disciples and said, "Behold the lamb (a soul which has sacrificed its human attributes for the sake of mankind) of God."

After visiting with his mother, Jesus went into the desert to look closely at the purpose which constituted his destiny. Leaving behind the fertile river banks and acres of cultivated land, he entered the wilderness on the far side of Megiddo, once the royal city of the Canaanites. Beyond lay the Kishon River, the Plains of Esdraelon, and Mount Carmel where Elijah led Israel back to Jehovah. Little by little the teeming animal life of the lower lands disappeared, until nothing remained except the soaring vultures overhead and occasional serpents and crawling centipedes. A no-man's land, the forbidding countenance of the hills stood starkly against the shimmer of the horizon, hiding many isolated recesses never touched by man. The silence of the vast waste fell upon the traveler, brooding heavily over him and the places where he walked.

On and on Jesus pressed, giving slight heed to the desolate scene which now showed little but gloomy hills, dark canyons, and bare rocks. At night, when the somber darkness descended over the stark terrain, he sought rest among the crevices beneath the dark peaks of sloping hills. There, under the night sky, he was watched over by the power which moves all heavenly bodies toward a predetermined rendezvous with destiny. In this silent land, the great Egyptian Pharaoh, Thutmose III, had fought the confederate princes of Syria and Palestine. Here also, King Saul had been slain by the Philistines, and the conquering Israelites faced the Canaanite kings. However, these apparitions of the past did not disturb the Master. When dawn etched its blanket of colored splendor across the sky, he boldly moved forward to the heart of the hills, where the Spirit guided him to the scene of some great spiritual struggle which he intuitively knew lay before him.

Alone now, somewhere within the protective custody of Mt. Tabor, the Hill of Moreh and Mt. Gilboa, the Master sought to find the appropriate means of fulfilling his mission. His descent through royal lineage offered him a temporal rulership over Israel if he so chose to accept it. The possibility of this prophecy had accompanied him since childhood, as the prophecies of the astronomers dwelled amid his youthful memories. On the other hand, to remain true to the narrow path of asceticism would ultimately fulfill the prophesy of ancient times and the Kingdom of Heaven would be brought to earth. Later this period of introspection into his soul's purpose would be referred to as Jesus' battle with Lucifer, or the final rendezvous with the material senses.

Ancient legend relates that two visions came to Jesus at this time. In the first he saw an image of himself descending the mountain to announce himself as the Messiah, the King of the Jews, later to lead a great conquering army in its march toward Jerusalem. The promise of a Messiah who would spring from the loins of David and take his rightful place as king, was imbedded in the heart of every Jew worthy of the name. Israel was oppressed by its conquerors and made subject to a foreign yoke, but when the Messiah came to deliver her, every Jew would rise to drive out the foreign invaders and conquerors; the yoke of Rome would be thrown off and the nation would once more take its place among the powers of earth. It is written that Jesus saw Israel's political sphere of influence extending in all directions, until at last Persia, Egypt, Greece, and even mighty Rome came under the dominance of Palestine; and the splendor of his royal court would exceed that of Solomon.

The other vision bestowed upon the man from Galilee showed a path true to his spiritual instincts. Throwing away the royal purple robe and the sceptre, he would accept the staff of the ascetic and render himself to the title of *a man of sorrows*. He saw himself continuing to sow the seeds of truth, which in later centuries would spring up, blossom, and bear fruit to nourish the world. At the same time, he also realized that such a path would place him in contention with those in power and authority, and that he would bring hatred and persecution upon his head. This would bind him to death by means of crucifixion. It has been written that never in the history of man had the powers of darkness so gathered together for attack upon the mind of a mortal man.

So the temptation of the wilderness failed, and Jesus descended down the mountain to return to the world of man. Before long, the desolate wilderness of his final temptation lay behind him, while the mud and sunburned structures of civilization containing his future rose quiescent before him.

In deep thought, the young Master reviewed the aspects of his decision as he gazed across the valley of Jezreel where the kings of Israel had once held court. During his travels, he had seen the rise and fall of numerous great empires. Even his own land had become a kaleidoscope of chaotic unrest, and the kingdom of heaven which was to descend upon earth was but a mirage in a distant dawn. Jesus knew that God must rise victorious and establish a spiritual kingdom on earth, if human evolution was to complete its journey through matter. Fulfillment of this predestined plan would manifest in the brotherhood of man and create peace among all nations. Service to this greater cause had been the supreme purpose of the spiritual giants of the past and would remain the ultimate goal of those not yet born. Although the outcome of his dilemma would long be known by the whole of earth, his reason for making this ultimate decision would never be fully understood until the mystery of the resurrection of the dead was made known to the masses.

Having completed his deliberations and made his decision, Jesus now had to formulate an effective course of action for accomplishing the great work. This would require moving mass consciousness out of its bondage of fixed precepts to allow the divine prophecy of a forthcoming Messiah to be fulfilled. Just as the division of Israel's Twelve Tribes had been established by Moses to correspond with the movement of the earth through the 12 celestial star clusters of heaven, the Master would select 12 disciples to bear testimony to his work. Like the rays of the sun, his teachings would then radiate outward and ultimately span the entire earth. With these things in mind the will of God played in celebration upon the harp of destiny, and Jesus, the Son of man, laid aside a human kingdom and went forth as Jesus, the Son of God, to bring the kingdom of heaven on earth. His crown was the illumined soul and his scepter the sword of truth and justice.

Leaving the wilderness behind, the Master prepared to return to the Jordan River where his cousin John was baptizing, thereby keeping the promise that he had made earlier. Traveling along the shores of Galilee, or *Bahr Tarbariyeh*, as it was called by the local inhabitants, afforded a welcome contrast to the expanse of the desert. Here the land was fertile, and many families sustained themselves through agriculture and fishing. The lake was 60 miles from Jerusalem, its depth 80 to 160 feet, and its waters were blue and sweet. Some distance away, the Jordan river entered the lake, flowing some 25 miles and descending at 60 feet a mile to complete its journey.

As Jesus neared his destination, he happened upon a man named Andrew, who lived in the town of Bethsaida near Capernaum. Andrew and his brother Peter were sons of Jonas, a fisherman of considerable skill. The fisherman immediately recognized the Master, for he had been present at the fork of the river when Jesus arrived and heard John speak of him as the one who was to come. As Andrew stood in the presence of the Master, he was not able to speak at first. Memory of the other time on the Jordan was still with him, and when he finally spoke, excitement spilled over in nervous utterances. This amused Jesus, who spoke kindly, and asked where he might locate his cousins, James and John, the sons of Zebedee. On receiving the information he requested, he turned and continued to ride southward along the sea. However, Andrew hastened to the place where he had last seen his brother to inform him that the Messiah had come.

Finding Peter was not difficult, for he had the fishing nets spread out along the shores of the sea and was busy making some necessary repairs. The circular nets were made of a fine mesh and were about 15 feet in diameter. Attached to the center was a long piece of fish line, while the margins were loaded with lead sinkers. During fishing, the line was held in the left hand, while the net itself was gathered up in the right and cast into the water by a broad sweep of the arm. Later the net was drawn up, and the fisherman waded into the water to secure the catch. From time to time, the fine mesh broke, and it became necessary to stop fishing long enough to replace the broken threads.

At the time, Peter was so intent on his work that he did not hear his brother approach him. However, when Andrew informed him that the Messiah had come, he looked up in surprise, wondering if this were true. He hastened with his brother to the spot where Jesus had last been seen that he might judge this revolutionary news for himself. He did not believe what he had heard, but he knew that his going would please Andrew. Too many rumors had floated across the land, and each had been as a tree withered in the hot sun. And as each rumor died, the spirit of the nation died a bit also. How then could he, Peter, a simple fisherman, be a witness to the fulfillment of such prophecy? But it came to pass, when Jesus beheld the two brothers approaching him, he said to Peter, "You are Simon Peter, the son of Jonas. Henceforth I shall call you Peter" (meaning rock).

Such a remark stunned the lowly fisherman and he looked at Jesus in disbelief, for no man except a prophet would speak in such a way. Although he saw the amusement in Jesus' eyes, he also felt something else, some intangible force unlike anything he had experienced before, emanating from Jesus' presence. "Could this be true," he wondered. "Is this man who stands before me indeed the Messiah, or some charlatan who has come to deceive the people?"

Inwardly Jesus smiled at the confused thoughts which were passing through Peter's mind, for as a sheep master knows his sheep so does a master know his disciples. Then his eyes became gentle and he looked at the brothers with deep concentration. He saw that their ways were as unpolished stones, but he was a craftsman, a jewel maker, and his cuts would be precise and accurate. After this he turned away that he might continue to search for his cousins, but Andrew and Peter came after him.

On the following day, Jesus went into Galilee where he met Philip, who had also been at the ford when Jesus was baptized by John. Immediately upon recognizing the Master, Philip began to ask questions concerning his teachings. After Jesus had spoken for some time the disciple fell silent. He no longer doubted that this was the indeed the Messiah, for he, like those the day before, felt the powerful inner presence which dwelled within the man from Galilee. Immediately after departing from Jesus, Philip went to locate his friend Nathaniel bar Tolmai to inform him that their search had ended. On seeing Nathaniel perched under a fig tree, Philip went up to him with great excitement, saying, "We have found him of whom Moses and the prophets did speak. He is Jesus of Nazareth, the son of Joseph the carpenter."

Shaking his head slowly from side to side, Nathaniel looked off in a distance at the lofty masses of Kurun Hattin and Mt. Tabor rising out of the desert plains where he had spent most of his life. He did not believe that one of their own countrymen had risen to such authority, although he had heard rumors from time to time. Questioning Philip, he asked, "Can there be anything good come out of Nazareth?"

And Philip looked down upon his friend sitting underneath the tree, barely able to contain his enthusiasm, and said, "Come and see."

Rising, Nathaniel looked at Philip with some concern. Yet, he saw it would please his friend if he went to see this person, and he stepped out on the road, lagging somewhat behind as Philip took the lead. Around them flowed the Jordan Valley, which at one time had been occupied by a great inland sea extending from Huleh to a point 40 miles beyond the present southern limit of the Dead Sea. Nearby, the hills closed upon the sea to the southwest and receded from the shore towards the north creating a great natural amphitheater, silent now, as the curtain of time waited to be raised upon a final drama.

When Jesus saw the two friends approaching he called out to Nathaniel Bar Tolmai, half seriously and half in jest, saying, "Behold here comes an Israelite in whom I can find no deceit."

Showing considerable surprise, Nathaniel inquired, "How do you know me, for we have never met? Are you then some prophet?"

Jesus smiled and he replied, "Before Philip called you, I perceived you sitting under the fig tree."

Considerably amazed because such things were not possible for ordinary men, Nathaniel said, "Rabbi (teacher), you must indeed be the anointed of God, the king who has been prophesied to rule Israel. No man could know that which you have spoken of, for I was not in your sight as I lay resting. Yet, your eyes saw me. How is this possible?"

A shadow of seriousness momentarily blanked out the amusement which had previously been on Jesus' face and he spoke, saying, "Because I have told you that I saw you under a fig tree, you believe. I promise you that you shall see greater things than these. One day you shall see heaven, and angels shall descend upon the Sons of men born of women's wombs and change them into Sons of God. Then shall the whole of earth become as heaven."

Kneeling down before the Master, Nathaniel pleaded, "Take me with you, Master. Although I am but a humble gardener and dealer of vegetables from the Garden of Hierocrates, I seek to learn and understand these things of which you speak. There will be no one to miss me, nor have I great possessions, but I will serve you in whatever way I can, even with my life."

As the gardener spoke these words, Jesus looked at his upturned face with deep sadness. By asking to become Jesus' disciple, Nathaniel had signed his own death warrant, and as with all disciples, Jesus lived a fleeting moment in an event which had not yet taken place. There in a foreign land he saw a cross and on its cross beam, upside down, hung the flayed body of the man who now knelt in front of him. Then another city, another cross, and another body superimposed itself over this scene, and on seeing this Jesus glanced over at Philip.

Motioning for the two friends to join him, Jesus told them that they would travel to where John was baptizing. As the men made their way up the Jordan River, the Master began the initial training which would transform them into forces of steel. By night they would sleep under the stars, by day they would learn the laws of nature, and when it had ended they would be as mighty swords, capable of breaking asunder the ways of the old. This would be no easy task, for the dead in them would have to be raised. And as he lifted, they would pull down, and the petty grievances which belonged only in the mortal world would make them argumentative and difficult to bear. Yet, the task would have to be accomplished, for these were the hands which would carry on when he no longer walked upon the earth. Therefore, he demanded asceticism, frugality, and obedience, even from the beginning.

After spending a brief time with John at the ford, matters of great urgency began to consume Jesus. Thus, he made preparations to depart. If a sense of heaviness pierced his heart, it was because the two men would never meet again in the human world, for soon thereafter John was to be imprisoned and executed. Sadly Jesus completed his farewells. Then the retinue turned and walked along the banks of the Jordan River in the direction of Capernaum.

At Scythopolis (Beth-shan) Jesus intended to veer off across the plains of Esdraelon and travel toward Nazareth. Scythopolis was an ancient fortress city which strategically commanded the valley of Esdraelon. It had been witness to several events which molded the history of Israel. After Thutmose III's great victory at Megiddo (B.C. 1482) it had passed into Egyptian hands, where it remained a garrison for Egyptian soldiers for 300 years. By B.C 1000, the land was in the hands of the Philistines, who fastened the bones of Saul and his sons to the wall of the city, and hung Saul's head in the Temple of the Dragon. As Jesus and his new disciples walked through its streets, the decadence of the past matched the sorrow in his heart over the forthcoming death of one whom he loved. Yet, he knew that John's work was almost finished and that the Master of Asha (movement of cosmic order) must take his knight from the cosmic chessboard. If he did not do so then the game would be lost to the forces of Ahriman (darkness and unknowing).

Shortly after Jesus returned to his family home in Nazareth, messengers informed his mother of the forthcoming marriage of a female relative who lived in Cana of Galilee. The prevailing customs required that the invitation to the wedding celebration be accepted. Also, the occasion seemed very important to Mary, so Jesus, his brothers, and new disciples prepared to escort Mary to the village. After packing the wedding gifts, the party prepared for their departure. The journey would not require a great deal of travel time, for Cana lay but a short distance northward along the road to the coastal village of Ptolemais. Therefore it was not long before the party reached the outskirts of Nazareth, at which point the route to the coast veered from the main caravan passage to Damascus. This would take them first to Sepphoris, then to the west of Kurun Hattin, which lay in the mountainous region between the Sea of Galilee and the Mediterranean.

According to the customs, the selection of a bride was negotiated by the male head of the household. After the formal espousal, or engagement, was finalized by a friend or legal representative, the bride became the recipient of many gifts. This constituted a portion of her dowry. In turn the father of the bride received a MOHAR, or payment, for the sale of his daughter. This contract was followed by the wedding ceremony. Usually the marriage took place at the home of the bride's parents and was celebrated by a feast to which friends, relatives, and neighbors were invited. As the wedding between male and female symbolized a spiritual union between God and man, the celebration usually lasted seven days to signify the seven phases of creation, or seven days of planetary progression. The pageantry was often enlivened with riddles and other amusements.

Since potable water was very difficult to find in the dry season, wine was pressed from the early grapes and served as the common drink. It was therefore not unusual for the host of the feast to be faced with the dual problem of an exhausted supply of drink and a number of intoxicated guests. Although Jesus taught continence and sobriety to his followers, he had both an understanding of, and a compassion for, the culture of his land. Thus, when during the wedding feast Mary came to inform her son that the wine supply had run out, Jesus sought to please her by changing the water into wine.

Following the wedding, the Master, along with his brothers, his mother, and his disciples, left for Capernaum. However, as they passed through Magdala, a small town on the west shore of Lake Gennesaret, Simon, a Pharisee and distant relative of the house of Joseph, invited Jesus and the others to dine at his home. While the meal was being prepared, there came a woman named Mary[6] from Magdala. She had known Jesus before when she had lived in Bethany with her sister Martha and brother Lazarus. Having heard of the Master's return to Galilee, she came bearing an alabaster box of ointment made up of olive oil, spices, myrrh, and nard. At first she stood behind Jesus, weeping, but when he paid heed to her she came and fell upon her knees and began anointing his feet. Immediately Simon took offense at this, saying to himself, "This man, if he were a prophet, would know what manner of a woman this is who now touches him; for she is a sinner."

The disciple's hostile thoughts soon drew Jesus' attention to him, and looking over at Simon with sternness Jesus spoke, saying, "Simon, I have something to say to you. There was once a certain man who had two debtors. One owed him much money while the other owed very little, but when neither was able to pay him the creditor forgave them both. Tell me, therefore, which of the two will love him more?"

Lowering his eyes in embarrassment because the Master had seen into his very thoughts, he finally replied, "I suppose that the one will love more who has been forgiven more. You have judged rightly so."

Those who gathered with Jesus in Simon's house did not know that this woman had once loved Jesus, nor were they aware of the unhappiness which possessed her during the long years of his absence. However, Jesus knew of those things in Mary's heart and he said to Simon, "See this woman? When I entered your house you gave me no water for my feet, but she has washed my feet with her tears. You gave me no kiss, but since I came in this woman has not ceased kissing my feet. Nor did you anoint my head, but she has anointed even my feet. Therefore, Simon, I would say to you, that her sins which are many are forgiven, for she has loved much. Not only has she loved man, but also the animals and birds and even the fish of the sea. To him of whom little is forgiven, he also has loved but little."

Looking down upon her with great compassion, he spoke gently, saying, "Your sins are forgiven."

As Jesus spoke these words, the disciples who sat with him began to ask among themselves, "Who is this that forgives sins?" and they were sorely troubled. Although he was aware of the doubts which now assailed these men, who had all too recently indicated that they would follow him forever, he paid little heed. He knew that they did not understand, and time and patience would cure the ignorance in their hearts. Nonetheless, he looked at them sharply, and feeling the penetration of his criticism they were silenced for a time. Then Jesus gave his attention to Mary and asked that she prepare to join them early the next morning, for he planned to turn her over to his mother who could teach her the ways of piety. Also, he had been somewhat concerned over the care of the woman who bore him because of his extensive traveling. The circumstances offered an opportunity to select a companion to tend her. He alone knew that Mary of Magdala would obediently bind herself to his wishes until her death.

On the following day, the party continued with their journey to Capernaum, now but a short distance away. Again, Jesus' disciples traveled with him, as did his mother, Mary Magdalene, Joanna, the wife of Chuza, Herod's steward, and Susanna. On arriving at their destination, arrangements were made for the women to stay at the house of Zebedee with Mary Salome, while Jesus went to seek out his cousins, John and James. He soon found them in the company of their father, mending nets along the banks of the harp-shaped sea. The surrounding hills were brown and bare except for the oleander which flourished around the shore, and tall papyrus plants could be found at the north end of the lake. Set deep among hills and consequently subject to sudden squalls and violent storms, fishing was not without hazard. The best view of the lake could be obtained from the top of the hills on its western shore, and looking down upon its glistening and sparkling waters, one could almost perceive some hidden promise of things which were yet to come.

Although Jesus hailed his cousins as he approached, it soon became apparent that the three men did not recognize him. James and John were greatly puzzled as they watched the white-robed figure coming nearer, and had they not been kept informed through family ties of Jesus' return to Judea, they would have thought him a stranger. However, when he came abreast of them, they recognized the youthful countenance of one with whom they had long ago played the games of childhood. They acknowledged him joyfully, and laying aside their nets, they sat down with Jesus and listened to the stories of his journeys.

The Master remained at Capernaum with James and John for several days, discussing his travels and his mission. His cousins never tired of hearing him discourse. As he had so many times during the long years of exile from his native country, he told them about earth's role in the systematic process of a progressing universe, how man's body was built from the forces of nature and his soul was woven in the tapestry of creation. He also began to teach them concerning the necessity of unity with God through the resurrection of the divine nature within. To this end, Jesus said, all humankind had journeyed through time and space, and only when they had reached this supreme goal would they achieve the peace that passed all understanding. He discussed his mission, which was to outwardly answer the request of the people for a Messiah. He explained that those who walked in darkness did not know that the fulfillment of prophecy would come through an inner awakening of the Law, but expected a human man. After this, he said that he had been sent by God to fulfill this purpose.

As Jesus explained the purpose of his mission and the mysteries of God, there remained little doubt in the minds of his cousins that their futures were linked to the man who now discoursed with them. Thus, when the Master prepared to depart, James and John also bid their family members farewell, accepting the cloak of asceticism in preparation of their entry into discipleship. During the next few months, five more men were accepted into initiation by the Master from Galilee. Among these were Matthew (known as Levi) and James, both sons of Alpheus, brother to Jesus' father Joseph. Then came Thomas Didymus who had been born in Antioch, Simon the Zealot, a member of a section of fierce advocates of Mosaic ritual, and Thaddaeus, a Hebrew youth born in Edessa and a disciple of John the Baptist.

As the winter rains began to abate and the Feast of the Passover neared, Jesus prepared to go to Jerusalem with his disciples, his mother, his kinswoman (mother of John and James), Mary Magdalene, and his brothers. Upon arrival in the Holy City, the women took leave of the men in order to visit with Elisabeth, while the men went to the temple where the Master would discourse in the manner of the learned doctors of his youth. Upon entering the temple, however, Jesus found merchants selling oxen, sheep, and doves for the evening sacrifice. His soul greatly disturbed, he fashioned a whip of cord and proceeded to drive both animals and men from the temple. He threw out the money changers and upset their trays, because their presence defiled the temple of worship and learning. Then Jesus spoke to those who sold doves, saying, "It is written, 'My house shall be called the house of prayer,' but you people have made it a den of thieves."

When the Jews questioned the Master's authority and threatened him by asking for a sign, Jesus answered, "Tear down this temple and in three days I will raise it up."

Then the Jews laughed and scoffed, saying to him, "It took 46 years to build this temple and you say you would raise it again in three days?"

Those who expected Jesus to continue in rebuttal were greatly disappointed, for he just looked at the people with some disdain and continued to make his way into the temple. Even some of his disciples were disappointed that he did not say more, but they managed to keep peace also and followed him. By now they had learned that his tongue could be sharp in chastisement and that there was a reason for his actions. It was well that they sought no explanation in spite of the conflict in their minds, for Jesus was not speaking of the physical temple which loomed before them. He spoke instead of another temple which would stand for all time, not one built of stone which could be destroyed by the hands of man.

Many who came to the temple during Passover heard the strange Master speak and believed in him so much they were desirous to follow him. Among these was Nicodemus ben Gorion, a Pharisee and member of the Sanhedrin, who was reputed to be one of the three richest men in Jerusalem. He said to Jesus, "Master, I have little doubt that you are a teacher who has been sent by God, for otherwise no man could perform the miracles that you do."

No one could approach Jesus without his deep penetrating eyes piercing the core of their soul, for his ability to discern spirit enabled him to clearly view the progression of every human. Neither could anyone lie, because even this was written in the actions of the past and in the destiny of the future. Now, observing the man who stood in front of him, Jesus' eyes took on a veiled look and he said, "No man can see the Kingdom of God who has not been born again."

The Pharisee, puzzled at how such a miracle should be wrought, inquired, "But how can a man be born when he is old? Can he enter a second time into his mother's womb?"

Jesus shook his head and commenced teaching concerning the mysteries pertaining to rebirth. "It is necessary that all people be born of water and come forth from the womb of woman, but there is another birth which comes forth from the womb of the spirit and rests in the hidden nature of mankind. This divine spark must be raised from its slavery to matter, or the soul cannot enter the kingdom of God. That which is born of flesh is flesh and walks in the dark shadows of ignorance, and that which is born of the spirit is spirit and walks in light more blinding than that of the sun. Do not marvel that I have said to you that you must be born again, for the wind blows where it lists and all hear the sound, but none can tell from where it originates or where it goes. So it is with human life, for all can see that which is evident, but few are there who can determine from whence the seed of man has come and where he is going."

Nicodemus, still greatly puzzled, asked him, "How can these things be?"

Jesus paused and looked at the Pharisee with great curiosity. "Have you become an elder of Israel without learning of this? Many speak the scriptures of men without either forethought or comprehension. We who know speak to reveal what we have seen, but many cannot understand because they live among the unawakened. If I have spoken to you concerning the laws of nature which are of the sun, the water, and the air and still you have not believed those things which are visible, how can you hope to understand that which dwells among the stars and is invisible? He who has opened the inner door of consciousness and ascended to the temple of the in-dwelling God, has also descended from heaven. Because the Son of man who has been born of the womb of woman has always resided there, he remains blind and unknowing in these matters.

"As Moses raised the divine nature within himself (raising the serpent in the wilderness) from the wilderness of human life, so must the Son of man, who is born of woman, be raised from his tomb of flesh that he may become the Son of God. Whosoever believes that the spark of God dwells within, nurtures it, and allows it to rule, shall not perish, but live forever in a kingdom not built by hands.

"God so loved all life, that he brought forth the light of consciousness in order that there be life. He established a Kingdom of Heaven within the world of matter, not to condemn, but so that the world might be saved. This divine spark of consciousness, which dwells in the temple of the soul, is the Son of God. He that serves and believes in him shall be raised from the prison of matter, for all power has been given to the Light. Those who cannot understand and do not believe in what I am speaking, condemn themselves even now. These are fated to walk in the way of unknowing until the veil which separates the mortal from the immortal has been torn away."

As Jesus spoke, his eyes gazed over the heads of those who sat around him as though he saw a new world not yet visible to man. Then he continued, saying, "And this is the judgment, that the Light which is the first manifestation of God has seen all things, knows all things, and is the guardian of each human. Yet people have loved darkness more than light, because they take delight in those things which destroy the body and the soul and bind the spirit.

"Anyone who misuses any law of God and nature, through what he eats, what he thinks, what he says, and what he does, despises the Light. These must suffer the infirmities of life, through illness, sorrow, pain, and death, because they choose the path of darkness and self will. But he who is good in all his ways comes before the Light and serves it, laying aside self will. His works shall be made known because his labors are done through God."

When Jesus had finished speaking in the temple, he and his disciples went into the land of Judea near Jerusalem to speak among the people. While he was there, many came to be baptized. After this he traveled to Engedi, the city of palms located on the edge of the wilderness of Judea, for he was in need of rest.

During this same period, John the Baptist was baptizing at the spring of Aenon near Shalem, where there was plentiful water. However, a dispute occurred between one of his disciples and a Jew concerning the matter of purification, and they brought their disagreement to John. "Teacher, he who was with you at the Jordan crossing also baptizes, but all men come to him."

Seeing that the people were questioning who was the greater, he or Jesus, John replied, "There is a spiritual law of progression, governed by a perfect law of cause and effect which results from the movement of cosmic order. You know I have said that I am not the Christ, but that I have been sent before him that his work be made easier and the kingdom of man become the kingdom of God. He who descends to dwell with the soul (bride) is that which is eternal. Thus a friend of the bridegroom who stands and listens to him cannot help but rejoice greatly when he hears the bridegroom's voice. Therefore, my joy is fulfilled, because he of whom you speak is the greater, so He must increase and I must decrease.

"When one comes who has united with God, he stands above all others. He that remains bound to the human senses is of the earth and speaks only of the matters of earth. He is less, but those who have pierced the doorway which rests between the two worlds have seen and heard and are taught from above. These speak the truth of the mysteries which pertain to both nature and God, for no man can receive these secrets who is not of heaven. Therefore, those who have achieved heaven are sealed by God who dwells with them. And those whom God has so anointed speak the words of God.

"The Father loves all who have risen and are united with his Son, into whose hand all power has been given. He who raises the Son of God and unites the soul shall have everlasting life. But those who do not believe shall not see the Light and the adversities of life (wrath of God) shall abide with them."

By this time, rumors of John's following had reached the ears of Herod Antipas, younger brother of Archelaus and son of Herod the Great. Herod, who was regarded as a sly, ambitious man and a lover of luxury, had begun to fear the popularity of John and the possibility that he might raise an army to overthrow the government.

However, because the Tetrarch's rulership had once been prophesied by the Essene prophet, Manahem (*Antiquities of the Jews and Jewish War*, Josephus), he had remained lenient toward those whom he felt might be affiliated, as a token of good will. Now the reports which reached him aroused great alarm. He was, therefore, moved to send his soldiers to arrest John and imprison him at Machaerus, a fortress located at Petraea within one of the valleys east of the Dead Sea. Although Herod undertook to do John no harm, at the same time he preferred to restrain him in a place where he could pose no threat to the government.

Cognizant of John's wisdom, Herod sometimes summoned his prisoner in order that the Baptist might counsel him on certain delicate matters. On one such occasion, this included the subject of his passion for his brother's wife, Herodias. John was quick to point out, however, that her marriage to Antipas while his wife lived, would be contrary to Jewish law and offensive to the people. He also explained that the situation would be aggravated even more by the fact that Herodias was a Jewess of royal lineage. As John extended his counsel against the marriage for the purpose of the ruler's protection rather than to condemn him, it created no undue friction between the two men.

Unfortunately, Herod's passion overruled common sense and before long he had accepted both Herodias and her daughter, Salome, into his stately palace. As Herodias was a selfish woman, although beautiful in a haughty way, she soon created numerous problems for her new husband. Thus it was not long thereafter that the Jewess, who had an eye for the more comely males, observed the attractive countenance of John the Baptist, which offered a pleasant contrast to the somewhat opulent and flabby figure of Herod. At times when the ruler was elsewhere occupied, Herodias sought to seduce John into laying aside his vows of asceticism and becoming her lover. Upon his refusal, she became hostile and, with the cunning of a woman scorned, awaited the opportunity to avenge herself.

John, recognizing that his death was near, felt a need to send a message to Jesus. He wanted to obtain a final assurance that the primary purpose for his life had been fulfilled in order that he might die in peace. Calling upon two of his disciples, he sent them to Jesus bearing the following message: "Are you he that is to come, or must we look for another?"

When the two men arrived in Capernaum they sought Jesus out to inquire concerning the information which John had requested, and Jesus said, "Go on your way. Tell John that these are the things you have seen and heard: those who were in darkness now see; those who were bound by mortal fetters now walk; those who were diseased of body, soul, and spirit are cleansed; those who were deaf now hear; and those who were dead have now been raised. To the poor, who cannot perceive all mysteries, the gospel has been preached, and blessed are those who are not offended by me."

On having sent an answer to John, Jesus turned and spoke to the people concerning him. "Whom did you seek in the wilderness, a man who could be shaken by deceit and ill gains, and dressed in soft raiment? Behold, such men who wear beautiful apparel and live delicately are found in the courts of kings. You say you went to see a prophet, but you saw much more than a prophet, for John was he of whom it was written, 'Behold, I send my messenger before your face, which shall prepare the way before you.' Among those who were born of woman, there is no greater prophet than John the Baptist. Yet he that is unawakened to the kingdom of God can become greater than John, for the capabilities of the spirit are without end. And if you will receive it, this was Elias who was to come."

In the meantime, the household of Herod had made plans to celebrate Herod's birthday. A great feast had been arranged, and many nobles of the land were invited. On the day of the festival, Herodias' daughter, Salome, who was also the wife of Herod's son, was called upon to dance for the congregation. So excellent and sensual was her dance, and so pleasing to the people that Herod offered her any gift if she would but name it. Seeing her opportunity, Herodias seized upon this moment to carry out her revenge upon John the Baptist and whispering in her daughter's ear, asked that the head of John be brought to her on a silver platter.

When Herod heard Salome's request, he felt inclined not to grant it, for John had done no harm to him. However, his promise had been made before the gathered noblemen of the country, and he was afraid of being ridiculed should he refuse. Therefore, Herod kept his promise and ordered the one man who had been honest with him to be put to death. He commanded a swordsman to go to John's rock-hewn dungeon and return with the prisoner's head.

Later John's disciples came for his body and buried it, and then went to inform Jesus. When the Master heard of his cousin's death, he knew that the time had come for the followers of John to be reconciled to him. He had now completed his quiet period of teaching among the people and was prepared to seek the more open arena of the multitude. Therefore, he went now into all of Galilee teaching in the synagogues, not as a priest, but as one of extraordinary wisdom. His fame spread quickly throughout the land.

1. Ledak, *Pali Cannon* (Notovich translation 1890).
2. It is not commonly known in modern times, even among the Buddhists, but the original Wheel of Life designed by Guatama Buddha contained 16 noble paths of peace; eight laws which per-

tained to the development of the soul, and eight others which pertained to the purification of the lesser nature. By proper practice of the 16 noble paths of peace, man escaped the wheel of Samsara (sorrow and rebirth) and reached permanent Nirvana (one with God).

3. The individual aspect of God which exists within each person.

4. Several translations of this letter exist within the library labyrinths at Dubonnet.

5. The dove, a current Christian emblem signifying the Holy Spirit, has been a highly revered symbol for many centuries. In many of the ancient mysteries it represented the third person of the Creative Triad, God (the Father), God the Son (the individualized aspect of God within each person, or the Christ Consciousness), and God the Holy Ghost (the movement of the divine nature within man). Because of its gentleness and devotion to its young, the dove was looked upon as the embodiment of maternal instinct, an emblem of wisdom representing the power and order by which the lower worlds are maintained and as a messenger of divine will.

6. Although theology has not acknowledged Mary Magdalene as the same Mary who resided in the home of Martha and Lazarus, the evidence of this relationship is now growing. It was Mary Magdalene who became one of the female disciples to Jesus, and it was also she who stood at the foot of the cross during the crucifixion. However, the most important evidence of this relationship is found in writings pertaining to the period immediately following the crucifixion, for it was Martha, Lazarus, and Mary Magdalene who set sail for England with the exiled Joseph of Arimathea.

PART II

SECRET TEACHINGS OF THE ELECT

Upon stepping into the open arena of public teaching, Jesus continued to come into open conflict with established Judaic conventions. As he had not been trained in accordance with the dominant culture of the land, many of the traditional scholars of Mosaic Law criticized him severely. In addition, as he walked the lands of Israel, he was challenged by each of the numerous sects which claimed to possess the only true way to God. From those who believed in the structured concepts handed down from generation to generation, Jesus' teachings evoked both jealousy and hatred. Nonetheless, it was obvious to all who actually tried to pit their knowledge against him that he was the greater.

It was from the common people, who sought a greater understanding than that offered by priestly dogma, that Jesus obtained his most sympathetic following; although there were among these a few of the more enlightened members of the Sanhedrin, such as Gamaliel, Nicodemus, and Joseph. The latter adherents did not demonstrate their interest too openly, however, lest it engender great dissension within the ranks of the court. The division between those members elected to the court by vote and those appointed through political influence had already created a volatile situation which might be sparked into an explosive uprising at any time. Such an open break would have been injurious to the whole of Israel.

Jesus' teachings were not confined to those laws prescribed by Moses, but also included the healing of man. He was able to perceive the effect of every cause rising through misuse of natural and cosmic law. He well knew that it was man himself who created his own illness because of the inability to work in harmony with the law, and that each also created his own hell. Therefore, the Master did not work his miracles in all who approached him, for directing the in-dwelling power of God toward the sick and oppressed often produced only temporary healing. Many returned to their old ways of life, at which time even greater ills would befall them. Yet for others, the requirements of their soul progression necessitated that the strict rule of non-interference be observed in order to allow them to learn their unlearned lessons. In rare cases, Jesus found it appropriate to perform miracles, meanwhile teaching others about bodily cleanliness, proper food, and the healing forces of sun, water, and air.

In due time, the teachings of the Master came to supplant the practices of Moses, reflecting a way of natural life which remains valid to this day. It was Jesus' cousin, John the Beloved, who carefully recorded the Master's instructions on health, nutrition, and angelology.

The Vatican manuscript on Jesus is not one which is commonly known by theological scholars today, and therefore some might consider it fraudulent. However, this would be an unfair assumption, primarily because the manuscript contains the secret teachings of Jesus which were not to be exposed to the masses. Therefore, before a declaration of invalidation can be formally made, the scholar would have to go directly to the Vatican in Rome and translate the original source material himself. The material contained in Part II, *The Secret Teachings of the Elect*, introduces a great deal of the Vatican manuscript, as well as the hidden teachings behind the traditional Gospel of John. In that there have always been two teachings to the Bible (as previously mentioned), one consisting of that which is literal, or fundamental, and the other which is hidden and mystical, the author feels that the latter is in keeping more with the intelligence of modern man.

CHAPTER IV

LAMP IN THE WILDERNESS

And when he was demanded of the Pharisees, when the Kingdom of God should come, he answered them and said, The kingdom of God cometh not with observation: Neither shall they say, "Lo here!" nor, "Lo there!" for, behold, the Kingdom of God is within you.

St. Luke
17:20-21

ollowing the news of John's death, Jesus returned to the desert where he was faced with the problem of integrating the works of his cousin into his own. He did not spend a great deal of time in Nazareth after this, but chose to teach in Capernaum, his second home, on the northern shore of the Sea of Galilee. Most of the inhabitants of the little town lived on the natural riches of the lake. Huts and houses in large numbers were nestled quietly on the gentle slopes which surrounded the centurion's synagogue where Jesus taught. Serving as the highway between Damascus and the Mediterranean, the land boasted of rich trade and fine fishing, while its hot springs drew multitudes to be cured. It was here, amid the dark greenness of the eucalyptus trees which enhanced the curving shores of the small bay, that Jesus prepared his disciples to carry on his work after his departure.

When this brief period of solitude was over, the Master visited with his mother, after which he traveled throughout Syria teaching in the synagogues. He taught not as the priests taught, but as a learned Doctor of the Law. His voice was strong, his bearing kingly, and his words powerful in comparison to those spoken by traditional Jewry. Soon his fame began to spread throughout Syria, moving from the northern frontier of Palestine westward. Great multitudes followed him, coming from Galilee, Decapolis, and even Jerusalem. To the masses Jesus taught redemption, that man's focus become centered in God, above all else. His mastery of natural and cosmic law appeared miraculous to some, yet others learned a new way of life which allowed them to overcome illness, retard the aging process, and delay death. To his disciples he disclosed the secret teachings which unlocked the unseen worlds of the soul. Among these were the mysteries of regeneration pertaining to the body, soul, and spirit, which occurred as the soul traversed the path of mastership over its lesser nature.

One morning, just as the sunrise kissed the waters of the sea with its pinks and golds, and parts of the land still lay in the shadows cast by the passing night, Jesus gathered his disciples in a grove of trees just outside the temple. As he lifted his face to the rising sun, its radiance filled his eyes, and as he sat silhouetted there for a moment he looked like he had descended from heaven. Soon the mirage of this moment passed, and the Master began to speak concerning some of those things which he did not teach openly, saying, "The spiritual nature within man can only be established by living in harmony with natural and cosmic law, through one's thoughts, and words, and deeds. Those who speak of things which are pure but deny them by their very actions, destroy the soul, even as the locust lays waste to the land. Utilization of natural and cosmic law serves as a passageway between man and the angels and must be established by effort, just as the steps leading to the Temple of Jerusalem were fashioned from stone. The laws pertaining to earth are seven and the laws pertaining to God are seven, the same laws which were established even before our forefathers walked upon the land."

Then one of the disciples asked, "Tell us, Master, how may we utilize these forces of which you speak and dwell in the kingdom of heaven while we live upon earth? We are but men and have not been able to walk in the ways of the angels as you do."

For a moment before answering, Jesus studied those around him and then smiled gently with compassion, for he knew the way was difficult for his disciples. They were born of woman and not yet raised by God. He knew that their minds were in a constant turmoil and filled with mundane thoughts wrought from the pangs of human attachments, and it would be long before the battle between light and dark would end. It was for this very reason that he now chose to introduce them to the secrets which were known only to those who had pierced the innermost sanctum of the in-dwelling spirit. As they learned to commune with the mighty forces of heaven and earth, their minds would become as silent as the calm at high noon.

But finally he spoke again, saying, "As a child becomes heir to the properties of his ancestors, we also inherit a holy kingdom from God. It is not as land to be furrowed and plowed, but a place within which we must erect an altar which is worthy of the Most High. Even as an altar must be carefully wrought out of stone, so will I give you the tools for building a stairway to heaven.

"The utilization of natural and cosmic law is a link between the world you know and the world you have not yet seen. You must think of your body as the trunk of a tree which is nourished by earth and all that she contains, while your soul is like the branches of a tree and nourished by the unseen forces of the Heavenly Father. Sun, water, air, preservation, health, and joy unite man with earth, while love, power, wisdom, eternal life, creative work, and peace unite man with the kingdom of heaven. This is the key to the mystery of the Tree of Life which stands in the Sea of Eternity.

"It is through love that God and nature become one. For the spirit of human life was created from the Spirit of God and your bodies were born of the elements of earth. You must therefore seek to become flawless, as the spirit of your Heavenly Father is flawless, and seek to transform your body into a holy temple. Therefore, you must love God with your hearts and your souls, and you must rejoice in the perfection of earth and abide by her will. After this, love those who walk the path of awakening, for they are your true brothers and one with the Holy Law. Since the beginning, when Kain (evil) slew Habel (good),[1] brother has fought against brother, and there has been no peaceful coexistence on earth.

"When your Heavenly Father has brought his spirit to life in you, then the Sons of man shall love and comfort one another, and your body shall become a holy temple wherein dwells the Kingdom of God. After this has come to pass, evil will also pass away, and there shall be no more sorrow on earth. Then the Son of man will come forth in all his glory to inherit the great kingdom, wherein there is no more darkness. And with the descent of heaven, shall come the end of time."

After this Jesus fell silent again and those who gathered around him remained silent also, although they expected him to continue discoursing. However, he chose not to do so, for he intended to introduce the communions one by one in accordance to their specific days. As he and his disciples traveled, he would wake them in the early dawn and sit with them in the sunset. When there were no rains, they would journey with him as he had journeyed with his camel over the sands of India and Egypt. And a great work would be wrought in them, for that which fettered their souls would fall away as rotted rope, and as the mighty eagle they would rise to the stars.

Finally he raised himself up, these thoughts still in his mind, and announced that they would journey to the southernmost Roman division of Palestine. Within him was a sense of urgency, for it was now time to go among the masses and teach concerning the Kingdom of God. Traveling from Galilee, through the wilderness to Samaria, and then on to Jerico and Jerusalem, his truth flowed unfettered over the land of his forefathers. For as a still pond which has no fresh water flowing into it becomes a breeding ground for disease and death, so it was with the people. Therefore, he constantly traveled from place to place, a living water in the midst of desolation.

During their journey the party stopped at Sychar, which was located on the eastern slope of Ebal, almost two miles east by northeast of Nablus and about a half mile north of Jacob's Well. The sun was now in its sixth hour since rising and the heat had greatly increased since the early morning dawn. Thirsting for water, Jesus walked to the well and sat down to rest, momentarily laying his head against the well's rough contours to listen to the soundless pause of high noon. While he sought respite, he sent his disciples into town to buy food. And it came to pass that while he was resting in this manner, a woman from Samaria came to draw water, and Jesus having no vessel to provide a drink for himself, asked, "Would you give me a drink?"

Looking at him with some astonishment, the woman replied, "How is it that you, being a Jew, should ask a drink of me, a woman of Samaria?"

Now there were grave differences between those of the traditional Jewish faith and the Samaritans, who were a mixture of races belonging to the tribes of Jeroboam. Ancient Samaria was located upon a hill at an elevation of about 300 feet, within a wide basin formed by a valley running from Shechem to the coast. While it had been the scene of the ministries of the prophets Elijah and Elisha, its worship centered around the pagan god, Baal, and the golden calves of Jeroboam which represented the God who brought the ten tribes out of Egypt. The orthodox Jews were, therefore, in horror of the rites of Jeroboam, which rejected the authority of the Old Testament, except for the Pentateuch. Moreover, the Samaritans claimed to possess an older copy of the Pentateuch than the Jews. Consequently, the Jews responded to the Samaritans with summary contempt and even hate, rejecting their right to claim Jewish descent.

Since the Master taught the brotherhood of all men, he perceived no differences between creed or caste. His journeys in India, Babylonia, and Egypt had long since revealed the common nature in mankind, and he was prone to be somewhat amused when he heard the people squabble among themselves over whose interpretation of the law was greater. Thus, because the woman who stood before him was a Samaritan only through circumstance and name, he spoke kindly to her, saying, "If you knew the gift of God and who it is that asked you for a drink, you would ask for a drink (to partake of the endless source of wisdom) from him and he would give you living water (the mysteries of life)."

The Samaritan woman was greatly puzzled and looked at Jesus with questioning eyes. Seeing that he carried no implement with which to draw water, she said, "Sir, you have nothing to draw with and the well is deep. From what source would you possess the living water? Are you greater than our father Jacob who gave us this well, having drunk from it himself, also his children, and cattle?"

Shaking his head in answer to the woman's question, Jesus replied, "Those who drink of this water shall thirst again, for this nourishes only the body. However, those who drink from the fountain of truth and knowledge shall never thirst, for that is of the soul. I promise you that he who drinks of that which is eternal shall find a never-ending spring."

By this time, the Samaritan woman perceived that Jesus was unlike other men, and she began to hunger for the unknown waters that she might never thirst again. However, when she asked him for this knowledge, the Master only shook his head, saying, "First go call your husband and then come to me."

Since Jesus was of comely countenance the woman was loath to admit that her life was encumbered by another. Therefore, she suddenly became somewhat flirtatious and looking at him through somewhat closed eyelids she said, "I have no husband."

Peering deeply into the finely etched consciousness of the past which had been woven on the looms of soul evolution, Jesus saw that the woman spoke true. Yet, he also knew that she lived in dishonor, for he was endowed with an ever present inner sight that always exists in a person of God. No one could hide their past, present, or future from one who possessed the power of discernment, for every deed was written in the pattern of the body, mind, and spirit and would bear fruit in the world of tomorrow. As Jesus was bound to God, so was he therefore connected to every human, so he recognized her flirtation and was amused by it. Although a ray of merriment momentarily touched his eyes, it passed quickly, leaving a touch of its final shadow in his voice as he said, "It is true that you are not married now, for he who dwells with you is not your husband. But in the past you have had five husbands to whom you have been married."

The woman realized that Jesus could not have known these things unless he were of a holy order, and her eyes became downcast for she felt shame over her senseless ways. Then slowly raising her eyes again she looked at him and quietly said, "Sir, I perceive that you are a prophet. You know that our fathers worshipped in the mountains, but now you are saying that we should come worship in the ways of the Jews whose temple is in Jerusalem."

Sending a piercing glance in the Samaritan's direction, Jesus spoke again, saying, "Woman, believe me, there will come a time when you shall not worship in the ways of the Samaritans or the Jews. While you do not understand the ways of your own worship, the Jews believe that salvation is found only in Jewry. However, a time shall come, and now indeed is, when the true worshippers shall worship the Father in spirit and in truth. He is the power who presides over all flesh, and they that love Him become obedient in His ways."

The woman, having heard the legend of her people concerning the forthcoming Messiah, and wondering if the Master might be he, now spoke concerning the prophecy, "I know that it is prophesied that a Messiah is to come which is called the Christ, and when he has come, he will tell us all things."

For a moment Jesus paused, his eyes looking out over the land where Abraham had pitched his tent and built an altar under the oak of Moreh. In turn, the rich plain of Mukhna looked back at him, echoing the blessings from Mt. Gerizim and the curses from Mt. Ebal where Joshua delivered his last counsels to the people. Up to now, Jesus had made no announcements of his mission except to his disciples, but it seemed applicable that he do so in this moment, for it was near here that the ten tribes renounced the house of David and transferred their allegiance to Jeroboam. Speaking as though his mind was in another world, another time, he said the words which lay claim to that which was lost so long ago. Although he spoke softly, his words resonated through the land with the formidable power of his ancestors, while the sun overhead bore witness to his oath. Looking again at the woman, he said, "I am he."

At this time, the disciples returned from the village with food and, seeing Jesus at the well with the woman, wondered that their master should speak with one of impure reputation. However, now more knowledgeable in his ways, they did not question the matter, for it was not the right of a disciple to do so. The woman, when she saw the approach of Jesus' disciples, left her water pot and went on her way into the city, her bare feet making no sound as she hastened away.

After she had disappeared from sight the disciples came to Jesus and urged him to eat, but he chose not to do so, saying, "Though you say that there are yet four months before the harvest, you see with human eyes only fields planted by man. Better are you to lift your eyes above these earthly limitations (four elements), that you may see the souls which are now full grown. These are also ready for harvest. He who reaps the harvest of the soul gathers eternal life, having grown his yield within himself, both good and bad. Know

you that it is the Heavenly Father who is the planter and man who
is the reaper. Now you have been called to reap the fields where
other men have labored. One day it will come to pass that God, who
is the sower, and man, who is the reaper, shall rejoice in the
harvest together."

Meanwhile, the woman reached the city and told many that she
had seen the Messiah, and great numbers of the townspeople came
believing in Jesus. Those who were converted asked that he remain
to teach them concerning the mysteries of life. And for a time he
tarried among them, that he might help them live a better life. He
also healed their sick, knowing that they would not believe his
words without some physical evidence of divine power.

At the conclusion of these teachings, Jesus went on to Galilee, after which time he returned to his place of rest at Capernaum. There
he healed the son of a nobleman. Also he discoursed at great length
with his disciples concerning the hidden teachings of the ancients,
as he had learned them.

One day, noticing that his disciples seemed troubled, Jesus asked
them the cause, to which one replied, "Master, please talk to us concerning the path of righteousness, for we do not wish to walk the
way of destruction."

Looking at them gravely, Jesus said, "Those things existing outside of you cause you to suffer, but that which lives within you
brings only peace and harmony. A child dies, a fortune is lost,
house and fields burn, and all men are helpless and cry out, 'What
shall I do now? What fate shall befall me? What will now come to
pass?' These are the words of those who grieve and rejoice over such
events as do befall them, events which are not of their doing. But if
we mourn over that which is not in our power, we are as the little
child who weeps when the sun leaves the sky.

"It was said of old: You shall not covet that which belongs to your
neighbor; and now I say to you that you shall not desire anything
which is not in your power, for only that which is within you belongs to you, and that which is without belongs to another. In this
does happiness lie: to know what is yours and what is not. If you
would have eternal life, hold fast to the eternity within you and
grasp not at the shadows of the world of men, which hold the seed of
death.

"Is not all that happens without you outside of your power? It is.
And your knowledge of good and evil, is it not within you? It is. Is it
not, then, within your power to treat all which comes to you in the
light of wisdom and love, instead of sadness and despair? It is. Can
any man hinder you from doing this? No man can. Why then
should you cry out, 'What shall I do? What shall now befall me?
Will this thing come to pass?' For whatsoever may come to pass,

you shall judge it in the light of wisdom and love and see all things with the eyes of angels. For to weigh your happiness according to that which may befall you is to live as a slave, but to live according to the angels which speak within you is to be free.

"You shall live in freedom as a true Son of God, and bow your head only to the commandments of the Holy Law. Know you that no man can serve two masters. You cannot wish to have the world's riches and have also the Kingdom of Heaven. You cannot wish to own lands and wield power over men and have also the Kingdom of Heaven. Wealth, lands, and power, these things belong to no man, for they are of the world. But the Kingdom of Heaven is yours forever, for it is within you. And if you desire and seek after that which does not belong to you, then shall you surely lose that which is yours.

"Know you, for I tell you truly, that nothing is given nor is it had for nothing. For everything in the world of men and angels, there is a price. He who would gather wealth and riches must run about, kiss the hands of those he admires not, waste himself with fatigue at other men's doors, say and do many false things, give gifts of gold and silver and sweet oils. All this and more must a man do to gather wealth and favor. And when you have achieved wealth and favor, what then do you have? Will this wealth and power secure for you freedom from fear, a mind at peace, a day spent in the company of the angels of the Earthly Mother, or a night spent in communion with the angels of the Heavenly Father? Do you expect to have, for nothing, things so great?

"When a man has two masters, either he will hate the one and love the other, or else he will hold to the one and despise the other. You cannot serve God and also serve the world. Perchance your well goes dry, precious oil is spilled, your house burns, your crops wither; but treat what may befall you with wisdom and love. Rains again shall fill the well, houses can again be built, new seeds can be sown. All these things shall pass away, and come again, and yet again pass away. But the Kingdom of Heaven is eternal, and shall not pass away.

"You must not barter that which is eternal and shall not pass away. Do you not then barter that which is eternal for that which dies in an hour. When men shall ask of you, "To what country do you belong?" say not that you are of this country or that, for of truth it is only the poor body which is born in one small corner of this earth.

"But you, O child of Light, belong to the Brotherhood which encompasses all the heavens and beyond, and from your Heavenly Father have descended the seeds not only of your father and grandfather, but of all beings which are generated on earth. In truth you are a Son of God, and all men are your brothers. And to have God for your maker and your father and guardian, shall not this release us from all sorrow and fear? Therefore, I say to you, take no thought to store up worldly goods, possessions, gold, and silver, for these things bring only corruption and death. For the greater your hoard of wealth, the thicker shall be the walls of your tomb.

"Open wide the windows of your soul, and breathe the fresh air of a free man! Why take you thought for raiment? Consider the lilies of the field, how they grow. They toil not, neither do they spin. And yet I say to you, that even Solomon in his glory was not arrayed like one of these.

"Why take you thought for house and lands? A man cannot sell to you that which he does not own, and he cannot own that which already belongs to all. This wide earth is yours, and all men are your brothers. There is no need for the son of a king to covet a bauble in the gutter. Take your place then at the table of the celebration, and fulfill your inheritance with honor. For in God we live and move and have our being. In truth we are his sons, and he is our Father.

"He only is free who lives as he desires to live, who is not hindered in his acts, and whose desires attain their ends. He who is not restrained is free, but he who can be restrained or hindered, that man is surely a slave.

"A merchant went to seek goodly pearls. When he found one pearl of great price, he went and sold all that he had and bought it. And if this one precious pearl be yours forever, why do you barter it for pebbles and stones? The Kingdom of Heaven is like that one precious pearl. Know you, that your house, your lands, your sons and daughters, all the joys of fortune and sorrows of tribulation, yea, even that opinion which others hold of you, all these things belong not to you. And if you lust after these things and hold fast to them and grieve and exult over them, then in truth you are a slave, and in slavery will you remain.

"My children, let not the things which are not yours cleave to you! Let not the world grow unto you, as the creeping vine grows fast to the oak, so that you suffer pain when it is torn from you. Naked you came from your mother's womb, and naked you shall return thither. The world gives and the world takes away. But no power in heaven, or earth, can take from you the Holy Law which resides within you.

"You may see your parents slain, and you may be driven from your country, but go you with a cheerful heart to live in another, and look with pity upon the slayer of your parents, knowing that by the very deed does he slay himself. For your true parents are your Heavenly Father and your Earthly Mother, and your true country is the Kingdom of Heaven. Death can never separate you from your true parents, and from your true country there is no exile. And within you, the rock which stands against all storms is the Holy Law which is your bulwark and your salvation" (Gospel of Peace, Section II, ch. XII).

For a few moments the disciples sat quietly. His words gave them much to think about, for each had attachments to the human world—families, homes, fear of death, and desires. Although they knew he spoke truth, their way of life created a deep inner feeling of inadequacy, and the path he spoke of seemed long and narrow. Yet in the heart of each lived a desire which went beyond all other desires, and that was to succeed in the world which seemed so far-away. Although the light of their master was greater and ground against the impurities of their souls, leaving them as trembling children, each knew that Jesus bore with them. Because of this, they believed and they dreamed. Finally one of them asked, "Tell us how our end will be."

As usual, when someone asked a question of which he knew a delightful answer, a touch of amusement cast a shadow upon his face, and he spoke, asking, "Have you discovered the beginning that you now look for the end? For where the beginning is, the end will be also. Blessed is he who takes his stand in the beginning. He will know the end, but shall not experience death" (Gospel According to Thomas, Log 18:10-16).

Pausing for a moment, the Master glanced at the far distant sun, for it was written in the movement of heavenly order that suns should produce planets and that planets should bring forth life. Therefore, the existence of each fragment of life was preordained and nothing could exist unless it was contained within the pattern of a greater plan. Looking down upon his seated disciples again, Jesus said, "Do you not know that earth is a reflection of the Kingdom of Heaven? Just as a child is born of the womb of woman, but grows into an adult, so too is your life on earth but the infancy of your destiny. Your toil upon the land prepares you for a greater kingdom which is yet to come, and one day you will return to your true home and become true Sons of God. Only through harmony with natural and cosmic law will we learn to see the unseen, to hear that which cannot be heard and to speak the unspoken word."

Then Jesus said to them, "Blessed is he who came into being before he came into being. If you listen to my words, these stones will also minister to you, for they are the beginning of life. These serve to mold the surface of earth and supply soil with minerals from whence our bones are born. Yet even these shall pass away. There are five trees for you in Paradise which remain undisturbed during summer and winter and whose leaves do not fall. Whosoever becomes acquainted with them will never again see death. With these words I speak to you in parable, for the five trees are the four elements which bind your immortal soul to the cycles of necessity. The Tree of Life does not shed, for it is eternal.

One day, when Jesus was with his disciples in Jerusalem, Mary Magdalene and his Aunt Mary came to be with him and his disciples. Although his aunt was knowledgeable in the story of his birth, and her own two sons were disciples, it was was still very difficult for her to acknowledge the divinity in her nephew. Raised in the more traditional Jewish customs of the family and espoused as it suited her parents, Mary questioned the possibility that one among their family could be the prophesied Messiah. In that Jesus had just made some reference to his destiny, she questioned him concerning this, saying, "Who are you, and whose son are you, if you are not of the seed of my sister, for you have taken your place upon my bench and eaten at my table many times as my nephew?"

Looking upon her with great compassion, for he well understood the strong tethers of tradition, Jesus replied, "Mary, I am a person who is one with God, and while I dwell in this world, I am not of it. That place where I dwell is a world unseen and unknown by those who have not rent its veil. You see, there are two natures which dwell together within all humans, and a time will come when one must die and the other live. When this thing has come to pass, then each person becomes one with God and is filled with light. We were created in this manner, but those who remain divided also remain filled with darkness."

While he was discussing these things, a Samaritan on his way to Judea passed by carrying a lamb. And with great amusement Jesus asked his disciples, "Why does that man carry the lamb?"

By this time the disciples were familiar with the Master's usage of parable and knew he had laid a trap. So for a few moments they were silenced, as they sought the meaning to his simple question. Finding none, one of them finally spoke up, saying, "In order that he may kill it and eat it."

This delighted Jesus, because he knew that he had caught them again in one of his subtle allegories. As usual his eyes took on the half penetrating and half roguish look which was so common to him at times like this, and further baiting the net, he said to them, "While it is alive, he will not eat it, but only when he has killed it and it has become a corpse."

Upon hearing this the disciples shook their heads, for they knew the expression on Jesus' face very well. Yet, none of them could see why the lamb was important, so John replied, "Master, he cannot really do otherwise."

This further increased the Master's pleasure and he prepared to draw tight the net, for the bait had been taken. "You must beware and seek the Kingdom of Heaven. If you do not, you shall be like the lamb which is being taken to his slaughter. You will die in the bonds of únknowing and your darkness shall consume your soul, even as the worms consume your body."

When he had finished speaking, another disciple asked him, "Describe the Kingdom of Heaven to us."

Looking up toward the unnumbered stars, the Master said to them, "It is like a mustard seed, the smallest of all seeds, and it dwells within man. But when the soul is prepared to receive the Kingdom of God through devotion, study, and meditation, it becomes like a great plant which becomes a shelter for other living things, even as I now give shelter to the world."

During this time, Mary Magdalene had sat quietly, listening to everything Jesus said. She was treated as an equal to the male disciples by Jesus, for she was both strong and dedicated to his ways, and, in her, his teachings had fallen on fertile soil. Yet he also liked to tease her, for sometimes she was too serious, as well as headstrong. Until now she had given much attention to the discourse, and her lips had remained silent. However, this was quite unusual, for she was generally full of wonderment and always asking about those things which perplexed her. Finally, unable to remain silent any longer, she asked, "Whom are your disciples like?"

Looking at her kindly, Jesus replied, "They are like children who have settled in a field which is not theirs (mortal world). When the in-dwelling God and owner of the soul comes, he will say 'Let us have back our field.' Then both of you shall labor to remove the impurities of the soul that it might take its rightful position in the Kingdom of Heaven. Therefore, I say to you, if the soul knows that the thief (worldly inheritance) is coming, it will begin its vigil and not allow him to plunder his house and carry away his goods. Therefore, you must be on your guard against the world. Arm yourself with great strength lest the robbers find a way to get through to you, for the difficulty which you expect will surely materialize. Let there be among you a man of understanding, when the good has been developed and the grain is ripened, go quickly with your sickle to reap it."

Simon Peter was also among those who sat in the group, and being one of the earliest disciples, occasionally felt that he was due more consideration than those who came later, and now he spoke out against Mary Magdalene, saying, "Master, why don't you let Mary leave us, because women are not worthy of the mysteries."

However, Jesus, knowing that God was neither male nor female and that he dwelled in both forms, turned his piercing eyes toward Simon and sent a slight look of warning. In rebuke, the Master could be as sharp as a blade of steel and his words abrupt. Now he rebuked his disciple, saying, "Then I myself shall lead her in order to make her male, so that she too may become a living spirit resembling you males. For it shall come to pass that when you make the two one, and when you make the inner as the outer and outer as the inner and the above as the below, and when you make the male and the female into a single one, so that the male will not be male and the female not be female, then you shall enter the kingdom of heaven" (The Gospel According to Thomas Log 22:24-30,34).

For a time the disciples remained silent. The concept that the souls of men and women were not only equal, but of nature neither male nor female, was unheard of. Women had always been considered less important in society and were expected to bear children and serve their husbands. They had never been admitted to the inner circles of the elders and priests, even in the time of Moses. Now Jesus not only allowed them to be present when he taught the mysteries of the universe, but he also spoke of impartiality. Such bold statements were difficult to accept, especially for Simon, but they knew that they must remain silent, for obedience was expected of them.

Upon seeing that Peter had been properly admonished, the Master turned and departed from their midst into the solitude of a world they could not yet know.

Sometime after this event had taken place, Jesus went to Jerusalem for one of the Jewish feasts. He arrived on the Sabbath which, according to Moses, was the weekly holy day signifying the seventh day of creation, or the day when God would gather himself together from all parts of the world and restore the earth. As the Sabbath was considered the holy day, the Jews forbade work and turned their attention toward the worship of their Creator as their Lawgiver had prescribed. It was, therefore, a day of rejoicing, prayer, and feasts to symbolize the great wisdom (manna) which is fed to man directly from God during the final phase of human transformation. The holy day began at sundown on Friday and was not only a day of rest but also a day to honor the eternal covenant made between God and his people. While sunset heralded the beginning of the holy day and signified the death of the old, sunrise the following morning signified new birth in which heaven and earth had become one.

The Jewish homes indicated the holy celebration by blowing on a ram's horn, a practice associated with the constellation Aries and often identified with the Lamb of God, or the Messiah, who would restore Israel. When the horn had been blown (the Lamb of God calling forth his people), the woman of the household lit a candle to signify illumination (the birth of God in man). The patriarch of the family then said a special blessing over the bread and wine, a custom denoting the soul's return to the one loaf (God) and its surrender of the personal life (wine represented sacrificial blood).[2]

Though the Sabbath contained much repetitious ritual, the rites had been ordained by Moses for the sake of the people. He realized that complete freedom would cause man to forget his Creator, and were this to occur, the pathway between the two worlds would close. This would have left only darkness, unknowing, jealousy, anger, hatred, war and death, and a far more degenerate world than that which came as a natural process of progression.

Having long observed the laws of nature and watched the winds blow, the plants grow, and children being born without cessation of creation, even on the Sabbath, Jesus rose beyond ritualistic practices. It was not uncommon to see him plucking ears of corn from the fields, healing the sick, discoursing, and administering to the needy, even on the holy day. For this reason he brought the ire of the Jews down upon his head and they sought to persecute him. Shaking his head when he heard that many were raising their voices against him, he said, "My Father works without end, and so, too, do I work without ceasing."

This did not stop the persecution, however, for many continued to relegate him to the level of an agitator. They did not understand his words and believed that, in claiming God as his Father, he was placing himself in a position of heavenly authority. Although he knew that the people walked in ignorance and that the world would not know his world for thousands of years, he gave no defense. When they insulted him he said, "Do you not know that he who is Son to God can do nothing of himself? Therefore, I can only do that which I see the Father do, as evident through natural and cosmic law. God's laws are just and beneficent and, when used wisely, allow man even greater words than these which you now marvel over. The Father raises up those who are bound by mortal ways, even as the Son also quickens those whom he wishes."

After this Jesus spoke concerning the dead, or those who were unknowing in the ways of heaven. These bound themselves to the darkness of human limitation without awareness of the wrongs they committed. Held fast by the chains of life and death, they faced constant illness and pain through misuse of natural and cosmic law and shed their blood on the battlefields of the world because of their hunger for power. Many also lived in lassitude and boredom because their greatness lay dormant in the deep recesses of the soul. Referred to as those bound to tombs (bodies) and lying in their graves (soul submerged in matter), these were the unawakened and unillumined, who dwelled in a temporal, ever changing world of matter without understanding their true purpose or reason for existence.

Finally Jesus said, "God judges no man, for he is a loving God and has so arranged the world that man's deviation from the good shall bring upon his head abhorrent sorrow. All men, therefore, should honor the inner spirit even as they honor God, for if you would know it, this is the Son in whom the Father has left all judgment. He who hears my words and believes that I have been sent shall learn the mysteries of the resurrection and remain no longer bound to the chains of darkness. The time is coming when those who are slaves to worldly ways will hear the inner voice of the Son, and they that do shall inherit the keys which unlock the gateway to heaven.

"Even as the Father contains all life within him, so has he given that which is divine in man the authority to execute all judgment. Do not marvel at this, for the future shall call forth all humans from their enslavement to matter, and all nations must heed the call. Even as good inherits good, so does evil inherit the pain and suffering of darkness and unknowing.

"I can do nothing of myself. As I hear, I judge; but unlike man, my judgment is more just, for it is that power within me which judges. If I try to bear witness of myself, my witness will not be true, for the eyes of the Son of man cannot see through a veil of darkness. However, there is the Other who dwells within me and sees all that I do and is a greater witness than John. The work which has been given to me to finish is the same work I do, and because it is for the good of humankind it bears witness that I have been sent by God. You who judge me have neither heard his voice nor seen his shape, but by your actions you are known. The deeds of evil are performed by those who do not know his spirit, or his word, which abides in them."

When he had finished teaching in Jerusalem, Jesus once more turned his attention toward the coastal cities located along the shores of Galilee. The first was Tiberias, which had been built by Herod Antipas and named by him in honor of the Emperor Tiberius, A.D. 14-37. It was one of the nine cities around the sea, each one having not less than 15,000 inhabitants. However, because Tiberias was situated on the edge of the ancient walled town Rakkath, or Hammath, whose cemetery lay beneath it, it was avoided by strict Jews. While this was of no concern to the Master, he still did not teach there because it was primarily occupied by Greeks and Romans. On the other hand, he did draw vast multitudes from nearby cities, such as Magdala, Chorazin, Bethsaida, and Capernaum.

The memories of Jesus' days and nights in the Midbar Pasture and the desert surrounding the Kuhha ye Zagros had been placed in the background now. Yet the harsh desert winds, the starlit nights, and the hot timeless wanderings which made him so much of what he was, were expressed through the discipline and wisdom which he administered to his disciples. Although he would have preferred to be understood by all men, he bore no direct malice. Yet neither did he avoid confrontation, for the truth he bore was greater than the pseudoknowledge of the masses. The power of his speech was like the mighty wind, strong, yet sensitive, impersonal, but personal, powerful, but gentle, and deeply penetrated the souls he touched.

Since most of the coastal cities were of similar size, the Master's coming always spread quickly by word-of-mouth and people gathered quickly, hoping to see a sign. Sometimes this distressed him, because illness was transmitted rapidly through the crowds due to the attendant neglect of natural law. Also, he would have preferred they live by his teachings, rather than reach out for the sense gratification of miracles. In spite of this, however, he tended to the needs of those who came to him in the form of teaching and healing, and his fame continued to grow.

Once, however, when he spoke out concerning the need to live in harmony with the forces of nature, Jesus saw that those who gathered around came only to bear witness to his miracles. This angered him and he spoke sharply to the people, saying, "You hypocrites, well did Elias prophesy of you, 'The people draw near me with their mouths and honor me with their lips, but their hearts are far from me.'"

Then Jesus called out to the multitude and said to them, "Hear and understand: That which goes into the mouth does not defile a man, rather that which comes out of the mouth defiles him."

After this the disciples came to him and said, "Do you not know that the Pharisees were offended at your words?"

Upon hearing this the Galilean threw back his head, and, looking upward toward the cloudless sky, he closed his eyes for a moment and shook his head. "And when have the Pharisees not been offended by my words?" he asked. "Let them alone, for they are blind leaders of the blind. And if the blind lead the blind then both shall fall in a ditch."

Now about this time a plot was born among some of the people that Jesus should be made king. Among these were young enthusiasts who considered the matter of a revolt exciting, for there were still those who believed the long awaited Messiah must take his place as ruler of Israel. Thus, an immediate plan was made to kidnap him during the night while he slept and then hold him in seclusion until he acquiesced to their desires. Naturally, they felt they would ultimately hold prominent positions in his court because of their endeavors. However, as the plot was being laid Jesus felt a heaviness descend over him, and he looked around to see the source of this new agitation. His eyes fell on a couple of the young men nearby, and in that moment he knew he had pinned down the culprits. As he perceived the plot which was being hatched, he became exceedingly delighted. Although he considered the idea ludicrous, he enjoyed the chess game of life and saw an opportunity to outsmart his potential kidnappers. When night fell, instead of going to sleep Jesus motioned to some of his disciples that he would like to go out some distance from the shore by boat. Later when all was quiet they made their way to Capernaum and settled down for a restful night.

On the following day, when the people saw that neither Jesus, nor his disciples, could be found along the shores of the village they hastened to Capernaum. When they found him there, one of the people asked, "Master, why did you come here?"

"You seek me because I have fed you food for the body," he replied. "However, you must not labor for that which perishes. Rather you must achieve great wisdom, which will endure even after the body has become dust. Listen to these things which I teach you. Although my body is born of woman's womb, my soul is born of the spirit and therefore sealed by God."

Then someone asked him, "What shall we do that we might do the works of God."

"First," Jesus replied, "believe in me whom God has sent." After this he tried to speak of the law of divine progression in which the least should serve the highest, thereby allowing the perpetual ascent of the soul from one level to another as it was earned. Even though he now spoke carefully, he knew that those who listened were unprepared to comprehend the unwritten law. Otherwise, they would not have asked for a sign.

When Jesus had finished, one of the multitude shouted out to him, "Our father ate manna in the desert, as it is written."

But Jesus shook his head and replied, "Moses did not give you bread from heaven, for heaven is within you. Verily, I say to you that those who hearkened to the teachings of Moses received a true understanding of the law as it is written in the hearts and souls of all men. These laws are the bread of life which was given to your forefathers. Now I give the same to you, that those who believe on me shall never hunger. But look at you. You see me, but you still do not believe, although I come from a kingdom which you do not know and serve the will of him who has sent me."

On hearing these words the people became greatly offended, for there were scribes and Pharisees among them. Their law did not extend to the possibility of someone descending from heaven by the command of God, and in their eyes those things which the Master said were blasphemous. So they began to murmur among themselves, calling up furtive memories of this human who stood before them. Since they knew he had been born of Joseph and Mary, now of Nazareth, they wondered how he could claim to have come down from heaven.

The Master looked at those standing near him, the stillness of the sea broken only by the sounds of their shifting bodies and the whispers upon their lips. "Murmur not among yourselves," he said, "for there does exist both a law of progression and a law of attraction. Therefore, no man can come to me except that the Father which has sent me draws him near. These will I raise up on the last day."[3]

As the whispering ceased, Jesus looked out upon the people, knowing that many were not yet ready to sacrifice human will to divine will. Yet he also knew that, in some distant future, God's divine plan would fulfill itself and bring forth heaven on earth. He spoke of this now, saying, "It is written in the Prophets, 'And they shall be all taught by God.' Those who have heard and learned of the Father come to me. None have seen God except those who are prepared to receive him, but these have seen him, and those who believe in these things which I teach shall find the key of lasting happiness and eternal life."

Jesus was speaking now of the authority which is given to one who has passed through the resurrection of the dead. Since most of the people who gathered around him sought only for a miracle and accepted what he was saying literally, dissension quickly arose among them. They believed that he was calling himself God, which was against the primary and first law which Moses had laid down before them, 'Thou shall have no other gods before me.'

Sorrowfully, Jesus saw the darkness in their hearts, but he continued his discourse, saying, "Your fathers were given these truths in the wilderness, yet many remained bound by human chains. This wisdom which I reveal is the bread of life which comes down from heaven, and those who partake of it will never die. My flesh is this living bread. He who eats of my flesh and drinks of my blood shall have eternal life."

With these words the Jews became even more offended, for they questioned how they could be given the flesh of the man who stood before them. Jesus was speaking of the soul's removal from the ways of flesh which bound man to death, old age, sickness, and birth, and he was saying that man must forsake any action which did not benefit all humans. However, the Jews believed he was saying that they must eat his body and drink his blood. Many in the crowd now became exceedingly disagreeable and departed, walking with him no more, and when they had gone Jesus looked at his disciples sadly, asking, "Will you also go away from me?"

It was Peter who answered him, saying, "Master, where could we go, for you speak the words of eternal life and we believe that you are the Christ and Son of the living God."

Then Jesus made reference to his disciples, among them the latest addition, Judas Iscariot, saying, "I have chosen you twelve, but even so, one among you is evil."

"Who is that?" Peter asked.

If Jesus heard him, he did not reply, but looked at all of those who were with him. As he glanced from one to another his eyes took on a look of seriousness, and he held Judas Iscariot in his gaze for one inscrutable moment. Then he allowed his eyes to pass on, his disciples taking no notice of the fleeting moment in time.

Only a short time had passed since Judas had been accepted among those of the inner circle of the Master's followers. Born in Kerioth, he was not only the son of Simon the Pharisee who had found early favor in Jesus' eyes, but he was also the nephew of Caiaphus, high priest to the Sanhedrin. He was slender, dark-haired, olive-skinned, a man of an unbridled disposition who dwelled in Jerusalem with his wife. His marriage was one of many thorns, for his wife was a selfish woman and her tongue was sharp. Never satisfied with her position in life, she constantly harangued Judas concerning the impoverished condition he had brought her into, although she was not responsible for her husband's occasional dishonesty. When Judas received compensation for a favor, he was prone to seek a means of cheating his wife out of it, which did not endear him to her. The couple had no children of their own, although his wife served as a foster mother for the seven-month-old child of Jesus' wealthy great uncle, Joseph of Arimathea. For this service, she received payment in gold coins, which she promptly secured from the reach of her materialistic husband (Revillout No. 5, Pg. 156).

Several factors were involved in Jesus accepting Judas as a disciple. One, of course, was that he was the son of Simon, and another was that Judas had sought admittance to the group, believing that they were going to bring forth a rich kingdom on earth. Although Jesus could have sent him away at any time and forced him to spy from the outer fringes of the multitude, he chose not to do so. By permitting Judas free access to his teachings, he was also assured that word of his works would reach the selfish ears of the political administrators of Israel. Although Judas was often somewhat quarrelsome and selfish, and on numerous occasions he acted in a manner which offended the closed brotherhood of disciples, the others tolerated him because of loyalty to their master. Besides, deep inside of Jesus there was a knowing that this intractable man held some key to the fulfillment of his destiny. Many who sought discipleship were turned away, but Judas was called forth by the Mover of all chess pieces, whose Son was the instrument of his will.

About this time, the disciples encouraged Jesus to move into Judea so that the people there might witness his miracles. However, he declined and continued to abide peacefully in Capernaum. It was here that he taught his disciples the mysteries written in the stars, wherein dwell the movement of universal order and nature's immutable laws. In the meantime the rains ceased, while the rich fragrance of another spring flowed down from the hills.

One day, while he was teaching along the shore of Galilee, one of the disciples asked the Master to tell them more about the Kingdom of Heaven, and Jesus replied, "The Kingdom of the Father is like a certain woman who was carrying a jar full of meal. While she was walking on the road, still some distance from home, the handle of the jar broke and meal emptied out behind her on the road. She did not realize it, and when she reached her house, she found the jar empty. This is like the person who carries the Spirit of God within him, but as he journeys through life he follows the path of destruction, and the seeds of wisdom fall useless behind him. Then when he is near death, he turns, only to find that his vessel is empty because that which was within him has fallen useless to the ground."

Then one of the disciples asked Jesus, "When will the Kingdom come?"

When he heard this, Jesus smiled mysteriously, while a familiar essence of mirth danced around the corners of his mouth. He always looked this way when he was about to move a chess piece in for a victory, and now with considerable amusement, he said, "It will not come by waiting for it. It will not be a matter of saying 'Here it is' or 'here it is.' Rather, the Kingdom of the Father is spread out upon the earth and men do not see it" (Gospel According to Thomas, Log 113: 14-18).

Finally Jesus rose, but those who gathered around him remained seated, for every man felt the power of his words. The full moon appeared between the breaking clouds and enfolded Jesus in its brightness, and his features disappeared into a halo of light. As he stood among them in the moonlight, a hush descended over the land, bringing the peace of the Heavenly Father into the hearts of those who sat motionless in a timeless sea of eternity.

At last Jesus stretched out his hands to them and said, after the manner of the Essenes, "Peace be with you." And he departed as a breath of wind swaying through the trees.

Soon after, the heat of July settled over the lands, and the Feast of the Tabernacles came upon the Master and his disciples. The feast was held following the gathering of the harvest and pertained to the first resting place of the Israelites in their march out of Egypt. Moses had originally designated this feast as the gathering of the laborers from the field to thresh the grain and tread the grapes into wine. This represented the purification (reaping) of man, as the spirit removed all things which bound him to the mortal world. Yet it was also a time of great rejoicing, for the feast began on the 15th day of July, five days before the Day of Atonement, in order to signify the five lesser mysteries pertaining to the descent of the soul into the flesh, and continued until the seventh day (the day when God would be born in man).

One of the highlights of the Feast of the Tabernacles was lodging for the celebrants. This consisted of booths constructed to serve as temporary dwellings, and according to tradition, their height could not exceed 20 cubit, to signify the two natures (mortal and immortal). Neither could the booths be less than 10 cubits, thereby signifying that spiritual rebirth could only occur by the return to the one God. The structures were comprised of three walls to remind the children of Israel that this great work could only be accomplished through the union of the body, soul, and spirit. The temporary lodgings also served to remind the people of the fatherly care and protection received by Jacob from God as he journeyed from Egypt to Canaan. In comparison with more permanent structures, representing bondage, the festival booths symbolized freedom from worldly attachments.

Each worshipper carried a myrtle bough in his left hand (the sorrows of human life), but the palm branch (victory over human bondage) was carried in his right hand. On the seventh day, these were tied together in a bundle, and at the conclusion of the festival the bundle was beaten upon the altar to represent the great threshing day in which the Lord God of Israel separated the good of man from the chaff of his impure nature. When this ceremony was completed, the pilgrims removed their belongings from the booths, thus signifying that victory over matter had been achieved. This celebration was therefore referred to as the great Hosanna Day.

Although there was yet much work for Jesus to complete before his fated death, he was not free to travel to the Feast of the Tabernacles openly, for some of the Jews already sought to slay him. As his disciples gathered in preparation for departure, he said to them, "My time has not come, and as yet the people do not seek to kill you. The world does not hate you, but I am despised because I speak truly of its works. Go you then to this feast, but I will not go forth with you lest my life be taken before it is time." And he remained in Galilee while his disciples departed.

As the festival began, some of the celebrants inquired after

Jesus, and among others there was much murmuring concerning him. Some contended, "He is a good man," while others condemned him, saying, "Nay, but he deceives the people." However, no one spoke openly in his favor because they feared reprisal from the other Jews.

Now it came to pass in the middle of the feast that Jesus, who had arrived in secret, went into the temple to teach. Taking his customary position by one of the temple columns, he began his discourse. It was not long thereafter that a substantial number of people gathered around him. As the Master taught differently, a great agitation arose among the noted Doctors of the Law who had been formally trained after the manner of the Jews. Their doctrine was structured about a rigid interpretation of Mosaic traditions, whereas that of the Master was based upon the eternal aspects of natural and cosmic law. Inasmuch as Jesus had not been trained in the traditional schools recognized by the Sanhedrin, he was not considered qualified to speak. Even so, it was clear to those who heard him that he spoke with great wisdom.

When the Master began to discourse, some of the Jews marveled over his ability to speak so eloquently and asked, "How can this man know the scriptures if he is not learned?"

And Jesus answered them saying, "The doctrine I offer to you is not mine, but His that sent me. If any man will do His will he shall come to know the doctrine, for it is both unchanging and written in the body, mind, and soul of man.

"Know you that the written word which comes from God is a reflection of the Heavenly Sea, even as the bright stars reflect the face of Heaven. As the ancient ones engraved the words of God on Holy Scrolls, so is the Law engraved upon the souls of all men. Thus, the written word is a clear pool of that which was revealed by the greats of old, even Enoch. He who has studied the teachings of the ancients through the mind, and contemplated upon them through the living things which surround him, has broken the mighty barrier between heaven and earth.

"Moses gave ten commandments to the children of Israel, but they could not keep them and complained that the laws were too difficult. Thus with great compassion, because of their suffering, he gave them many laws. Although these were derived from the original commandments, they were easier to follow, for Moses did not wish for the people to wither away. But, the scribes and Pharisees have made hundreds of new laws and have placed an intolerable burden upon you, one which they do not carry, for the nearer you are to God the less you need of numerous laws. Therefore, the laws of the Pharisees and scribes are multitudinous, while the laws of the Son of man are seven, (seven cosmic laws); of the angels, three (body, soul, spirit), and of God, one (return to the one God).

"Thus, I speak only of those laws which are familiar to you, so that you may become spiritual beings and comply with rules of nature. It is only then that God's Holy Spirit can descend and lead you to the greater laws, for it is difficult for you to interpret those things which have been written in words when you are yet in darkness.

"There is little advantage in reading scriptures, if by your actions you deny them. However, the law is present in all living things, in the plants, in the fish, in the animals, and in you, for Moses did not receive his legislation through the written word, but rather through the living God. Therefore, do not seek the law in your scriptures, but through the contemplation of life."

As the people gathered in the temple to listen to Jesus, they felt great hostility because they could not understand his words. They had long rehearsed the written letter of the law and paid homage to those who bore the spoken word. Now at Jesus' statement they began to feel even greater antagonism welling up inside them, for he seemed in opposition to their beliefs. This caused them to plot his death and blame the devil for his teachings. Calling out, one accused him saying, "You have a devil; it is he who seeks to kill you."[4] Jesus looked at the crowd and, seeing into their minds, answered them, "I have done but one work and you all marvel. Moses gave you circumcision, not because it is of Moses, but of the fathers. However you circumcise on the Sabbath[5] so that the Law of Moses will not be broken, yet you are angry at me because I have made a man whole. Why do you not judge a person's work by what you see, rather than by arbitrary laws which are written by man according to his inexplicit understanding?"

On another occasion, Jesus spoke to his disciples in private concerning the custom of circumcision in a somewhat different way. "If circumcision were beneficial, would not the children be born circumcised from their mother? True circumcision in spirit has become completely profitable."

The disciples knew that he spoke not of the physical circumcision, but of raising that which was immortal in them in order to cleanse and purge the soul through spiritual regeneration. Regarding the physical practice of circumcision, however, Jesus remained silent. To speak against the ancient ritual would only incite the people against him all the more. Since the male organ symbolized regeneration and life's continuity, the descendants of the Tribes of Israel had suffered their children to endure the rite of circumcision as a penance for any misdeeds committed against the Lord God of Israel. It would have been difficult for him to explain the significance of this practice to those who still walked the path of conventional Judaism, for their eyes were clouded by priestly ritual. Indeed, some citizens of Jerusalem were even now beginning to talk among themselves, asking, "Is this not he whom the multitude seeks to kill? Yet look how boldly he speaks and no one says anything to him. Is it possible that our rulers believe that he is the anointed one? Now we know this man and where he was born, and he cannot be the Christ, for it is said that when he appears no man will know from whence he comes."

When he heard the discord of the people Jesus felt betrayed, for he had walked among them, healed their sick, and done all manner of good. Even though it was the work he had been assigned to do, he saw that little had changed since the days Moses journeyed in the desert with the children of Israel. Then, as now, the people reprehended the good and turned against the proffered hand of peace because their hunger for worldly things outweighed their desire to seek the way of the righteous. A heaviness settled over him, and he finally spoke to those who murmured, saying, "You know me and those things which I have done and that I have not come of myself. He that has sent me is true and yet you cannot see this."

After this the people sought to take Jesus, but no one could yet lay a hand on him, for it was the will of God that another harvest should pass across the face of the earth before his life should end. And it came to pass that on the final day of the Festival of the Tabernacles, after the Musaph (special sacrifices of the day), the children threw away their palms and ate their citrons. Then came the Roman officers, together with the chief priests and Pharisees, and the people inquired of them, "Why have you not arrested this man?"

The officers replied, "Never has a man spoken like this one."

But the Pharisees persisted, "Are you also deceived? Can you not see that none among the rulers and Pharisees believe him? These people who do not know the law are cursed."

About this time Nicodemus, a Pharisee and a member of the Sanhedrin council who had secretly become a sympathizer of the Master, spoke out in an attempt to still those who spoke against Jesus. "Does your law judge any man before it hears him and knows what he does?"

The troublemakers laughed scornfully, "Are you also of Galilee? See for yourself, out of Galilee there arises no prophet."

Nicodemus knew that further confrontation at this time would not be wise, and he stepped back quietly into the crowd. This action later gave rise to the illusion that he was a cowardly man. However, as one of the three wealthiest men in all of Jerusalem, he possessed not only great power, but also was a learned man who carefully sought to adhere to the Laws of Moses. By this time, the council of the Sanhedrin, in whose ranks had stood the greatest men of Israel, was no longer the exalted source of law which had prevailed in the past. Its effectiveness had begun to lessen with the addition of inferior men appointed by Valerius Gratus, curator under Pontius Pilate. Among those with political appointments were the selfish and greedy Caiaphus and his father-in-law Annas. Therefore, Nicodemus sensed that the great days of the Sanhedrin priesthood were numbered, and he reasoned that to allow himself to be removed from his position, or to be killed, would only hasten the disease which had already undermined the dignity of the council.

When Jesus had finished his discourse in the temple, he lifted himself up and departed toward the Mount of Olivet, which rose 2,680 feet above sea level. Facing the temple mount at Jerusalem on the east, it was separated only by the Vale of Kidron, *Jebel et-tor*. The garden was one of the Master's favorite places to discourse with his disciples in private, and he made the trip frequently when he was in Jerusalem. Walking along in a surefooted manner, he came to a place where the path branched in two directions. Selecting the one going to Bethany, a village situated on the eastern slope of Mount Olivet, he hastened toward the home of his friend Lazarus that he might dine with him.

The sun had just set over the symmetric hills of Palestine, bringing forth the dusk to herald the dying day. The next day Jesus intended to return to Jerusalem for the eighth day of the feast. This part of the celebration was observed by rest and holy convocation, as opposed to the pageantry of the preceding days. Although the feasts and celebrations were of little interest to him, they did lend an opportunity to speak to the multitudes. Many came to the temple to listen to the various men of learning who expounded the law. As the last rays of sun danced across the sky, they momentarily caught Jesus' hair and turned it into a reddish-gold halo, not unlike the Himalayas against Apollo's rise. Then, as though also wearied, the sun dropped behind the distant hills, leaving the words of Enoch's vision whispering within the subtle stillness.

Behold, the Lord cometh with ten thousands of his saints. To execute judgment upon all, and to convince all that are ungodly among them of all their ungodly deeds which they have ungodly committed, and of all their hard speeches which ungodly sinners have spoken against him.

Jude:
14-15

When the eighth day of the festival dawned, Jesus left the house of Lazarus and returned to the temple in Jerusalem. First, however, he stopped at the Mount of Olivet for a few moments of seclusion. He often sought these brief interludes of quiet in order to remove the clinging shadows of the human world. During his discourses, he sensed the thoughts of those who bathed their bodies with water but were content to leave their unclean minds to create chaos in the hidden consciousness which lay beyond the view of human eyes and the hearing of human ears. Frequently, his disciples also displayed unbridled minds, characterized by skepticism and discord. As their minds were linked to his own by the higher law which prevailed between master and disciple, he was the bearer of their indifferences. Lest the collective force of these unbridled thoughts decrease his virtue, he retired to the hills and streams for regeneration.

Looking over the Kidron Valley toward Jerusalem from 2,000 feet above the sea, Jesus sensed the tides of controversy engulfing him. Yet, as he rose to resume his journey along the path toward the temple, he also accepted the sands of destiny which had bequeathed him this role. Therefore, he was not unhappy, for in him there was no loneliness, lack of purpose, fear, malice, or discontent. Those who schemed against him were bound by the earthly fetters of illness, old age, and death. They would have to endure the chains of evolution until the hatred and discord etched in their souls were left behind in the passage of the sun.

It was still early in the morning when Jesus arrived at the temple, and taking his customary position, he prepared to speak. However, the priestly scribes, who laboriously endeavored to preserve the ancient Hebrew icons, and the Pharisees, sought again to lure him into controversy. Having found a woman of ill repute on the streets, they laid hands on her and brought her into his presence, that he might judge. They wished to see if he would violate the Mosaic tradition concerning adultery, calling for the punishment of stoning.

At first the Master ignored those who had come to test him, and he reached over with his finger and began to etch ancient symbols upon the earth. As the taunts and jeers continued, Jesus raised himself up and said, "He who is without sin among you, let him first cast a stone at her."

Again Jesus stooped down to write upon the ground. He knew that every human had misused natural and cosmic law at some time, even though it may have been in ignorance. Under natural and cosmic law, resulting from the perfect forward motion of the divine plan, the soul was subject to an exacting penalty for each infraction and did not escape the consequence of any action. Therefore, the judgment of man was inferior.

When Jesus finally looked up from his writing, the accusers had all dispersed and no one remained but the woman. A slight smile took over the seriousness of his eyes, and he asked the woman, "Woman, where are those who were accusing you? Has no one condemned you?"

And she replied, "No, my Lord."

"Neither do I condemn you," Jesus said kindly. "Now go and sin no more."

As the morning passed, the Master continued to speak, frequently pausing to answer some question posed to him by a scribe or a Pharisee. As midday approached, the discussion began to center on Abraham, who was regarded as the sacred father of the children of Israel. Still seeking to trap Jesus into committing blasphemy, those who had gathered pursued their probing, saying, "Abraham is our father."

However, Jesus shook his head and replied, "If you were Abraham's children, you would do the work of Abraham. But you seek to kill me, a man who has told you the truths which have been passed down to me by God just as they were to Abraham before me. Your deeds are of the mortal world and born of mortal fathers."

These words brought great rebuttal and the argument began to wax strong, for the Jews believed Jesus was saying that he was of God, but they were not. Having heard it said that Jesus was born of immaculate conception, many of the Jews believed he had been born through the immoral actions of his mother. Therefore, in their eyes, he was overshadowed by fornication, which was in direct violation of their law. Mocking him, one of the scribes counterattacked by innuendo, "We are not born of fornication. We have one Father, even God."

Shaking his head, Jesus wondered if it would always be the same, the ignorant seeking to destroy the good. Now the scribes and Pharisees had come to destroy his words like animals drawn to the carcass of a kill, seeking to partake of the meat and blood of their victim. He gave careful consideration to the next words he would speak, aligning himself consciously with the power which abided in him. Such challenges were usually not offensive, for he was a master swordsman and his sword of truth and justice had been scrupulously sharpened. Finally, speaking with solemnness, he said, "If God were your Father, you would love me, for I have come from him. Why is it that you cannot understand my speech? Is it because you do not listen? You have been born of human fathers and their lusts are yours also, and you abide by the path which leads to destruction and not in the ways of truth. When man utters a lie, it is of his own making and he is the father of it. Yet, I tell you the truth, and you do not believe me."

By this time, a great number of people had been attracted by the dispute. It was these who now accused him of being the devil as well as a Samaritan, but Jesus immediately took issue with this statement, saying, "I am not a devil, but I honor my Father and you do dishonor to me. I say to you that I do not seek my own glory, but the glory of him who will be raised within all men, and is the judge. If you can understand these words, then you will never see death."

It was not uncommon for someone in the crowd to incite revolt when the Master spoke, and it was no different on this day. Delighting in doing mischief, there was one who taunted, "Now we know it is you who has a devil. Abraham is dead and the prophets are dead, but you say that one who keeps your sayings shall never taste of death. Are you then greater than our father Abraham, and also the prophets?"

Like a warrior, Jesus side-stepped the blow which had been dealt and decided to further confound them. This time he spoke to them in mystical terms, saying, "If I boast of myself I have little honor, but he who tells others of his greatness deserves no reward, for he has given it to himself. My rewards come from my Father, who you claim is your God. Your father Abraham rejoiced to see my day; the day when all men stand as brothers and peace has come to earth. He saw it and he was glad."

As Jesus used the term *my day* the Jews thought he was saying that he had seen Abraham and they broke out in raucous laughter, scoffing, "You are not yet 50 years old, yet you are claiming you have seen Abraham?"

With sorrow in his heart because of the treachery of his tormentors, Jesus replied with yet another mystery, "Verily, I say to you that before Abraham was, I am."

Although Jesus referred to the eternal selfhood, or the immortal aspect of man's essence which existed in the beginning, the Jews became incensed. Picking up stones, they began to throw them at him. Standing up quickly, he stepped behind a pillar for protection. Then he passed through his tormentors and left the temple.

Legends which float on the winds of time and carry memories of events long past say that Jesus exerted all his powers in self-defense, and controlled the crowd with his piercing eyes. In them was reflected a powerful will, developed only through mastership and containing a great power, little understood by ordinary men. It was further said that the mob, sensing the presence of a mighty force, experienced fear and began to scatter, leaving a wide path for the man in the scarlet robe who strode through their ranks. Perhaps this legend born by the wind is true, for the Master indeed returned to the shores of Galilee without suffering harm. In his heart abided the Law of the one God and the vision of salvation for all mankind in a world yet to come.

1. Fabre d'Olivet, *Hebraic Tongue Restored* (Maine: Samuel Weiser, Inc. 1976).

2. As mentioned before, the hidden meaning to Jewish ritual is not commonly known among the Jews, or the Rabbi. As with most religions, the spiritual experience of many things is relegated to outer, or exoteric, practice and ritual. The Sabbath is such an example, obscure not only in Judaism but virtually all religions, including Christianity.

3. The term *last day* is usually misinterpreted to mean the end of earth. However, this is not what Jesus referred to. The transformation of human to divine, or the resurrection of the dead prescribes that the Christ nature in man be raised through devotional surrender to God. When this feat is accomplished, then man is freed from his imprisonment to matter. In that all souls are united by a common thread of divinity, then one who has already reached this height also lifts others. One can perhaps say that the weaker is enhanced by the mere presence of the stronger.

4. The term devil is a matter of scriptural symbolism. It is considered as an anthropos, or composite figure, signifying the unrestrained lesser nature of man, although many believed him to be real and have blamed him for all their misguided actions.

The concept for this symbolic figure is derived from the idea that within the soul, God created both a predestiny of perfection for every human, and simultaneously, the obstacles to be overcome before such perfection could be achieved. This antithesis later became known as the war between Lucifer and Christ, or the battle of the soul between good and evil, an evolutionary conflict. Through this pattern of seeming contradiction woven by God, man can attain salvation. Therefore, while the devil, also known as Satan, was believed to be evil, he was also an essential instrument by which progression was assured.

5. Sabbath represents the day of divine man in which the indwelling God is raised from its tomb of matter and finally separated from its mortal counterpart in order to become whole. In this final phase of planetary progression, heaven and earth become one, thus the fulfillment of prophecy, or the descent of the new Jerusalem.

Angel of Power   Burrows (cc)

You, O great Creator, have made earth by your power, have established the world by your wisdom, and have stretched out the heavens by your love.

Gospel of Peace
Vatican MS./Szekely
Section. II, ch. XI: 48

CHAPTER V

THE FOOTSTOOL OF GOD

My children, know you not that the earth and all that dwells therein is but a reflection of the Kingdom of the Heavenly Father?

Gospel of Peace
Vatican MS./Szekely
Section II, ch. XI:3

aving departed from the house of Lazarus with some of his disciples, Jesus prepared to return to Capernaum along the silent desert shores of the Jordan River. After walking some distance the group made a sharp left turn, following the old boundary line which separated the tribe of Judah from the tribe of Benjamin. The long descent was bounded on the south side by the wild gorge of the Kelt, and across the barren plains lay the sparkling Dead Sea. Its water was perfectly clear and transparent, but its taste was bitter and more salty than the ocean. For those who dared to sample it, the water acted upon the tongue and mouth like alum, smarted the eyes like camphor, and produced a burning, prickling sensation. The atmosphere was like a vast funeral pall let down from heaven, and it hung heavily over the lifeless bosom of the mysterious lake before expanding over the entire area below Jericho.

As the small group descended into the desert, the profound gorge of Wady Kelt lay beneath them, and on the north towered the ridge of Quarantana, with its caverns, cells, and rock-hewn chapels. On the left was the southern face of Jebel Kuruntul, which presented many utterly inaccessible places between its dark perpendicular cliffs. The impenetrable silence of the land seemed to forbid speaking and so the small group made its way quietly without conversation. The Master was also silent. Here in the desert he was free from the raucous vibrations of the cities, and a deep peace flowed through his soul. He drank heavily of the isolation, for his nomad years had made him kin to the intense heat, sifting sands, and moving winds. In no other place did he feel so free and yet so one with the powerful forces of nature and the universe. While many bemoaned the loneliness of seclusion, and others became lunatics, he alone, as had

Moses before him, surrendered to the desert's rule.

On arriving in Jericho, Jesus and his disciples prepared to spend the night. As they reached the high plateau, known as the Tell es-Sultan, the Master stopped for a moment to view the panorama of the valley below him. The remarkable city rested between the wide plain where the Jordan Valley broadened between the Moab and Edom precipices. From here he could see the vast area of plain and mountains which were crowned with the ancient memories of some of the grandest events in history. Then, setting their feet in motion once more, they went into the city to seek food and lodging, satisfied with a frugal fare and a palate of straw under the stars. However, before night fell, word had gone out through the city that Jesus had come, and some people came to him that they might be healed.

And it came to pass that he taught for several days, and then taking his disciples, he departed for Capernaum. Descending down the Tell es-Sultan, they entered the Jordan Valley which ran 65 miles between the Lake of Galilee and the Dead Sea. Although much of the valley had abundant vegetation, particularly in the spring, this did not hold true for the entire land. There was a portion which was shrouded in desolation, where the land was sour, and the jungle obtrusive marl, and the parched hillside earned the undisputed title of desert. For a time, the river retired far to the eastward and the only variation in the dreary monotony was a necessary detour westward in order to get around deep gullies, which led some 200 feet down to the river. After walking for several hours in this part of the wilderness plain, the retinue reached the Wady el Faria and stopped for water. When their thirst was quenched, Jesus rose and motioned to his disciples that they should continue with the journey.

On arriving at Kurun Hattin, near Capernaum on the west side of the Lake of Galilee, Jesus retired with his followers and prepared to teach again. Word spread quickly to the surrounding countryside that the Master was there, and soon people began to arrive from the nine villages which surrounded the sea. One of these was a man with grievous plagues, and he came to kneel before Jesus, asking, "We know that you have it within your power to heal all manner of diseases and we ask you to free us from Satan and from his great afflictions. If you know all things, tell why we must suffer and why we are not whole like other men?"

Answering the question with great kindness because of the man's sorrow, Jesus said, "It is right for you to be seekers of the truth, and I will fill you with the same wisdom which Moses gave to your forefathers. Happy are you also who knock upon the door of life, for it is the violations of natural and cosmic law which cause all affliction. Come to me, and I will lead you into the earthly kingdom and her angels, where the power of disease cannot enter."

Although they had heard of the kingdom of God, many did not know this earthy kingdom of which Jesus spoke, nor were they familiar with the laws of nature. Looking at him in amazement, one man asked, "Where is this earthly kingdom?"

With great patience, as though he were teaching a small child, Jesus began to speak of the kingdom of earth from which the substance of man's body was made, saying, "God is the God of the living, and Satan that of the dead. Serve, therefore, the living God, that the eternal movement of life may sustain you, and that you may escape the gripping stillness of death.

"Work also, without ceasing, to build the kingdom of God, lest the earth become a slave to darkness. As you build, so will the Heavenly Father and Earthly Mother send their angels to teach, to love, and to serve you. For peace proliferates within the lands of our Heavenly Father, while sorrow darkens the empire of death. Be, therefore, true sons of the kingdom of earth and of your Heavenly Father, that you descend not into the caverns of Satan.

"After this manner, therefore, pray to your Heavenly Father: Our Father which art in heaven, hallowed be thy name. Thy kingdom come, Thy will be done on earth as it is in heaven. Give us this day our daily bread, and forgive us our debts, as we forgive our debtors. And let us not be led into temptation, but deliver us from evil. For thine is the kingdom, the power, and the glory, forever. Amen.

"And after this manner, pray to your Earthly Mother: Our Mother which art upon earth, hallowed be thy name. Thy kingdom come, and thy will be done in us, as it is in thee. As thou sendest every day thine angels, send them to us also. Forgive us our sins, as we atone all our sins against thee. And lead us not into sickness, but deliver us from all evil, for thine is the earth, the body and health. Amen." (Gospel of Peace, Section I, ch. VIII: 9-24).

When he had finished praying, the Master raised his head and opened his eyes. Then he looked quietly at those who gathered around him and spoke again, "Your body is comprised of the elements of earth and is part of it, just as your spirit is of God. From the beginning you have gathered the dust of earth to form your bodies, and one day you will return it. Wise is the man who learns obediency to natural law, for he shall never see disease. The power of earth is above all things and destroys that which is unclean, for it is the kingdom of the living God and therefore rules over life.

"The blood which runs in us is born from the water of the earthly kingdom, which rises as mist from the sea, descends as snow on the distant summits, flows in the mighty rivers, sings in the bubbling streams, and gleams as dew in the morning sun.

"The air which we breathe is born by the movement of the earth on her predestined journey through the unnumbered stars. It flows through majestic trees, sings in the tops of the mountains, moves the wheat grass as it wills, and nurtures life in man. Truly, the Son of man is born of earth and shall not find happiness until he venerates its laws. Otherwise, the shadow of death reaches out and entices him to its dark bosom.

"He who seeks harmony with the laws of earth shall be healed of illness and live a very long life. And he shall be protected from fire, from water, from attack by poisonous reptiles, and the sting of the scorpion. For the love of earth for her children is greater by far than the love of a thousand mothers by blood."

After this he sat silent for a time. Since his early training, his journeys, and his observation of the movement of heavenly bodies, Jesus had come to recognize the suns and their corresponding earths as integral aspects of the evolution of the universe. For this reason, he tried to teach those who so often gathered around him that the consciousness of God was expressed in and through all living things including the earth upon which they walked, and that those who worked in harmony with earth would learn the ways of the Heavenly Father. In spite of the fact that people all too often failed to understand, he still felt deep empathy for them. Most could not comprehend these things he spoke of, any more than had the children of Israel who traveled with Moses in the desert. Thus, because nature was evident in all living things, he sought to explain through simple parables, teaching that the Son of man would learn joy from the flowers, healing from the sun, regeneration from the grass, and life's continuity from the grain of wheat.

When Jesus finished teaching the people, he withdrew from them and went into solitude with his disciples. Although the people did not try to follow him, neither did they leave. For a time they sat and talked of his wonders, many believing that he was the Messiah. Others, still questioning, sought a miracle. Some even waited through the night, and he did come among them the next day and the next, teaching many wonderful things.

One hazy rain-filled morning in the month of Tebeth (December-January), just as the flocks left the highlands for the Jordan Valley, and the lower districts were green with grain, Jesus gathered his disciples in private to instruct them in some of the mysteries of old. Those who were now with him were considered the elect; they had risen above the patterns of fundamental Jewish beliefs and would lay the cornerstone of the future. In them, the shadow of the cross seemed less menacing, for they above all others had earned the privilege of abiding closely to him. On the distant horizon, their destiny lay as tiny flecks of sand, and the faint outline of their work was written in the pages of eternity.

On this particular day, the Master chose to meet them underneath one of the ancient trees which dotted the countryside. Those who came approached him quietly, for he appeared to be concentrating deeply on a small vessel which he held in his hands. However, as they neared he looked up at them kindly and motioned for them to be seated near him, saying, "It is good that you have chosen the path of righteousness, for you have entered in the ways of immortality and walk in the path of truth, even as your ancestors did before you. You have learned to see and hear with the eyes and ears of spirit, where the air flies high against the azure sky, where the sun reigns supreme above the clouds, and where the glistening water flows in the streams of life.

"The time has come when I can speak to you of deep and mysterious things, for the grass which grows in this earthen pot is more powerful than the mighty thunder. It hides its grandeur after the manner of a great ruler of old, who once disguised himself as a beggar and visited the village of his subjects. He knew that they would open their hearts to a simple man, but if they knew who walked among them, they would fall at his feet in fear. I tell you truly, that the blade of grass carries a force of life which sustains all living things, even as it endures the ravages of the wind and fire. It was brought forth with the seas and the mountains and has lived since the beginning of earth."

Then one of the disciples who sat near him looked upon the earthen pot which Jesus held in his hand and saw that it contained some wheat grass like that which grew in the lower valleys, and he asked, "How is that which you hold within your hand different from that which surrounds us in the distant fields?"

"It is not different," Jesus replied. "Every growing thing is a part of nature. Yet, when we separate these blades of wheat from the fields, it is possible to touch the Holy Stream of Life which has brought forth creation. This is invisible to those who cannot see with the eyes of spirit, for they walk in darkness in the light of the sun and beneath the gleaming stars of night. And as they walk they do not know the powerful forces which constantly surround them.

"Take this earthen pot and place your hands gently around the growing grass. Then close your eyes and breathe deeply, and you shall feel the force of life flowing from the grass into your own body, and you shall know its power of regeneration."

When he had finished these words he took the wheat between his hands, and as he closed his eyes waves of light radiated around him, shimmering in the sun. Those who were with him bowed their heads in reverence before the power of light which poured forth from his seated figure. Then he handed the earthen pot to one of those who sat near him.

As the earthen pot was passed one to another, each of the disciples shut their eyes in order to see with the eyes of spirit. And as they followed the gleaming blades of grass to their roots they merged with the Holy Stream of Life and knew that it carried the mystery of earth's beginning. Even as the shadow of day lengthened, Jesus continued to sit so silently that every living thing around ceased paying him heed. And it came to pass that the souls of the elect became free from the agitations of the outer world, and they united with a moment in infinite time when the world began. No longer aware of sitting beneath the tree, they became conscious only of the Holy Stream of Life which flowed from God to man.[1]

After this Jesus returned to the Sea of Galilee to minister to the people again. As he walked along the shore, his white apron created a sharp contrast against his dark skin. As he moved, he held his body very erect, his feet moving soundlessly against the earth. Silhouetted against the sparkling sea and the brown hills, he portrayed a certain unity with the forces which surrounded him, and there was no doubt in the minds of those who saw him that he was unlike other men. As always, the news traveled quickly that he had come, and it was not long thereafter the people came. When he had settled himself, he began to speak, saying, "Many unseen dangers lie in wait for the Sons of men. The ruler of death, lord of illness, takes form in the desires of men. He tantalizes them with power and riches, strong drink and rich food, and idle days. And because his seat is in the center of their hopes, he leads them to that of which their heart is most inclined.

"In that time when the Sons of men become submissive to his vanities and harmful desires, then in payment Beelzebub, the prince of devils, takes away the things to which nature supplies in abundance. And man becomes short of breath, full of pain, suffers stiffness in his bones, and his body is wracked with illness. At last his eyes grow dim, till dark night enshrouds them, and his ears become stopped, like the silence of the grave. When these things have come to pass, then he dies without memory of having lived.

"But if the Son of man learns where he has erred and returns to the way of nature, and if he lives in harmony with natural law, he will free himself from the fangs of darkness. Then abundant health and long life become his heritage, and he shall become very happy indeed, for the angels of sun, water, air, life, health, and joy will serve him all the days that he lives. Peace and prosperity shall follow those who live according to the law of life, for they are like the mighty mountains which rise to greet the heavenly stars."

Those around Jesus listened intently to everything he said, for his words were powerful, and he taught differently than the scribes and Pharisees. Even though the sun had begun to wane, causing the evening shadows to strengthen their hold over the dying day, the people still did not depart for their homes. Instead they continued to sit around him in silence. Finally one of them spoke, "Master, remain with us longer and teach us that we may be healed."

As the Master looked around these people whose trust had been placed in him, he felt great reverence. They would be the light of tomorrow's world, the strength of nations and the foundation for peace. Tonight they were his children, tomorrow they would be adults, living and dying for their noble causes, therefore he smiled at them with understanding and spoke again, his words coursing through their minds like liquid silver, "Seek always to live in harmony with the air which is all around us. It bounds in the forests and passes silently over the distant field, even as it rests within your bodies. Go and remove all your clothing, that your bodies may unite with the Angel of Air that you be made pure. Holy is the air which purifies all unclean things and makes sweet their smell. Learn to breathe long and deeply, and allow the air to flow within you, for no man can achieve atonement with God who has separated himself from the forces of nature.

"Honor your Heavenly Father, whose forward thrust has set all things in motion and brought forth the air which you breathe. Behold, in the vast universal empire which exists above and around us, lives the holy breath which gives you life. I say to you that, in the moment between your breathing in and your breathing out, is hidden the mysteries of creation.

"Know, you who have walked the ways of truth so long and bear the light, that the forces of nature are messengers of God, for they are within you and without you. We do not think of this when we breathe, for we breathe without thought, as do the sons of darkness who live without thought. But every time you petition the Angel of Air, your body is regenerated and you come closer and closer to the heavenly kingdoms which reside within your Heavenly Father.

"And when you have breathed deeply of the Angel of Air, cast yourselves into water and embrace the seas, the rivers, and the streams, and remember to stir the water with your body. As you do so, the Angel of Water will clean you within and without, and all that is unclean which remains with you shall be carried by the rivers to the sea. I tell you truly, holy is the force of water which makes the flowers bloom, turns the blossoms of a tree into fruit, and cures the illness of man. Each must be purified by water and truth. As your body bathes in the rivers and streams, so must your spirit bathe in the light of God.

"And if afterward there still remains any past uncleanness within you, seek the Angel of Sunlight. Remove your clothing and allow the sun to embrace all your body. And the sunlight shall cast out of your body all things which defiled it without and within. And that which is unclean shall depart from you, even as darkness of night fades before the brightness of day. Abide by these things I say to you and illness shall flee from you as night flees before the rising sun."

Finally the crescent moon rose over the mountains and rays of silver light danced in the waters of the river, and those who were with Jesus became joined as one man. Then they knelt in reverence and offered thanksgiving for the words of their master as he taught them in the ancient ways of their forefathers. After this Jesus said to them, "Peace be with you," and slipped away into the silence of the night.

As the months passed, the Master continued to teach in the areas between the Lake of Galilee and Jerusalem. As he walked along the deep valley of the Jordan River, with its curves and twists, he could see the hills of Galilee and Samaria, yet he never forgot the majesty of the great Himalayas which had once stood over him in shrouded mystery. Those years, now past, lived in the deep silence of his innermost thoughts. Few would ever know these things which Jesus held dear to him, for he was a person who gave, and his private world was as mysterious as the mighty mountains themselves. He was a master and the world of mastership could only be understood by those who pierced its iron doors.

The Jordan itself was from 90 to 100 feet across, rapid and often muddy. Its depth varied from three feet at some fords to ten or twelve feet. Over the 65-mile course the descent of the river averaged 14 feet a mile. It was said that to pass the Jordan was like crossing the Rubicon, and many of the most remarkable events in the history of Israel were associated with the fording of the Jordan: Joshua, who led Israel into the promised land; the parting by Elijah; and the escape of Elisha and David from the rebellious Absalom. As Jesus traversed the ancient land after the manner of his ancestors, he worked endlessly to build a foundation which would endure until mankind evolved beyond human existence.

Through the Master, the Holy Spirit wandered also, touching the hearts of those who sought the deeper truths and causing the blind to see. Jesus knew no separation from this ancient bearer of light, for they had dwelled as one since his birth. Neither did the memories of childhood weave their way into the pattern of his soul any longer. He had become an ageless grain of sand in the pages of eternity. His spirit would live forever in the hearts of those who sought to know him and abide by what he taught. Even from beyond the stars and from the kingdom of the immortals, his hand would reach out to guide those who sought mastership through his teachings. Through the work of his followers in a later age, his secret teachings would be liberated from their imprisonment and carried freely upon the winds of time, and God would finally descend to live on earth. For now, he was satisfied to walk upon the earth with sandaled feet, occasionally stirring up the dust before him.

Sometimes Jesus paused to rest in the solitude of the peaceful hills that he might be made anew, for he gave much and much was taken. Among those who came to him, many were not seeking the wisdom of his words, but rather merely to ask for a favor or to be healed. He understood their childlike way and granted them favors or performed an occasional miracle, that his greater purpose might be known. But for each of these he paid a price in the weakening of his body, even as those who were ill became strengthened from it. Sometimes he even experienced a temporary lessening in his consciousness, as others were thereby raised. For these things he sought no personal gratitude but requested only that all honor and glory be given to God, whose power flowed through him.

During these periods when Jesus went into seclusion to regenerate himself, he communed with the angels, both those who guided his earthly steps and those who restored power to the body, soul, and spirit. His greater rewards came as he sought the presence of the Heavenly Father, that his spirit might rise above the coarser vibrations of earth and dine at the hidden table of God. The life he observed around him was also precious to him; he understood the tiny souls of the plants and the little scurrying creatures of the desert.

One morning, just as the sun was rising over the rim of the earth, those who were purifying themselves by the river bank saw Jesus coming toward them from over the mountain. The brightness of the rising sun circled about his head, and when he at last arrived, he greeted them according to his custom, saying, "Peace be with you."

The people could not speak, but cast themselves down before him that they might touch the hem of his garment in recognition of their healings.

Jesus halted momentarily to touch one of them on the head who knelt before him, saying, "Give thanks not to me, but to your Heavenly Father. Go now and remain obedient to the laws of nature, that you may never again see disease. And allow the healing forces to remain your guardians."

Then another asked him, "Where should we go, Master, for you possess the words of eternal life? Can you not stay and speak to us concerning those things which bring us illness?"

Kindly Jesus answered him, saying, "Be it as you have asked," and then he sat down among them and taught.

"While a child is yet small, his place is with his mother and he must obey his mother. When the child is grown up, his father takes him to work by his side in the field, and the child comes back to his mother only when the hour of supper has come. His father teaches him, that he may become skilled in the works of a man. And when the father sees that his son understands his teaching and does his work well, he gives him all his possessions, that they may belong to his beloved son and his son may continue the father's work.

"Happy is that man who accepts the counsel of his mother and walks as she has taught. And a hundred times more happy is the man who walks also in the counsel of his father, for Moses said to you that you must honor your father and your mother. Now I say to you, honor your Earthly Mother that you may have health and long life upon earth, and honor your Heavenly Father, that you may find the path of immortality and walk in the Kingdom of Heaven forever.

"Your Heavenly Father is greater than those which are joined to you by seed and blood, and greater also is earth, which has nurtured you since its beginning. The Son of man is loved a hundred times more by God and earth than by his parents of blood and seed. These words which I speak to you come through the Holy Spirit of our Heavenly Father. There are none among you who can understand all that I speak, but you can understand those words which are spoken through a diseased and mortal body. Few are those who seek the light of life.

"If the blind lead the blind, both shall fall into the ditch, for a blind man leads others into illness and into death. I have been sent to you by the Father, to make the light shine upon the darkness. Just as the sun lightens the day, the light lightens the darkness, but darkness knows only itself and knows not the light. I have many things to say to you which you cannot yet understand. However, since it is easier for the Son of man to follow that which is visible to the eye, go and renew your body that you might perceive the light of God."

Two young men came seeking Jesus one day and saw him sitting among his followers by the bank of the river. Their hearts filled with hope when they heard his greeting, as they were desirous of asking him many questions. However, as they approached him they looked at him with great amazement, for no words came to their lips and no thoughts to their mind. Then, with great amusement, Jesus said to them, "I am here because you need me."

And one cried out, "Master, we do indeed; come and free us from our pains."

Then Jesus replied, speaking to them in parable: "You are like the prodigal son, who ate and drank for many years and dwelled among those who dwelled in insurrection and corruption. And it came to pass that all which his father gave him he frittered away and gambled without his father's knowledge. However, the money lenders continued to loan him money because they knew that his father was a very wealthy man and had always paid the debts of his son. The father often admonished him and suggested that he cease his constant intemperance and return to the fields that he might watch over the servants. Although the son promised him everything if the father would pay his old debts, the next day the son would turn again to the path of iniquitous ways.

"For more than seven years the son continued his riotous living. But, at last, his father lost patience and would no longer pay the money lenders for the debts of his son. 'If I continue always to pay,' he said, 'there will be no end to the sins of my son.' Then the money lenders, who felt that they had been deceived, took the son into slavery in their wrath and forced him to repay his debts by daily travail. This put an end to his lavish eating and intoxicating drink, and he was compelled to eat dry bread with only his tears for water. From morning to night he labored in the fields, until his body was wracked in anguish, and after three days he suffered so much from the heat and torment that he said to his master, 'I cannot work any more, for all of my limbs ache. How long will you continue to torture me?'

'Until the day when you pay men in full for all your debts,' the creditor cried, 'and when you have labored with your hands for seven years.'

"Then the son, with his limbs aching, went back in despair to the fields to continue his work. Already he could hardly stand upon his feet because of his weariness and his pain. When the seventh day came, the Sabbath day in which no man worked in the field, the son gathered the remnants of his strength and staggered to the house of his father. He cast himself down at his father's feet and said, 'Father, believe me for the last time and forgive me all my offenses against you. I swear to you that I will never again live in lawlessness, but will be your obedient son in all things. Father, look upon my sick limbs and harden not your heart.'

"Tears came into the father's eyes and he took his son in his arms, and said, 'Let us rejoice, for today a great joy is given me, because I have found again my beloved son who was lost.' He clothed his son with his choicest raiment and they made merry all day. On the morning of the morrow, he gave his son a bag of silver that he might pay his creditors all he owed them. In time the son repaid tenfold all that he had squandered and helped his father's vineyard to prosper. When his father saw this, he gave him all his possessions, after which the son also forgave all those who were indebted to him."

Looking down upon those who had come to be with him, Jesus said, "I speak to you in parables that you might understand the Kingdom of Heaven. Seven years of eating, drinking, and riotous living are the sins incurred by the soul as it passes through the seven cycles of necessity. The wicked creditor is Satan. The debts are diseases. The heavy labor is pain. The repentant son is yourselves, but payment of the debts occurs when you cast out the desires of wrong doing, and purify the body, the mind, and the soul, and sin no more. Silver represents the soul and the liberating power of the cosmic forces which emanate from the throne of God, and the father of the wayward son is none other than God. The field is the world, which is changed into the Kingdom of Heaven as the Sons of men work together.

"It is better that a son obey his father and keep watch over his father's servants in the field than become a debtor of the wicked creditor and toil and sweat in serfdom to repay all his debts. It is better, likewise, that the Sons of men obey the laws of their Heavenly Father and work together with His angels in His Kingdom, than to become the debtors of Satan, the lord of death and disease, and suffer with pain and sweat until they have repaid for all their misuse of natural and cosmic law. Great and many are your debts, and many years you have yielded to the enticements of the human world. Now you must repay them, and such payment is difficult and hard.

"Therefore, do not be impatient after the third day when you have raised the body, soul, and spirit like the repentant son, but wait for the seventh day —when God is resurrected in man; and then go with humble and obedient hearts before the face of your Heavenly Father, that he may forgive you your sins and all your past debts.

"Your Heavenly Father loves you without end, for he also allows you to pay in seven days (final phase of human evolution when human and divine become one) the debts of seven years. Those who owe the sins and diseases of seven years, but pay honestly and persevere till the seventh day, our Heavenly Father will forgive their debts of all the seven years."

"And if we have sinned for seven times seven years?" asked a sick man who suffered horribly.

"Even in that case, the Heavenly Father will forgive you all your debts in seven days," Jesus replied.

Those who had gathered about Jesus were amazed at his words and at his power. And they said, "Master, you are indeed God's messenger, and do know all secrets."

"You must become true Sons of God," Jesus answered, "that you may also partake in his power and in the knowledge of all secrets. It was said in olden times, 'Honor your Heavenly Father and your Earthly Mother, and do their commandments, that your days may be long upon the earth.' Afterward, this commandment was given, 'You shall not kill.' Since all life is given by God, let not man take it away, for from one Mother proceeds all that lives on earth.

"Therefore, he who kills, kills his brother, and from him the Earthly Mother will turn away. Learn therefore, the laws of God."

After this, the Master remained silent for a time and neither did those around him speak. They knew that his ways had brought them healing, although they could not fully understand the reasons why. He had forbidden meat to those who were seriously ill and this was difficult to accept. Meat had been an integral part of both sacrifice and diet since the time of their ancestor's ancient journeys. Now a new law was given to them by Jesus, saying that dead food brought death and illness.

Lost deeply in thought, it was some time before the people could open their mouths. Others turned against the Master because his ways meant surrender of some of their uttermost desires. Finally one of those present called out, "What am I to do, Master, if I see a wild beast rend my brother in the forest? Shall I let my brother perish? If I kill the wild beast shall I not transgress the law?"

Accepting the challenge of the question proffered in such a rude and arrogant way, in the manner of all such questions, Jesus replied, "It was said to them of old time: 'All beasts that move upon the earth, all the fish of the sea, and the fowl of the air are given into man's power.' Truly, of all creatures living upon earth, God created only man after his image. Wherefore, beasts are for man, and man for beasts. You do not, therefore, transgress the law if you kill the wild beast to save your brother's life. For man is more than the beast."

Some in the crowd which gathered around Jesus were so sick and tormented with pain that they had to crawl to him because they could no longer walk. Showing him their feet and the twisted and knotted bones, they said, "Neither air, water, nor sunshine has assuaged our pains. Even though we have cleansed ourselves with water and fasted and prayed and followed your words in all things, we are overcome with disease. Master, tell us what to do."

Looking closely at the arthritic conditions which besieged the bodies of those who lay helpless at his feet, the Master was still for a brief moment. Then drawing upon that wisdom which rested in him, he replied, "Your bones will be healed. Be not discouraged, but seek your cure from the earth, for thence were your bones taken and thither will they return."

Then he pointed to where the running water and the sun's heat had softened the earth by the edge of the stream and turned it into mud, saying, "Put your feet in the mire that they embrace it, and the living forces of the earth will draw all uncleanliness and disease from your bones. Your pains will disappear, the knots of your bones will vanish, and they will be straightened."

Upon hearing this, those who were diseased did as the Master had told them, for they knew that they would be healed. And it came to pass that those who were obedient to Jesus' instruction discovered life's hidden mysteries, revealed only to the children of the Law. Their quiet minds became disciplined instruments of contemplation and their bodies a finer vibration, less subject to heat and cold, pain and illness, old age and death. Their souls, no longer driven by heavy human passions, became capable of playing hide-and-seek with the ever-elusive God of their forefathers who ruled the unnumbered stars. Having found the pathway of the immortal, many did not stray again. To deviate from it would mean remaining bound to a world of darkness and unknowing. After this Jesus returned to Jerusalem.

During this time Pilate, Roman procurator of Judea (Lower Galilee) and a descendant of Pontii, had removed his army from Cesarea to Jerusalem to take up winter quarters. In doing so, he carried ensigns with Cesarea's effigies and brought them into the city. Since this was against Jewish law, it was natural that the Jews wished to rise up against him, particularly since he was the first one to bring such images into Jerusalem. He had accomplished this feat during the hours of darkness, without the knowledge of the people. As soon as the Jews discovered this, they went in multitudes to Cesarea to intercede with Pilate. Although they continued in their attempt to have the idols removed, Pilate refused their requests, and on the sixth day ordered his soldiers to have their weapons ready. When they petitioned him again, he gave a signal to his army to encompass them and threaten them with death. However, the people threw themselves on the ground and laid their necks bare, saying that they would take their deaths very willingly, rather than have the wisdom of their laws transgressed. The procurator was so deeply affected by this that he finally commanded the images to be carried out of Jerusalem and back to Cesarea.

It also occurred about this same time that Valerius Gratus, procurator of Judea prior to the appointment of Pontius Pilate, had given the office of high priest to one Joseph Caiaphas. Although Caiaphas had been given this high office in place of Annas, his father-in-law, Annas still possessed a great deal of influence and control in sacred matters. When the men heard rumors of the great miracles which were being performed by Jesus of Nazareth, plans were formulated to dispose of him. Already, there were dissidents gathering at the public places where the Master taught, and rumors of his possible arrest were spreading throughout the countryside.

Not all of the officials were against him, however, for some had been converted. Others heard of his miracles and requested help, among these Abgarus Uchama, who wrote the following letter regarding his illness to Jesus:

"Abgarus Uchama the toparch to Jesus the good Saviour that hath appeared in these parts of Jerusalem, greeting: I have heard concerning thee and thy cures, that they are done of thee without drugs or herbs: for, as the report goes, thou makest blind men to see again, lame to walk, and cleansest lepers, and castest out unclean spirits and devils, and those that are afflicted with long sickness thou healest, and raiseth the dead. And having heard all this of thee, I had determined one of two things, either that thou art God come down from heaven, and so doest these things, or art a Son of God that doest these things. Therefore now have I written and entreated thee to trouble thyself to come to me and heal the affliction which I have. For indeed I have heard that the Jews even murmur against thee and wish to do thee hurt. I have very little, but it is sufficient for us both.

Abgarus

Since the threat of his destiny weighed heavily upon him and there was still much to do before his death, Jesus felt that a journey to visit Abgarus at this time would impede the progress of those things now confronting him, so he replied, saying:

"Blessed are you who has believed in me, not having seen me. For it is written concerning me that they that have seen me shall not believe in me, and that they that have not seen me shall believe and live. But concerning that which you have written to me, to come to you; it must needs be that I fulfill all things for that which I was sent here, and after fulfilling them should then return to him that sent me. And when I am taken up, I will send you one of my disciples, to heal your affliction and give life to you and those that are with you.

Ecclesiastical History
(i.13) Translated by
Euseius from Syriac.

As the northeasterly winds blew across the bleak hills, now dry from months without rain, the land was in great turmoil and unrest. It was not a good time for political offenders, or those who took a stand against the gradual invasion of the political power of the Romans. Even so, this did not stop Jesus from teaching. If anything, he increased his efforts to prepare man for the Kingdom of God and to heal the sick. As he walked among the sick, he said to them, "Happy are those that persevere to the end, for the devils of Satan (illness, pain, and old age) write all your evil deeds in a book, in the book of your body and your spirit.

"No human makes an error, but that it is written in their souls. You may escape the laws made by man and kings, but none can escape the laws of God and nature. And when you have raised the veil of immortality you come before the face of God, and all which is written in your souls shall bear witness of you, both good and evil. If you then atone for those things written in your body and your spirit through good words, good thoughts, and good deeds, God and his angels shall forgive all your sins and prepare a place for you in the Kingdom of Heaven and make you ruler over many things on earth.

"If, afterward, you do not err, but pass your days in doing good deeds unto all men, then your good deeds shall fill the book of your body and spirit. No good deed remains unnoticed by God. From kings and governors you may wait in vain for your reward, but never do your good deeds want their reward from your Heavenly Father. Happy is he who can enter into the Kingdom of God, for he shall never see death."

And a great silence fell at Jesus' words. And those who were discouraged took new strength from the things he said and continued to fast and to pray.

One time Jesus spoke to those who gathered near him, saying, "I teach you only those laws which you can understand so that you may become men and follow the seven laws of the Son of man. Then shall the angels further reveal their ways, and God's Holy Spirit will descend upon you and lead you to his Law."

Then, as was often his habit, Jesus spoke in parable. "Be not like the foolish husbandman who sowed cooked and frozen and rotten seed in his ground. And the autumn came and his field bore nothing, and great was his distress. Be you instead like that husbandman who sowed living seed in his field and whose field yielded living ears of corn, repaying him hundredfold for the seeds which he had planted. It is better to live only by the fire of life and prepare not your meals with the fire of death, which kills your food, your bodies, and your souls also.

"The living angels of the living God serve only living men," he cautioned. "For God is the God of the living, not the God of the dead. Eat always from the table of God, the fruits of the trees, the grains and grasses of the fields, the milk of beasts, and the honey of bees; for everything else leads to the way of disease unto death. If all of your life you eat at the table of the Earthly Mother, you will never know want. And your days will be long upon earth, for this is pleasing in the eyes of the Lord."

After this Jesus discoursed on the importance of eating foods in their season, when they were fresh and consequently the most living. Since the Israelites divided their Sabbatical year according to

natural phenomena exclusively, combining both the solar and lunar year, the months began with the new moon. The first month
was fixed by the ripening of the earliest grain (barley). While the lunar month averaged 29 1/2 days, a year consisted of twelve months
of 30 and 29 days, alternately. Therefore, the first month of the
Hebrew ecclesiastical year was Abib or Nisan, which covered the
last half of March and the first half of April. This was also the
period of the spring equinox and melting snows of Lebanon, as well
as the celebration of the Feast of the Passover.

During Ijar (April-May), the Little Passover was celebrated by
those who were unable to participate in the earlier festival. Summer began as the south winds destroyed the vegetation across the
Jordan Valley. At this time the Israelites still harvested barley in
the lowlands, while the wheat and apricots ripened in the highlands. Therefore, Jesus instructed the people, saying: "From the
coming of the month of Ijar, eat barley; and from the month of
Sivan (May-June) eat wheat, the most perfect among all seed-bear-
ing herbs. And let your daily bread be made of wheat, that the Lord
may take care of your bodies.

"From Tammuz (June-July), eat the sour grape, that your body
may diminish (i.e., lose winter fat). In the month of Elul (August-
September), gather the grape that the juice may serve you as drink.

"In the month of Marcheshvan (October-November), gather the
sweet grape dried and sweetened by the sun, that your bodies may
increase (i.e., add body fat in preparation for colder weather), for
the angels of the Lord dwell in them.

"You should eat figs rich in juice in the months of Ab (July-
August), and Shebat (January-February), and what remains, let the
sun keep them for you. Eat them with the meat of almonds in the
months when the trees bear no fruit.

"And the herbs which come after rain, these eat in the month of
Thebet (December-January), that your blood may be cleansed of
that which is unclean.

"And in the same month begin to eat also the milk of your beasts
because for this did the Lord give the herbs of the field to all the
beasts which render milk, that they might with their milk feed
man.

"I tell you truly, happy are they that eat at the table of God, for
their lives shall be long upon earth, their health will blossom as
the fields of Lebanon, and their minds will be like unto the wind.
Eat not those foods brought from far countries, but eat always that
which your trees bear. Your God knows well what is needed for you,
and where and when. And he gives to all people of all kingdoms
food which is best for each.[2]

When Jesus completed his instructions concerning the months

and their corresponding foods, he said to those who had gathered near him, "The powerful forces of nature enter your body with the living food which is served you from the royal table of your Heavenly Father. And if you eat with the Angel of Air above you and the Angel of Water below you, then shall the Angel of Health bless you twice and you shall experience oneness with the living God. And chew all of your food well with your teeth, that it become as water and enter the holy stream of blood which flows through your body."

Although Jesus taught the people many things to prevent illness, he spoke to his disciples in private, saying, "See how the branches of the tree reach upward toward the Kingdom of Heaven, and see how the roots of the tree sink deep into the bosom of earth. Even so it is with man, for his soul, like the branches of the tree, reaches upward to his Heavenly Father, and the life in his body, like the roots of the tree, reaches far into the earth that it might live.

"You have sought to work in harmony with nature by day and sleep in the consciousness of your Heavenly Father by night. Now you are ready for the gift of tongues which shall allow you to draw the blinding glory of God and have dominion over all kingdoms. These words are not given to you lightly, for he who misuses any power becomes no more than a creature of darkness. Therefore, hear me well, for by communing with the forces of nature in the morning and with the powers of God by night you will become one with the Kingdoms of Heaven and earth, the oneness which has been destined from the beginning.

"Say these words, let them echo in that spirit which makes its abode in the heart of the soul, for words without thought, or power without action, are like a dead corpse which contains no life. Close your eyes, and say, 'I now enter the eternal and infinite world of God, which is without end. My spirit is one with God and my heart is in harmony with all mankind. I dedicate my soul, my mind, my heart, and my body to all that is good, after the manner of the great ones before, even Enoch.'"

As the disciples journeyed with Jesus he joined them in the early morning and sat with them in the evening, continuing to teach them things in secret which could not be taught to the multitudes. When they practiced the disciplines of those things he taught, they found that a certain unity existed between themselves and those forces which surrounded them. This transformation set them apart from the people. Even as the first faint glimmer of new birth fell upon them, their bodies began to regenerate with little effort, they knew not illness, the wild animals were stilled, and the poisonous creatures of the desert ignored them. Yet other things occurred also, for communion at sunrise brought the disciples a strength and oneness with God which few people had ever experienced, and wisdom began to penetrate their unbridled minds. During this awakening, the Master observed his disciples with the pleasure of a father, the kindness of a brother, and the power of a teacher. Yet, they did not often know this, for his pleasure over their progress was hidden beneath the controlled outer mask of one who knew there was yet much for them to learn.

One day, as the dew lay upon the tender plants, Jesus spoke to those who were with him concerning joy, "Go forth into the fields of flowers after the rains and give thanks to the Holy Mother of Earth for the sweet odor of blossoms; for a flower has no other purpose than to bring joy to the Son of man. Listen with new ears to the sound of the birds as they sing in the morning's dawn, and see the wonder of sunset with eyes not shadowed by the darkness of ignorance. These things have been given to you to make joyful your life on earth, and no one comes before the Heavenly Father whom the Angel of Joy has not touched. In joy did God create the earth, and in joy did the holy earth bring forth all life."

After these words he said, "God comes in the glory of dawn to wake you from your sleep. Therefore, obey his command and do not lie idle in your beds, for the miracle of life awaits you without. Work in the vineyards of the world all day with a happy heart and allow the power of love to flow from your heart. It is then you come to understand these things which I teach you. And when the sun is set, and your Heavenly Father brings you his most precious gift, sleep, then will his unseen angels teach you many things concerning the Kingdom of God which is without end."

Then the Master departed from them, saying, "Give to everyone your peace, even as I have given my peace to you. For my peace is of God. Peace be with you."

It so happened that Jesus was with his disciples in the Garden of Gethsemane when he said these things, and when he turned from them he moved off in the direction of Jerusalem. As soon as they realized where he was going they raised themselves up also and prepared to follow him. Soon the southeastern part of the city appeared, although the northern portions were still hidden by the slope of Olivet on the right. After this the road descended a slight declivity and the entire city was again hidden behind the ridge, then the path mounted again, climbing ruggedly until it reached a ledge of smooth rock. In that instant the entire City of David burst into view. Immediately below was the valley of the Kidron, here seen in its greatest depth as it joined the valley of Hinnom, giving the illusion that Jerusalem was a dark mirage rising from a deep abyss. When he reached the ledge, Jesus paused for a moment to observe the impressive panorama, and then he moved swiftly on, his disciples hastening lest they fall behind.

On arriving at the temple, Jesus situated himself and began to teach, and soon a number of people gathered around him, among these the usual scribes and Pharisees. The presence of these always produced a challenge, one which he found in no other part of Israel. They came not to listen, but to trap him, for they were deeply envious of the knowledge which flowed from his lips. Also they could not understand how he, the son of Joseph, born in their native land, could know those things which no man seemed to know except their lawgiver. On this particular occasion, one of the Pharisees asked, "Is it lawful for man to cast out his wife for any cause?"

Immediately Jesus realized that another snare had been set, for Moses had written in his commandments that one should not commit adultery. Now this man who stood mocking him sought to prove that he spoke against the law, but Jesus replied, "Have you not read that he who made them in the beginning made them male and female? For this cause shall man cleave to his wife and they shall become one flesh. Wherefore, they are no more two but one, and that which God has joined together, let not man part."

Yet the Pharisees were not satisfied and continued their questioning, "If what you say is true, why did Moses command the husband to give a letter of separation and then divorce his wife?"

At times like this, the Master's eyelids would drop slightly and he would look at his opponent as a master swordsman coming in for the kill. Circumventing the thrust, he answered with great skill, saying, "Moses, considering the hardness of your hearts, gave you permission to divorce your wives, but it was not so in the beginning. Now I am saying to you that he who leaves his wife without just cause and marries another commits adultery, and he who marries a woman who was cast out because she was an adulterer, also commits adultery."

Then one of the disciples, even more curious why this was so, inquired, "If there is so much difficulty between man and woman, is it worthwhile to marry?"

Greatly amused, Jesus answered, "This does not apply to every man, but to those whom it is given. There are eunuchs[3] who were so born from their mother's womb, and there are other eunuchs who either were made by man, or made themselves such for the Kingdom of Heaven. To him who can comprehend, these words are alone sufficient."

During this time the Sadducees also came to question Jesus concerning the law of marriage, asking with regard to Moses' teachings, "Teacher, Moses has told us, if a man dies without sons, let his brother take his wife and raise up offspring for his brother.

"Now there were among us seven brothers. The first married and died, and because he had no sons, he left his wife to his brother.

"Likewise the second, also the third, up to the seventh. And after them all, the woman also died. Therefore, at the resurrection, to which of these seven men will she be a wife, for they all married her?"

Again Jesus's eyes took on the look of knowing, and again he prepared to thrust the sword blade deep in his opponent's heart. They could never defeat him, for he had been assigned his task by a power greater than any who walked in darkness could ever possess. He was confident, yet without ego, delighted to thrust, yet mercy flowed also from the knife's sharp blade, and he replied, saying, "You err because you do not understand the scriptures, nor the power of God. For at the resurrection of the dead, men neither marry women, nor are women given to men in marriage, but they become like the angels of God in heaven."[4]

Now when the Pharisees heard that Jesus succeeded in silencing the Sadducees, they gathered together and selected one among them who knew the law to step forward and challenge him, asking, "Teacher, which is the greatest commandment in the law?"

Jesus said to him, "Love the Lord your God with all your heart and with all your soul and with all your might and all your mind.

This is the greatest and first commandment.

"And the second is like it, love your neighbor as yourself. On these two commandments stand the law and the prophets."

Then Jesus spoke to the people and to his disciples: "The scribes and the Pharisees sit in the chair of Moses. Therefore, whatever they tell you to obey, obey and do it, but do not do according to their works, for what they say and do are two different things.

"They bind heavy burdens and put them on men's shoulders, while they themselves are not willing to touch them, not even with their fingers."

Then Jesus departed from them, and as he traveled with the wind from town to town, his fame continued to spread throughout all of Israel. Although he knew that the world was not yet destined for peace, because those who knew the deeper mysteries of life were still few, he also knew that such a fortune was written in the soul of mankind. Time and again his ways came into conflict with those of the priesthood, whose members sought to do him harm. In spite of this, however, some still wanted to enter discipleship under him that they might come into the ways of those who followed him. On these he bestowed additional attention, but his tests were firm. Since he would have to pay a price for every disciple he accepted, by raising them up, his ways were for the obedient. To each of those who came seeking the narrow gate, he said, "He that loves his father or mother more than me is not worthy of me, and he who does not take up his cross and follow after me is not worthy of me. Everyone who has forsaken house, or brethren, or sisters, or father, or mother, or wife, or children, or land, for my name's sake, shall receive hundredfold and shall inherit the Kingdom of Heaven. Therefore, if any man will come after me, let him deny himself and take up his cross and follow me, for whosoever will lose his life for my sake shall inherit all things."

Many turned away from Jesus when he said these things, because their ties with the human world were yet strong. Yet he was patient with them, for he knew that the chains of earth cast a shadow of darkness and unknowing over their eyes, and they were blind. Late one day, while teaching among his elect, Jesus said, "Follow the example of the angels of the Heavenly Father and of the Earthly Mother, who work day and night without ceasing within the Kingdoms of Heaven and Earth. Receive also into yourself the strongest of God's angels, the Angel of Work, and together build the Kingdom of God.

"Follow the example of running water, the wind as it blows, the growing plants and trees, the beasts as they run and gambol, the waning and waxing moon, the stars as they come and go; all these move, change, and perform their labors. For all which has life moves, and only that which is dead is still. I tell you truly, God is the God of the living, and Satan that of the dead.

"Serve, therefore, the living God, that the eternal movement of life may sustain you, and you may escape the eternal stillness of death (those who are bound to matter). For eternal joy abounds in the living Kingdom of God.

"Be, therefore, true sons of your Earthly Mother and of your Heavenly Father and become not slaves to that which destroys. Then your Earthly Mother and Heavenly Father will send their angels to teach, to love, and to serve you. And their angels will write the commandment of God in your mind, your heart, and in your hands, that you may know, feel, and do God's commandments.

"And pray every day to your Heavenly Father and to your Earthly Mother so that your soul may become as perfect as your Heavenly Father's Holy Spirit is perfect, and that your body may become as perfect as the body of your Earthly Mother is perfect."

Then Jesus seemed to disappear into the dancing shadows which separated night from day. The elect were hushed as the crescent moon which governs the ebb and flow of the seas rose above the distant hills. As both men and creatures slept in accordance with the laws of nature, the elect also closed their eyes in peaceful surrender to the sweetness of rest. But unseen, the Holy Spirit danced in the shadows created on the higher ridges of the distant hills. He swayed with the wind, leapt in the brooks, and sang with the birds, for he alone was free for all time from the chains of limitation and misunderstanding. Playing hide-and-seek with the moon while Jesus slept, he moved without ceasing, keeping time with the ever changing movement of cosmic order. At dawn he would return to live in the flesh, as he and the Master roamed earth together, raising the dead and helping the blind to see. But for now he flowed at one with God, while the Harp of Destiny continued to sound its rhythm among the stars.

1. This ability to merge the finite mind into the infinite signifies union with God and has been experienced by many great people. However, it is recognized more fully by the Christian world as that state which was achieved by Moses on Mt. Sinai. In that it is a state which will be experienced by all people, it is natural that some of the disciples reached it. Among these was John the Beloved, who outlined the precise details of the transformation in his *Revelation*.

2. The Law of Harmonics, or similarities, should be stressed here, for it applies to the food which we consume. If one does not fully understand this principle, it is then difficult to comprehend why Jesus taught in the foregoing manner. Each food has its own cell frequency, or vibration, and is thus connected or attuned to all things of similar nature. For example, the cells of all carrots are of common frequency. Without such similarities and differences, a carrot would not be a carrot, and a tomato would not be different from a carrot. If, therefore, a person consumes a tomato, the digested aspect of the tomato in his body will correspond by vibration to all living tomatoes. In this manner that which is without will be drawn to that which is within. Thus, if many different foods are eaten at one meal, a war can ensue within the body because there is a lack of harmony.

3. Jesus spoke in parable, for the word eunuch refers to the barbaric practice of castration. Using this term more in the context of circumcision, he indicated the separation of man from God, for some of those who served God preferred celibacy to conjugal love. Although some of the disciples were married, others, such as John the Beloved, chose to channel their efforts exclusively toward serving as co-creators to God.

4. These scriptures bring to light the hidden law pertaining to the resurrection of man. This concerns the holy union between God and man, by which the human nature is united with its Christ counterpart and returned to its heavenly estate. Once this union has been consummated, man is no longer man and woman is no longer woman. Therefore, human marriages are reflections of this final ascent and are binding only on earth.

Kingdom of the Heavenly Father   Burrows (cc)

He is covered with Light as with a garment. He stretches out the heavens like a curtain. He makes the clouds His chariot, and he walks upon the wings of the wind. He sends the springs into the valleys and His breath is in the mighty trees.

Gospel of Peace
Vatican MS./Szekely
Section II, ch. XIII 8: 12-13
Psalms 104: 2

CHAPTER VI

KINGDOM OF THE HEAVENLY FATHER

Three are the dwellings of the Son of man, and no one may come before the face of God who knows not the Angel of Peace in each of the three. These are his body, his thoughts, and his feelings. When the Angel of Wisdom guides his thoughts, when the Angel of Love purifies his feelings, and when the deeds of his body reflect love and wisdom, then does the Angel of Peace guide him unfailing to the throne of his Heavenly Father.

Gospel of Peace
Vatican MS./Szekekly
Section II, ch. XIII: 14

s the grains of sand containing Jesus' destiny fell, he persevered with his work. For the most part, his travels, took him from Engedi to Capernaum, encompassing the territories of Judea, Samaria, and Galilee. During the few months before his recorded last and triumphal entry into Jerusalem, he became more acutely aware that his life was nearing its close and that little time remained. However, he spoke of it lightly, lest his disciples become sorrowed. On the other hand he still wanted them to listen to his words carefully, for the continuation of his work to build the Kingdom of Heaven on earth would have to be left in their hands.

By this time his mastership, as it would be remembered, had been completed by the events of his life. He was of truthful countenance, possessed a high-minded and freedom-loving nature, and he had a tendency to overrule traditional domination. Neither rich nor poor by material standards, Jesus had the most remarkable mind in all of Israel, as well as an ability to speak several languages fluently, some of which he had learned during his travels. Possessing total integrity, he did not experience any separation between the two natures inherent in all men (human and divine), while his intuitive powers were so strongly developed that he did not distinguish between thinking and knowing. At the same time, he remained a sober seeker of even greater truths and was always able to prove his words by reference to natural law. He showed no favoritism among those who came to learn, for he treated all people kindly and equally. For physical exercise, he swam along the shores of Galilee, climbed the nearby hills, and walked great distances.

One day in the month of Elul (August-September), during the celebration feast of the restoration of the walls of Jerusalem by Nehemiah, Jesus came again to his disciples. The heat across Israel was still intense, and while there was much lightning, there was very little rain. The wind blew from the northeast, and in the distant fields, which were almost transparent in the shimmering haze, the harvesting of the dourra and maize had started. But even as the Israelites sweltered from their labors, fields of cotton stood white headed against the sun, and pomegranates began their seasonal change to ruby red. As Jesus approached his disciples, wearing his usual white robe, he too looked like a stark mirage against the shimmering landscape. However, when he reached those who were seated in the shade of the trees, he sat down among them and carefully crossed his legs, saying, "I will make the deep and mysterious things which are hidden from the eyes of darkness known to you. Truly, all things exist by God and there is no power beside Him. Turn your hearts toward Him that you might walk the true path where His presence dwells."

Then Thomas, who was seated with the group on this day, asked Jesus, "How, then, may we bring peace to our brothers, Master? We would that all mankind walk in harmony."

The Master felt great tenderness as he looked at Thomas, for he knew the fate of each of his disciples. This one who now sat near him would die in the faraway land where he, Jesus, had witnessed the splendor of the great mountains. Such a short time to comfort them, he thought, but he finally answered, "Only he who is at peace with himself can shed the light of peace on others, for the winds of a storm trouble the waters of the river and only the stillness that follows can calm them once again. Achieve, therefore, inner peace, for then your peace will be as a fountain that replenishes itself with the giving. The more you give, so the more will be given, for such is the law.

"Three are the dwellings of the Son of man, and no one may come before the face of God who knows not peace in each of the three. These are his body, his thoughts, and his feelings. When wisdom guides his thoughts, when love purifies his feelings, and the deeds of his body reflect both love and wisdom, then do his peaceful ways guide him unfailingly to the throne of his Heavenly Father.

"It is well that you ask concerning peace, for peace is what the world yearns for most. It is the lack of peace that troubles kingdoms, even when they are not at war. For violence and warfare can reign in a kingdom, even when sounds of clashing swords are not heard. Though no armies march one against the other, there is still no peace when the Sons of men walk not with God.

"Many are those who do not know peace, for they are at war with their own bodies; they are at war with their own thoughts; they have no peace with their fathers, their mothers, their children; and they have no peace with their friends and neighbors. Neither do they know the beauty of the teachings of the wise ones, for they do not labor through the day in the kingdom of their Earthly Mother; nor do they sleep at night in the arms of their Heavenly Father."

When these words had been spoken, the Master sat silent for a time and gazed quietly over the land he knew so well. He enjoyed such interludes, for he perceived a perfection in all living things and desired that his disciples do likewise. Those who were seated waited patiently for him to continue, for they had learned that they should not speak during his discourses unless he first spoke to them. After a brief time, he returned to them from his unknown world and spoke again, saying, "After this you must seek peace with others who dwell on earth, even with the Pharisees and priests, even with the beggars and homeless, and even with kings and governors. All of these are the Sons of men, whose souls rest in the heart of God, whatever be their place in life, whether their eyes have been opened to the light of the Heavenly Father, or whether they walk in darkness and ignorance. Although the law of men often punishes the innocent and protects the undeserving, the Holy Law, which abides in the spiritual nature of all beings, is without flaw, and each receives accordingly. Therefore, seek peace with those who walk on earth, and let it be known to those who follow me that we have abided in the Holy Law since the time of Enoch of old, and before.

"Blessed are those who build the Kingdom of Heaven on earth, for they shall come to dwell in both worlds. However, each must follow the Law of the Brotherhood (those who work for the good of mankind) and work together, even though each follows his own path and worships God after the manner of his own heart. There are many diverse flowers in the infinite garden, and who can say that one is more beautiful than another, or that one is greater than another? Though men may be of different complexion, yet do they all toil upon one earth, and seek the same God.

"There shall be no peace among nations until there be one Garden of the Brotherhood covering the earth. Therefore, you must gather with your brothers and then go forth to teach the mysteries of heaven and earth to those who will listen. Those who have found peace with themselves and with earth have made themselves co-creators with God."

After this Jesus departed from them that he might dine at the home of his family. As his disciples watched his figure diminish against the horizon, they remembered the wonders they had experienced with him. Also, they remembered their chastisements, their lessons, and the common thread which bound them. Occasionally, the path became difficult for them, because the purification of the body and soul caused that which was less in them to run undisciplined and unbridled like a wild animal. This brought with it darkness and discouragement. Even when these times fell upon the disciples, Jesus encouraged them, saying, "The Son of man must seek peace with the Kingdom of his Heavenly Father. For truly the Son of man is born of his father by seed and his mother by the body, that he may find his true inheritance and know that he is the son of a king. God is the Law which fashioned the stars, the sun, the light and the darkness, and that divinity within our souls. Everywhere is He, and there is nowhere He is not.

"All which is in our understanding and all we know not, all is governed by the Law. The falling of leaves, the flow of rivers, the music of the insects at night, all these are ruled by the Law. There are many mansions in heaven's kingdom, and many are the hidden things you cannot know yet. Truly, the domain of God is so vast that no man can know its limits, for there are none. Yet the whole of his kingdom may be found in the smallest drop of dew on a flower, or in the scent of newly cut fields under the sun. Truly, there are no words to describe the Kingdom of Heaven."

When the disciples heard these things, they were heightened again and the clouds of darkness passed like a storm across the tumultuous sea. When Jesus saw that their discouragement had passed, he began the disciplines once more, that their weakness be made strong. He knew they had many things to bear, including the pangs of death, and he would be there to comfort them only in spirit. During his most demanding moments, he wove a strong net to keep those who loved him from sinking into the unknown marshes of the future.

After a time, Jesus departed from Galilee and went into Samaria to teach in the settlements near the rocky peaks of Mt. Ebal and Mt. Gerizim. There were three cities—Samaria, Shechem and Sychar—and all were beautifully situated in the wilderness of the hill country. As Samaria stood four miles above the rolling hills, Shechem (the village of Nablus) slept in the peaceful Mabartha Valley. About a mile from the latter was Sychar, the nearest village to Jacob's Well where Jesus had met the Samaritan woman.

Although Jesus went to and from the three cities, and even as far as Bethany, to the home of Lazarus and his sisters, he did not go to the Temple of Jerusalem, because there was grave danger that he would be taken before it was time. It came to pass that during one of his discourses a young man approached him, asking, "O good teacher, what is the best thing that I can do to achieve eternal life?"

When people came to him in this manner, the Master sent a deep and penetrating gaze into the very heart of their souls. There he could discern the reason and pattern of life progression. With such discernment and insight he chose his disciples, and because of this ability, he was able to afford wise counsel to those who were in need. Such a power, when used in the hands of the wise, was as strong as those of healing and prophecy, for no human being could deceive another. Although a mouth could speak with euphonious words, the words were only as true as the goodness of the soul. When one claimed to love, but their nature was filled with animosity and hatred, the shadow of this truth overruled the spoken word. Thus, as he pierced the heart of him who now stood before him, Jesus spoke, asking, "Why do you call me good? There is not one who is good except God. However, if you would find the key to eternal life, you must obey the commandments."

"And what commandments are these?" the youth questioned.

"They are the Laws of Moses," Jesus answered, "You shall not commit adultery, you shall not steal, and you shall not bear false testimony against another. After this, honor your father, your mother, and your neighbor as yourself."

"But, Master," the young man replied, "I have obeyed all of these from my boyhood, and yet I walk in darkness. What other things must I do to break the barriers of death?"

Still half studying and half analyzing the young man's countenance, Jesus became grave, for many were called to enter the narrow gateway to eternal life and few were chosen. Speaking kindly, he said, "If you wish to learn the mysteries of eternal life, go and sell all your possessions and give them to the poor. Then you will have a treasure in heaven. When you have done this, come and follow me."

Sorrowfully the young man shook his head and walked away, for he had great possessions.

Turning to his disciples, Jesus said, "It is very difficult for a rich man to enter into the Kingdom of Heaven, for his attachments in human life bind him to earthly things. I tell you truly, it is easier for a rope to go through the eye of a needle than for a rich man to enter the Kingdom of Heaven."

When the disciples heard this, they were exceedingly astonished and James, Jesus' cousin, asked, "Who then can be saved?"

Gazing at his disciple intently, a familiar ripple of merriment danced across Jesus' heart, although he did not allow this to touch his lips as he answered, "It is impossible for people to raise to such heights alone, but as God dwells in all mankind, everything is possible."

Then Peter spoke to him with some agitation, "Behold, we have left everything and followed you; what will we have?"

Shaking his head, surprised that his disciples yet sought personal gain, Jesus answered, "In the new world, when the Son of man has brought forth his divine glory, you who have followed me and accomplished this great work shall also sit in the seat of mastership and shall judge.

"Every person who leaves houses, or brothers and sisters, or father and mother, or spouses and children, or fields, for my namesake, shall receive back hundredfold all that which they have given. They shall know no more darkness, nor have any further interruption of life because of death. In spite of this, many of those who speak first in my name shall be last, for they do not understand those things I teach in secret. But many who come at the end of time shall understand what I say in secret and shall come first, for they will have passed through the resurrection of the dead."

After saying these words, Jesus left them, his mind in a place which they could not yet enter, while his eyes seemed to pierce a world too far away for them to follow. His feet made no noise upon the ground as he disappeared, and soon he faded from their vision, like the mirages of the distant wilderness.

Then the rains began their descent upon the land, and the Feast of the Trumpets,[1] celebrating the second advent of man, passed. The soil, which was hardened and cracked by the long summer, drew moisture like a dry sponge. This was a period of transformation; for evaporating within its temporal nature, the water rose as mist toward heaven. Later it returned to earth, according to its predetermined nature. Occasionally, a rainbow arched from land's end to land's end and confirmed the covenant God had made with Noah.

During the late fall, the Master returned to his beloved Capernaum and to the small synagogue which overlooked the sparkling waters of the Sea of Galilee. By this time most of the vegetation had disappeared and the moon was on the wane. The wind blew from the north-northwest and northeast much of the time, although an occasional day of fair weather occurred amid the early rains. It was the last winter Jesus would spend in his beloved homeland. In spite of this, he was able to remove his thoughts from death and give his attention to the living. This was not too difficult, for there was a sense of inner joy over the work he was doing. If he thought about the moment of departure from the human world, he thought also of its continuation in worlds unknown by man and the temporal existence of all matter. As the waters of the sea glistened in the fall light, turning silver beneath the clouds, he saw only the majesty of the future. Here, not far from the spot where the fast running waters of the Jordan poured into the lake, amid eucalyptus bushes and gentle slopes, he continued to impart a heritage of rich wisdom to those who shared their lives with him.

Most of the disciples were with him this final year, and as they gathered near he continued to temper that part of them which was still lesser. Seating himself in their midst one afternoon, he said, "They are blessed who seek peace with the knowledge of the ages before them, for the Holy Scrolls contain a treasure a hundred times greater than gold and fine jewels. They are more precious because they contain all the wisdom which God has passed down to the Sons of Light. They came to us through Enoch of old, and even before him, for the path of wisdom has existed since the beginning. This is our inheritance.

"Through study of the teachings of ageless wisdom, we come to know God, for the great ones saw him face to face, and when we study the Holy Scrolls we touch the feet of God. When we see with the eyes of wisdom and hear the ageless truths of the Holy Scrolls with understanding, we must go among the Sons of men and teach them. Those who jealously hide this holy knowledge, pretending that it belongs only to them, become like one who finds a spring high in the mountains and rather than let it flow into the valley to quench the thirst of man and beast, buries it under rocks and dirt, thereby robbing himself of water, as well.

"Go among those who war in darkness and instruct them in the Holy Laws, that they might thereby save themselves and also enter into the Heavenly Kingdom. But, tell them in words they understand and in parables which reflect nature, for noble desire can live only in the awakened heart. He is blessed who reads the Book of the Law, for he shall be as a candle in the dark of night and an island of truth in the rampaging sea of falsehood. The written words which come from God are a reflection of the Heavenly Sea, even as the bright stars reflect the face of Heaven, and as the words of the ancient ones are etched with the hand of God on the Holy Scrolls, so is the Law engraved upon the hearts of the faithful who study them.

"It was said of old that in the beginning there were giants on earth and mighty men of renown. Thus, the holy teachings must be preserved by the Children of Light, lest we become again as beasts, and find not the Kingdom of Heaven which rests within and around us. Through the written word, you will find the unwritten Law which lives in your spirit and flows like a spring from the secret depths of earth. This written Law is the instrument by which the unwritten Law is understood, as a mute branch of a tree becomes a singing flute in the hands of the shepherd.

"There are many who would prefer to stay in the tranquil valley of ignorance, where children play and butterflies dance in the sun for their short hour of life. But no man can remain there long, and ahead of him rise the somber mountains of learning. Many are called and few are chosen, for many fear to cross, and many have fallen bruised and bleeding, from the steep and rugged slopes. Faith is the guide over the gaping chasm and perseverance the foothold in the jagged rocks. Beyond the icy peaks of struggle lies the peace and beauty of the Infinite Garden of Knowledge, where the meaning of the Law is made known to the Children of Light. Here in the center of its forest stands the Tree of Life."

After this Jesus withdrew from his disciples, again entering into communion with worlds few people ever saw. Here he was administered to by the higher angelic regions; these were also, in part, the source of his power and his miracles. Like a great pianist, he touched the keyboard of creation with dexterity and accuracy. To the poor he brought hope, to the sick, wellness, and to those who sought knowledge he poured forth the mysteries of all that was hidden. Even so, he knew that some of the seed would fall on fertile ground, and that in ages yet to follow others would come to master the cosmic chess board and strike the same notes.

The days passed and the trees became bare, even as the plains and deserts became green pastures. The snows fell upon the mountains of Lebanon, and the time rapidly approached for the Feast of Dedication. During this period, Jesus spent much of his time in Galilee. From Nazareth to Magdala, from Philoteria to Capernaum and Bethsaida, he healed the sick, gave comfort to those in poverty, and strength when the burden of human life bowed the spirits of those who walked in darkness. While many of the scribes, Pharisees, and Priesthood continued to develop even greater hatred and animosity toward him, the people loved him. He was brother and sister, friend and confidant, teacher and master, father and mother, to all those who came and loved him. However, to his disciples he was even more. He was the reflection and tangible evidence of God.

One day after Jesus had withdrawn from the multitude that he might administer again to his disciples in private, he brought forth secret teachings pertaining to the angelology of the Tree of Life. As he did so, he asked that the disciples reveal these mysteries to no one, lest they be cleaved by the people as a wild animal rends a carcass. When he mentioned the great and mighty forces which were administered by the powerful will of God, Philip asked him, "Master, all men can see the light of the sun and feel the water which flows from rivers and springs. They can even see the golden wheat bowing to the winds, or see the fruit of the tree change color, but these forces are visible. However, the forces of God are not visible, and we cannot touch them, smell them, or feel them. How then is it possible for us to speak to them?"

Boldly the morning sun touched the auburn hair of the man from Galilee, and as he stood in its rays it was as though time was suspended. Finally he answered, "Do you not yet know that earth and all that dwells therein is but a reflection of the Kingdom of God? As you are carefully tended by your mother during your youth, you grow into a man, and leave the innermost dwelling of the home that you might work in your father's fields. It is the same with earth and God, for the Earthly Mother guides your steps toward Him who is your Heavenly Father and all His hosts, that you may know your true home and become true Sons of God.

"While we are children, we can see the rays of the sun, but we cannot understand the power that created it, any more than we can see the love which springs from the flowing brook. Nor can a child see the great hand which scattered the stars throughout the universe. Only through communion with these great and mighty cosmic forces, can we see the unseen, and hear that which is not spoken.

"The first communion is with power, for creation was naught until there was power, the same power which flows through a man in his fields and a fisherman at sea. I tell you truly, God did order a path for each of us. There is no power save that from the Heavenly Father. All else is but a dream of dust, a cloud passing over the face of the sun, and there is no man who has power over the spirit; neither has he power in the day of death. Only that power which comes from God can carry us out from the city of death's worldly ways and unknowing.

"As there is no life on earth without the sun, so there is no life of the spirit without the Angel of Power. What you think and what you feel, they are like the dead scriptures, which are only words on a page, or the dead speech of dead men. However, a man of Light will not only think, will not only feel, but will also do, and his acts will fulfill his thoughts and feelings, as the golden fruit of summer gives meaning to the green leaves of spring.

"The second communion is with the Angel of Love, whose healing waters flow in a never-ending stream from the Sea of Eternity. Let us love one another, for love is of God, and everyone who loves is born of the Heavenly Order and knows the angels. Without love, a man's heart is parched and sterile, and his words are empty as a hollow tomb. Loving words, on the other hand, are sweet to the soul and bring unmeasured joy, for it is like a deep sea and the kiss of dawn. It was said in ancient days to love your Heavenly Father with all your heart, and with all your mind, and with all your deeds.

"If any man says, 'I love the Heavenly Father, but hate my brother,' then he is like a parched desert which has had no rain, for he who does not love his brothers whom he has seen, cannot love God whom he has not seen. You shall know those who walk the path of good by their fruit, for these shall love the Heavenly Father, also their brothers, and they shall keep the Holy Law. Every night when the stars gambol in the heavens and the moon sends its soft rays over the darkened land, those who seek the Kingdom of Heaven should bathe in the holy stream of love, that the Angel of Love may immerse the Sons of men with kind deeds and gentle words.

"During the daylight hours, our feet are on the ground and we have no wings with which to fly. However, our spirits are not tied to the earth, and with the arrival of night we overcome our attachment to earth and join that which is eternal. I tell you truly, the Son of man is more than he seems, and only with the eyes of the spirit can we see those golden threads which link us to life everywhere."

After this Jesus departed with his disciples and went to the home of his aunt, where his mother and Mary Magdalene waited to tend him. As was the usual custom, everyone gathered around the Master after the simple repast, hoping that he would again teach and tell them of strange and wonderful things. Sometimes during such periods he talked of his travels, other times he spoke concerning Rome's influence on Israel, and occasionally he just remained silent, basking in the gentle care of loving people. On this evening, as night fell upon them and the lamp caused flickering shadows to dance on the wall, he was of serious nature. For a moment he paused and looked with deep affection upon those who sat with him, even as the fleeting shadows of somberness echoed within his mind. Finally he spoke to them, saying, "The Son of man must seek peace with his own thoughts that the ways of wisdom may guide him. Truly, there is no greater power in heaven and earth than the thoughts of the Son of man. Though unseen by the eyes of the body, each thought has mighty strength, even such strength as can shake the heavens. The power of thought is not given to any other creature on earth, for all beasts that crawl and birds that fly love not of their own thinking, but of the one Law that governs all. Only the Sons of men have been given the power of thought, even thoughts which can break the bonds of death. Do not think because it cannot be seen that thought has no power. The lightning that cleaves the mighty oak, or the quaking tears that open the mighty earth, these are as the play of children compared with the power of thought.

"Each thought of darkness, whether it be of malice, or anger, or vengeance, wreaks destruction like a fire which sweeps through dry kindling under a windless sky. But man does not see its carnage, nor does he hear the piteous cries of his victim, for he is blind to the world of spirit.

"But when this power is guided by Holy Wisdom, then the thoughts of the Son of man lead him, and he shall build a heavenly kingdom on earth; then the thoughts of men shall uplift all souls, as the rushing stream revives your body in the summer heat.

"When a fledgling bird first tries to fly, his wings cannot support him and he falls again and again to earth. But he continues to try and one day he soars aloft, leaving earth and his nest far behind. So it is with the thoughts of men.

"The day will come when man's thoughts will overcome death and soar to everlasting life, to a world he now only dreams of. When man is guided by Holy Wisdom he builds a bridge to God."

When the Master had finished saying these things, he sat quietly and a great stillness stole over his disciples, for no one wished to break the spell of his words. The shadows of early evening played upon the distant river, still and silvery as glass, and in the darkening sky the crescent moon cast its subtle light upon the land. Then the great peace of the Heavenly Father descended over them.

After a time Jesus opened his eyes and looked over the still heads of his followers. During his years of Essene training, he had studied the deep mysteries pertaining to merger with the holy streams of life, sound, and light, and now he spoke of this softly, for the darkness of night had completed its pursuit of day, and merger with the Holy Stream of Light was the most sacred of all teachings. "When darkness overshadows the light of day and all creatures close their eyes, then shall you also sleep that your spirit may join the unknown angels of the Heavenly Father. In the moments before sleep think of the bright and glorious stars which contain many deep and unknown mysteries of life not yet discovered. Your thoughts just before sleep are like the bow of the skillful archer, and you dwell in that land of your dreams until the hours of night are spent. Allow your thoughts then to be with the stars, for the stars are light, and the Heavenly Father is light, even brighter by a thousand times than the brightness of a thousand suns.

"Therefore, unfold your wings of light and in the eye of your thought, soar with the stars into the furthest reaches of heaven where untold suns blaze with light and you shall become one with it. This Holy Stream will carry you to the endless Kingdom of the Heavenly Father, there blending into the Eternal Sea of Light which gives birth to all creation."

Then Jesus rose quietly, leaving those he loved in the shadows of the dying embers of the fire, their eyes closed, and their faces radiant from his presence. They did not see his tender smile, or feel the gentleness of his love, as he retired for the night.

Endless Light   Burrows (cc)

And soar into the paths of the stars, the moon, the sun and the
endless Light, which move around their revolving circle forever.

Gospel of Peace
Vatican MS./Szekely
Section II, ch. XI: 28

On the following morning, Jesus took his disciples and departed from Galilee. Those who had joined their families in Jerusalem would await him there. Neither his mother nor Mary Magdalene came to attend him. They would wait for his return and then travel with him to Jerusalem for the Feast of the Passover. Because winter had descended on the land and the north winds were very penetrating, Jesus decided to journey along the inland route through Samaria where he knew they would be given shelter according to their needs.

During this time, Upper Galilee was still under the authority of Herod the Tetrarch, the younger brother of Archaelus. Sly and ambitious, he was intriguing with a Roman officer of the army named Sejanus and confederating with the King of Parthia against the Roman empire. This was creating great unrest among the people, which led to frequent uprisings. These acts of defiance, in turn, produced a constant fear among the sympathizers of Herod, as well as those politically appointed to the council of the Sanhedrin, and greatly increased the danger for Jesus. His many followers attracted much attention, and in the eyes of the authorities, his popularity was construed as sedition.

As winter grasped the countryside in its cooler hands, Jesus spent many days in seclusion with his followers. When the rains increased and the seasons changed into deep winter, it became necessary for him to seek frequent shelter. During this period, he spent a great deal of time back in Ephraim, the land which once belonged to the second son of Joseph by Asenath, daughter of Potipherah. Symbolically, it was a fitting place for them to gather, for it lay in the wilderness northeast of Jerusalem, near the center of Palestine, in an area about 40 miles from east to west and varying from 6 to 25 miles from north to south. Even the gold tribal standard of the descendents of Ephraim, bearing a head of a calf signifying sacrifice, seemed to boldly declare the fulfillment of the prophecy Moses made on Mt. Hor.

Occasionally, the Master also traveled to the city of Samaria, which was separated from Ephraim by the Kanah River. Nearby stood the historical Mt. Ebol and in a distance lay the Plains of Sharon, part of the coastal plain of Palestine extending from Joppa to Mount Carmel. Since Samaria rested between Nazareth and Jerusalem, it offered a central location, thereby enabling Jesus to journey easily in any direction. Standing upon a hill about 300 feet high, the city rested in a wide basin which extended from the city to the coast. Surrounded by mountains on three sides, Samaria offered a great view of the west. The broad vale was visible for eight miles, then a low range of hills, and over them the sea about 23 miles away. This particular period in Jesus' life was to earn him the title *Rose of Sharon,* after the fragrant pink Rosa Phenicia growing along the coast and in the mountains. Later, many who followed his teachings would elect to remove the symbol of the crucified man on a cross and replace it with the full-blown rose, to symbolize the future birth of the Christ in all mankind.

And it came to pass that, in the year of 26 A.D. as the end of winter approached, Jesus returned to Capernaum for a brief sojourn. The Feast of the Passover was very near, and the disciples were being prepared to relinquish their beloved teacher to a greater realm, that even a greater work could be accomplished. As they were traveling through Galilee, Jesus said to them, "This body which has been born of woman will soon be delivered into the hands of men and I will be killed. Then it shall come to pass that these three worlds consisting of mortal, soul, and spirit shall be raised and united in the one world which is eternal, and I shall dwell thereafter in the Kingdom of Heaven."

After they arrived on the shores of Galilee, Jesus retired to the house of Simon the Canaanite that he and his disciples might dine. While he was there some of the men who collected silver coins for head tax came to Peter and asked him, "Would your Master give his tax coins?"

"Yes," Peter replied, and turning away from them he entered the house where they were staying. He found to his surprise that Jesus already anticipated the reason for his approach, for he asked, "What do you think, Peter? From whom do those who rule over earthly things collect their duties and taxes, from their own sons or from strangers?"

For a moment Peter paused. He had all too often been trapped by the Master, and he knew that this was one of those times when Jesus was as the cat which toyed with the mouse. However, he finally answered, saying, "From strangers, for no father collects taxes from his children."

"Then," Jesus remarked, "the sons are free."

After this, not wishing to offend those who received their living by collecting taxes, he said to Peter, "Go out into the world and teach. You will find that the first person who comes to you and speaks will give you a coin. Take it and give it to the tax collectors, so that we might be counted among those who have no wish to deny those of this world."

The fact that the Master seemed to know these events which were to take place no longer surprised those who journeyed with him, as he had stunned them many times with just such subtle comments. It always amused him to do so, for he caught them by surprise, and they were always both amazed and delighted. Therefore, Peter just looked at Jesus for a moment, and then turned away to do as he was bid.

Going to the nearby road the disciple began to teach, and there came then a man to the grove and situated himself among the onlookers. Immediately the stranger began to ask questions concerning the strange doctrine coming from Peter's lips. When these had been answered, the man forthwith handed the disciple a gold coin which was equal to several pieces of silver, after which he continued on his way. Then Peter quickly followed his Master's instructions and gave the coin to those who were collecting taxes, that he and his Master should be counted as honest men. However, when he returned to the house to report to Jesus, he could speak no words, for silent laughter had taken over the countenance of his teacher.

By this time it was spring. The cultivation in the valley of Jordan had drawn to an end, even as the barley bowed its ripened heads in the west wind. A trumpet sounded thanksgiving on the eighth day of Adar, twelfth month of the sacred year and sixth of the civil year, and before long the people gathered to celebrate the Feast of Purim. A heaviness descended upon Jesus, much like the dark shadow of a world which knew not the presence of light. Usually, he could shake this heaviness by utilizing the forces of natural and cosmic law, but for now the shadow remained relentless. With this also came the knowledge that it was time to depart from this land which had given him birth. Therefore he instructed his disciples, saying that they were to return to Galilee to prepare for the journey to Jerusalem and the Feast of the Passover.

The travelers did not tarry along the way, as was their usual custom, but made their way directly to Nazareth and Capernaum. Passing through the low ranges which were separated by broad fertile valleys did little to dispel the burden hanging over Jesus. He was sharply aware that the sun had reached its zenith, and the hour of twelve had gathered its momentous force to fulfill destiny. While there was no fear in him, he knew that he must bid farewell to those whom he loved on earth, and that he must endure great pain before the curtain fell upon the final act. In spite of this, he still attempted to lighten the spirits of those who were counted among his disciples, and as they returned to Capernaum and the Sea of Galilee they were of easy conscience. Jesus was glad to see this and watched after Peter, John, the son of Tholmai, and James, as a shepherd watches over his flock. And it came to pass that his love flowed through them as dry earth touched by rain, and they felt the special closeness which existed only between master and disciple. To them, the agony at Golgotha was yet no more than a faint outline in some misty shadow. It did not touch the promise of spring blowing in from the south or in the shadow of the sun against the melting snows of Lebanon.

Shortly after their return, Jesus and John helped their kinsmen make ready for the yearly pilgrimage to Jerusalem. Although the older women were placed upon the backs of burros, Mary Magdalene chose to walk beside the animal carrying Jesus' mother. Her comely countenance and her strong-boned cheeks were more clearly defined because of the dark shawl covering her head and shoulders. Although she might have been considered voluptuous, her form was now encased within modest attire which lent her dignity and commonness. Her brown hands were strong upon the lead rope as she pulled at the head of the animal with firm determination, causing it to move forward with surefooted steps.

Six days before the Feast of the Passover, Jesus and his party arrived at Mt. Olivet. As usual, he stopped for a moment to view the panorama of Jerusalem which lay below, and he marveled over these wonders man had wrought through the strength and power of the intangible spirit in him. This time, however, the Master also felt the icy fingers of finality. Although the combination of human ending and the beginning of a new existence among the stars was not new to him, he never ceased to marvel over the inseparable duality. Immediately he pushed these thoughts of destiny away, lest he bring a moment of pain to those who journeyed with him. Turning toward Bethany, Jesus and his followers made their way toward the home of Lazarus in order to dine there that evening.

That night the women prepared supper for the Master and served him, and when he had eaten they gathered around him as usual to listen to him speak. As he did so his voice was gentle as a mother speaking to a new born infant, and he said, "The Son of man must seek peace with his own feelings, that his family may bask in the light of loving kindness. Although your Heavenly Father is a hundred times greater than all fathers by seed and by blood, and the Earthly Mother is a hundred times greater than all mothers by the body, and your true brothers are all those who do the will of your Heavenly Father and of your Earthly Mother, and not your brothers by blood, you must learn to see God in your father by seed and nature in your mother by the body, for these are also the children of God.

"You must learn to love your brothers by blood as you love all your true brothers who walk with the angels, for these too are children of God. It is easier to love those newly met than those of our own house, who have known our weaknesses, heard our words of anger and seen us in our nakedness, for they know us as we know ourselves. However, if we call on the Angel of Love to enter into our feelings and purify them, then our impatience and discord will turn to harmony and peace, as the arid plains drink in the gentle rain and become green and tender with new life.

"Many and grievous are the sufferings of the people when they fail to administer love to all others, for he who is without love casts a dark shadow on everyone he meets, most of all upon those with whom he lives. His harsh and angry words fall on his brothers like fetid air from a stagnant pool, and he who speaks them suffers most, for the darkness that encloses him is full of the dank smell of a musty tomb and the rampant forces of evil.

"Blessed is he who is pure in heart, for he shall see God. Even as the Heavenly Father has given you his holy spirit, your Earthly Mother has given you her holy body. Therefore, give love to all your brothers, and let your love be as the sun which shines on all the creatures of the earth and does not favor one blade of grass for another. Let this love flow as a fountain from brother to brother, and as it is spent, it shall also be replenished. If man has not love, he builds a wall between himself and all the creatures of earth, and therein he dwells in loneliness and pain. Or he may become as an angry whirlpool which sucks all that floats too near into its depths.

"The heart is a sea with mighty waves, and love and wisdom must temper it, as the warm sun breaks through the clouds and quiets the restless sea. He who has found peace with his brothers has entered the kingdom of love and shall see God face to face. When people love, then darkness is dispersed and the light of sunshine streams from him and the colors of the rainbow swirl about his head. Gentle rains fall from his fingers and he brings peace and strength to all those who draw near him.

"After this manner, therefore, pray to your Heavenly Father: Our Father who art in heaven, send the Angel of Peace to all the Sons of men, and send the Angel of Love to those of our seed and blood, that peace and harmony may dwell in our house forever."

After this Jesus fell silent and bowed his head that he might join those around him in communion. While they were gathered thusly in the peaceful silence of the early evening, Mary Magdalene rose and went to get a pound of costly spikenard (an aromatic oil extracted from a plant in eastern India). Then she came and knelt in front of her beloved teacher and began to anoint his feet. Now it happened that Judas Iscariot, the son of Simon and the nephew of Caiaphas the high priest, was very displeased that such an expensive oil should be used in this way, and spoke up with great aggravation, saying, "Should this ointment not be sold for 300 pence and the proceeds given to the poor?"

On hearing these words, Jesus looked at the slender dark-haired man, who had become his last disciple, with considerable perspicaciousness. He knew that Judas' mercenary tendencies were fed by the illusion that he, Jesus, would usher in an earthly political kingdom and appoint this provocateur to the post of secretary of the treasury. Although he had made it quite clear that his intent was not to bring forth an earthly kingdom, he knew that Judas still maintained considerable hope that this kingship would be formed. However, Jesus shook his head and said, "Let her alone. She has kept this for the day of my burial. The poor will always be with you, but you will not always have me."

Even as the Master spoke, some distance away word had spread among those arriving in Jerusalem that he was in Bethany, and many came to the house of Lazarus that they might speak to him. After this, they returned to the temple to inform others that Jesus would appear to them on the following day, which was the fourteenth day of Nisan and the first day of the Feast of the Passover. Some began to prepare for his coming by cutting branches from the palm trees. These would be laid in his path to pay homage. Frequently referred to as *goodly trees*, the branches were used to signify prosperity of the godly.

To fulfill the final mystery of the descent of God to live in human sheath, Jesus sent two of his disciples to bring him a colt tethered nearby. By riding into Jerusalem in such manner, he would demonstrate supremacy (Christ) over the human world (burro— beast of burden). This would emphasize the fulfillment of the prophecy and the time when mankind would rise victorious from the ashes of worldly existence. Therefore, he said to John and Peter, "Go into the village. As soon as you have entered it, you will find a colt tied up which no man has sat on. Bring him to me, and if any one asks you 'Why you are doing this?' tell them that the Lord needs him."

After their teacher had finished speaking, the two disciples departed and went into Jerusalem to secure the colt. They had not traveled far before they found one tethered by the side of the road. However, when they started to untie it, the owner of the animal approached and asked why they were taking his property. Then, remembering what Jesus had told them, they said that their Lord had need of him. Forthwith permission was given to take the creature, after which the disciples returned to Bethany. Jesus was waiting for them outside of Lazarus' home when they returned, and when they saw that he was ready to depart, they cast their garments over the back of the colt that he might ride more comfortably.

At first the procession consisted only of those who had come with him from Galilee, as well as those disciples from Jerusalem who had arrived in Bethany the night before. Soon the Queen City appeared before them in all her splendor, a city built neither by nature nor by the wisdom of man. Below them a number of people waited, and as the procession neared, these laid down their cloaks in front of Jesus, while others waved palm branches and chanted, "Hosanna, Hosanna," (meaning save now). These familiar words were from the 118th Psalm of David, forming a part of the traditional scriptures recited each Feast of the Passover. Now they were used to greet the Master as he began one of his last pilgrimages to the temple. His mood was solemn, but it touched not those who were with him, nor those who had come to greet him. Therefore, he allowed the animal to walk along peacefully under him, knowing that destruction of that which could no longer live would become the foundation of a new world in which all people would live as brothers. He knew not that the memory of this day would remain etched in the winds of time and heal all generations.

Hosanna: blessed is the King of Israel that cometh in the name of the Lord.

St. John 12:13

And when he entered into Jerusalem, all the city was moved, saying, "Who is this?"

1. This festival signified the father of Israel for the second advent. The first advent was looked upon as the descent of the soul into matter, while the latter represented that period when God in man would raise from his tomb of flesh and bring the Kingdom of Heaven to earth. At that time, the silver trumpets, signifying the call of the soul, would sound, and man would enter into the final battle between the two natures, mortal and immortal. (Since the time of Moses, brass has indicated the base, or lesser, nature, or humankind; silver, the soul; and god, the indwelling spiritual nature).

PART III

VIA DOLOROSA

(PATH OF SORROW)

Twenty centuries have now passed through the dusty labyrinths of Israel's dead, since the man from Galilee rode his beast of burden into Jerusalem and passed through the Gennath gate that fateful morning in the month of Nisan. Since then war and bloodshed have poured down the steps of the Temple of Jerusalem, and the echo of many battles has created dark clouds of conflict. In 66 A.D. the Jewish Zealots revolted and held Jerusalem for four years, but in 70 A.D. the Romans again took over occupancy of the Queen City and the temple was destroyed. Even as the city was laid to waste, her people were taken captive and sent to Rome. By 135 A.D. the Romans decreed that no Jew be allowed into the city under the penalty of death. Two hundred years later, Jerusalem came under the rule of the Christian Emperor Constantine, thereby changing the outer face of the Christian religion for 1700 years. Before long Christian churches began to spring up everywhere, yet the Jews were forbidden to enter the city except on the ninth of Ab when they were allowed to lament the destruction of the temple.

The exile of the Jews continued, for on June 7, 632 A.D. a member of the Koreish tribe, and the son of Abdullah and his wife, died. His name was Mohammed, a gentle philosopher who claimed to be the mouthpiece of God. During the 60-plus years of his life, he drew thousands of followers, who later under the guise of Muslim Arab armies conquered Jerusalem and further exiled the Jews from their homeland. Today, in the Muslim sector, the threads of the past are no more, for modern buildings have been erected over the ancient decay of past glory. Although Mohammed was a good and noble man, his followers represent a somewhat violent religion in today's world, much resembling the warring Christians during the Dark Ages. For in July 1099 A.D. the Christian Crusaders entered Jerusalem and massacred Muslims and Jews alike, even though many of the latter were killed in the protection of their synagogues. The Crusaders made Jerusalem the capital of their kingdom.

Following the Crusader's entry into Jerusalem in 1099 A.D., all the Jews in the city were either murdered, sold into slavery in Europe, or ransomed to the Jewish community of Egypt. The Crusaders then brought Christian Arab tribes from east of the river Jordan and settled them in the former Jewish Quarter, between St. Stephen's Gate and the Valley of Jehoshaphat. Once Jerusalem had been conquered, as many as 10,000 Christian pilgrims made the journey every year, some from as far away as Scandinavia, Muscovy, and Portugal; and each year a small number of these pilgrims decided to remain permanently in the city. However, no man, nor nation, nor religion can reign supreme forever, as there is but one earth governed by a single power beyond human intelligence. This law prescribes equal rights for all people. Therefore, almost 100 years later, the Crusaders were driven from Jerusalem by Saladin. This was followed by the invasion of Kharezmian Tartars, who sacked the Queen City and massacred the Christians. The tables had turned, and within the next century the Muslims murdered the monks on Mount Zion and destroyed the Chapel of the Holy Spirit, while the monks of the Monastery of the Cross were massacred by Arab marauders.

Today Christians, Jews, and Muslims live together in Jerusalem, yet still separated from one another by ideology, sometimes violent, sometimes pacific. Christians journey to Bethlehem every Christmas eve to worship in the Holy Shrine of the Nativity, but even they are separated by ropes, one denomination from another, because of religious differences. Even to walk where Jesus once walked is difficult now, for the narrow Via Dolorosa is lined with merchants who barter their wares, and their raucous voices impose their seduction on one's quiet wish to remember another time, another place. The imprint of his feet along the shores of the Jordan River has long ago been washed away by the bloodshed of war and violence. Yet, something strange and mysterious still exists amid the winds of destruction and distant sound of rolling drums. It is a promise of a world yet to come, echoed amid the darkness of the death-filled tomb which held him and the martyrdom of those who loved him. Although his body was burned in the fires of persecution his teachings still live and will continue to live more powerfully tomorrow than ever before. And because of this, the love of humans for one another will one day be without boundaries.

CHAPTER VII

THE ARREST

When I shall have gone into the Light, then herald it unto the whole world and say to them cease not to seek day and night. And remit not yourselves until you find the mysteries of the Light, which will purify you and make you into light and lead you into its kingdom. Say to them: Renounce the whole world and the whole matter therein and all its cares and all its sins, and all its associations which are in it, that you might be worthy of the mysteries of the Light.

Pistis Sophia 111—102:1-2
St. John 3:19-21

urefootedly, the procession wound its way down the hillside, passing through the narrow streets of the Holy City as it moved toward the temple. The temple and its courts occupied a 500-cubic-foot area. Arranged in terrace form, one court was higher than another, with the temple itself highest of all so as to be seen easily from any part of the city.The outer court was surrounded by a high wall, with several gates on its west side, and porticoes went around it which rested on highly finished pillars. These were covered with cedar and supported by marble pillars, 25 cubits high. The women's quarters, where Jesus' mother had been raised, could be approached by the east gate, or the great gate, while the temple stood at the western end of the inner court upon a foundation of massive white marble. The temple was constructed in three major divisions: the outer court to symbolize the *body*, the Holy place to symbolize the *soul*, and the Holy of Holies to symbolize the indwelling spirit which contained the Ark of the Covenant, or Law of God. The building proper was approached by climbing 12 steps to signify the return of the two natures of man to the one God (1-2).

It was early morning when the caravan halted at the base of the court steps and Jesus, still astride the beast of burden, prepared to dismount. As he did so, he turned and approached the temple. He walked slowly, his back straight, that those who watched him saw naught but the power of one who walked with God. As he passed the Pharisees, who were watching nearby, they spoke one to another, saying, "Perceive how you prevail nothing? Behold, the world is gone after him."

Among the Pharisees there were certain Greeks who had arrived to worship at the feast, and they came to Philip of Bethsaida asking if they might see Jesus. Immediately, in reply to their inquiry, Philip went to tell Andrew of their request. By this time Jesus had already situated himself in preparation for discourse, and when he saw the two disciples coming toward him he felt a certain sense of unreality. Even though he had been born for this purpose, it was hard to believe that the ebb and flow of life for him was ending. Although the finality was so poignant, contact of the physical senses was also very real, and he found it necessary to cast his will over the moment in order to cease thinking and wondering. However, as Philip and Andrew approached, he spoke to them kindly, saying, "The hour is come when the Son of man will be glorified. Forget not the earthen pot which contained the wheat, for one grain must fall to the ground and die to produce 20 grains. If it does not fall, it is but a single grain and must dwell alone, for it can produce no fruit. The Son of man is also like the single kernel, for while he is human he is relegated by mankind to human status, but when he dies he is no longer hindered by physical boundaries and becomes greater.

"Any person who loves his life must lose it, because he does not know the Kingdom of God which cannot be seen. Yet one who hates his life in this world shall seek the secrets of that kingdom which cannot be seen, for though he dwells in this world, he is not of it, but has discovered eternal life. If anyone desires to serve me, let them follow me, and where I am, they shall be also, and if someone surrenders their personal life, which is of this world, in order to serve this greater cause, they will be honored by my Father. Now my soul is troubled, and what should I say? Father save me from this hour, when it is for this purpose I was brought into the flesh."

For a moment Jesus sat silent, then he lifted his eyes toward the sun filled sky and prayed, "Father, glorify your name."

In that instant, the consciousness in Jesus' soul and that which existed throughout the universe became as one. Those who were around him could not understand this undefined power which seemed to embrace them. They could not believe that oneness with God could be possessed by other than Moses. However, Jesus felt it flow through him and it spoke with a voice unlike a voice. Its depth and breadth resonated on the ears of the people and some thought it had thundered, while others said, "An angel spoke to him."

Then Jesus dropped his head toward the ground. As his eyes closed he knew that the pusillanimous aspect of man would continue to dominate the world for centuries. Their unenlightenment would continue to breed doubt and hostility, and they would condemn all who, like him, had found the path to God. As the scribes and Pharisees mocked him this day, so too would the rancorous aspect of humankind mock those who rose tomorrow. Yet, he knew that all these things must come to pass, and when he raised his head and spoke, it was with great compassion, "This which you have witnessed did not come because of me, but for your sakes. The world has judged that the prince (one who has raised the divine nature and rules over the worldly nature) shall be cast out. But I, by departing from human life, shall draw all men to me."

Even as Jesus spoke, he felt the fire of the living God consuming his sorrow like a flame against the tallow, bringing peace where mortality raged. This was reward sufficient unto itself and he asked for nothing else, although someone cried out, "We have heard out of the law that Christ will live forever, but you say that the Son of man must be lifted up?[1] Who, therefore, is the Son of man?"

Jesus did not answer the question directly, but continued with that which he was saying before, adding, "You only have the light (illumined consciousness) with you for a short time. Walk in this light while it is possible or darkness will overcome you, for those who walk in darkness do not know where they are going. While you have light with you, believe in the teachings which are derived from it, that you also become children of the light."

With these words the Master departed from the people and hid himself for a time. Walking unhurriedly, in a deeply contemplative state, he went into the olive groves located at the foot of the Mount of Olivet. There he sought to quiet the unrest in his soul, for resistance to death was instilled in all men, although its shield assured the continuity of life. There were times during this day of finality when he had great calm and peace, but other times the events which were to take place came stealthily upon him and took away the peace. He did not fear as ordinary humans might fear, but there was wonderment and question. These were also the last hours of unchained movement over earth, and there was a closeness as well as a heightened sense of clarity pertaining to all life. At the same time, he had never felt greater oneness with God. It was as if the entire cosmos was raising, strengthening, and sharing each single moment of destiny's great triumph.

Some time later, as the Master sat in the Garden of Gethsemane, the disciples came to him in private. Finding him of serious countenance they approached quietly and with some concern. Here in the solitude his death seemed far away, yet its threat hovered over them like a dark shadow. Seating themselves around his feet, they asked him concerning the last days, or the time when men would raise the divine spark of God in them and become no more. "Tell us," one of the disciples asked, "what shall the sign of your coming be, and the sign of the end of the world?"

In beginning his apocalyptic discourse, Jesus set a precedent which would later be emulated by a number of followers. His cousin John's Revelation would confound the world for 20 centuries, while the versions of the end times as told by Simon Peter, James, Paul, and Thomas would be submerged among the lesser writings of the church under the title of Apocryphal New Testament. In spite of the latter, however, the tantalizing fragrance of apocalyptic teachings would trigger mankind's investigative nature for all time, and the fulfillment of God's divine plan on earth would remain the prophecy of all prophets. This mystery of the final death struggle between human and divine had been, and always would be, the last frontier of human will.

Although Jesus did not respond to his disciple's inquiry immediately, he finally set those thoughts from his mind which had occupied him these last hours. Raising his eyes he looked at them, speaking at last as a father speaks to a child. First he cautioned them against being deceived, saying, "Many will come in my name saying that they are of me, and many will be deceived, for many whose eyes are bound by darkness and know not of the mysteries of the resurrection shall lead others into darkness. Although you shall hear of wars and rumors of wars, be not troubled, as these things must come to pass. However, the end is not yet, for the end shall come only when there is peace, and there can be no peace among people till there be one garden of the brotherhood over the earth. The kingdom is not brought into being by expectation, nor can they say, 'See here, or see there,' but the Kingdom of the Father is spread upon the earth and men do not see it."(Gospel According to Thomas, Log 113:14-18).

"Nation shall rise against nation and kingdom against kingdom," Jesus continued, "and there shall be famines and earthquakes in divers places. All these are but the beginning of sorrows, for they shall raise up against those who carry the light and some will be killed because they have been my followers. Even many of the common people shall be offended and will turn against one another in hatred and malice.

"Many will preach in my name, but because they walk in darkness they shall also deceive many, and because ignorance will abound, the love of man for one another shall wax cold. Yet he who remains true to the laws of life, which are to love God and love each other, shall pass through the resurrection and be saved. These tidings of salvation concerning the Kingdom of Heaven must be taught throughout the world, and you who have followed me must become way-showers for all nations.

"When you have witnessed the desolation of the soul and entered into the final battle to transform human into divine, as spoken by Daniel the prophet, you must remain centered in the Spirit of God within you. Otherwise, your abyss shall be deep, your pain without measure, and your nights filled with unfathomable darkness."

And in the days of these kings shall the God of heaven set up a kingdom, which shall never be destroyed: and the kingdom shall not be left to other people, but it shall break in pieces and consume all these kingdoms, and it shall stand forever.

Daniel 2:44

And some of them of understanding shall fall (dark night of the soul), to try them, and to purge (purify), and to make them white (purity of the soul when it has become one with its immortal counterpart), even to the time of the end; because it is yet for a time appointed.

Daniel 11:35

Many shall be purified, and made white, and tried; but the wicked shall do wickedly: and none of the wicked shall understand; but the wise shall understand. Blessed is he that waiteth, and cometh to the 1,290 days (1000-body, soul, and spirit return to the one God 200 separation of the two natures, mortal and immortal soul has been reborn through the resurrection, or atonement with God).

Daniel 12: 10,12

And it came to pass that part of this prophecy pertaining to the outer world would be fulfilled during the ensuing years, for the Romans were to gain power over the Israelites and great rebellions would follow. This brought much destruction to the Holy Lands. In A.D. 66-70, the religious community of Jerusalem, which was to condemn Jesus to death, would be all but extinguished as a result of the Jewish war. Rising up against the Romans, the Queen City was first to fall into the hands of a rebel zealot. Although C. Cestus Gallus, the Roman governor of the province of Syria, would march to the rescue, he would be forced to retire due to heavy losses. Then another rebel named Josephus, who later became recognized as a great Jewish historian, would be appointed commander-in-chief of Galilee.

After this, Emperor Nero was to entrust the Roman command to General Titus, who would counterattack Galilee from the north. The villages on the shores of Lake Gennesaret, which Jesus loved so much, would see the first of the war, and by October A.D. 67, Galilee would be subdued. Among those taken prisoner by the Romans, was Josephus, the commander-in-chief, and not long thereafter Nero committed suicide. Vespasian, father of Titus, was to become ruler of the Roman empire.

During this time Marcus Vissanius Agrippa, general and colleague of Augustus Caesar (60 B.C.-14 A.D.) was to order the death of Simon Peter, who at his own request, was crucified upside down. Andrew would be crucified by order of the Aegeas the proconsul of Patrae in Achaia, and Philip stoned and crucified in Hierapolis, a city in Phrygia. Nathaniel, known as Bartholomew, a gardener and dealer of vegetables from Hiercrates, taken, flayed, and beheaded, while John, Jesus' closest disciple, would be ordered into imprisonment and hard labor on the Isle of Patmos. James the Great, Jesus' cousin, would be decapitated by Agrippa in A.D. 44, and Thomas, called Didymus (meaning twin), killed by lance and buried in Edessa. Judas Iscariot would commit suicide.

By the spring of A.D. 70, Titus would arrive outside Jerusalem with his army of 80,000 men and when the Holy City refused to surrender, the Roman artillery would begin to batter the north wall. Soon the entire city was to be cut off from supplies, and famine would reach its long tentacles in brutal attack, bringing pestilence and disease. Galilee's commander, Josephus, whose own family suffered with the defenders, later spoke of the siege of Titus on Jerusalem, saying, Because I tell of things unknown to history, whether Greek or barbarian, it is frightful to speak of it and unbelievable to hear of it. I should gladly have passed over this disaster in silence, so that I might not get the reputation of recording something which must appear to posterity wholly degrading. But there were too many eye-witnesses in my time.

Finally, in the year of A.D. 71 Titus would overcome the Zealots and march through the city in victory. Among his prisoners, the famous Zealot rebels, John of Gischala and Simon bar Gion, were both transported in chains. Two other costly trophies of pure gold would be among the plunder carried off by the Romans: the seven-branched candlestick representing the seven cycles of creation and their corresponding laws, and the table of shew bread symbolizing the two natures of man, mortal and immortal, bound to the world of matter. Remaining remnants of the population of the *Promised Land*, who were neither slaughtered in the Jewish war of A.D. 66-70, nor in the Bar Kokhba rebellion of A.D. 132-135, were to be sold into slavery. Yet the power of Jesus, the Master, was to prove greater, for in A.D. 325 Emperor Constantine the Great would choose Christianity as the religion of the Roman empire.

Now, however, as Jesus sat with his disciples in the Garden of Gethsemane discussing those things which were to come, his concern was not for the outer world. Most of what he was teaching referred to the final days of human evolution when man would surrender, not to the world of matter, but to the world of God. Therefore, after he finished speaking about the forthcoming trials of the downfall of Israel, he said, "In the end, great tribulation unlike anything since the beginning of time shall befall the soul of man. And nothing which is adverse to the ways of God will remain within any creature. But for those who raise the dead (the elect, or those who raise the in-dwelling Christ), the days shall be shortened.

"If anyone should say to you, 'Here is Christ, or there is Christ,' do not believe it. For there shall arise many unillumined, who have not yet awakened the dead, and they shall show many signs and wonders, and will deceive many people. However, their powers and their signs shall be less, in that people can only manifest in the outer world according to their inner spiritual evolution. Even when they say, 'Behold, he is in the desert, or he is in the secret chambers,' do not believe it. The light comes from the east like unto the morning star, bringing new birth, or the rains which bring forth new life upon earth, and it shall shine even in the west upon the aged and the sick. So shall be the coming of the Kingdom of God (St. Luke 17:20-21 and Revelation 1:7).

"Wherever man's ways are contrary to natural and cosmic law, there will the ideals of perfection gather together and consume the remnants of past misdeeds. Immediately after the tribulations of these days, the spirit shall be darkened as a sun is darkened amid the storm clouds, and the mind shall become as black as the moon on a moonless night. Even the aspirations of self will shall be shaken by the powers of heaven. After this there will appear a great light in the soul, which comes forth with power and great glory, and God will send forth his purifying forces to call the soul into battle. He shall call forth those who are ready to free themselves from the bonds of earthly attachment.

"Learn the parable of the fig tree, for when the branch is yet tender it shoots forth new leaves and you know that summer is near. So too, when you see these things of which I have spoken, you will know that the end is near, even at the doors, nor can any person pass from human generation until all these things have come to pass. Although heaven and earth shall pass away, these things I am saying to you cannot pass away, because the laws of God and the laws of nature are unchanging. No individual knows the day in which Christ shall awaken, not even the angels of heaven, but God knows."

Again Jesus fell silent for a time, while the aged olive trees cast their shadows over the silent and solitary ground. Only a herd of goats fed not far off, and a few flocks of sheep appeared on the side of the mountain. High above towered the dead walls of the city, through which penetrated no sound of human life. It was almost like the stillness and loneliness of the desert. Neither did the disciples make a sound, but waited as they had so many times for him to continue teaching. When he saw that some still did not understand the full implications of his words, he said to them, "Then shall the Kingdom of Heaven be likened unto ten virgins (10-when the in-dwelling spiritual nature has been resurrected, or returned to the one God), which took their lamps (light) and went forth to meet the bridegroom (the in dwelling Christ). And five (the soul-1, bound by the four elements-4, to the progression of a corporeal world) of them were wise (that aspect of the soul which has never descended into the corporeal form), and five were foolish (that aspect of the soul which is bound to the world of matter). They that were foolish took their lamps, and took no oil with them (the portion of the soul which journeyed through matter in darkness and unknowing). But the wise took oil in their vessels with their lamps (the portion of the soul which has not been imprisoned to the corporeal world).

"While the bridegroom (indwelling Christ) tarried, they all slumbered and slept (bound to matter). At midnight (12-signifying the time when the two natures, mortal and immortal, would seek release from the corporeal world and return to the one God) there was a cry made. Behold the bridegroom cometh (the indwelling Christ appears); go ye out to meet him (raise the dead).

"Then all those virgins arose and trimmed their lamps (the soul seeks its return to its heavenly state which has now been illumined by the Christ Light). And the foolish (that which is bound to the corporeal world, or body) said to the wise (that which has remained liberated from the body), 'Give us of your oil; for our lamps are gone out' (darkness and unknowing). But the wise answered, saying, 'Not so; lest there be not enough for us and you' (the awakened soul now becomes fearful, lest the body draw it into worldly ways).

"And while they (the unawakened) went to buy oil (purification of corporeal parts), the bridegroom came (the resurrection of the divine nature) and they (the awakened) that were ready went in with him to the marriage (the unaffected aspects of the soul seek union with the inner Christ). Afterward came also the other virgins (mortal counterpart), saying, 'Lord, Lord, open to us.' But he answered and said, 'Verily I say to you, I know you not.'

"When the Son of man comes in his glory and all the holy angels with him (through the indwelling Christ, the soul is united with the Kingdom of Heaven), then shall he sit upon the throne of his glory (his temple shall then abide in the soul). And he shall set the sheep on his right hand (those who are obedient to his ways), and the goats (those who resist his ways) on his left."

Again the Master stopped speaking, but now his eyes closed and he rested his head against the strong and powerful tree which stood behind him. By this time, the sun had set in great splendor over the edge of the distant hills and its myriad colors enhanced the shadows of night, which were prepared to descend over Israel. Jesus would live to see but two more sunsets, for in 48 hours he would surrender his earthly life to the cross that the world would rise out of ignorance and unknowing. Destiny had decreed that he would be delivered into the hands of the Sanhedrin following the Feast of the Passover, scheduled for the next day. Once again the Holy Spirit would drift freely within the consciousness of its Creator, awaiting the time when others would bear Him. In the meantime it would work through the hearts of men, that they might bear forth fine grapes. When the fruit was ripe, the harvest would begin and the water (mortal nature) would be turned into fine wine (divine nature) as the grapes were pressed (purification of the soul) into a drink worthy of God.

Moving unhurriedly through the olive trees, Jesus made his way to Bethany for the last time. He wanted to spend these final hours with Lazarus and his sisters, who were so close to his heart. Even as he turned in that direction, the chief priests, scribes, and elders were gathering in council at the palace of Caiaphas, the high priest. The meeting had been called for the purpose of deciding how to take Jesus and kill him. It so happened that the death penalty presented grave complications, for the laws of the people resisted capital punishment. The maximum penalty, which was usually stoning, could be administered by the court, but this would not necessarily remove the threat of the new kingdom which Jesus and his disciples had prophesied. If the Master were to be executed, it would be best to have him prosecuted by Rome, whose maximum penalty was crucifixion.

Obtaining a death warrant from Rome would be difficult for the priesthood, as it was not the customary practice of Roman officials to intercede in the proceedings of the Jews. In order to succeed, the Sanhedrin would be required to prove that Jesus had plotted against Caesar and attempted to overthrow the Roman government. At the time of this preliminary meeting of the Sanhedrin, a number of the senior members were not present. Among those absent were Gamaliel, whose own son was named Jesus after his former prodigy;[2] Nicodemus, a Pharisee, who later took up Jesus' defense at the trial; and the Master's uncle, Joseph of Arimathaea,[3] one of the wealthiest men in all of Israel.

Discussions concerning the death penalty of Jesus went far into the night, under the direction of Caiaphas and his father-in-law, Annas. As Caiaphas became progressively more determined, the younger malcontents began to feel exaltation over the idea of condemnation.

However, it was finally decided that Jesus should not be arrested during the feast, for this might arouse the people against them and hinder the verdict they sought. Therefore, they mutually agreed that it would be best to make the arrest in private. They would need the aid of Judas Iscariot, Caiaphas' nephew, for this purpose.[4] It would be his responsibility to lead them to where Jesus was secluded, thereby removing any danger of public arrest. When this had been accomplished, the final goal would be to convince the officials of Rome that Jesus was a traitor to their empire.

While the meeting of the Sanhedrin was taking place, Martha and her sister, Mary, went about preparing the Master's evening meal in Bethany. When they sat down to eat, Lazarus, their brother, sat with them, but since there was not sufficient room for all of the disciples to be seated with Jesus, some sat crossed-legged nearby, balancing their plates in their hands. Although Jesus sought to ease the seriousness of those whom he loved, he was aware of the distant meeting which would determine the events of his destiny. As he looked at those gathered around him, he felt a sense of sorrow, for their time together was now very short. In turn, the disciples were also quiet, knowing that if his statements concerning his death came to pass, he would walk among them no more. Some hoped that he would be reprieved in the final hour. For a time, Jesus felt the thoughts and actions of those who held council against him, and the burden of the forthcoming events weighed heavily on his soul. Yet, even while the priesthood was unconsciously releasing its invisible forces of hatred and discord, the power of God also lifted his spirit that in his suffering he might also rejoice.

No hand could hold back the passage of night, and all too soon the pink fingers of dawn enfolded the darkened horizon. Before long, the light of morning fell upon the home of Lazarus and the birds began their morning ritual, unaware that a great drama was to unfold in the human world. Two miles away in the city of Jerusalem, many rose to prepare for the celebration of the Feast of the Passover. There being no fixed sanctuary, the houses were converted into such places of grace, or altars, and the blood from the paschal lamb was put on the posts and lintel of the doors as a sign that the house was to be spared. With the sparing and reconciliation accomplished through forgiveness of sins, the meal became the *sacramentum*, the sacrificial flesh a means of grace. The unleavened bread symbolized spiritual purity, or the purification of the mortal nature through removal of all things which brought harm to itself or to others; and the bitter herbs were intended to call to mind the sorrowful experiences which the Israelites suffered in Egypt after the Exodus.

As the disciples rose, Peter and John went to Jesus, asking, "Where would you like us to prepare the Passover?"

Wishing to spend this last night alone with those who had walked with him in life, Jesus looked at his disciples with great gentleness and said, "Go into the city and you will meet a man bearing a pitcher of water. Follow him and say to the owner of the house that the Master wishes the guest chamber prepared that he might have the Passover with his disciples. He will show you a large furnished upper room. You are to make this ready for us."

As soon as Jesus had finished speaking, Peter and John hastened to follow his instructions. Upon entering the Coenaculumn which the Master had described, they approached Irmeel, the good man of the house. He led them to a large, but dreary upper room, 50 to 60 feet long by 30 feet in width. Selecting a long table, the disciples began to make preparations for the Feast of the Passover.

Although traditional Jewish observance always began with the killing of the paschal lamb, the feast was not to be celebrated by the Master according to Jewish law, but rather according to ancient rituals pertaining to the resurrection. The table was, therefore, adorned simply with unleavened bread made from flour and water and a bottle of fermented grape juice. Next they placed a large cup in front of the place where Jesus was to sit, that he might drink. When these arrangements had been completed, the two disciples departed from Irmeel's house and headed in the direction of the temple where Jesus was now discoursing.

When the day drew to an end, Jesus raised himself from the hewn stones of the outer court of the great temple and motioned his disciples to follow him. Departing from the multitude which had gathered around him, he made his way once more to the Garden of Gethsemane. The declining sun poured a flood of golden light into the lower valley of Jehoshaphat and over the western face of Olivet as the group began to climb. Jesus felt very exhausted after this day, for his spirit had been tried mightily. To know of death, yet to will its seeping tentacles into submission, that the day appear no different than any other day, had cast a heavy burden. Gratefully he sank to the ground, closed his eyes, and leaned his back against one of the ancient trees. As they watched his eyes close, they knew that he would not speak now and had need of rest and regeneration.

Although some remained with him for a time, Peter and John made their way back to Jerusalem to insure that everything was in readiness for the Passover.

As the sun went into final wane and the shadows of the night played hide-and-seek with the last rays of day, Jesus raised himself up and began to walk quietly toward the city. When he entered the upper room which had been prepared for them, he asked his disciples to be seated, while he took the place which had been set for him. After this he seated himself, and picking up the bread, he began to break it.

The unleavened bread was made without leaven, or yeast, and then formed into thin round cakes, or loaves, about four inches in diameter and one half inch in thickness. The bread was baked on heated sand or flat stones by covering it with hot ashes. Although this was a common food for the poor, it also represented a much deeper mystery to Jesus and his disciples. The flat bread signified the human soul which had not yet pierced the divine nature (yeast) within it, and as Jesus broke one of the cakes, that he might share it with his disciples, he offered them the mystery of regeneration (resurrection). Each disciple, in accepting his allocation, agreed to return to the one God (one loaf) via sacrifice and purification, or union of the mortal nature (water) and the immortal nature (wheat).

And it came to pass that after Jesus had blessed the bread and broken it, he gave a piece to each of his disciples, saying, "I have desired to eat this Passover with you before I suffer. I will not be able to eat any more until it be fulfilled in the kingdom of God, and heaven and earth become one. Therefore, take and eat. This is the body which is given for your sake."

Then each disciple took the proffered bread and ate it, to signify the reunion of the indwelling light within them with the one Light, that the world should be made whole.

Next Jesus reached for the grape nectar contained in the silver cup in front of him. This, too, he offered his disciples, for it represented blood sacrifice and atonement to God, Father to all people. By sacrifice of its heavenly abode to fulfill the will of the Creator, light had descended into all flesh to guarantee the redemption of every human. Now the soul must surrender to the divine will in order to take its rightful place in the heavenly abode, just as the grapes must sacrifice their outer skin in order to be made into fine wine. Next it would be purified by the indwelling light, after the manner of the grapes which were placed in a wine press and pulverized. Therefore, with this understanding of the mysterious metamorphosis which had consumed his own soul and governed his life, Jesus picked up the cup and passed it to the closest disciple on his right hand, saying, "Take, drink of it, all of you. This is my blood of the new testament (new teachings) which is shed for the remission (purification) of sins."

In these final words, Jesus spoke of the individual aspect of the in dwelling God (Son of God), who turned the wheel of the wine press, stripping every soul of those things which brought it old age, sickness, and death. By accepting a drink from the cup as it was passed from hand to hand, each disciple agreed to surrender his personal life to serve the world, that all men, and women, and generations yet unborn, might achieve the resurrection. This mission was, and would remain, the common purpose of all illumined souls.

When the Lord's Supper, as it would hereafter be called, was finished, Jesus rose from the table and laid aside his garments, and taking a towel, he girded himself. Then he filled a basin with water, knelt down, and began washing his disciples' feet. This was also a rite of purification, signifying the raising of God in man who would come forth to cleanse the temporal world. Kneeling now in front of them, Jesus represented the risen Christ who would purify the unclean aspects in man, that he might walk anew.

And it came to pass that when Jesus came to Simon Peter, the disciple asked him, "Are you, my Lord, going to wash my feet?"

And Jesus answered, saying to him, "What I am doing, you do not understand now, but in the days which are yet to come you will remember this moment."

However, Simon Peter said to him, "You will never wash my feet." Then Jesus spoke in a gentle, but commanding voice and said, "If I do not wash you, you have no part of me.[5]

"Then, my Lord," he answered, "wash not only my feet, but also my hands and my head."

In a slight voice of admonition, Jesus replied, "He who has bathed does not need but to wash his feet for he is already clean. And all of you are clean, because you have lived the way of the Law except one."

After this he refrained from speaking further and continued washing the feet of his disciples until every one of them had been ministered to. The flickering light from the candles cast shadows of moving dancers on the wall, but beyond that the hall was dark and musty. A lamp at the entrance of the doorway also added its own silent specters, silhouetting them amid the unseen forces of life and death. Jesus was bare to his waist, his lower torso girded only with the towel. His legs were also bare, but his feet remained shod in the usual leather sandals, tied with leather thongs which wound around his ankles. Every movement of his body was performed with the grace of a dancer upon the winds of spring, and although strong in this humble gesture, he was also filled with great power and love.

When he had finished washing the feet of his disciples, Jesus put on his robes and sat down, saying to them, "Do you realize what I have done? You call me Master and Lord; and you speak well, for so I am. If, therefore, your Lord and Master has washed your feet, you should then wash one another's feet, that you do to others as I have done to you. You see, a servant is not greater than his lord; neither is he that is sent, greater than He who sent him. If you know these things, happy are you if you do them.[6]

As Jesus looked at each of those who sat with him, his heart was moved by immense feelings, for these alone, with the exception of one, had risen beyond the chains of earthly bonds. They had possessed the forbearance to endure the tests he had given them, and for this each had paid a price. Then his eyes fell upon Judas Iscariot, who had been bribed to betray him. Even now Judas carried 30 pieces of silver in the treasury bag in payment for this treachery. When Jesus' eyes fell upon him he said, with great sorrow in his voice, "Truly, I say to you that one of you will betray me."

The disciples were saddened to hear this and began to ask him, one by one, "Is it I, my Lord?"

Then John, the brother of James, knowing that the time remaining with his master was short, came forward that he might kneel at Jesus' feet. For reasons of obedience and loyalty he had become the Master's favorite disciple, and later the responsibility of spearheading the great work would be passed on to him. Now, he knelt at Jesus' feet seeking to comfort him in some small way and letting him know of his loyalty. Jesus, perceiving the cause of his disciple's concern, reached out and momentarily drew him close to his heart.

When Peter observed the moment of passing affection between the two, he beckoned to John to inquire of whom the Master spoke. Jesus noticed this and for a moment a shadow of mirth touched his lips, the first for many hours. Unfortunately, the seriousness of the situation forbade a smile and Jesus replied, "It is he to whom I shall give a sop after I have dipped it."

Now a sop was a piece of bread which had been dipped into a sauce, or in this case, fermented grape juice. It was common practice for a host who wished to honor a guest to personally offer a dainty morsel to him. However, as Jesus dipped the bread to give to Judas, he did so to signify betrayal. The bread, representing the physical body, was being dipped into the blood of sacrifice in order to fulfill the ancient rite symbolizing death of the mortal nature. It was the Master's lot not only to foretell his own end, but also to show that his death was for the purpose of sacrifice in order that a greater work might live. As he handed the sop to Judas he said, "That which you must do, do quickly."

No man at the table knew for what reason the ritual of the sop had been administered. Some thought he spoke this way because Judas kept the money bag and was being instructed to buy provisions for their keep, or to give something to the poor.

However, after Jesus had spoken to him in this manner, Judas slipped out into the darkness to inform his relatives of his master's whereabouts. A strong wave of doubt assailed him as he left and a sense of separateness followed as he moved quickly through the narrow streets toward his destination. He did not know that this journey would cost him, not only the life of Jesus, but also his own. Even his wife, who had little respect for him, often taunted him, and it was she who had encouraged him now to become the betrayer for monetary gain. (Revillout, Suppl. 1, pg. 195). As a traitor to one man he would never be trusted by others, especially those who held authority in the Sanhedrin. He would never again walk among those of spirit nor with dignity among those in the world of man.

When Judas departed from the upper room, Jesus began what would be his last discourse. He spoke at great length to his disciples concerning his impending separation from them. "Little children, yet a little while am I with you. You will seek me, but as I have said to the Jews, where I go you cannot come. Now I ask that you love one another as I have loved you. By this all men shall know that you are my disciples."

Upon hearing this, Peter immediately interrupted, asking, "Lord, where are you going?"

Patiently, as though Peter was a young student, Jesus replied, "Where I am going you cannot follow now, but you will follow me afterward."

Affronted, Peter, who had followed his teacher over mountain and valley, through rain and hot summer winds, and abided close to him whenever it was permitted, could not comprehend that this closeness was now to end, and he questioned, "Lord, why cannot I follow you now, for I would lay my life down for your sake?"

Sadly Jesus looked upon this brother to Andrew, for Peter had been among the first of his followers. Although he knew that Peter would deny his affiliation with him three times before the night had passed, he also recognized the bitter burden which would hang like a millstone around his disciple's neck because of it. Therefore, he cared not that Peter's fervent loyalty would be betrayed, but rather that Peter would later fall beneath death's dark omen and be crucified. Thus, Jesus shook his head at his disciple's dismayed look and spoke kindly, "Would you really lay down your life for my sake? I say to you that the cock shall not crow until you have denied my name three times."

The disciple looked back at his teacher aghast, but he spoke not again. Too long had he journeyed with this man from Galilee and yet he did not know him. Jesus had many intangible qualities, nor was he ever the same; yet he was unchanging. He would help a tiny bird return to the nest of its mother, but the sword of his words could pierce the most studied priest. However, this Peter did know, the now firm line of his teacher's jaw forbade him further words.

For the next two hours, the Master spoke to his disciples concerning their inevitable separation. He first described the unseen kingdoms (mansions) where the continuity of life assured each living creature of its rightful place according to the law of progression. Jesus knew that he would ascend into the higher angelic kingdom following his death and would be free from all earthly chains. Then, with the assistance of the angelic kingdom, he would continue his work toward the brotherhood of men. He assured his disciples that he would come again through the subtle inner worlds to anyone who dared to step beyond the limitations of human understanding.

Now Thomas, who was also very devoted to Jesus, could not interpret what the Master was saying and needed to ask him, "Lord, if we do not know where you are going, how can we know the way?"

"Have you been so long with me Thomas and yet cannot understand these things I say?" Jesus questioned. "Those things I have taught you are as a light which shines in the shrouded night and guides your way up the rock-hewn mountain of learning. As I have climbed, so must you climb, for I am an example of the path which all people must walk. No man can come to the Father, except through the Christ which has been raised in me and must be raised in you. If you have known me, you have known my Father also. Although he is not visible, he is manifest in all living things. How can you say to me, 'Show us the Father'? Is He not present in the opening of the lily, the cry of a newborn child against its mother's breast, the mighty storm clouds against the silver sea, and even in the hearts of a master and his disciple. Can you not believe therefore, that I am in the Father and the Father is in me? Even these words I speak to you I do not speak of myself. They come from the Father who dwells in me and it is He who does the works.

"Believe me when I say these things, but if you cannot do so, then believe in me for the work's sake. He who believes in me, the works that I do he shall do also; and greater works than these; because I must leave you and go to my Father. And whatever you ask in my name, I will do, that God may be glorified through the Son in all man.

"If you love me, keep my commandments; love God and love each other. I will pray to the Father and he shall give you another comforter (raising the divine nature), that he may abide with you for ever. He is the Spirit of Truth, whom the world cannot receive because it cannot see him and does not know him. But you know him, for he dwells with you and shall be in you. Nor will I leave you comfortless, for I will come to you.

"In just a little while, the world will see me no more, but you shall see me because I shall continue to live, even as you shall live. In that time you will understand what I am saying now, that I am in my Father, you are in me, and I am in you. He who keeps my commandments is he that loves me, and he that loves me will be loved by God. I will also love him and manifest myself to him.

"These things I speak in your presence. However, the Comforter, which is the Holy Ghost (the Spirit of God in man), whom the Father will send in my name, shall teach you many things. He will bring forth all remembrance of the teachings you have received.

"If I had not come and spoken to the people they would have remained blameless for their errors. Once, they walked in ignorance and darkness, unknowing of life and all its causes. Now they have no cloak under which to hide. If I had not done those works which had never been done before, none would now be counted among the ungodly. However, those who walk in darkness cannot be condemned because they are one with the nature of things. Yet they have both seen and hated me, as well as God, for my words have revealed the error of their ways.

"It has been a long journey through the unknowing era of human beginning, and if the world is to change, the written Law must be fulfilled. The Comforter will guide you in all truth. He will not speak of himself, but will show you many things which are yet to come. He will glorify me and reveal my ways, that you might bear witness to these things you have been taught. From among all people, you who are with me now have been selected for this cause, for you have been with me since the beginning."

As the Master continued discoursing with his disciples he spoke one last time of the trials before them. Although he cautioned that they would suffer pain, he consoled them with a promise of a greater destiny. In spite of his careful instruction, they still could not fully fathom that which they had not yet seen and did not yet know, and as he sat among them they wanted to struggle against the hands of fate which would tear him from them. Yet, even now the Mover of destiny drew the inner senses of the Master toward the invisible hourglass which ruled over the seasons of all people, and he saw that it was time for life to yield under its invincible will.

A moment of quietude and Jesus raised his eyes to heaven and began to pray, "O, my Father, the hour has come. Glorify your Son, so that your Son may glorify you. You have given the Son power over all flesh and have sent him to abide in all souls, that they be given life eternal. You have given him to mankind so that all people can come to know you and that you are the only true God, even the One who sent me. I have already glorified you on earth and the work which you have given me is finished. Now, my Father, glorify me with the same glory I knew with you before the world was made."

Into Jesus' thoughts entered the memory of this world born without conscious awareness of itself so long ago, the perfection of its plan, and the individual role each must play. As he existed then, so had all others, although no more than an idea living in the mist of molten fires. "It was good," he thought, "Mankind was born from God and when the resurrection of the dead has been accomplished they too will enter the Kingdom of Eden and become one with each other, and one with Him. This was the covenant of Jehovah, a promise blowing in the subtle winds of endless time."

Then he began to pray again, "Hereafter, I will not be in the world, but these who have come to me must continue to dwell amongst worldly things. Now I am coming to you, O Holy Father, protect those which you have given me so they may become one even as we are one. I shielded those you brought to me in this world and none are lost, except those who remain in darkness in order that the mysteries might be fulfilled. Now I am coming to you and I speak these things while I am in the world, that my joy may be complete in them. I have taught these disciples your word. However, people have hated them because they are not of this world, any more than I am of this world. I am not asking that you take them away from the task which rests before them, but that you protect them from evil. Neither am I asking for them alone, but also for the sake of those who believe in me. I desire them to know the glory which you have allowed me, so that they may be one as we are one. Even as I am in them, you are in me, so all may be made perfect in one. I ask that the world will one day know that you sent me and that I have loved all humans as you have loved me.

"Father, I would those whom you have given me be with me where I am going, in order to behold the glory which has existed since the beginning and know of the love you have given to me, and to them, since the foundation of the world. Oh, righteous Father, the world has not known you, but I have known you. I have declared your name to them, and now I ask that your love be in them as it is in me."

Jesus' heart had grown heavy, for life is preserved by Him who gave it, but in each human there remains a thread of human attachment in the final hour. This was established forever by divine order, to insure that mankind valued life upon earth as an integral part of progression. Since Jesus knew that he must suffer much pain before sunset the next day, he felt the need to be strengthened by the power which brought him into being, for these final hours had to bear forth its ripened fruit. And it was written in the code of life that even death should not be of darkness, but so arranged as to benefit the whole world.

After a brief pause, Jesus spoke softly, saying, "Peace I leave with you. Even so it is my peace which I give to you, not the peace which the world gives. Let not your heart be troubled and do not be afraid. Hereafter, I will not have much of an opportunity to speak to you, for the prince of this world (death which consumes the mortal body) will come soon, yet he is nothing to me. Arise now and let us go hence."

As they departed from the building, the angel of darkness moved swiftly across the land and its shadows brought forth a kiss from the lord of death, who even now sought to bury it in the dark minds of the Sanhedrin. Walking through the hushed streets toward Gethsemane, Jesus felt the final curtain begin to fall on the last act of his role in human life. He knew he had played his part well, but the icy fingers which haunted him throughout the day could no longer be buried beneath the subtle practice of daily work. Now it crowded upon him with its fullness, and its heaviness became so intense it almost bowed his back. The night was in its zenith when he and his disciples arrived at his favorite place in Gethsemane. Above his head the stars looked down, seemingly suspended in time, waiting the close of a dying era.

Feeling the need to pray, Jesus instructed some of those who were with him to sit nearby under one of the aged trees and commune with God. However, he asked Peter, John, and his brother James, to be near him during these final hours, for they were closest to his heart. Lifting his eyes that he might pierce the unseen power and Ruler of the universe, he asked, "If Thou but will, remove this cup from me; nevertheless, not my will, but yours be done."

Strengthened by the power that flowed through him, the Master raised himself up. Death was inevitable; it was decreed that destiny should be fulfilled. Even now, accompanied by Sanhedrin guards, Judas moved through the night preparing his kiss of betrayal and triggering the flow of the last 24 grains of sand in the hourglass. With the descent of the final granule, Jesus would bear no more pain and the history of tomorrow would begin.

Author's Addendum:

THE PATH OF CHRISTIAN MASTERSHIP VIA THE DOLOROSA

(ALSO KNOWN AS THE RESURRECTION OF THE DEAD)

But Jesus said unto them, "Ye know not what ye ask: Can ye drink of the cup I shall drink of, and be baptized with the baptism that I am baptized with?"

St. Mark 10:38

Since the ancient times of Enoch, Abraham, and Moses, those who choose to seek the mysteries of heaven have had to undergo and surmount trial by water, trial by fire, and the last great hurdle, crucifixion of the soul. While there is mention of these in the form of outer initiations and rituals going back 6,000 years, the ultimate battle lies within man himself. In Zorastrianism this conflict is depicted as the battle between the mighty Devas and Ahuras; in Hinduism, as the great war between the Pandavas and Karavas; in the Essene tradition, as the conflict between the Sons of Light and the Prince of Darkness; and in Christianity, St. John's Armageddon battle. Contrary to popular concepts, the *resurrection of the dead* still lies far ahead for most people. Its powerful inner drama takes the strong and molds them from mediocrity into greatness, but leaves the weak to remain in the embrace of earthly evolution until they also become strong enough for the long journey of transformation. For those who have followed the teaching of the man in the scarlet robe through 2,000 years of spiritual evolution, the cross awaits them in the distant shadows of a world which cannot be pierced by mortal eyes. However, if Christianity is to ever fulfill its true destiny, then it must leave behind its false utopia and accept the need for transcendence through walking the Via Dolorosa. As it was said in an ancient Egyptian manuscript, "No man escapes death; every living soul is destined to resurrection."

For Christians, the first symbol is the five-pointed star, which leads the body, mind, and soul to the manger of the inner Christ. Their second symbol is the cross, representing the four elements which comprise the physical body, their tomb since the beginning of earth. Before entry into the sacred chambers of the resurrection, each must retire to the desert (solitude of the soul) to fight Lucifer (personal life versus impersonal life). There each will make a final decision whether to remain bound to the personal life or accept the role of co-creator and help bring forth God's divine plan to earth. No one is allowed to progress further unless the impersonal life is selected, for caste systems, lack of universality, and narrow concepts have no place in the new world of tomorrow.

The journey has already been a long one for those who have reached the stage of the conflict with Lucifer. Having moved from mass consciousness and its secular devotional surrender, they now seek admittance into the deeper mysteries of life. These have been carefully observed by the inner Christ, and with the aid of unseen forces, each Christian who would seek supremacy over the lower nature will be tested now to determine if he, or she, is worthy to walk the Via Dolorosa. If the probationer surmounts the obstacles placed in front of him, the narrow gateway leading to Golgotha will be opened. This is the narrow gate to which many are called but few are chosen.

THE FEAST OF PASSOVER

As a person steps from the mortal world through the gate of no return, he experiences a series of illuminations. These reveal the destiny of the initiate, the ideal to be achieved, and how each came into being. There is now no turning back to the mortal life, for the narrow gate closes. It has been determined by a greater power that the divine-elect is ready to walk the Via Dolorosa, just as Jesus did before. The initiate's personal life must now die in order for the individual to rise victorious and immortal.

The great Feast of God (illumination) is symbolized in Judaism as the Feast of the Passover and in Christianity as the Christmas Dinner. These festivals are both celebrated for a period of seven days, symbolizing mastership over the seven cycles of creation and of necessity. Each initiate who has been admitted through the narrow gate has partaken of the bread and wine. Therefore, each has agreed to die to the personal life and to seek atonement through wisdom and dedicated service.

THE FOURTEEN STATIONS

Although the way to divine transformation encompasses 14 symbols, the first two stations are preliminary to the process itself and the remaining 12 comprise the actual journey of the Christ-initiate. Therefore, two numbering systems are used—one representing the 14 stations as a whole and a second representing stations 3 through 14, known as the Via Dolorosa. Moreover, within the 12 stations of the Via Dolorosa, there are three successive phases: 1 through 5—walking the Via Dolorosa; 6 through 9—purification and rebirth; and 10 through 12—final struggle leading to the resurrection.

Symbol 1

And they stripped him, and put on him a scarlet robe

Judgment has been rendered. The divine-elect must die. Now the immortal and Holy Spirit descends from the subtle unseen worlds where it has dwelled throughout the eons to make its abode with the mortal self. Incarnated, he is the Christ, who immediately prepares war against man's human ways that the lesser be glorified. He rides forth upon his white charger (the newly illumined soul) with his purifying force to open the doorway to the three worlds: the body, the soul, and the spirit. The gateway between the initiate and the personal life he once lived is closed, and he is now scourged as the inner forces cause him to remember all the errors of his past days.

Symbol 2

The Christing of Man And when they had plaited a crown of thorns, they put it upon his head

The conflict between the personal and impersonal life, also known as the struggle between the Christ and antichrist, begins. A crown of thorns descends upon the initiate's head. Though the crown cannot be seen by others, it is nonetheless real to those who bear it. This shall not be removed from the head until resurrection from the dead is completed. Though the Christian initiate has eaten of the Feast of the Passover, has been scourged and wears the crown of thorns, he must still die. There are 12 further stations of the cross still before him, which will ensure that his lesser nature shall live no more and that the body, soul, and spirit shall be united for all time (St. John's 12,000 in his Revelation). The scarlet robe is now removed to signify the sacrifice of the personal life.

Symbol 3 Via Dolorosa (1)

Walking the Via Dolorosa

The time has arrived for the Christian initiate to begin the steep ascent toward Golgotha. His cross, or mission on earth, has been revealed to him and he must die of the personal life, as Jesus did before him. This station, and the four succeeding stations, signify collectively the removal of all personal attachments to the human world. The number five is the symbolic number of the crucified man (materialization of the flesh body from the four elements), and the process of dying to the personal life will consume not less than five years of the resurrected's life.

Symbol 4/Via Dolorosa (2)

Simon the Cyrene Helps Carry the Cross

Simon represents the lesser nature which must become an instrument of divine will. The mission of the Christ, whose work is to bring forth the brotherhood of man, can only be fulfilled through a physical vehicle. This burden is almost too heavy for the Christian initiate, who stumbles again and again as he winds his way toward Golgotha.

Symbol 5/Via Dolorosa (3)

Condemnation Along the Way

Now the initiate, having been given his cross, must continue his course in spite of all adversities. The way is narrow and steep and lined with those who will condemn. Many come who declare his work to be that of Satan (the symbol for the finite self) instead of God. As Jesus before him, he must learn to ignore the outer world, which would seek to distract him from the path.

Symbol 6/Via Dolorosa (4)

Veronica Wipes Christ's Face with Water

One by one the bonds of the outer desires are severed as the immortal Christ oversees the purification of the soul which is to become his bride. He requires that the initiate become centered in him and that the inner contemplative life begin. The body is purified in order to make it a worthy temple for the immortal self, or living God. The mind is also mastered so that it too becomes a fit vehicle, while the soul is cleansed of the lusts of passions collected during its pilgrimage through matter.

Symbol 7/Via Dolorosa (5)

Christ Is Given Vinegar and Gall

The Christian divine-elect is walking a difficult path, one which is little understood by those who still dwell in darkness. He experiences the hurts and disappointments of the Christ, who also tried to teach mankind a better way of life, only to experience the bitter dregs of persecution.

Symbol 8/Via Dolorosa (6)

The Crucified Is Nailed to the Cross
and Raised in Front of the Multitude

Having successfully walked the Via Dolorosa, the Christian initiate graduates to a higher order. The voice of the Christ speaks, saying, "The doorway of higher learning is now open to you." There is a brief period of rejoicing as the lesser mysteries have been mastered and the steep climb from the bottomless pit has been completed. However, many difficulties still lie ahead, for the initiate has at least four more periods remaining before him until spiritual rebirth is completed. Stations 6 through 9 of the Via Dolorosa represent years of purification and balancing between human and divine will.

Symbol 9/Via Dolorosa (7)

Two Thieves Are Hung with the Christ

As the immortal self descends to live in the flesh, it assumes both a lesser mind and a corporeal body. These two thieves stole the divine inheritance from the immortal self and bound it with many chains (desires) to the temporal world of matter. These thieves must die if the Christ aspect in man is to rise victorious and again walk on earth.

Symbol 10/Via Dolorosa (8)

The Soldiers Divide Christ's Garment into Four Lots

Though the initiate has long been governed by the inner Christ and undergone many disciplines, the final death of the lesser self is not yet assured. The two thieves can only be sacrificed through purification by the four elements. These elements signify *earth*, or the body, which is cleansed with *water*; and *air*, or mind, which is cleansed by *fire* (white Christ light). The difficulties attendant to the resurrection of the dead continue.

Symbol 11/Via Dolorosa (9)

Death on the Cross

Spiritual rebirth is at last accomplished and the Christ speaks saying "It is finished." At last the Christian initiate will be taken down from the cross and laid to rest in a new tomb. This station of the cross signifies completion of the crucifixion of the soul. Although the doorway to victory is now opened, the initiate must not become too jubilant, for it leads to a tomb. Nine periods of trans-formation have passed since the *resurrection of the dead* began.

Symbols 12, 13 and 14/Via Dolorosa (10), (11) and (12)

The last three symbols represent the final death struggle. The Christian divine-elect strives to loose the last chains of human bondage and rise victorious over matter in conquest of the cycles of necessity. The crucified is now laid in the tomb, and a great stone is rolled across the entrance. As in the beginning, there is no turning back. Station 10 refers to the initiate's return to the One (10=1) through the power of love which is the cohesive force of the universe. Next he will enter station 11 (11=2), at which time the doorway to higher power awaits him. And finally, the number 12 (12=3) is achieved, signifying victory. Love and Power, now gov-erned by Wisdom, roll away the great stone representing the last remnant of human will. The immortal one is at last free to walk upon earth, and the *resurrection of the dead* is complete. The newly arisen goes forth from the tomb to pursue his mission for a period symbolized as 40 days. This signifies the divine nature still encased in a sheath comprised of the four elements (corporeal body), but no longer governed by mortal boundaries.

1. The Christ (Gr. *christos*; anointed), meaning the individual and indwelling aspect of God in every human, is to be raised and re-united with the omniscient. This transformation must take place if the Son of man is to be transformed into the Son of God, thereby transcending worldly attachment.
2. Josephus, *The Antiquities of the Jews and the War of the Jews* (Michigan: Kregel Publications, 1963).
3. Emperor Heodusia, *De Santo Joseph at Arimathea*, A.D. 379.
4. Revillout 5, pg. 156.
5. Whenever a student, or disciple, is severed from the emanating consciousness of his teacher, the door between the two closes and the disciple must then walk alone and without support from his master. Simon Peter, therefore, realized that to be excluded from the presence of his teacher would be a fate worse than death, for he loved Jesus very much.
6. These words were spoken so that those who sat with Jesus would always remember that a perfect servant was also a perfect master. In heaven even the archangels, who represent the highest authority between God and man, remain ever subservient to their Creator. Those who continue to move only within the limitations of their own ways separate themselves from others, and from this separa-

tion is born hatred, anger, revenge, and selfishness. Thus, to serve the greater with calm resolution was not only pleasing in the eyes of the Master, but also one of the first requirements of anyone who seeks to pierce the deep inroads of the soul.

The Pieta   Burrows (cc)

And when darkness gently closes the eyes of the angels of the Earthly Mother, then shall you also sleep, that your spirit may join the unknown angels of the Heavenly Father.

Gospel of Peace
Vatican MS. /Szekely
Section II, ch. XIV: 20

CHAPTER VIII

THE COURT TRIAL OF JESUS THE CHRIST

All ye therefore that read this and translate it into other books, remember me and pray for me that God will be gracious unto me and be merciful unto my sin which I have sinned against Him.

Annas, the Protector
of praetorian rank
Acts of Pilate, Prologue

s dusk approached and day surrendered to the shadows of darkness, the moon cast its light over Jerusalem.[1] Its pale light danced across the distant mountain peaks in somber beauty, playing its eternal game of victory and surrender. In the distance, Jesus saw the faint outline of ghostly figures winding their way toward the sanctuary of Gethsemane, their burning torches lighting the way before them. He knew that they were coming for him, and if he had chosen, he could have escaped by taking one of the small pathways leading to the other side. However, if he were to follow the way of man, his work would die in the fires of forgetfulness. By living, the task which had been assigned him would fail. Therefore, he waited with calm fortitude as the tiny band of Sanhedrin guards led by Judas Iscariot moved ever closer to him.

Although Annas and Caiaphas had intended to hand Jesus over to Rome, no attempt had yet been made to effect this plan. It was arranged that the Master would first be tried before the official court of the priesthood, then taken to Pilate where a death sentence could be rendered. This would not be easy to obtain, as the jurisdiction of the priestly court was restricted to the 11 toparchies of Israel; hence, it had no authority over Jesus if he departed to Upper Galilee. At this time, however, he was within their dominion, so they had no alternative but to order that his arrest be made by their own officers. While the court was allowed to dispose of any case not involving a penalty of death, capital punishment could only be ordered by an edict from Roman authority. This limitation did not exist because the Sanhedrin lacked the necessary judicial right, but because their law forbade crucifixion.

As the entourage approached the place where Jesus stood, he said to his disciples, "Rise now and let us be going, for he who is to betray me is now at hand."

Even as he spoke, the Master saw Judas coming toward him, followed by the centurions, and stepping out from behind the shadows of the ancient olive trees which stood sentinel over the garden retreat, he asked the guards, "Whom do you want?"

"Jesus of Nazareth," they replied quickly.

Moving slightly ahead of his disciples, who now stood close to him, Jesus embraced this moment of betrayal and said, "I am he."

Upon hearing these words, the guards stepped forward to take him, but Peter drew his sword and cut off the right ear of Malchus, one of the high priest's servants who had been assigned to assist in the arrest. On seeing this Jesus chastised him, saying, "Put your sword into your sheath. Would you not have me drink from the cup which the Father has given me?"

After this, the soldiers placed Jesus between them and turning back toward the Holy City, began their descent toward the courts of Caiaphas. During this time, Judas, who had witnessed the arrest with averted eyes, slouched off into the night, his punishment having already begun. He would henceforth be cut adrift from the circle of disciples who had followed the Master, and from the one man who had treated him as an honorable human being. In spite of this treachery, however, he did not believe his kiss of betrayal would actually result in Jesus' death, nor did he know he had also signed his own death warrant.

As the guard unit made its way toward the palace of the Sanhedrin, the prisoner heard only the occasional cry of a child who was not yet asleep and the rhythmic beat of the guards' feet shuffling against the earth. Except for these sounds, the night was still and gave little indication of the drama to be enacted within the next 19 hours.

The judicial procedure of the Sanhedrin court required that it assemble under the leadership of the acting high priest, who also served as its presiding officer. At the time of Jesus' arrest, Caiaphas was acting in this capacity, having been appointed to this position by the reigning political authorities, rather than through the standard practice of election by a majority vote of the members. It was also an established procedure that an acquital required a simple majority, but a judgment of condemnation had to be rendered by a majority of two. Therefore, if 12 of the 23 judges forming the court voted for acquittal and 11 for conviction, the prisoner was discharged. However, if 12 were for a conviction and 11 for an acquital, the number of the judges was increased by adding two. This process was repeated until either an acquittal or a conviction was obtained. Under no circumstances could the number of judges exceed 71 (70 officiating priests and one high priest).

As previously arranged, Jesus was first taken to Annas, who was regarded as the high priest, *jure divine,* and had authority over spiritual matters. As the prisoner was brought before him, Annas inquired of Jesus concerning his disciples and his doctrine.

Jesus answered him, saying, "I spoke openly to the world; I even taught in the synagogue and in the temple where the Jews always gather. In secret I have said nothing. Now why do you ask me these things? Ask them who have heard me concerning that which I have spoken, for they know what I have said."

And when he had finished saying these things, one of the officers standing nearby struck him with the palm of his hand and asked, "Answer you so to a high priest?"

Not moving, Jesus replied, "If I have spoken evil, then you speak well, but if I have not, then why do you strike me?"

During this cursory interrogation of Jesus, only John the Beloved, the captain of the guard and his soldiers, a few servants, and one aide were allowed to witness the proceedings. Although John and Peter had both followed after the Master, John was the only one to be received into the inner chamber. His admittance was primarily due to the political influence of his father, Zebedee, who maintained some control in the decisions of the Sanhedrin. Since the nights were still somewhat chilly and a strong loyalty existed among the disciples, John went to the portress at the door to arrange for Peter to join him. When Peter saw the portress silhouetted in the lighted opening, he was filled with deep fear lest he was being summoned to defend his teacher. He was afraid that under such implications he would also be arrested. This did not stop the feeling of shame which coursed through his body, and when the woman spoke, asking if he were not a disciple of the prisoner, he replied that he was not. He was not aware that this act merely denied him admittance into the council room. Neither did he realize that his denial would become a burden which he would carry with him all his life, for the memory of this night would forever haunt him as the shadows of night cast their timeless vigil over the sleeping. Dropping his head against his chest in order to preclude recognition, he turned toward the fire which was being tended by the servants.

The place where Jesus awaited interrogation had once belonged to Herod the Great who had a passion for ostentatious display in the direction of magnificent architecture. Encompassed by a wall, the edifice portrayed unspeakable riches, particularly on the north side. However, Jesus had been taken through one of the side doors into the general council chambers, where he was first interrogated by Annas. After this he was bound and delivered to Caiaphas, who was not only designated as official high priest for the Sanhedrin, but also recognized as Pontiff by the Roman government. Although Annas' great age, ability, and influence, as well as being Caiaphas' father-in-law, gave him much authority, he was not equal to the power which had been assigned to his son-in-law. Therefore, it would fall upon Caiaphas to render sentence. It had been prearranged that a verdict of guilty would have to be administered before the senior members of the Sanhedrin, such as Gamaliel and Nicodemus, became aware of the meeting. Some, particularly the high priest, believed that these men were sympathizers of the Galilean. Also, Caiaphas was afraid that if too many of the more influential members of the court were present during the trial, others might be persuaded to favor an acquittal.

The traditional judicial procedure required that the members sit in a semicircle, enabling each person to see the others. At the front stood the two clerks of the court, one on the right and one on the left. It was their duty to record the votes of those in favor of an acquittal on one hand, and those in favor of a condemnation on the other. Customarily, three rows of learned men faced them, each of whom was assigned a special seat, and any prisoner who was to stand trial was expected to approach the court in a humble attitude and dressed in mourning. An unusual sequence was observed in capital cases. First came the arguments for the defense, followed by the arguments of the prosecution. If anyone spoke favorably concerning the accused, he was compelled to remain true to his decision throughout the trial. After both sides had been heard, a vote was taken. Beginning with the youngest, each member stood in turn, although on rare occasions the voting did begin with the council's most distinguished members.

It was approaching midnight when the guards led Jesus into the praetorium, where Caiaphas sat waiting for him. A number of the seats within the hall were conspicuously empty, particularly those of the senior Doctors of the Law. This, of course, would greatly facilitate a verdict of condemnation. If the accused was to be turned over for capital punishment under Roman law, then time would become a major factor. Delay could mean interference from those who would seek to release Jesus and remove him from the territorial jurisdiction of the Sanhedrin. One of the main purposes of the prosecution, of course, would be to prove that the accused claimed to be the Messiah. According to Rabbanical belief, such a person was to come forth as a powerful king and save the people from the hands of their oppressors. Thus, the council would argue that this man who drew people to him by performing miracles could not be the prophesied one, for he was not a powerful king. Were he really the Christ, he could have expelled the Romans and assumed the Jewish throne with ease and splendor.

While these events were taking place, Peter, who had continued warming himself over the open fire, began to ask questions concerning the penalties to be imposed upon the prisoner. One of the nearby guards took notice of the disciple's undue interest pertaining to the accused and began questioning him, asking, "What! Are you not also one of his disciples?"

Although Peter immediately denied any affiliation with the prisoner, one of the servants of the high priest who had been in the entourage during the arrest then inquired of him, "Did I not see you with him in the garden when he was arrested?"

Still fearing reprisal, the disciple again denied any affiliation with the Master, an action which would later cause him great sorrow. Unfortunately he, like Judas, did not believe his teacher's arrest was a matter of great seriousness and thought that he would soon be released. Although Jesus had spoken to the disciples concerning his death on several occasions, it was not a reality which Peter could understand. He had seen only the living, and the slender thread of a heart beat appeared strong and powerful, particularly in the young strength of a man who had done no wrong.

By this time Jesus had entered the court room. Caiaphas was in good humor as he faced the prisoner, for he had just finished the opulent feast prepared in anticipation of his forthcoming victory. He sat casually in front of the room with his gold embroidered cape partially draped over his shoulders. As he began to speak, the light from the evening candles and torches played upon the faint lines of self-centeredness and cruelty which were etched across his face, and his voice betrayed his arrogance.

The trial had not been in progress very long before the high priest perceived some difficulty and knew that he would have to exert pressure if he were to have the pleasure of Jesus' condemnation, for no witnesses came forward immediately to accuse the Galilean. Glaring down from his raised position, he looked at those in assemblage as a general looks at a coward. Squirming under such direct scrutiny, two of the lesser council members came forward with some bravado and said, "This man said that he was able to destroy the temple of God and then rebuild it again in three days."

On hearing these words the high priest rose and asked Jesus, "Answer you nothing concerning this charge which has been brought against you?"

However, Jesus held his peace, and Caiaphas, greatly agitated, admonished him, "I adjure you, by the living God, that you shall tell us whether you are the Christ, the Son of God."

The accused now raised his voice and spoke for the first time since being brought into the praetorium: "It is you who have said these things, for my kingdom is not of this world. Hereafter, you shall see that which is born of woman's womb sitting on the right hand of power and coming in the clouds of heaven."

Taking this statement quite literally, Caiaphas was greatly vexed, for he thought that the accused was saying that he expected to arrive in the physical clouds which floated over Israel. Turning to speak to the council, the high priest said, "This man has spoken blasphemy. What further need have we of witnesses? He cannot be the expected Messiah, and his reception by the people in this manner arouses the Romans against us and causes them to take away the rights we now enjoy. By now you must realize that it is expedient for us that one man should die for the people, so that a whole nation does not perish.

"I, Caiaphas, believe that the nation will be in jeopardy should the people follow the teachings of this man, and that his death would save this country from danger. Behold, now you have heard his blasphemy. What think you?"

And the court replied, "He is guilty and must be sentenced to death."

Following this decision, some of the members of the court spit in the accused's face, while others smote him with their hands, saying, "Prophesy to us, you Christ!"

Little realizing what they had done, the council now initiated a series of events which would lead to the eventual downfall of the glory of its nation. By 70 A.D., the Sanhedrin would be abolished, Jerusalem destroyed, and its people massacred by the Romans. Under Hadrain, the Romans would refortify Jerusalem as a Gentile city and hold it against its former inhabitants. Nor did Caiaphas realize that, as he spoke the words of accusation, he too had sealed his own fate, for he would be arrested later, along with Archelaus, Philip, and Annas, and taken to Rome for prosecution under an edict issued by Tiberius Caesar. Tortured at the hands of Roman soldiers, he would die on route, while Annas, his father-in-law, would be sewn in a fresh bull's hide and suffocated by the contraction of the drying animal skin.

The following letter from Tiberius which was delivered by Rachaab, Tiberius' messenger, explains the nature of these orders:

Since you have given a violent and iniquitous sentence of death against Jesus of Nazareth, showing no pity, and having received gifts to condemn him, and with your tongue have expressed sympathy, but in your heart have delivered him up, you shall be brought home a prisoner to answer for yourself. I have been exceedingly distressed at the reports that have reached me: a woman, a disciple of Jesus, has been here, called Mary Magdalene, out of whom he is said to have cast seven devils, and has told of all his wonderful cures. How could you permit him to be crucified? If you did not receive him as a God, you might at least have honored him as a physician. Your own deceitful writing to me has condemned you.

As you unjustly sentenced him, I shall justly sentence you, and your accomplices as well.

(Recension B of the Acts of Pilate, Pll: 6).[2]

After the meeting with Caiaphas, Jesus, who was still bound, was held in an area directly adjacent to the praetorium chambers. The room where he was detained somewhat resembled an antechamber and separated the street outside from the main council room. He was to wait here until morning, for it was now the intent of those who had presided at the council to take the prisoner to Pilate at the earliest possible moment. While Jesus awaited this move, he was subjected to a great deal of ridicule, but as yet he had not been harmed. However, as sunrise approached, he knew that the finale of his life on earth and his destiny was now close at hand.

In the meantime, John had left the chambers of the Sanhedrin to inform Jesus' family of the Master's arrest. Mary, the accused's mother, became greatly distraught when she heard the news, for Jesus was not only her teacher, but also her beloved son. She instructed John to go directly to her uncle, Joseph of Arimathea, who was also a member of the priestly council and possessed both wealth and considerable personal influence. She hoped that he might be able to intercede on her son's behalf. (*De Sancto Joseph at Arimathea*, Pynson).

It was still early when John arrived at Joseph's house and informed him of Jesus' arrest. The news did not come as a great surprise to the elderly statesman, as he was well aware of Caiaphas' hatred toward his nephew. Upon receiving the news, Joseph instructed John to return to Mary and leave the work of obtaining Jesus' release in his hands. Following the disciple's departure, Joseph hastily dressed, and on leaving the house, he went to contact Gamaliel and Nicodemus. He was greatly concerned over the illegality of the proceedings which had transpired during the previous night, for there had long been a thread of conflict between the members of the priesthood who had received their appointment by political means and those who had descended through royal lineage. It was, therefore, not only Jesus' arrest which occupied his mind, but also the corruption of the legal system within Israel.

A major part of the early morning had passed by the time Joseph was able to reach the other senior members of the court who had been excluded from the meeting the night before. Upon entering the chambers of the high priest, he and Nicodemus learned that Jesus had already been taken to Pilate. The two men then made haste to Herod's castle, arriving barely in time to witness the inauguration of the proceedings. Gamaliel, having come earlier, met them outside the entrance of the judgment hall and, by the seriousness stamped on his face, Jesus' uncle knew that the course of events was not going well.

Pontius Pilate, a descendant of Pontii, was procurator of Judea at the time of Jesus' arrest. As an illegitimate son of Tyrus, king of Mayence, he had originally been sent to Rome as a hostage. Later, having committed a murder, he was banished to Pontus where he subdued the barbarous tribes and in so doing earned the honorable appointment of governor of Judea under the reign of Tiberius. Since it was customary for the procurators to reside at Jerusalem to maintain order during great feasts, Pilate was at this time in residence at Herod's palace.

Caiaphas and his supporters, as well as Jesus and those who guarded him, arrived at Herod's palace expecting Pontius Pilate to command the death penalty without extensive inquiry. Unfortunately for them, Pilate had developed some respect for the utility of justice and understood his business too well to wantonly provoke rebellion. For this reason, he decided that the accused would stand formal trial.

It was still early morning when Jesus was led into the procurator's judgment hall, where the chief priests and scribes had now assembled and were waiting formal trial. Since it was the last day of the week, as well as the end of the Passover, some of those attending refused to enter the judgment hall, lest they defile themselves. Among those present, of course, were Annas and Caiaphas, along with Somne, Dothain, Gamaliel, Judas Levi, Nepthali, Alexander, and Jairus. Also present were Daniel, Joannus, and Raphal Robani, the Pharisees who would ultimately sign the official death warrant.

As soon as the opening formalities of the official court were over, those who had been chosen to lead the prosecution instigated by Caiaphas came forward before Pilate to accuse Jesus, saying, "We know this man, he is the son of Joseph the carpenter, begotten of Mary. But he says that he is the Son of God and king. Moreover, he pollutes the Sabbath, thereby destroying the Law of our fathers."

Now it came to pass that Pilate had heard many rumors concerning the man from Nazareth, and because of these he was possessed by considerable curiosity. Looking with some interest at the dissidents who stood before him, he inquired, "And what things does he do that destroys the law?"

In response to the question, the accusers replied, "We have a Law that states we should not heal any man on the Sabbath. But this man by his evil deeds has healed the lame and the bent, the withered and blind and paralytic, the dumb and those possessed, all on the Sabbath day."

With some surprise, Pilate asked, "By what evil deeds?"

By this time, those who had been appointed as spokesmen were showing great enthusiasm toward the task assigned them, and responded quite vehemently, saying, "He is a sorcerer, and by the power of Beelzebub, the prince of devils, he casts out devils which are all subject to him."

In some ways Pilate found this response highly amusing, and looking down at them with a hint of mirth in his eyes, he astounded them by stating, "It is not possible to cast out devils by an unclean spirit, but rather by the god Ascipius."[3]

It became increasingly apparent during this early part of the inquiry that Pilate might not consider interrogating the prisoner, let alone condemn him to die. Clearly, this would pose a serious threat to Caiaphas' plan. Therefore, the prosecution saw that they would have to move quickly now and demand a full scale trial. Looking toward the high priest for their next instructions, they saw him motion for them to keep silent, and stepping aside they made room for him to pass between them. Once Caiaphas approached the judgment seat, he looked up to the king and said, "We beseech your majesty that Jesus appear before you and be examined."

However, Pilate now motioned for the priest to come even nearer to him, and in half humorous quiescence, asked, "Tell me, how can I, who am a governor, question a king?"

Quickly Caiaphas replied, "We do not say that he is a king, but he claims it for himself."

When Pilate heard these words, his curiosity became intensified, and calling one of his messengers forth he asked that Jesus be brought to him. According to his instructions, the courier departed and went to get the prisoner, but when he came to Jesus he took out his kerchief and spread it upon the earth, saying, "Lord, walk on this and enter, for the governor has called you."

This action aroused great tribulation among those who sought Jesus' death, and one of the accusers cried out to Pilate, "Why did you not summon the accused by a herald rather than a messenger? When he saw him, the messenger worshipped him and spread out his kerchief upon the ground, and made him walk upon it like a king."

Therefore, Pilate summoned the messenger to him and asked, "Why did you spread your kerchief upon the ground for the accused to walk upon?"

In response to the governor's inquiry, the messenger looked up toward the praetorium seat and said, "Sir, a few days ago, when you sent me on a trip from Jerusalem to Alexander, I saw this man sitting on a burro and the children of the Hebrews paid great homage to him by bowing before him and waving palm branches. Others spread their garments beneath, crying out, "Save now, you who are of the highest, blessed are you who come in the name of the Lord."

These words caused even further agitation to the prosecution, and one of the Jews challenged the messenger, "The children of the Hebrews cried out in Hebrew, therefore how could you possibly know what was being said?"

Constraining himself from derision, because there were certain rules regarding conduct during legal proceedings, the messenger replied, "I asked one of the Jews what was being said, and he interpreted for me."

When the messenger finished speaking, Pilate, who had been intently listening, turned toward the high priest and those with him and asked what had been said in Hebrew. And the Jews replied, "Hosanna membrome barouchamma adonai."

"Hosanna and the rest," the Governor questioned, "how is this to be interpreted?"

"It means, save now, thou art the highest; blessed is he who comes in the name of the Lord," one of them interpreted.

By this time, Pilate had some difficulty maintaining his normal dignity, for the charges lacked any criminal action. So far they had been amusing, so he asked, "If you yourselves bear witness to the words which were said by the Hebrew children, how then has this messenger sinned?"

For a brief time, the prosecution held its peace, so the governor spoke again to the messenger, "Bring the prisoner in after what manner you will."

Once again the messenger stepped into the adjacent room to summon Jesus, and again laying his kerchief upon the floor before the accused, he said, "Lord, enter; the governor calls for you."

While this preliminary dialogue between Pilate and the prosecution had been going on, Jesus remained quietly outside the judgment hall, for he alone knew what decision the court must ultimately render. No individual could change the course of events, as the outcome of the trial was under the control of a power greater than any person now present in the courtroom. Three years earlier, during his solitary struggle on the Mount of Temptation, this day had been revealed to him. Now that the vision had come to pass he accepted its challenge, just as he had then, that the world might be a better place to live for all mankind. As yet he suffered no pain, but those final hours of surrender still lay before him.

By this time some of the disciples, including his mother and Mary Magdalene, had gathered outside the palace, where John instructed them to remain. He felt it best that they wait there, lest the sight of the proceedings cause too much sorrow. After he had insured their welfare, he then went into the palace to obtain news of the proceedings. He met briefly with Joseph, Gamaliel, and Nicodemus before they entered the judgment hall, where Nicodemus was later to plead Jesus' defense. John saw by their serious demeanor that the situation was not favorable; yet there was little he could do about it.

Unfortunately, when the senior members of the Sanhedrin entered the hall, John was restrained from accompanying them and compelled to wait outside the room with various supplicants seeking an audience with the governor. He remained calm, for Jesus had made all his disciples aware of his impending death. On the other hand, facing this possibility was difficult and he hoped that his Master's prophecy was not yet to come to fruition. In the event he could be of some assistance, the disciple decided to remain near the praetorium, rather than return to those at the gate.

While this was taking place, Jesus was before Pilate. On seeing the prisoner, Pilate immediately turned to the prosecution and asked, "Why have you brought me this man?"

Seeing that things were not going as quickly as he had planned Caiaphas, who had assumed the duty of representing the prosecution, now stepped forward to state the charges: "I found this man perverting our nation. He says that he will destroy our temple and abolish our religion. Many times has he spoken blasphemy, saying that he is the Messiah king."

The charges which the Sanhedrin had just related to the governor meant little to Pilate. He had been sent to Israel to prevail over Roman interests, and whether the Jewish temple and Jewish law were abolished meant nothing to him. However, since the trial had officially begun, he was inclined to see it through lest he offend the priestly representatives of the people of Israel. To do so would have made his work more difficult, and neither was he above the favors which the prestige of his office bestowed upon him. So, calling the prisoner toward him, he asked, "What do these people have against you? Will you not now speak in your defense?"

As Jesus stood before the governor, he was complacent and without fear. His kingly bearing, along with the power developed with his years of mastership, gave him an appearance of elegance and control which set him apart from those around him. He paused but a moment before he replied, and then he said, "If these people had not been given the power to speak, they could say nothing. Good or evil, every man has power over his own mouth."

On hearing these words Pilate observed the accused with even greater curiosity. Now, more than ever, he preferred that the matter not be brought before him, for he was fearful of its consequences. However, since he had been appointed to this uncomfortable position of mediator between the political authority of Rome and the supreme religious power of Israel, he felt it would not be wise to offend the prosecution. Already those in the courtroom were becoming restless, and it was quite clear to them that this unseemly matter was not being disposed of as expediently as they had hoped. The strategy of the accusers now turned to discrediting Jesus by innuendos about his birth.

With great braggadocio, one of the spokesmen for the Sanhedrin pushed his way to the forefront, and standing before Pilate, he pointed an accusing finger at Jesus, saying, "What do we see? First, this man was born of fornication; second, that his birth in Bethlehem was the cause of children being slain; third, that his Father, Joseph, and his mother, Mary, fled to Egypt when the accused was born because they had no confidence before the people."

No sooner had these words been uttered, when there was a commotion in the praetorium, and one of the devout Jews stepped forward, saying, "We say that he is not born of fornication, for we know that Joseph was betrothed to Mary in the manner of the law."

At this outbreak Pilate looked first at the man who had come forth to defend Jesus, and then he shot a questioning glance at Caiaphas, who had incited the charges. Shaking his head over the inconsequential nature of the argument, he asked, "Now one of you claims that there were espousals, while the other says that there were not. Who may I ask is right?"

Both Annas and Caiaphas reacted quickly to the governor's question and, with considerable arrogance, they replied, "The multitude of us say he was born of fornication, yet we are not believed. Those others are mere proselytes and disciples of his."

"Come close to me, Annas and Caiaphas," Pilate instructed, "I wish to know what you mean by the term proselytes."

Now this question posed some difficulty to the prosecution, for there were two classes of proselytes: first, Gentile strangers who, while living among the Jews, had bound themselves to observe the seven Noachian precepts against idolatry, blasphemy, bloodshed, uncleanness, theft, eating flesh with the blood, and obedience; second, proselytes of righteousness who, having been formally admitted to participation in the theocratic covenant, professed their adherence to the doctrines and precepts of the Mosaic Law. If any of the Gentiles wished to become citizens, the law sanctioned their admission on the condition they be circumcised. In view of such complexities, it seemed more expedient for Caiaphas to reply to Pilate's question by simply saying, "They were born of Greeks and have now been Jews."

Turning his head in the direction of those who seemed to be defending the accused, Pilate asked, "And how do you answer your priesthood on this matter?"

For a moment there was silence, for there were those in the hall who knew that Mary and Joseph had descended from the blood lineage of King David and had been married in the Temple of Jerusalem by Zacharias. Some had even witnessed the espousal.[5] Among those who had was Mary's uncle, Joseph of Arimathea. (St. Joseph of Arimathea at Glastonbury, Lewis). Stepping forward for the first time, Joseph spoke quietly saying, "We were not born proselytes, but are of Jewish lineage, and we speak the truth. We were present at the marriage of Joseph and Mary."

Now Pilate, having been a man of devious ways himself, well understood the trickery of Annas and Caiaphas. For this reason, he decided to select 12 men to represent the accused, and when this had been accomplished he said to the 12, "I adjure by the safety of Caesar, are these things true which you have said, that he was not born of fornication."

"We have a law that we swear not, because it is a sin," one of them replied. "Therefore, we suggest that you allow the accusers to swear by the safety of Caesar that if it is not as we have said, we will be guilty and subject to death."

On hearing these words the governor turned directly toward Annas and Caiaphas, inquiring of them, "Answer you nothing to these things?"

By this time it had become quite obvious that the two high priests were not pleased with the way the hearing was progressing. Their hope for an expeditious death penalty was not bearing fruit. And, it was also apparent to them that the attempt to discredit Jesus' lineage was also failing. Therefore, Caiaphas, feeling that he had more authority with the Roman officials, decided to take over the primary arguments of the prosecution. Responding to the governor's inquiry he stated, "These 12 men are believed who say that Jesus was not born of fornication. Even though the whole multitude of us cry out that he was born of an unmarried woman, is a sorcerer, and claims he is the Son of God and a king, we are not believed."

With great agitation now, Pilate commanded the hall be cleared with the exception of the 12 men who spoke on Jesus' behalf. Among those who had been chosen to remain were Eleazer, Asterius, Antonius, Caras, Samuel, Crispus, and of course, Gamaliel,

Joseph, and Nicodemus. Next Pilate commanded Jesus to be set apart and, turning to the 12, asked of them, "For what cause do they desire to put this man to death?"

"I am afraid, sire," replied Gamaliel, "that there is great envy toward this man because he has many powers and has healed on the Sabbath."

"Are you saying then," Pilate continued, "that for good work one must be put to death?"

By now Pilate was becoming incensed, and making his exodus from the judgment hall, he went into the outer chamber where he said to those awaiting his verdict, "I call the sun to witness that I find no fault with the accused."

In reply, Caiaphas spoke up rudely, saying, "If this man were not a malefactor, we would not have delivered him to you."

"If this be so," the governor stated firmly, "I suggest that you take him and judge him according to your own law."

Ever shrewd with the tongue, the high priest persisted in his effort to obtain a verdict of death and retorted, "It is not lawful for us to put any man to death."

"Then," asked Pilate, "has God forbidden you to slay and allowed it to me?"

With these words he returned to the praetorium, and taking his seat, called Jesus forward to interrogate him further. "Jesus, I have watched you during these past three years and examined your teachings and actions," Pilate said quietly. "You are a liberal and I am not sorry for that, for your uprightness is well known. I do not know whether you studied Socrates or Plato, for as it has been reported to me I see that your simplicity is combined with both the teachings and actions of a philosopher. Yet, you well know that your uprightness has caused many to conspire against you. In Socrates' case, the mob rose up against him and he was persecuted and put to death by poison for dissenting from the polytheism of the Greeks. But Socrates was an old man, while you are still in the prime of your youth. Moreover, you see the people also clamor against me and charge me with taking your part. I must, therefore, ask you some questions in order to better render a decision."

Throughout the preliminary skirmishes which had taken place before him, Jesus had retained dignity and silence. However, now that he had been asked a direct question by the governor, he replied with calm fortitude, saying, "Governor, you are not capable of stopping the river from its course. If you command a river which is cascading down a mountain to stop and run backward, it instead obeys the laws of the divine power. In this case, I am afraid that the blood of the innocent must be shed before the fruit can ripen on the tree.

"Will you then answer this question, Jesus of Nazareth," the governor queried, "Are you really a king?"

"You ask me whether I am a king in the sense you would understand," Jesus replied, "yet my present condition should answer you plainly. Were I a king in this respect, the Jews could not have brought me before you in such a manner."

"Jesus," Pilate said, shaking his head, "you do bring great problems for your own nation, and for the chief priests who have delivered you to me. What have you done?"

"My kingdom is not of this world," Jesus answered. "You ask if I am a king, yet it is for this cause that I was born and came forth, that everyone who is of truth shall hear my voice."

"Then what is truth?" Pilate questioned.

"Truth is of heaven," Jesus replied.

"Are you saying that there is not truth on earth then?" asked Pilate with eager curiosity, for he was somewhat of a student of philosophy and it pleased him to discuss such matters. Very few who came into his presence could discourse on life and death, and in this respect the governor found the accused exceedingly challenging.

"You can see how those who speak the truth are judged by those who have authority on earth," Jesus answered.

Once more Pilate rose from his seat in the judgment hall and went to address those who were waiting in the outer room. On arriving there he announced, "I find not fault with the accused."

Then one of the contenders quickly rose and avowed, "But this man said, 'I am able to destroy this temple and in three days to build it up.'"

"What temple are you speaking of?" Pilate asked.

Although Jesus had referred to the temple of the living God, or the body, when he had spoken, this man was not yet awakened and could not therefore understand such a sublime mystery. He, as had others with him, thought that the Master had spoken about the Temple of Solomon and had been greatly offended. Thus, he answered the Governor's question, saying, "We speak of that which took 46 years for Solomon to build. However, this man said he will destroy it and then rebuild it in three (resurrection through the union of body, soul, and spirit) days."

Looking at those who had gathered, Pilate spoke again, "I am guiltless of the blood of this just man. See you to it."

And the Jews replied, "His blood be upon us and on our children."

Next, Pilate called the elders, the priests, and the Levites into the judgment hall that he might speak to them privately. "Do not do this," he cautioned. "There is nothing worthy of death in your accusation, for it pertains only to healing and profanity of the

Sabbath."

"Are you suggesting then," asked Caiaphas, "that if a man blasphemes against Caesar he is not worthy of death?"

And Pilate shook his head, for that was not so, and he replied, "He is worthy of death."

"So," Caiaphas retorted, "a man is worthy of death if he blasphemes against Caesar, yet this man has blasphemed against God."

By this time the governor was highly incensed, and turning away from the priests, he quickly strode back into the judgment hall. It was quite obvious that the Sanhedrin would settle for nothing less than death of the accused. On the other hand, he saw that the charges were weak and not within the jurisdiction of Roman law. Once again, shaking his head, he commanded the Jews to depart from the judgment hall and called Jesus to him, asking, "What shall I do with you?"

During Pilate's discussion with the Sanhedrin, Jesus had remained bound between two guards in the praetorium, his countenance calm and unconcerned. A man of few words, and one who frequently spoke in parable, his reply to the governor's latest question was brief, "Do as it has been given you."

"And how has it been given me, Jesus?" the Governor asked.

Then Jesus spoke of Moses and his prophecy concerning him. Those who were seeking his execution overheard this and interrupting Pilate's questioning inquired of him, "Why do you have to hear more of this blasphemy?"

Pilate, turning to those who again contrived to sway his judgment, spoke sharply, "If his words be blasphemy, you take him to your synagogue and judge him according to your law."

"It is contained in our law that if one man sins against another, he is condemned to receive 40 stripes, save one," one of the Jews argued. "But he that blasphemes against God should be stoned."

"Then," replied Pilate, "take him and avenge yourselves of him in whatever manner you will."

"We want him to be crucified," responded Caiaphas quickly.

As the governor looked upon the people standing by, he saw that some of them were weeping and he said, "He does not deserve to be crucified. You can see that some of the multitude does not share your desire for his death."

But the Jewish elders countered, "To this end have all of us come to you, that he should be put to death."

"Why should he die?" Pilate once again questioned.

"Because he calls himself the Son of God and a king," was the reply.

At this point, Nicodemus ben Gorion presented himself before the governor to plead the defense of Jesus. He was not only a respected member of the Sanhedrin council, but also a fine orator. His own appointment to the supreme court had come through family lineage, as well as popular vote, and his wealth and influence made him very powerful. Addressing the procurator, he said, "I entreat you, righteous judge, that you favor me with the liberty of speaking a few words."

Looking on Nicodemus with some favor, Pilate acknowledged this request and motioned for him to speak. He hoped that a solution to the difficult situation would somehow be forthcoming from the mouths of those who appeared to defend the Galilean. He was well aware of the fact that the trial had taken a more serious turn, and he sought some opening which would enable him to dismiss the entire matter.

Now, having received the governor's permission to speak, Nicodemus approached the judgment seat with great dignity, saying, "I spoke to the elders and the Jews in their assembly. What is it you would do with the man who is now accused? He is a man who has wrought many useful and good works on earth. Let him go, and do him no harm. If the signs he gives are of God, they will stand, but if they are of men, they will come to nothing.

"Verily, when Moses was sent by god into Egypt, he also performed many signs which God had commanded him to do before the Pharoah of Egypt; and there were certain other members of the royal court who did likewise. Though the Egyptians held them as gods, the signs of the royal courtiers perished, as did those who believed in them. So I urge you to let this man go, for he is not deserving of death."

Nicodemus' speech was not received well by Caiaphas and Annas. They had sought a quick verdict for this very reason, hoping to avoid confrontation with the senior members of the court. Even now, some of the prosecution was weakening, for Nicodemus had approached them in the assembly room outside of the praetorium.

Caiaphas, now hoping to show bias on the part of the defense, interrupted, "You have been his disciple and for this reason you speak on his behalf."

However, Nicodemus countered this remark quickly, saying, "Has the governor also become his disciple that he speaks on his behalf? Or did Caesar appoint him to this dignity?"

When the high priest heard these words, he was consumed with rage, for if his attempt to obtain a condemnation of the accused failed now, a trial at some future time could also be barred. The thought of such a prospect was not at all pleasing to him, nor to the others who thirsted for blood. A change of strategy would now be required and a trap for Pilate would have to be set. Within a brief period, although he did not presently know this, Caiaphas would be successful in an attempt to maneuver the governor into the desired position.

During the interim, however, others came forward to plead Jesus' defense, among them a man who had lain on his bed with palsy for 38 years before being healed by the Master. Also, Veronica, who had been cured of a blood issue, stepped forward as well. However, others mocked them saying, "This man is a prophet, and the devils are subject to him."

At this innuendo Pilate commented sarcastically, "If devils are subject to him, are not your own teachers also?"

By this time, the governor could see that further testimony would be of little value. Already the trial had become a mockery. Finally, thinking to free himself from an awkward situation, he authorized the accused to be taken to Herod, saying, "As long as this man's actions are known in Galilee and he is from Galilee, then he should be tried there. Since the tetrarch is now in Jerusalem, indeed in this very castle, I will send him to Herod that he might do what he thinks best. It is my duty to observe the laws and rights of local officials."

In spite of the fact that many people continued to call for an immediate verdict, Pilate instructed his secretary, Manlius, to escort the entourage to Herod forthwith, with a message that he should try the case according to justice and the laws of the Roman empire. Having set this plan in motion, Pilate immediately withdrew from the judgment hall and retired to his private chambers where his wife, Lady Procla, awaited.

"Oh, Pilate," she pleaded, "I have dreamed that the ravens gathered together in a tree under whose shade a man took shelter. In the meantime, the sun was darkened and a great storm seemed to uproot the tree, and a voice cried out, 'Innocent blood is shed in the Valley of Kedron.' I saw the face of Caesar besmirched with mud, for the authorities had acted unjustly against the innocent, and a babe spoke from his cradle to wise and learned men. I awakened to hear the barbarous Jews saying, 'He deserves death.' Again I slept and beheld a great crowd being tried before a just and righteous king, and I saw you standing among the condemned. For this reason, I beseech you to ponder these things, lest the wrath of Caesar fall upon you."

Even as Pilate and his wife sat at the table, one of the attendants came to him and said that the Jews had returned with Jesus and were nearing the judgment hall. Then Manlius delivered a note from Herod saying, "Jesus, who is accused by the Jews and condemned by their council, was born in Bethlehem of Judea. Since his prosecution is taking place in Judea, it is the responsibility of the governor of Judea to see to his trial. The tetrarch of Galilee has no jurisdiction over the case."

This left Pilate with no alternative, but to return to the judgment hall. Upon entering, he paused for a few moments to speak to Nicodemus, who was standing nearby, "What am I to do, for I risk sedition among the people?"

As Pilate took his seat, he looked upon the scene before him with deep concern. Although some time had elapsed since the guards had taken the Galilean to Herod, little appeared changed. The courtroom was once more filled with the irascible faces, and the issue which gathered them together like vultures still needed to be resolved. However, believing that it might be possible to bargain for the Galilean's life, the governor said, "You know you have a custom that at the Feast of the Unleavened Bread I should release a prisoner to you. Now I have a prisoner under condemnation, a murderer, Barabbas, by name, and this Jesus who stands before you, in whom I find no fault. Which one shall I release to you?"

A furor broke out among the dissidents, among them some who had been bribed, and they shouted out, "Barabbas."

Although this answer did not particularly surprise Pilate, it did not please him, and staring down upon the multitude he asked, "What then shall I do with Jesus, who is called the Christ?"

The moment had arrived when the prosecution could spring its trap, for they too had been able to formulate a new plan. Stepping out to face the governor, Caiaphas spoke boldly and arrogantly, saying, "You are no friend of Caesar's if you let this man go, for he has called himself the Son of God and a king. Will you, therefore, have him for king and not Caesar?"

These words were to seal the fate of the accused, and a short time later a death warrant was issued. Pilate was greatly vexed when he heard Caiaphas' words, for he realized he had been trapped and that further defense of Jesus would make him appear a traitor to the Roman Empire. Speaking almost sadly, he said, "Your nation has always been seditious, and you rebel against your benefactors. Even as your God delivered you out of Egypt, nourished you with manna and gave you a law, you provoked him to anger. Moses supplicated on your behalf and you were not put to death, but now you accuse me of hatred for the emperor."

And Pilate rose up from the seat of judgment and prepared to leave. But the Jews cried out, "We know our king, even Caesar and not Jesus. This was he whom Herod sought to slay, and when his father Joseph heard it, he and Mary took Jesus to Egypt. And when Herod learned of it, he destroyed all the children of the Hebrews that were born in Bethlehem."

On hearing these words, Pilate was even more distraught, and

DEATH-WARRANT OF JESUS

THE CHRIST

Sentence rendered by Pontius Pilot, acting
governor Lower Galilee, stating that Jesus
of Nazareth shall suffer death on the cross.

In the year 17 of the Emperor Tiberius Caesar, and the 27th day
of Nisan in the city of the holy Jerusalem-Annas and Caiaphas
being priests, sacrificators of the people of God-Pontius Pilate,
Governor of Lower Galilee, sitting in the presidential chair of the
praetory, condemns Jesus of Nazareth to die on the cross between
two thieves, the great and notorious evidence of the people saying:

1. Jesus is a seducer.
2. He is seditious.
3. He is the enemy of the law.
4. He calls himself falsely the Son of God.
5. He calls himself falsely King of Israel.

Orders the first Centurion, Quilius Cornelius, to lead him to the
place of execution. Forbids any person whomsoever, either rich or
poor, to oppose the death of Jesus the Christ.

Signed: Daniel Robani (a Pharisee)
Joannus Robani
Rapheal Robani Capet (a citizen)

The foregoing words were engraved in Hebrew on a copper plate,
on the reverse side of which was written, "A similar plate is sent to
each tribe." It was found by Commissioners of Art of the French
army while excavating in the ancient city of Aquila in the Kingdom
of Naples.

silencing the people, he said, "So then, this is he whom Herod sought."

And he took water and washed his hands before the sun saying, "I am innocent of the blood of this just man; see you to it."

Now Pilate commanded the veil to be drawn before the judgment seat, and he said to Jesus, "Your nation has accused you of claiming to be king. Therefore, I decree that you should first be scourged according to the law of pious emperors. Then you shall be hanged upon a cross in the garden where you were taken, and let Dysmas and Gestas, the two malefactors, be crucified with you."

As Jesus was taken from the hall of judgment, he was led past his sympathizers, and he paused momentarily to gaze upon them with compassion. Then the soldiers rudely shoved him forward, that they might continue on their way. Those who loved him knew that it was as he had prophesied, he was to die. John, his cousin, who had patiently kept the all-night vigil, went to notify those who waited outside the gates that it was over, that the Master was to be crucified.

In the meantime, the soldiers of the governor took Jesus into the common hall, and summoning more guards, stripped him and began to scourge him. This was done with thongs, or whips, made of leather straps. The ends were tied either in single or multiple knots, referred to as a scorpion. Although the customary form of scourging called for the accused to be stretched out on a frame, in this case the prisoner was taken to a stone wall just inside the courtyard. Here his hands were tied with leather bands and secured to iron rings. Dressed only in a loincloth now, the accused was compelled to face the wall, leaving his back exposed to the soldier to receive the prescribed 40 lashes.

The condemned allowed no flinching as the whip struck its first blow, and then the next, and the next. His mind focused only on remaining one with the Infinite who had assigned him this destiny. In this manner, he could remain removed from the events happening to the outer body, rather than bound to it. Therefore, the cracking sound of the whip as it lay against him held no dominion over him, and he was able to bear his affliction without acknowledgement of its intent. He would maintain this kingly bearing throughout the remaining hours of his life, and would ask no mercy. To do so would lessen the purpose for which he had lived and show weakness in accepting the allocation of God.

When the scourging was completed, the Roman guards who were responsible for administering the penalty freed Jesus, while others who were present put a scarlet robe on him to signify the royal status of a king. Then they placed a crown of thorns on his head, which had been made of intertwining branches of the paliurus shrub after the manner of the garland accorded to Roman heroes, that they might ridicule him. By this time, Jesus' back and legs were not only covered with small, deep cuts, but the thorns were beginning to dig deeply into his forehead. Next, the soldiers put a reed in his right hand to represent the royal scepter, after which they bowed their knees before him and mocked him, saying, "Hail, King of the Jews." Spitting on him, they took the reed to smite him on the head and removed the robe. Then his own raiment was returned to him and he was led away to be crucified.

Crucifixion required that the condemned carry his own cross, or at least that part of it called the cross beam, in which case another was compelled to share the burden. Upon arriving at the place of execution, the accused would be stripped of his clothes and drawn up on the perpendicular beam which had been previously erected. There he would be secured by cords and nails. Before the nailing or binding took place, a medicated cup, usually a mixture of wine and soporific myrrh, would be offered to confound the senses and deaden the pains of the sufferer. The limbs of the crucified generally remained hanging about three or four feet above the earth.

As Jesus was led away to his execution, the soldiers brought his cross, called an *immissa*, or a straight beam with an interlocking cross beam. This death was befitting a master who had sought to fulfill the ancient mysteries, for the cross represented the bondage of the soul by its corporeal body comprised of the four elements. Removal of the temporal body sheath signified return to one's heavenly estate, or the Garden of Eden. Exactly what circumstances originally caused the Romans to adopt this form of torture as capital punishment for their criminals is not fully understood. However, it may be assumed that the punishment is related to the mysteries of immortality and sacrifice. Used for 6,000 years in ancient rites to represent bondage and resurrection, the cross has always stood as the emblem of man's suffering.

As the procession surrounding the condemned Jesus and two thieves wound its way out of the palace entrance toward the valley leading from Jerusalem to Golgotha, the site of the execution, the Master passed near his mother. She was standing just outside the gate of the judgment hall with Mary Magdalene and some of the other disciples who had gathered to await news. Following John's announcement of Jesus' impending death, the women were urged to return home, for the disciples feared that the sight of the crucifixion would be too painful for them. However, neither of the Marys adhered to this suggestion, but chose to remain nearby, in desperate hope that there might be a last minute reprieve from the judgment.

When Jesus' mother saw her son in pain, bleeding, and secured to his cross, she nearly swooned. This was actually the first moment she fully realized that the child to whom she had given birth was to die. In spite of this, however, she still refused to leave and leaned on John's arm as she and others who loved her son followed behind. Beside her, Mary of Magdala, also stunned by the sight, began to weep. The sight of the weeping women, accompanied by his disciples, caused the wounded man to stumble. As the soldiers noticed Jesus' weakness, they spotted Simon the Cyrene returning from the country, and ordered him to help bear the cross. After Simon's aid had been solicited and he had picked up the lower end of the cross beam, the column continued on its way. Prodded by the guards, the people and the condemned slowly made their way along the steep, narrow streets of Jerusalem. Later, these streets would be named the Via Dolorosa, or trail of mourning.

The Master, who had been allowed little or no sleep during the previous 24 hours, was nearing exhaustion. He experienced deep pain in the upper part of his thighs, which was caused by the heavy weight of the cross and the steep path leading to the site of execution. This pain caused him to falter again, but those who came to help him were pushed back by the guards. Many whose homes and shops lined the path came out to watch, and the swarm of people grew in number. Even those who had once gathered to hear him discourse in the temple shouted blasphemies, and occasionally children threw stones. Behind him, the two malefactors, Gestas and Dysmas, struggled with their own crosses and fared little better.

Arriving at the barren mountain summit of Golgotha, the procession halted and Jesus fell to the ground. In the meantime, the Roman soldiers went about selecting places in which to erect the crosses. According to custom, when this was done they offered the sufferers a drink of wormwood and wine, called Toska, to render the condemned unconscious before crucifixion. However, Jesus refused it, for he chose to do nothing which would lessen the afflictions imposed upon him. To have done so would mean he had shirked the full responsibility of the greater work, which was now nearing its earthly completion.

After the erection of the crosses, it was time for the final punishments to be inflicted. The first ceremony entailed tearing the clothes of the condemned, leaving each bare except for a loincloth. Because the Romans made mockery of the Sanhedrin's allegations that Jesus called himself a king, he was to be elevated in the middle between the two thieves to denote that he was the greater. His cross was even distinguished from the others, in that the perpendicular beam extended well above the cross beam.

Then the guards laid hold of Jesus and, lifting him up, laid him upon the cross beam. Next they tethered his arms and legs with strong cords. This was done tightly so that the circulating blood would flow back to the heart, thereby causing the breath to become more labored. Lastly, they drove thick iron nails through his wrists and feet. Although he almost swooned as the spikes pierced him, unlike Dysmas and Gestas, whose unearthly screams rent the air like tortured specters, he made no sound. When this ritual had been completed on all of the condemned, the crosses were lifted into their respective positions. Later in the day the heat of the sun would add to their agony.

After the three men had been secured, the soldiers took possession of Jesus' clothing and ripped them into four pieces, with the exception of the tunic which was not torn. Then they cast lots for his garments.

By now, many curious people had been drawn to the site of the execution, among them several priests who had come to ridicule the condemned Jesus and to exhort the people to mock him. The Romans, in derision of the Jews, had fixed a tablet on the cross over Jesus' head which designated him *King of the Jews*. This deeply angered the priests, but inasmuch as they still possessed some fear of Pilate, they swallowed the insult. Victory, after all, was theirs and the enemy of the priesthood was being removed. Instead, they sought to amuse themselves with mockery, and one passerby jeered, "You who say you can destroy the temple and build it again in three days, save yourself. If you be the Son of God, come down from the cross."

Another in the crowd added, "He saved others; but himself he cannot save. If he is the king of Israel, let him now come down from the cross, and we will believe him. He trusted in God, so let God deliver him now, if He will have him. For he said, 'I am the Son of God.'"

Later in the day, others of the priesthood, who were still not fully satisfied by their success, arrived to look upon the crucified. The noise of their arrival all but drowned out the sound of those weeping near the cross. They were adorned in great splendor, so that all might see and recognize that their power extended even over rulers. Then they too began to mock Jesus. Gestas, one of the thieves, joined in, for he still hoped that he might be spared by some miracle. "If you be the Christ," he said, "save yourself and us."

However, Dysmas rebuked him, saying, "Do you not fear God, seeing that you are also condemned? And we justly, for we receive due reward for our deeds, but this man has done nothing."

Then he said to Jesus, "Remember me, Lord, in your kingdom."

On hearing this request, Jesus replied, "Verily, I say to you, that today you will be with me in paradise." He said this that those who suffered with him might be comforted, for they could not know that pain, death, and old age did not exist beyond the corporeal world.

Finally, darkness began its descent upon earth, and many of the people returned to Jerusalem. However, Jesus' family, friends, and disciples remained at Golgotha, while some of the Pharisees also stayed hoping the accused might still come down from the cross. When this did not happen they felt deceived and angry. For the most part Jesus suffered quietly, but as evening approached he quietly began to recite parts of the twenty-second psalm: "My God, my God, why have you forsaken me? Why are you so far from helping me, and from the words of my roaring? My strength is dried up like a potsherd; and my tongue cleaves to my jaws; and you have brought me into the dust of death. For dogs have compassed me; the assembly of the wicked have enclosed me, and they have pierced my hands and my feet. They part my garments among them, and cast lots upon my vesture."

At this time one of the centurions, being a noble man of compassionate nature, allowed John to conduct the mourning women to the foot of the cross. As Jesus looked down upon his mother, his Aunt Mary, Mary Magdalene, and his disciples, he said to his mother, "Woman, behold your son," and to John, his beloved, he said, "Behold your mother."

It was growing darker now and Jesus realized that the time for deliverance was near, so he said to the guard, "I thirst." After this, one of the centurions prepared a sponge dipped in vinegar and placed it on a long hyssop cane (ancient rite symbolizing purification). The vinegar (representing the bitter dregs of persecution) was a strong and intoxicating beverage called *Sikera* which was made from a mixture of sweet ingredients and designed to dull the senses. This he raised to the lips of the condemned.

As the evening progressed, the earth began to shake, and the terrified guards turned to pray to their gods, believing now that Jesus was beloved of them. Even in these final moments of life, the Master spoke on behalf of the people, saying, "Father, forgive them, for they know not what they are doing."

Then a thick red fog moved out from the Dead Sea and the mountains around Jerusalem continued to shake violently. In these last moments the Master was free of pain, and with his final words the world would know that he had seen the magnificent finale of his earthly mission.

1. This chapter is taken from the Gospel of Nicodemus, or Acts of Pilate; Dr. M.R. James, *Apocryphal New Testament* and Hennecke Schneemelcher, *New Testament Apocrypha* ,Vol. I.

2. The same facts concerning the life of Mary Magdalene are revealed in the Greek Holkam, translated by Dr. M.R. James, former provost of Eton University.

3. The name Ascipius was derived from the Egyptian culture and originally signified the divine spark of the Godhead incarnate in all men, as did the Greek work *Christos* in later periods. One such man believed to have attained this supreme state of transformation during the great period of Egyptian civilization was Hermes, also identified by some with the personage of Enoch. That Pilate should now speak of Ascipius indicated that he had either read the Divine Pymander, one of the sacred Hermetic records, or had in some other manner become familiar with the Egyptian Mysteries.

Eli, Eli, Lemana Shabakthani
My God, My God, for this I was spared.
Translated from Peshitta

Matthew 27:46

Gloria

Burrows (cc)

Eli, Eli, Lemana Shabakthani My God...My God...for this I was spared.

CHAPTER IX

RESURRECTION OF THE DEAD

Lay hold of the wings of the Angel of Eternal Life, and soar into the paths of the stars, the moon, the sun, and the endless Light which move around their revolving circle forever, and fly toward the Heavenly Sea of Eternal Life.

Gospel of Peace
Vatican MS./Szekely
Section II, ch. XI: 28

s the last threads of human life ebbed from Jesus' body, his soul slipped out of the heavy body sheath into the descending darkness. The faint image of the hourglass which was etched in the disappearing sun showed that the last grain of sand had fallen. Although human lives would come and go, before the man from Galilee lay only timeless eternity and a history not yet written. Truth and justice have been his two-edged sword, light his shield, and while his life on earth was finished, the battle of darkness and light had just begun. High in the angelic kingdom he would continue the work he had started on earth, that the brotherhood of man be hastened. Freed from the earthly shackles which housed life and death, old age and pain, he could walk once more among the souls of Abraham and Moses. And never would he forget the vision of man's future world, when it would unite with the Light, and peace would come to earth. His cousin, John the Beloved, would write about this later, saying:

And I heard a great voice out of heaven saying, Behold, the tabernacle of God is with men, and he will dwell with them, and they shall be his people, and God himself shall be with them, and be their God.

Revelation 21:3

By this time the air had become stilled, as though it was holding its breath for the final moment, and then the earth began to quiver like a woman in grief. The ground heaved, the mountains shook, the rocks cracked, and the temple gave way. As the Creator of the universe took his beloved son to his bosom, and Jesus drew his last breath, it was as though the grief of God stretched out across the land and gave one last thunderous tremor. After this there was an awful silence, almost as though he asked, "How many more lives will you waste before you live in harmony with one another?"

One of the Roman centurions who had taken the women to the foot of the cross in the last hour, now believed in both the divinity and the innocence of the condemned, and sought to comfort Jesus' mother. About this time also, four soldiers came to break the legs of the three men who had been crucified. This was done to insure that the lord of death could complete his work, for with the descent of night came the Sabbath. Since the law of the Jews prescribed that no one should be left hanging on the holy day, it was necessary that the cruel task be expedited. Otherwise, the condemned sometimes lived several days and suffered greatly.

Earlier that afternoon, when it became obvious that Jesus was to die, Joseph of Arimathea had gone to Pilate to ask for his body. It was normally the Roman custom to allow the crucified to hang until death, then bury them in a potter's field without markers. However, in this instance, Pilate, who was aware of the influential position Joseph maintained in the political life of Jerusalem, was predisposed to grant him permission to bury the body. Posthaste, he sent a messenger to the site of the execution to learn if Jesus was dead, and to instruct the guards that his legs should not be broken. On his arrival, the messenger approached the centurions and inquired concerning Jesus. He was told that the condemned was no longer alive, and that the bones had not yet been broken.

Then one of the soldiers pierced the body of the crucified with a spear, allowing the point to pass over the hip into the side. As the corpse did not convulse, the centurion accepted this as verification that Jesus was indeed dead. However, blood and water flowed from the wound.[1]

By this time, Joseph had returned from his visit to Pilate and had been informed that his nephew was no longer alive. Nicodemus, having arrived at Golgotha earlier, was standing nearby with a burial ointment of aloes and herbs. Together the two men examined the body, somewhat surprised that Jesus was already dead, for he had hung less than nine hours. Hoping that there might be a thread of life remaining, Joseph said to the soldiers, "We must immediately have the body, that it might be buried with the bones unbroken."

Hastening to the cross, Joseph and Nicodemus slowly untied

Jesus' binds, pulling the spikes out of his hands and feet first. Then they carefully laid him on the ground and covered his body with powerful spices and salves. Next, they applied balsam to the wounds left by the large stakes, but felt it unwise to dress the wound in the side because the flow of blood and water might be beneficial if, indeed, any life force remained. After this, the two men bound Jesus in linen clothes and spices after the manner of the Jews and had the body carried to a new sepulchre which Joseph had built. When the grotto had been smoked with aloes and other strengthening herbs they gently placed the body, now stiff and inanimate, on a bed of moss-like substance. Having completed this task, they rolled a large stone in front of the entrance. The night was exceptionally humid, and there were a series of after-shocks from the earthquake, offering a bizarre conclusion to the day's strange events.

Although the next day was the holy day and consecrated to God, it did not stop the chief priests and Pharisees from coming together for another meeting with Pilate. They were concerned that the disciples might attempt to steal Jesus' body and spread some rumor that he had risen. Therefore, when the conspirators finally gained an audience with Pilate, they said, "Sire, we remember that the deceased said he would rise again in three days. For this reason, we are asking that the sepulchre be made secure until the third day, lest the disciples come by night and steal him away and then tell the people that he has risen from the dead. We are saying to you that such a second error would be worse than the first."

Pilate longed to put the trial of Jesus behind him, for it had brought him much discomfort. Always aware of the cunning and trickery of Caiaphas, however, he proceeded with some measure of caution to avert further trouble. Addressing those who stood before him, he said, "You have a watch of your own, so I suggest that you go on your way and make it as secure as you can."

Although the governor's answer did not particularly please the priesthood, they left the auditorium and returned to their own quarters. Once there, they made arrangements for their guards to make the sepulchre secure by sealing the stone and setting a watch.

As these events were taking place, Joseph and Nicodemus deliberated together concerning protection of the tomb. They were afraid that the townspeople, who had been incited earlier, might return to break into the tomb and mutilate the body. In order to avert this, they decided that they should also have someone stand watch over the tomb until the body could be prepared for proper burial. Therefore, they sent one of the young officiates at the temple to ensure that everything in the tomb remain untouched.[2] When the soldiers saw the unidentified robed intruder approaching, they were overcome with great fear. It had already been a troublesome night for them, and since they were very superstitious, the death watch stimulated their imagination with eerie possibilities. In spite of this, however, the officiate did as he had been instructed and sat down near the entrance of the tomb to await those who would later come to prepare the body for proper burial.

Unfortunately, as the dawn of the Sabbath approached, it became apparent that the priesthood had not yet finished its mischief. Now they conferred with Caiaphas to see what could be done to thwart Joseph of Arimathea, who was still causing them much concern, and Nicodemus, whose fine oratory at the trial had turned the minds of many. And it came to pass that they first went to the synagogue to search for Nicodemus, where he was performing the usual priestly oblations.

When Nicodemus saw them approaching, he asked, "Why have you come to the synagogue?"

In answer to his question, the Jews retorted, "And why are you at the synagogue? You are a confederate of him who was put to death. Surely his portion shall be with you in the life which is to come."

On hearing this, Joseph, who was also at the temple, spoke up, saying, "Why are you vexed with us? Is it because I asked for the body of Jesus? You know that I simply placed it in my own tomb, wrapped in clean linen, and that a stone seals the door of the cave. You do not deal justly with me because you are not satisfied to have only crucified him."

The Jews, fearing that Joseph would incite Jesus' disciples against them, grabbed hold of him and ordered that he be held in custody until the first day of the week. They said to him, "You know that today is the Sabbath and we cannot do anything against you, but you shall not bury Jesus, for we will feed his flesh to the fowls of heaven."

Calmly Joseph answered, "Yours are the boastful words of Goliath, who reproached the living God and the holy David. But one among you who was circumcised in the heart took water, and washed his hands before the sun, saying, 'I am innocent of the blood of this just person, see you to it.' And you answered Pilate, saying, 'His blood be upon us and upon our children.' Now I fear for you lest the wrath of God come upon you and upon your children."

Joseph's words made the priests angry, and they carried him off to a windowless room in the palace and locked him up. Since the law required that all offenders be tried before the court on the first day of the week, the council convened the following morning. It was their intent to secure another death warrant. As soon as the council was seated they commanded that Joseph be brought before them in dishonor. However, when they unsealed the door to the room where he had been imprisoned, he was gone, for Nicodemus had obtained his release during the night. Since they dared not lay a hand on him who had defended Jesus so ably before Pilate, they could do nothing more. (Gospel of Nicodemus, or Acts of Pilate XII:I).

Approximately a day and a half after the crucifixion, another blow befell the priesthood. When Mary Magdalene, Mary the mother of James, Salome, Joanna, Lia, and Bernice arrived at the tomb to prepare the body of Jesus for final burial according to the custom, they discovered that the stone had been rolled away and the body was gone. In the place where Jesus had lain there remained only the burial cloth, some remnants of byssus wrappings, and, further away, the customary face cloth. As they stood there amazed, two white robbed figures came from the tomb and asked of them, "Why do you seek the living among the dead? He is not here but is risen."

Deep sorrow was etched across Mary Magdalene's face, and turning, she hastened toward the city to notify the disciples that the Master's body had been taken. She had gone but a short way when she came upon Peter and John walking toward the tomb. Approaching them with great emotion, she cried, "They have removed the Lord from the tomb, and we do not know where he has been taken."

When they heard this, the two men also hastened to the sepulchre. They saw the scattered linen clothes and that the napkin, which served as a face cloth, was not with the other linen, but folded separately. Now they also became greatly concerned, for they believed that the body might have been stolen and destroyed by enemies of their work. However, one of the white-robed figures who appeared to be watching over the tomb spoke to them kindly, saying, "Jesus has risen; therefore, do not seek for him here, but go to his disciples and tell them that he goes before them into Galilee."

Although these instructions left John greatly perplexed, he and Peter did as they had been instructed and returned to the city to gather the other disciples and determine what should be done. After they departed, Mary continued to remain standing outside the grave, weeping. Peering inside the cave again, she saw that the two men were now putting the tomb in order, and when they heard her weeping they turned and asked, "Woman, why are you weeping?"

"Because they have taken away my Lord," she replied. "And I do not know where they have laid him."

Yet even as she spoke she saw another person, a stranger dressed as a gardener, approaching the entrance of the tomb. Believing him to be a caretaker of the graves she said, "If you have taken the body of Jesus away, please tell me where you have put him, and I will remove him."

Then, the stranger called her by name, his tone greatly changed.

Immediately, Mary recognized the voice and ran toward him quickly, crying out, "Rabboni" (meaning Rabbi or Master).

Fearing that she would touch him in her enthusiasm, Jesus quickly said, "Do not approach me. Still I live, but soon I must return to our Father in Heaven. I want you to go to my disciples and tell them that you have seen me, and that I will come to them soon."

Greatly excited by what she had witnessed, Mary turned and hastened along the dirt road leading into Jerusalem to carry out the instructions of the Master.

Some moments later, as Jesus walked along the wall, he reached the small gate which led into the valley. As he neared it, he overheard two of the women who had come to attend to the burial talking among themselves concerning the disappearance of his body. With some amusement, he stepped out of the shadows and approached them quietly. However, when they saw him they were greatly alarmed, for they believed they were seeing an apparition. However, he spoke to them, saying, "Tell my friends that I will go into Galilee, and that you will see me there."

After this, he turned in the direction of Upper Galilee and his beloved Capernaum. As he walked along the road, he chanced upon two men who appeared to be in deep conversation. It so happened that he knew them quite well, and when he overheard one of them lamenting over the fact that the resurrection had not been fulfilled, he inquired, "What are you discussing with each other that makes you so sad?"

The men did not indicate that they recognized the stranger as he spoke these words, for the hood of Jesus' robe was pulled down about his face lest he be recognized by those whom he wished to avoid. Now it happened that one of them was named Alpheus, father of James the Less, and he answered Jesus, saying, "Are you a stranger to Jerusalem that you do not know what has happened these past days?"

With the same amusement he showed to his disciples during the years of his journeys with them in Galilee, he inquired with great seriousness of what things they spoke.

"We refer to Jesus of Nazareth, a man who was a prophet, mighty in word and deed before God, and before the people. The high priests and the elders delivered him up to the judgment of death, and they crucified him. We were hoping that he would rise again that he might save Israel, but it has been three days since these proceedings were inaugurated and he has not been seen. Earlier today some of our women went to the tomb, and when his body was not found they came and said to us that two angels had told them that he had risen."

With some of the mischievousness of old, Jesus continued walking with them, expounding upon the law from Moses up through all the prophets, and interpreting the scripture. On hearing these things, the two travelers began to take great interest in this man who walked with them, for they had heard such teachings from only one other. And it came to pass that, as they neared the village of Emmaus, their destination, they constrained Jesus, saying, "Abide with us, for it is nearing evening and the day is spent."

And the Master entered their home that he might take meat with them, but when he took the bread, blessed it and broke it, and gave it to them, they recognized him. After this, they talked for some length and then he left them. With great excitement, Alpheus and the other man then departed for Jerusalem to confer with the disciples and tell them what they had seen. They found the 11 gathered together, as well as some of Jesus' close followers (Mary Magdalene, Jesus' mother, and Mary, the mother of James and John). Immediately, they related the events of the day, saying to the disciples, "The Lord is risen indeed, and has appeared to us."

One disciple was missing from those who gathered, and this was the betrayer, Judas. After learning that a death warrant had been issued against Jesus, he sought to return the 30 pieces of silver to his priestly relatives, hoping to purchase back the life of his Master. This was to no avail, for even Annas and Caiaphas knew that a betrayer to one man would betray another. And when they refused his offering, he threw the silver down at their feet, after which he left the praetory with the echo of their mockery still ringing in his ears. On returning to his home, he found his wife sitting by the open fire and roasting cock for their meal. He said to her, "Rise up, wife, and provide me with a rope, for I would hang myself as I deserve."

Shaking her head over such silliness, his wife said to him, "Why do you say such things?"

"The truth is," he answered, "I have wickedly betrayed my Master, Jesus, and allowed the evil-doers to take him before Pilate and put him to death." Then he removed himself from the house that he might make a halter of rope, and went out and hanged himself. (Acts of Pilate, Recension B of the Greek).

Even as these events were taking place, things were also becoming increasingly more unfavorable for the priesthood. The Sanhedrin guards who had been assigned to watch the tomb where Jesus had been placed, arrived at the castle and reported the disappearance of Jesus' body to Caiaphas. The high priest was greatly angered, for not only had Joseph of Arimathea eluded them, but also their greatest fear had become a reality. Hoping to avoid reprisals from the priesthood, the guards told of a great earthquake, after which an angel descended from heaven, rolled away the stone, and sat upon it. They said that they had heard the voice of the angel speaking to the women, "Do not fear, for I know you seek Jesus, who was crucified. He is not here, for he has risen. Go quickly and say to his disciples that he has risen from the dead and is in Galilee."

The priest looked at the guards with considerable disbelief and inquired of them, "With what women did he speak?"

"At what hour was this?" another priest questioned.

"It was at midnight," the guards replied.

These words caused Caiaphas to become exceedingly angry. Although he certainly did not believe what he was hearing, he knew that such a rumor could cause great trouble. Inquiring further, he asked, "Why did you not take the women?"

"We became sick with fear," the men complained, "and how could we take them when there was no light?"

Disdainfully the priest frowned upon the men, deep suspicion crowding at his soul, for he felt they were trying to escape punishment. With great sarcasm, he said, "I do not believe you. Take heed lest this report be heard, or the public might begin to find favor with the Galilean."

After this, the priesthood convened in council to decide the best course of action. It was finally arranged that a considerable amount of money was to be paid to the guards and that they were to be instructed to respond to any inquiry by saying that, while they slept, Jesus' disciples came and stole his body away. The council also finally agreed to protect them in the event the matter come up for hearing before the governor. Placated by the bribe, the guards took the money and did as they were instructed. However, as with all evil, the matter was to worsen, for one deceit bred another. Finally the entire deception collapsed, and the legends and stories of Jesus of Nazareth went on to survive the supreme test of time.

In the meantime, while these events were taking place, Mary Magdalene arrived at the house where the disciples were gathered and notified them that she had seen the Master and he had spoken with her. This message came as a great surprise to those who were assembled, and some doubted its truth. Most assumed that Mary had been caught in a fanciful dream born of her great sorrow, for they knew she had loved Jesus deeply. However, as darkness fell and they gathered behind closed doors to partake of the evening meal, Jesus came and stood in their midst, saying, "Peace be unto you." After saying this, he showed them his hands and his side in order to dispel any doubt remaining.

As they gathered joyfully around him, he instructed them saying that they were to fulfill the great work and bring forth the Brotherhood of Man, and he urged them not to give up hope. He asked that they be of good cheer. Then he blessed them, and said he could not tell them where he was going, for he must go alone, but when they wanted him he would come, for he yet had much to say to them. At last departing from their midst, he went through the door, quickly disappearing into the shadows of the night.

Now it happened that Thomas, one of the 12, called Didymus, was not among the disciples on this particular occasion, and when he heard that they had seen Jesus, he said, "Except I see the imprint of the nails in his hands and put my finger into them and thrust my hand into his side, I will not believe."

Eight days later, as the disciples again gathered, and Thomas with them, Jesus entered through the door and stood in their midst, saying, "Peace be unto you." Then turning to Thomas with a faint flicker of amusement, he said, "Reach forth your finger and behold my hands, and reach out your hand that you might thrust it into my side. Don't be faithless, but believing."

Following this, Jesus disclosed to his disciples that they were not safe because of his presence among them, after which he commissioned John to go to the house of Lazarus to see his mother and his other friends and tell them that he would soon be with them. Shortly thereafter he appeared in Bethany, asking that those who awaited him there believe in truth, and warning them of false expectations. When he departed this time, he further advised them that he must now go to Galilee to strengthen his disciples in the good work, for he knew that they had come to believe that he would be with them forever, now that he had risen. This was not to be, of course, for his final earthly appearance came on the fortieth day after his crucifixion.

It was not long before rumors began to circulate through Jerusalem that Jesus had been seen. Although Caiaphas spread the word that the disciples had stolen Jesus' body and invented a miraculous story, many citizens were prepared to believe that Jesus had indeed risen by the hand of God. They began complaining of the injustice done to him, and the high priest feared a rebellion.

While the rumors flowed like rampant rivers over dry land, the disciples departed for Upper Galilee. As they gathered there, they asked one another, "Where shall we go? Our Master has fixed neither time nor place."

While this discussion was taking place and there was a question of whether to search for Jesus in Nazareth or Capernaum, Peter suggested that they seek to provide sustenance and not be idle. Skillful at fishing, he invited the others to go to sea with him that evening. So, Thomas, Nathaniel of Cana, John and his brother, James, and two others joined him in the boat. They anchored a short distance from the shore and cast out their nets. When morning came they saw a figure standing on the shore, but they did not recognize him for he was a distance away.

"Boys, have you got anything to eat?" the man called out. And they replied that they did not.

"Then set your net on the right side of the boat and there you will find fish," he instructed.

Immediately, the disciples threw the net over the right side of the boat, and when they sought to haul it aboard, it was filled with many fish. And John looked at those in the boat with great joy, exclaiming, "It is the Lord." Whereupon he dived into the sea and swam ashore.

The others followed by boat. When they landed, they found a fire had already been laid, and Jesus said to them, "Bring the fish you have caught and let us dine." They dared not question his instructions, for they knew it was the Lord. This was the third occasion upon which Jesus had shown himself to his disciples since he had risen.

After they had dined, Jesus turned to Peter and asked, "Simon, son of Jonas, do you love me more than you love these fish?"

Nodding his head up and down in the affirmative, the disciple felt much like he had when he first met Jesus, inept and childlike. Noting this, Jesus laid his hand on his shoulder, and spoke to him kindly, "Then go forth and teach. Verily, I say to you, when you were young you clothed yourself and walked where you wished, but when you are old you must stretch out your hand and allow yourself to be clothed by light, that you walk where the footsteps of darkness cannot reach."

Sometime after this, the disciples gathered together in the grove of palm trees near the Sea of Galilee, and Jesus came again and stood in their midst. It so happened that only minutes before this, Thomas had questioned the subject of truth. Now the Master spoke to him, saying, "Truth is in God alone, for no man, nor any body of men, knows that which God alone knows. To man truth is revealed according to his capacity to understand and receive it. Truth has many aspects and one person may see a single side only, someone else another side, but some see more than others, as it is given to them.

"Behold again, when one begins to climb a mountain, seeing a peak, he says, 'This is the top of the mountain; let us reach it.' Yet when he has reached that height, lo, there is another beyond it. He who is in the valley does not have the same view as he who is on a hilltop. But to each his perception is the truth, as his mind sees it at that time, and so remains until a higher truth is revealed. And to the soul which receives a higher light, more light shall be given. Therefore, do not condemn others, that you be not condemned.

"As you keep the holy laws of life which I have given you, so shall greater truth be revealed to you, and the Spirit of Truth (the Holy Spirit) which comes from above shall guide you through many wanderings. Be faithful to the light you possess until a higher light is given to you. Seek more light, and you shall have it abundantly, and rest not until you find it."

After saying these things, Jesus announced that he would meet with them again in Jerusalem.

Continued rumors of the resurrection scattered far and wide over the land. People claimed to have seen Jesus here, and sometimes there, although other times the sightings were mere figments of overactive imaginations. Anyone who observed a white-robed figure thought himself to be witness to the miracle of him, he who had risen from the dead. Soon eyewitness accounts began to filter back to the priesthood, eventually descending upon them like a swarm of devouring locusts, and the stories lay waste the fields of careful planning which Caiaphas had planted.

It came to pass during this time of miracle and turbulence, that three men from Galilee also arrived in Jerusalem: Phinees, a priest; Addas, a teacher; and Aggaeus, a Levite. Their stories added yet more kindling to the already raging fire, for when they entered into the city, they immediately sought out the elders of the synagogue and said to them, "We saw Jesus and his disciples sitting upon the mountain which is called Mamilch, and he said to them, 'Go into all the world and preach to every creature; he that believes and is baptized (ritual to symbolize the purification of the lesser nature of man) shall be saved, but he that does not believe is condemned.' Even while he was still speaking to his disciples, we saw him taken up into heaven."

The wrath of the priesthood waxed strong when they heard of this, and they spoke to the visitors in great anger, "Come you here to pay your vows to God? If so, to what purpose is this idle nonsense which you have babbled to the people?"

However, one of the men stood his ground, saying, "If these words which we have spoken are sinful, then do to us that which seems appropriate in your eyes."

In reply to this insolence the priest took out the Book of the Law, and after reading from it, he admonished them to speak no more on such matters. Then he ordered them to leave Jerusalem. When the three had departed, he set out for the temple, that he might discuss the matter with Annas and Caiaphas.

"Why are you troubled?" Caiaphas asked. "Do you not know that Jesus' disciples gave much gold to those who watched the sepulchre, and taught them to say that an angel came down and rolled away the stone?"

"That may be so," the priest replied, "but how did his soul return to his body, and why was he seen in Galilee?"

In reply to this inquiry, Nicodemus arose and addressed the council, reminding them that within their own scriptures there were those whom God had taken up also, such as Enoch and Elias. He therefore suggested that a thorough investigation of the matter be commissioned. This idea greatly pleased the priesthood, who immediately dispatched members of the order to search the coasts of Israel. Although no one found Jesus, they did encounter Joseph of Arimathea, but dared not take him.

It was not many days thereafter before Jesus appeared to his disciples in Capernaum and announced that he would see them again in Bethany. And when the disciples had gathered at the house of Lazarus, he came among them for the last time, saying, "Verily, I say to you, the Kingdom of Heaven is within you. But the time will come when that which is within will be made manifest without, for the sake of the world. Love you one another, and by this shall all men know that you are my disciples."

When evening fell, Jesus went with his disciples to the Mount of Olivet. Passing over the Kidron River, he stopped and wept for Jerusalem, then continued in silence. Coming to the place he had enjoyed most, he halted and urged his disciples to be of good cheer, and firm in their faith. He prayed for the friends he had to leave, then lifting his arms he blessed them. As he did so a mist rose around the mountain, tinted by the descending sun, and when the disciples, who had knelt down, lifted their eyes, they saw that he was gone.

Investigation into the disappearance of Jesus did not prevent the stories from spreading even further, and the traditions established at that time would long outlive the rivalry of the Sanhedrin court. Although centuries later, many were to ponder over the missing pages in the life of the man from Galilee, the answer to the puzzle was obvious. Annas and Caiaphas issued an edict, admonishing the public that Jesus' words were the false teachings of a heretic.

Because it was mandatory in those days that all Jews abide by the rule of the priesthood, the man in the scarlet robe might have disappeared in obscurity but for the work of his disciples. John the Beloved was to pierce the center of Asia Minor, and build the seven churches of Ephesus. Joseph of Arimathea, forced into exile, along with Lazarus, Martha, and Mary Magdalene, went on to establish the Christian teachings in England and convert the powerful Celtics, while a later convert named Paul started the first church in Rome. Thomas traveled to India, Simon taught throughout Maurelanta, Libby and among the powerful southern Yorkshire Celts, while Nathaniel journeyed into Armenia. The fields they planted brought forth a fertile harvest, for the teachings of Jesus of

Nazareth could no more be suppressed than the rains of Lebanon.

As a result of the trial and crucifixion, an incurable rift began to eat its cancerous way into the priesthood. Although it was still Annas and Caiaphas who whispered into the ear of imperial Rome, the traditional aristocracy of Nicodemus ben Gorion, Joseph of Arimathea, and Gamaliel held the temple, as well as the ear of its people. These two forces were destined to battle again and again, with neither winning a complete victory. Although the two priests responsible for Jesus' death eventually defeated most of their principal adversaries, a triumphal victory was denied. For it came to pass that, after the death of Gamaliel and Nicodemus and the banishment of Joseph into exile, the Sanhedrin became imprisoned by the newly enthroned emperors of Rome, who hungered for complete control over the land. By 70 A.D. the supreme council of Israel was little more than a shredded remnant of its former glory, and in the end, the just hand which guides the universe had dealt out chastisement for the unjust.

There shall be no peace among peoples till there be one garden of the brotherhood over the earth.

Gospel of Peace
Vatican MS./Szekely
Section II, ch. 62:1

1. This fact would later cause many scholars to question whether Jesus was actually dead when his body was removed from the cross. Later, because of his numerous appearances, extensive rumors would flood Israel. Some believed he had resurrected, some believed he never really died, and others believed that it was not his physical body which appeared to his disciples, but a semi-material, or immortal light body.

2. Crucifixion, Austin Publishing Co., Los Angeles, Calif. 1919. A translation of a letter written by an Essene Elder to one of the Essene Communities in Alexandria, seven years after the crucifixion.

Lying in State   Burrows (cc)

And no one knew if an hour had passed, or a year, for time stood still and it was as if all creation held its breath.

Gospel of Peace
Vatican MS./Szekely
Section I, ch. 26:3

IN MEMORY OF THOSE GREAT MEN
WHO FOLLOWED JESUS OF NAZARETH
AND GAVE THEIR LIVES FOR
THE BROTHERHOOD OF MAN

JOHN THE BAPTIST: Son of Zacharias and Elisabeth, cousin to Jesus of Nazareth, John the Beloved, James the Great, James the Less, and James the Just. Native of Judea. Beheaded by the edict of Herod the Tetrarch.

JOHN THE BELOVED: Son of Salome and Zebedee, brother to James the Great and cousin to Jesus of Nazareth, James the Just, and James the Less. Native of Bethsaida. Served imprisonment on the Island of Patmos under the edict of Domitian. Died of natural causes in the service of God.

JAMES THE GREAT: Son of Salome and Zebedee, brother to John the Beloved and cousin to Jesus of Nazareth, James the Just, and James the Less. Native of Bethsaida. Slain by sword by command of Herod the Tetrarch.

SIMON: Called Peter, son of Jonas, brother of Andrew. Native of Bethsaida. Crucified head downward in Rome under the edict of Nero.

ANDREW: Son of Jonas, Brother to Simon Peter. Native of Bethsaida. Scourged and crucified by the Aegeates of Patrae under the edict of Agrippa, grandson of Herod the Great.

PHILIP: Originally, a disciple of John the Baptist, brother of Mariamne. Native of Bethsaida. Stoned and crucified in Hierapolis, a city of Phrygia.

MATTHEW: Son of Mary and Alpheus, brother of James the Less and cousin to Jesus of Nazareth, John the Beloved, James the Great, and James the Just.

Native of Capernaum. Died a natural
death in the service of God.

JAMES THE LESS: Son of Mary and Alpheus,
brother to Matthew and cousin to
Jesus of Nazareth, John the Beloved,
James the Great, and James the Just.
Native of Capernaum.
Hurled from a pinnacle of the temple
to his death in A.D. 62.

THOMAS: Called Didymus. Native of Antioch
Imprisoned in India and taken to a
mountain where he was pierced by spears
until dead.

THADDEUS: A Hebrew, originally a disciple of John the
Baptist. Died of natural causes in Beirut in
the service of God.

JAMES THE JUST: First Bishop of Jerusalem,
son of Joseph and stepson of Mary of
Nazareth, half brother to Jesus of Nazareth,
cousin to John the Beloved, James the
Great, and James the Less. Stoned to death
by order of Ananus, a high priest of the
Sanhedrin.

SIMON: The Zealot, the Canaanite. Native of Cana
of Galilee. Taught throughout Maurelania,
Libby, and among the powerful southern
Yorkshire Celts. Crucified by the Romans at
Caistor, Lincolnshire under the edict of
Ratus Decianus.

NATHANIEL: Bar Tholmai (Bartholomew). Originally, a
disciple of John the Baptist. Native of Cana
of Galilee. Flayed alive and crucified head
downward in Armenia.

PAUL: Saul of Tarsus, a Pharisee. From the tribe
of the city of Cilecia. Chained and beheaded
under the edict of of Agrippa.

JOSEPH: of Arimathea, a Sanhedrin,
uncle to Mary of Nazareth and
great uncle to Jesus of Nazareth.
Exiled from Israel. Died of natural causes
on English soil after founding the first
church in Britain.

BIBLIOGPAPHY

Anglo-Saxon Chronicles King Alfred the Great, England 891.

Apocrypha Cambridge at University Press, Great Britain.

The Apocryphal New Testament translated by Dr. Montague Rhode James, Litt. D., F.B.A., F.S.A., Provost of Eton, Oxford University Press, London, England 1926.

The Apocryphal New Testament by William Wake, M.R., D.D., Archbishop of Canterbury, and Rev. Nathaniel Lardner, D.D., published by Simkin Marshall, Hamilton, Kent and Co., Glasgow, Scotland.

The Apocryphal New Testament Simpkin, Marshall, Hamilton, Kent and Co., London.

The Archko Volume or The Archeological Writings of the Sanhedrin and Talmuds of the Jews translated by Drs. McIntosh and Twyman. Keats Publishing, Inc., New Canaan, Connecticut 1975.

Astrologers Pew in Church by Reverend John Jacobs, ordained Methodist Minister and major in Bible studies at Wheaton College, the National Bible Institute, Perkins School of Theology, Southern Methodist University and University of Southern California. Published in Honolulu, Hawaii 1979.

Augustine Robert Meagher, New York University, 1978.

Augustine of Hippo Peter Brown, University of California Press, 1969.

The Babylonian Genesis Alexander Heidel, University of Chicago Press, Chicago and London, 1942.

The Bible as History by Werner Keller, 1909, translated from German by William Neil., William Morrow and Co., Inc., N.Y.

The Book of Enoch by R.H. Charles, D. Litt., D.D., Clarendon Press.

The Book of the Secrets of Enoch by W.R. Morfill, M.A. Clarendon press, 1964.

Chronicle of Fabius Ethelwerel King Lucius, England, 975-1011.

Complete Works-The Second Birth Omraam Mikhael Aivanhov Prosveta, U.S.A. edition, 1976.

Confession of Pontious Pilate by Fabricus Albinas, translated into Arabic by Jerasimas Jared, late Bishop of Zahleh in Lebonon. Translated from Arabic into English by Beshara Shehadi, Interpreter of Arabic for the Government of Australia, 1893.

The Crucifixion of Jesus by an Eyewitness, Austin Publishing Co. Los Angeles, California, 1919.

The Crucifixion by an Eyewitness, Indo-American Book Co., 1972.

The Day Christ Died Jim Bishop, Harper and Row, San Francisco.

The Dead Sea Scrolls Edmund Wilson, Oxford University Press, 1969.

The Dead Sea Scrolls and the Bible Chas. F. Pfeiffer, Baker Book House Co., 1969.

The Dead Sea Scrolls and the Christian Myth John M. Allegro, Westbridge Books, 1979.

De Santo Joseph at Arimathea Emperor? Heodusia (found in Pilate's Praelorium in Jerusalem-AD 379).

Discovery of the Essene Gospel of Peace of Jesus the Chris by Professor Edmond Bordeaux Szekely, Ph. D. Designed by Golondrina Graphics and Published by Acadamy Books, Division of I.B.S., International.

The Drama of the Last Disciples by George F. Jowett. Published by Covenant Publishing Co., Ltd., London, England, 1975.

Gospel of Peace of Jesus the Christ According to John original Hebrew and Aramaic texts translated and edited from the Archives of the Roman Vatican by Professor Edmond Bordeaux Szekely, Ph. D., University of Paris, Vienna and Liepzig. Section one published 1937, C.W. Daniel Co., Ltd., London, England. Section II privately published in 1981 by Acadamy Books, San Diego, California.

Eusebius, History of the Church from Christ to Constantine translated by G.A. Williamson, Penguin, 1965.

The Forgotten Books of Eden edited by Rutherford H. Platt, Jr. Asst. Editor J. Alden Brett, Bell Publishing Co., New York, 1980.

The Galilean-A Life of Christ Albert DePina House-Warven Publishers, Hollywood, California, 1951.

Gods, Graves and Scholars, The Story of Archaeology C.W. Ceram, Bantam Books, 1967.

The Gospel According to Thomas Translated by A. Guillaumont and Yassah Abd Al Masih, Harper and Row, New York, 1959.

The Gospel of the Essenes translated by Edmond Bordeaux Szekely The C.W. Daniel Co., Ltd., England.

Harper Bible Dictionary by Madeline S. Miller and J. Lane Miller Harper and Row, New York, 1973.

The Hebraic Tongue Restored Fabre d' Olivet, Samuel Weiser, Inc. York Beach, Maine, 1976.

Hermes and Plato by Edouard Schure translated by F. Rothwell, B.A. William Rider and Son, Ltd., London, 1972.

History of the Britons Nennius, England, 796.

History of the First Council of Nice Dean Dudley, Attorney at Law Copyright A.D. 1886, Peter Echler Publishing Co., 1925.

The Holy Bible from Ancient Eastern Manuscripts translated from the Peshitta by George M. Lamsa, 1933. A.J. Holman Company, Nashville, Tennessee.

The Holy Bible translated out of original tongues by His Majesty's King James special command. Printed by His Majesty's Printer, Eyre and Spottiswoode, Ltd., London, England.

The Holy Kabbalah by A.E. Waite, University Books, Citadel Press.

The Hymn of Jesus G.R.S. Mead, John M. Walkins, London, 1963.

An Introduction to the Cabala -Tree of Life Z'ev ben Shimon Halevi Samuel Weiser, Inc. New York 1972.

Israel and the Dead Sea Scrolls Edmond Wilson, published by Farrar, Straus and Giroux, New York, 1978.

The Israelites Time Life Books.

Jerusalem History Atlas Martin Gilbert. Macmillan Publishing Co., Inc., New York.

Jesus Michael Grant, Weidenfeld and Nicholson, London.

Joseph of Arimathea Skeats, University Press, 1871.

Josephus Complete Works. The Antiquities of the Jews and the War of the Jews translated by William Whiston, A.M. Republished in 1963 by Kregel Publications, Grand Rapids, Michigan.

The Koran translated by N.J. Dawood, Penguin Books, 1956.

Letter a transcript of a letter written by an Essene doctor in Jerusalem to a brethern of the Order in Alexandria. Originally translated from Latin into German, then from German into Swedish by J.F. Sasberg, 1880. Published by the Austin Publishing Co., Los Angeles, California, 1919.

The Letters of the Younger Pleny translated by Betty Radiel Penguin, 1963.

Life in Ancient Egypt Adolph Erman, translated by H.M. Terard Dover Publications, Inc., New York.

Life of St. Mary Magdelene Maurus Rabanus, Archbishop of Meyenie, England.

Lives of the Saints translated by J.F. Webb, Penguin Books, 1965.

The Lost Books of the Bible Bell Publishing Co., New York, 1979.

The Lost Years of Jesus Revealed Rev. Dr. Charles Francis Potter Fawcett Publications, Inc., 1962.

Magna Tabula Glastoniae Pynson (currently in possession of the House of Howard in England).

Metrical Life of St. Joseph Pynson, England 1520.

Morals and Dogma of the Ancient and Accepted Scottish Rite of Freemasonry prepared for the council of the Thirty-third Degree. Entered into the Library of congress at Washington, D.C. 1871, published by L.H. Jenkins, Inc., Richmond, Va.

The Mystical Doctrine of St. John of the Cross selected by R.H.J. Stewart, Sheed and Ward, London.

Nag Hammadi Library translated by members of the Coptic Gnostic Library Project of the Institute for Antiquity and Christianity, 1977 Harper and Row Publishers, New York.

New Testament Apocrypha edited by Professor Wilhelm Schneemelcher.

University of Bonn. English translation edited by R. McL. Wilson, Ph.D., D. Theol., 1963, Westminister Press, Philadelphia, Penn.

The Odes of Solomon: Original Christianity Revealed Robert Winterhalter, Llewellyn Publications, St. Paul, Minn. 1985.

Old Testament Light George M. Lamsa, Harper and Row, 1893.

Old Testament Wisdom-Key to Bible Interpretation by Manly P. Hall The Philosophical Research Society, Inc., 1957.

Origin of Christianity, Books I and II by Professor Ednond Bordeaux Szekely. This manuscript was based upon the author's research in the archives of the Vatican and was published originally on meat wrapping paper under the subtitle Dialectical vs Chaotic Exegesis.

The Orthodox Church Timothy Ware, Penguin Books, 1963.

The Oxford Dictionary of Saints David Hugh Farmer, Oxford University Press, 1978.

Pagan and Christian Creeds: Their Origin and Meaning by Edward Carpenter, Harcourt, Brace and Co., New York.

Pali Scroll of Mount Marbour Library of Lhasa, translated into Tibetan language sometime during the third century A.D.

The Passover Plot Dr. Hugh J. Schonfield, Bantam Books, 1966.

Philo of Alexandria Samuel Sandmel, Oxford University Press, New York, 1979.

Pistis Sophia extracts from the Book of the Savior and excerpts from a cognate literature by G.H.S. Mead, M.A., 1896, published by John M. Watkins, London, England.

Primitive Christianity - Vol. I, II, III and IV by Otto Pfleiderer, D.D. Reference Book Publishers, Inc., New Jersey, 1965.

Saints-Their Cults and Origins Caroline, Williams St. Martin's Press, New York, 1980.

Secret Teachings of All Ages an encyclopedic outline of Masonic Hermetic, Qabbalic and Rosicrucian Symbolical Philosophy. CVIII The Qabbalah, CXII-Fundamentals of Qabbalic Cosmogony, CLXXVII-Mystic Christianity, and CLXXXI-The Cross and the Crucifixion, Manly P. Hall, 1978. Philosophical Research Society, Inc., Los Angeles, California.

Shroud Robert K. Wilson, Bantam Books, 1977.

The Shroud of Turin Ian Wilson, Doubleday and Co., Inc., New York 1979.

Southern Palestine and Jerusalem W.M. Thomson Harper and Brothers, 1882.

St. Francis of Assisi by Morris Bishop, Little Brown and Co., Boston 1974.

St. Joseph of Arimathea at Glastonbury by Kiovel Smithett Lewis late Vicar of Glastonbury 1922, published by James Clarke and Co. Cambridge, England.

Unger's Bible Dictionary by Merrill F. Unger, 1957-1980, Moody Press, Chicago, Illinois.

The Trial of Jesus of Nazareth S.G.F. Brandon, a Scarborough Book, Stein and Day Publishers, New York 1968.

The Westminister Dictionary of the Bible John D. Davis, Ph. D., D.D., Westminister Press, Philadelphia, 1944.

Wild Branch on the Olive Tree Father William Treacy and Rabbi Raphael Levine in collaboration with Sister Patricia Jacobsen, Binford and Mort Publishers.

The Wycliffe Bible Commentary edited by Chas. F. Pfeifer Old Testament and Everett F. Harrison, New Testament, Moody Press Chicago, Illinois, 1962.

INDEX